RESOLVE

RAEGAN OF RUIN BOOK FIVE

A. L. ROOK

PLAYLIST

Unstoppable - Hidden Citizens
Ocean - Martin Garrix
Everybody Wants to Rule the World - Lorde
Infinity - Jaymes Young
Never Surrender - Liv Ash
Monsters [feat. Katie Sky] - Timeflies
War in Your Bedroom - A Change of Pace
Welcome to the Fire - Willyecho
New Kings - Sleeping Wolf
Get Ready - Rayelle
Fallout - Unsecret & NEONI
Immortals - Fall Out Boy
Dreamin - The Score ft. blackbear
In My Bones - The Score
Revolution - The Score
Dusk Till Dawn - ZAYN
Made For This - The Phantoms
Alkaline - Sleep Token

Unbreakable - Telykast

RISE - League of Legends

Girl on Fire - Alicia Keys

Burn It All Down - League of Legends

Phoenix - League of Legends

Heroes - Zayde Wolf

Easy - Camila Cabello

Fire on Up - Paper Kings

My Songs Know What You Did in the Dark - Fall Out Boy

Coffins - Bohnes

Wolves - Sam Tinnesz

Fight Song - Rachel Platten

Rise - Katy Perry

Legendary - Welshly Arms

Legends Never Die - League of Legends

Spotify

TABLE OF CONTENTS

CHAPTER ONE

JACKSON

THE COPPERY TANG OF blood blends with salt and brine on the ocean breeze. The others must be in the thick of taking down GE agents since we split up. Kellan escaped with Dane to the base of the cliffs while Raegan and Aiden block agents from chasing after them. I'm still stuck on the other side of Royce's beach house at the top of the cliff, hidden from the rest while I fight to save Reid. The agents I'm facing would be dead already if they were on their own. Paired together, they're troublesome.

Once I've knocked the woman with paralysis-inducing nails to the ground, I reach toward the second agent and fist my hand. He runs at me, swinging punches that I easily evade while keeping his flow of oxygen suspended.

The female tries to sneak up behind me, as if I would somehow forget that she was there. I'm keeping her in my peripherals as I dodge the other one. His movements slow at an exponential rate the more he attacks me. I just need her to keep her distance until I've taken him out.

She raises her arm, and I push off the sandy grass, using my gift to glide out of range before her nails swipe across where I'd been standing. The move unfortunately forces me to drop my focus on the male agent, and he gasps for air.

I land in front of Reid. He's still frozen in place by the venom that woman injected into his neck. I'm guessing only she can free him from it, either by choice or her death.

I'm aiming for the latter, but the male agent has continuously intervened in my attempts so far, which has driven me to shift my attention to him. I slip my hands into my hoodie pocket and finger the remaining blades as I tilt my head and smile at them both.

"As much as I enjoy a good fight, you're keeping me from the others. I can't promise a clean death the longer you draw this out." Licking my lips, I add, "I'm losing my patience," in a darker, serious tone.

"You're the one dying here today," the guy says, sneering and then wiping his mouth with his sleeve.

I chuckle. The sound is hollow and devoid of any humor. Seeing them shiver in response ratchets my smile to a maniacal grin. "Those are unfortunate last words."

Plucking two knives free, I toss them at the venomous agent with my gift boosting their speed. As expected, the male dives between them and the blades clatter against him and drop. His body is hard and sharp like jagged rock, his skin jutting out in strange angles that are just as likely to stab or cut me if I were to attack him directly.

Which is exactly what I'm going to do now.

My wind attacks have proved fruitless against him, just like throwing any sharp projectiles. The only attack that works is limiting his air, but his partner has intervened every time, and I'm not practiced enough on this newer technique to hold it without full concentration. And I can't get to her without him getting in the way, so he dies first.

While he'd moved in front of my knives, I jumped high above them, drawing another knife free. I drop onto his back, slamming him to the ground with my thick boots. I grab his hair and yank back, then drive my knife through his eye. It plunges deep enough that it's lights out for good.

The woman screams behind me. I roll off the dead agent in time to miss her pointed nails. Now that her partner is gone, she's an easy kill.

I wave my hand in a sweeping motion. All my fallen knives rise and surround her. Wrenching my blade free of her partner's eye, I stand and offer her another smile. "Release Reid, and I'll consider letting you live."

She scowls, eyeing the knives hovering in a circle around her. "And if I don't?"

"Then you die right now. I don't care for prisoners."

I give her until the count of three to think about her choices. I'm already pushing my patience the longer Raegan's out of my sight. We've just defeated Royce and all the strings attached to him—Thorne, Vera, and a horde of zombies—only to have Charles appear and kidnap Dane. I'm not worried about the agents with him, but I know the GE president will be hard to beat. The sooner I get back to her, the better.

Aiden's with her.

It should settle the frenetic energy coursing through my veins to get to her, but it doesn't. Nothing will soothe it until I see she's safe and unharmed. I'd also like a front row seat to watch her eviscerate our enemies, and these two agents have been delaying me for too long.

"You can have him if you swear to let me go. I'm not buying your consideration crap," she snaps.

"I swear to let you go."

Her eyes narrow, but she walks to Reid. I mirror her on his other side, staying out of her reach but keeping close to Reid so I can monitor what she's doing. My knives clear a forward path and maintain their distance around her.

She wraps her hand around Reid's shoulder and leans in, her eyes closing as she drags her tongue over the area she'd punctured.

Hm. Probably a good idea I hadn't killed her right away, then. Luckily, she values her own life over taking down one of our allies with her.

"There." She steps back from Reid.

His surprised expression melts back to its usual stoicism. As he blinks, I take the opportunity to shove the woman over the cliff with a burst of air.

The only promises that mean anything to me are the ones made to Raegan and my brothers.

"Who was that?" Reid questions, though his tone is indifferent.

"The enemy."

Something flies past the tip of the headland.

A person?

Could be from Kellan, but he should be at the base of the cliff and not up here. I focus more on the body and freeze when I notice the suit.

"Is that..." Reid trails off.

Aiden.

Realization hits me like a brick.

I won't make it in time.

I lift my hands as if I'm holding an invisible ball and start pulling in and gathering air between them. This isn't anything I've tried before, but I'm acting on instinct now to do whatever it takes to give us time. I seal it, then shoot it out at Aiden to cover his face.

It could pop when he hits the water. It might not stick to him at all.

It reaches him just before he disappears in the water.

He doesn't come up.

There's no time to think about whether that worked or not. I balance on the edge of the cliff, building the air needed to launch myself skyward, when a scream pierces the air and echoes in my bones. The sound of her voice—drenched in pain and fury—seizes my soul in an iron fist, and I nearly fall.

At the same time, the smell of burned wire, a sharp metallic taste that clings to the back of my throat, warns me what's coming next.

Reid grabs my arm. "She's with Charles. I'll bring us there."

"No." Breaking his grip, I run along the cliff and stop when I see Kellan and Dane still fighting off agents. "Get them to the Guild. Then bring Cassandra to the zombie caves."

Raegan's gift bursts out of her as a shockwave of power. Reid stumbles back but manages to keep his balance while my gift holds me to my perch. The headland collapses to rubble, and she and Charles descend through the destruction. Red lightning arcs and ripples around her, further decimating the broken rocks to dust until they're surrounded by a cloud of dirt and powder.

Reid vanishes, reappearing on the beach in a split second to reach the others, and then the three of them are gone.

Charles hits the ocean first, and it disperses outward and upward like a stone dropped in water until his back impacts with rocky and saturated sand. The sea rushes against an invisible barrier surrounding them, steam hissing and rising where it makes contact.

I sprint to the beach house and kick the already-broken door off its hinges, sending it down the rockslide where the remaining GE agent won't spot it. The agents up here are all dead, Aiden's slashes clearly marked in red on every body. A single bush clings to the cliff above Raegan and Charles, halfway over the edge from the headland collapse with its roots struggling to hold on. I duck behind it and crouch on the precipice to reassess.

Even though my body vibrates with the need to go to her, I keep still, ready to move at a moment's notice.

If any one of us is going to defeat Charles, it's her.

It's the only win I can see for us. The only gift that can break through all his imitated powers. She's underestimated her gift at every turn, and I think she's finally starting to realize how powerful she is. How strong she can be, if she uses it right.

The sweltering heat radiating from them at the base of the cliff reaches me even up here, making me sweat in my hoodie. We're losing daylight, losing time. My chances for rescuing Aiden are narrowing with every breath. I know I need to find him, but I can't leave her with Charles. Aiden would understand.

Charles's voice carries on the wind.

"Is this all you have?"

I fist my hand, accepting the time to beat him isn't today.

Not yet. But soon.

He continues, "I'm going to take Dane now and kill the rest of your friends. You should thank me for a poetic ending. I'll let you die in the same watery grave as your lover."

I'm relieved that Dane and the others are gone, stealing that prize from Charles. He thinks he's won, but if I can get Aiden back, it'll be a draw at best.

"Sleep." Charles palms her face, wielding the same gift he'd used to knock Kellan out in the bunker, and her eyes close.

The president is too impatient to follow through on his promise to recapture Dane that he doesn't deal a killing blow with his telekinesis. That would have compelled me to intervene before the attack could land, and I'm not sure if I could escape him. It's a mistake on his part. A flaw in how he thinks during a fight. I wouldn't have hesitated to go for the kill.

My muscles tense, desperate to go to her, but I can't let him see me. Saving Raegan and Aiden are my priority.

I force myself to wait.

To be patient.

Even when he teleports away and her gift dissipates.

Even as the water floods the crater, crashing over her, and swallowing her from my view.

Every nerve ending burns to move; to save her.

Wait.

Charles reappears by the beach house, and I tuck in closer to the bush. He surveys the dead agents, then strides to the cliff to peer below. He teleports to the remaining agent, speaking a few words back and forth. Hopefully telling him that Dane and the others are gone. The GE president turns, and the agent places his hand on his back.

They vanish.

I dive, thrusting the wind at my heels and splitting the air with my hands. The buffer of air lasts until I slide beneath the water. The cold temperature skitters over my skin, inducing a shiver, but it's not a muscle-binding chill.

Moving through water is a heavy, claustrophobic experience for me. I'm used to air at my fingertips. That invisible, endless freedom and lightness which constantly surrounds me. But underwater, it's muted. Smothered. As if I'm trapped in a thick, wool blanket.

I'm slow. Weak. Cut off from the gift that I've interwoven into every fiber of my being. I fight against the instinct demanding I return to the surface and swim harder instead.

The warmth from her gift beckons me to her, growing in temperature the closer I am until I see her. She's floating just above the softened sand, the setting sunlight reaching for her with slender orange fingers.

I shove myself toward her, wrapping her in my arms even as her heat scalds my skin.

I swim toward the shore, wishing I could control air underwater—use it to propel us into the sky or increase my speed. But I'm as restricted in the water as anyone. I bundle her to my chest once I can keep her head above water, progressively shifting to a run until I lay her on the sand and start CPR.

I'm sure there's a way I can use my gift to clear the water from her lungs, but I haven't tried it before, and I'm reluctant to try anything for the first time with her. I save it as a backup option if this doesn't work, continuing the compressions and guiding air into her lungs with my gift.

Come on, little one. Breathe.

After a minute with no results, I debate switching tactics, panic bleeding into my composure the longer she's not breathing. My compressions become rougher; my own breathing clipped as my heart races.

Her body jerks, and I quickly help her to her side as she coughs water. Once it's all out, her breathing slows, and her eyes remain closed. I check her pulse, then palm her forehead.

She's still burning up from her gift.

Lifting her in my arms, I fly us to the rockslide where Reid's supposed to be with Cassandra.

Neither of them is there.

Something's wrong.

If he's not back by now, they ran into trouble at the Guild.

I take a calming breath, releasing the frustration that keeps trying to take over. Cassandra can't heal her from this anyway. I need her for Aiden. Hopefully, they'll be here before I get him back.

There are mini tide pools on this side of the beach formed by the broken rocks and boulders from the rockslide Raegan created and filled in during high tide. I slip Raegan into one of those, away from the waves, but still in the cooler water to help regulate her temperature. I shift the larger boulders around her, blocking her body from view unless someone gets close enough, then find the door I'd dropped around here.

"I'll bring him back to you," I promise, hopping on the hovering door. A quick burst of air shoots me over open water as I fight the strong ocean breeze. I lie on the door to reduce air resistance and keep myself low to the water. The winter sun sinks below the horizon, darkness creeping over the sky and shadowing much of the sea.

I try not to consider the possibility of not finding Aiden or him not making it.

I promised Raegan that we would all make it through this war.

I already failed her with Gordon.

I won't do it again.

My chest tightens as those thoughts percolate. We all need her, but the same is true for the rest of us.

Our family won't be whole without him, either.

She's the glue to our broken pieces, but we won't fit together with a piece missing.

It has to be all of us. Together.

I'll find him and bring him home.

Chapter Two

AIDEN

Stinging pain from the back of my shoulders to my legs slaps me awake in an instant. I open my eyes and gasp on reflex, just in time to witness a wave devour and shove me underwater.

Instinct snaps my eyes and mouth closed as I'm forced down. The pain builds to a burning ache. Through the insistent throbbing, there are two sharp reminders of the bullets I'd taken in my shoulder and side. Then the three bruising strikes to my chest that had knocked me out rather than killed me, thanks to the metal plate I'd formed.

I'd just finished off the last of the agents when I saw Charles appear on the headland. When I saw his arm raise, gun pointed at her, I reacted on instinct.

Using my whip sword, I'd smoothed it in an instant and stabbed it into the ground, vaulting myself over Charles and sending whatever remaining metal I had left to protect my chest.

I wasn't thinking about how I was going to stop him or what to do next.

I wasn't thinking about death.

All that mattered was her.

Because I will always stand between her and danger.

I open my eyes, giving myself a second to adjust to the salt water, but it's a pointless effort. It's too dark to see much of anything from however deep I've sunk, all the shades of blue blurring in every direction.

I'm being dragged down, down, down.

I'm too heavy.

All the metal that saved my life a minute ago is now my downfall.

I need to dump it all.

I can't breathe.

My chest burns and tightens. That last gasp of air I'd stolen is almost gone, and my lungs are fit to burst.

Something sways in front of my face and I expel the last of my air before I can see what it is. It shakes and wobbles, then continues to float in place.

Is it...an air bubble?

I breathe in slowly.

Air.

Logic urges me to draw a small breath, but my body takes over in survival mode. I wheeze, gathering air back into my lungs in a wasteful but necessary catch-up, then take another deep breath.

The air bubble shrinks closer to my face.

However Jackson managed to do this, I need to make it count.

Drawing all the metal to each of my hands, I let it fall free until there's nothing left. No whip sword. No metal jewelry. No metal plate full of bullets.

But I don't stop there.

I wince at the excruciating pain in my back and side as I unbutton my jacket, then methodically strip it from each arm. I don't squander air and energy trying to rush it off. Next is my shirt, shoes, and pants, lightening my weight as much as possible before I begin my struggle to the surface.

I'm compelled to take another breath, then watch the tiny bubble of hope dwindle further.

I'm far from the surface, but being pulled down gave me a hint of direction, so I stroke and kick as fast as I can. There's no light around me. No sight or sound to tell me if I'm getting close.

Just endless sea.

Chapter Three

Kellan

The agent's neck snaps with a sharp twist, and he crumples to the ground. When I turn around, another three are running toward us, adding to the three still fighting.

Where the hell are they coming from?

I'd thought bringing Dane down to the beach would help divide their forces, but I must have miscounted. Every agent who shows up is one more obstacle between me and Dane should Charles appear.

To make matters worse, my gift is running out. I can feel the strength thinning with every blow. And attacks that would normally slide over scales now land with full force. I may have gotten the hang of activating it, but holding onto it for extended periods of time is still a work in progress.

I check on Dane, who's holding his own against an agent. "Get on my back!" I shout, punching the agent trying to attack him from behind and then shoving his face into my knee.

Dane throws his fist at the agent, knocking him back and then following up with another blow that drops him to the ground. "Fuck off!" he growls, kneeing the agent on the ground and laying into him.

I lock my arm and clothesline the next agent, then stomp my foot on his chest to keep him down. "Charles could show up to grab you any second."

He leans back on his heels, panting. "Any of these fuckers have guns on them? I'll stay close, but I'm not going to be a backpack."

The approaching agents surround us before we get a chance to check. Dane shoves himself to his feet, fists up.

And then I hear her voice.

Her *scream*.

I whip around, frantically searching for her even as the agents start their attacks. The world around me sharpens as my fading gift resurges with a vengeance. I can feel the pull of scales covering the backs of my arms when I clench my hands. The newfound strength thrumming through me. A burning scent fills the air, and something about it has alarm bells ringing in my head.

Protect. The instinct roars through me, demanding action. I barely feel the strikes from the agents surrounding me. Flies to a dragon who aren't worth my attention when my girl's in danger.

A blast of power rocks the beach, sweeping over us. I brace myself through it, positioning my arms in front of me and widening my stance as Dane and the GE agents are knocked to the ground.

The headland collapses beneath her and Charles.

"Rae!" Dane yells, then grunts at my side.

I grab the agent trying to grapple with Dane by the face. He shrieks with pain before I throw him to the side, then reach for the next nearest agent and slam my scaled knuckles into his jaw, causing a loud *crack*. Another agent tries to run, but I fist his hair and drag him back, snapping his neck.

Dane's already racing to where Raegan and Charles are falling. I catch up to him in a few running strides before Reid appears in our way.

"Move!" I snarl, raising my arm to swipe him to the side.

His hand meets my arm halfway.

And the world tilts.

We land in the center of the Guild Hall at the Tower, still riddled with zombies and destruction from the fight. The off-balance I ordinarily feel from his teleportation isn't here this time with my gift active.

Dane wobbles on his feet beside me, and Reid...

Fury electrifies my blood as I realize what's happened. At where we are and where *she* is. I lift Reid by the throat, my grip twitching with the desire to squeeze tight enough to make his eyes pop. "What have you done?!" I roar. "Bring me back!"

"Reid!" Tinsley beats my side and pulls on my arm, but I don't budge. "Let him go! Whatever it was, he was *helping you*! Put him down. Right! Now!" She emphasizes her words with punches that I hardly register.

Reid's face is pinched, his fingers digging into mine as if trying to help support himself more than trying to break free. He's smart enough to know he's not getting down unless I decide it. "...J-Jack ..."

"Rae was fighting the president alone. We have to go back!" Dane argues, panicked. He, too, grabs Reid's arm. "Now!"

Reid gives the barest shake of his head, and my grip tightens involuntarily, making him choke.

"Stop! Stop it! You're going to kill him!" Tinsley screams, pounding at my scales. She disappears, then slams into me with enough force that I slide a few feet across the floor.

Cibrina and Evie run over.

"What's going on?" Cibrina asks, sounding breathless. "Kellan? What are you doing to Reid?"

Reid vanishes before I can answer.

"NOOO!" I whip my head around to see where he teleported to. "Reid!"

Dane's face pales. "Fuck! Where did he go? She needs us, Kell, and we're *not there*."

"I have him," Evie says, lifting her hand to show a miniature Reid in her grasp. "What happened?"

"Reid!" Tinsley reaches for him, but Evie pulls her hand in.

"I didn't free him. I'm just trying to get answers without Kellan killing him first."

"Make him big again," I demand. "He can't teleport us in that size, and Raegan's fighting with Charles. We need to go back."

"We'll go with you," Silas chimes in from behind us, Fabian and Gabe standing with him.

A tiny voice chirps from Evie's hand. She releases Reid, and he drops to the ground back to his regular size. "If you have a problem with this plan, take it up with Jackson," he remarks, accepting Tinsley against his chest and holding her there.

Dane steps toward him. "What's that supposed to mean?"

"He's the one who told me to bring you here."

"You didn't see what was happening with Raegan—" Dane starts, but Reid cuts him off.

"Don't assume it was easy for me to leave her there, either. But I trust Jackson will keep her safe. It's Aiden you should be worried about."

Aiden?

Reid jerks to the side, staring at something in the room. "Someone's coming. Grab him and get down!" he shouts at me, indicating at Dane.

I do it, and then we teleport again. It's not far. We reappear behind the bar in the same room seconds before a deafening silence overtakes the Hall. Followed by the crunch of broken glass.

Crawling to the end of the bar, Reid hisses at me to stay hidden over Tinsley's head, who is still tucked against him. I peek around the edge, and my blood chills, dread hardening my gut.

Charles.

It can't be.

He wouldn't have left unless he'd won. Unless Raegan...and Jack and Aiden...

Dane shakes, his expression muddled with fear, anguish, and anger.

Charles waves his hands, and the zombies and debris on the floor sweep to either side to clear a path for him. The Guild members dodge or move around it. Cibrina and the others are grouped in the middle of the room, only a short distance from him, and I notice a GE agent standing behind Charles, who must've arrived with him.

All the other agents are dead.

I have to get everyone out.

But I also have to go back to find Raegan, Aiden, and Jackson.

Damn it.

"Still cleaning up, I see," Charles begins, his voice carrying easily in the vast room. "I hate to be the bearer of bad news, but your Guild Master is dead. He threw himself in front of a bullet not meant for him."

Gasps erupt in the room, and Dane throws me a stricken look. I shake my head. We can't believe a word he says. *I* won't believe a goddamn thing unless I see proof of it.

Aiden's alive.

He has to be. So are Raegan and Jackson.

"I'm here looking for a colleague of yours. Dane." He strolls forward, approaching Cibrina and the others. He stops in front of her. "You haven't seen him, have you?" His smile stretches as he zeroes his gaze on her.

My muscles tense, preparing to launch myself at him if he touches her. Dane shifts behind me, then grunts softly.

"Sit down and stay quiet," Reid whispers. To both of us, I think. "He's trying to lure you out."

That's fine. Dane can stay here. I'm not going to sit still and watch Charles hurt anyone in the Guild while I'm here.

"No," Cibrina answers, her voice remaining calm and collected.

"Hm..." Charles lifts his hand as if he's going to touch her face, and the others in the group shove forward to get between them.

"He's not here," Silas snaps, and the GE president looks between the others before landing on Silas. He drops his hand.

"I see. You think I'm the bad guy, don't you?" He steps away, turning to address more of the room. "But who's really the villain here? Your Guild Master killed his predecessor, then took the Guild for himself. He pockets money from your pay, controls the jobs you take, and trains you to take the lives of other people like you."

Charles places his hand over his heart. "I've always instructed my agents to never kill. To avoid harm as much as possible."

I clench my jaw to restrain the urge to go out there and beat the shit out of him. But with my gift in his veins, it wouldn't do anything more than prove I'm here and that Dane might be, too. If he's not hurting anyone, then it's not worth that risk.

"Between the Guild and GE, who has murdered hard-working gifted people and who hasn't taken a gifted life?"

Of course, he'd word it that way, considering all the non-gifted families they've murdered to kidnap the gifted children. But I'm sure even this is a lie. What about those gifted we'd seen comatose in beds? How many have died in training or experimentation? Or from defiance?

He even killed Harvey, though most of the Guild doesn't know it yet.

He continues, "Are you sure you're on the right side?"

Silas scoffs. "Do you hear yourself? You kidnap gifted kids! I've seen and rescued some of them, asshole!"

Charles smiles. "Are we not the ones rescuing them? Giving them a chance at a better life, free from living job to job. Paycheck to paycheck, just to give the money to your Guild Master. People like us—we're not meant to steal and beg for scraps." He gives Silas a knowing look and the latter looks away.

This bastard has our files. Only a handful of us know where Silas came from, what he'd been doing illegally with his gift just to make ends meet for his family. How he's always putting every penny he makes into an account to support them.

Vera.

When they'd attacked the Tower and she'd hacked the network, triggering Dane's virus to shut everything down. Once it was back up, there was no stopping her from grabbing whatever information Charles wanted.

"I'm giving them a purpose to use their abilities to build a better world. To free them from human shackles that bind them to rules that are not meant for gifted like us. I've spent the last decades protecting children from non-gifted families who wouldn't understand; who would ridicule or shame those of us with gifts; who would despise and fear you for what you can do. I'm building a world where you can control them instead of the other way around."

"No one should control anyone," Evie counters.

"In a perfect world, I agree. However, if it ever gets out that people like us exist, that result is inevitable. Either they control you because of their fear, or you control them with my method, where there will be no resistance and no fighting as they remain blissfully ignorant of who holds the power in this world."

The Hall is silent.

My heart pounds the longer he talks, and the condition of Raegan and the others stays unknown. *Leave.* The sooner he goes, the faster Reid can bring us back. But I can't abandon the Guild to this man. And if Reid was able to sense his arrival, then he might be able to sense us leaving if we go before him.

Charles's expression never changes as he scans the room, and no one agrees or steps forward. "Your loyalty is admirable. I'll admit, I'm envious. It would be an honor to accept you into the fold at Gifted Enterprise, should you be willing."

Cibrina straightens, shifting to the front of the group. "Please leave."

"I'm aware that losing someone important to you can be... *emo-*

tional," he says. "It can make people become irrational and make poor choices. Of course, you still need time to accept the unfortunate passing of the Guild Master, someone you hold in such high regard. I could never ask anyone to rush a decision as important as this. Take your time. Say your goodbyes. And truly consider my offer."

Charles looks to the GE agent he'd arrived with, and the other man crosses the room to place a hand on his back. "I'll give you until the end of the month to make your decision, as I assume you'll be coming upon a new month of bills and debts to be paid. Join GE, and you'll have a better place to call home. Or decline, and I'll be forced to see you as an enemy and potential threat to GE."

They disappear.

"Is he gone?" Tinsley whispers to Reid, staring at him like he's her knight in shining armor.

Reid closes his eyes, his brow pinched with concentration, then nods. "He's gone." He stands, bringing Tinsley with him, while Dane and I follow suit.

Dane grabs Reid's arm. "Take us back to the beach house!"

"Jackson wanted you both here. I need to find Cassandra and bring her back."

He yanks himself from Dane's grip, but I snatch his wrist and squeeze. "We're not asking," I growl. All I can think about is what Charles said about Aiden. How we'd last seen Raegan fighting with the GE president, and yet he was able to appear here, unscathed and without her. "You're wasting time."

Reid releases Tinsley from his other arm, gently pushing her behind him. She grips his shoulder anyway. "I'm not going anywhere without Cassandra. Aiden won't survive without her, if he isn't dead already."

"She's in the infirmary helping the ones you rescued or who were hurt here," Cibrina says as she rushes by, her heels clicking on the floor. "I'll get her!"

"Is what he said about Aiden true?" Evie demands, running up to the bar with the others close behind. "Where is he?"

"Where's Raegan?" Gabe adds. "And the ninja?"

Dane takes Reid's arm again. "Infirmary, then beach house."

Reid nods, and the four of us reappear in the middle of the infirmary.

Cassandra jumps at our arrival, her hand flying to her chest in a gasp before scanning a critical gaze over each of us. "If you aren't severely injured or dying, we have a door," she admonishes, returning her attention to a patient in bed. "We've got five rescued members, six still out from that sleeping mist and tranquilizers, and another four with significant zombie-related injuries. Thankfully, Holly's here to help, but—"

Tinsley uses her gift to reach Cassandra and pull her to our group, and we teleport before she can finish.

Chapter Four

JACKSON

Being out on open water is like being lost in a void. There are no markers to act as a guide or tell me where I've been. The deep blue ocean looks the same in every direction once the beach and cliffs are out of sight. Now that the sun's dipped below the horizon, taking its light with it, my chances of finding Aiden slim even more.

I'm reaching the limit of my gift before I'll need to pass out for a day to recover. My fight against Thorne, against zombies and GE agents, plus keeping the weight of me and the door airborne over an ocean of combating wind, is taking its toll.

Even with that looming expiration, I refuse to give up, expanding my search with every loop over the area where I think he dropped. Sending out sharp whistles and waiting for the slightest sound over the waves.

It's after one of my whistles that I hear something.

Drawing it closer, I focus on the sound of splashing water. It's similar to the crash of waves, but too close together to be natural.

Then, it stops.

I turn to follow the sound with a burst of speed. Something bobs in the water, and then the next roll of waves pushes it under.

Aiden.

I shuck my clothes off and leave the door hovering in place as I dive into the water. It's even darker underwater where the moon's glow is barely visible. It takes a second to find Aiden's shadow, then I swim as fast as I can to reach him. He sinks at a steady pace, but I'm catching up with every forceful stroke.

I grab his arm, pulling him up and then dragging us back to the surface.

The door hovers in the distance, showing how far we've moved already, and I send it to us on a gust of wind and drop it on the water. I climb on first, an awkward endeavor while keeping Aiden above water with one hand, then pull him up and start CPR.

His body jerks after the fifth compression while I feed him air and then I roll him to his side. He chokes, then coughs, and water releases from his mouth.

I drop on my backside, knees up, and throw my head back as relief sweeps through me in a rush while he catches his breath.

I made it, little one.

Aiden returns to his back, panting and eyes closed. His body shivers hard enough that I can feel it through the door. There's a bullet hole in his shoulder and his side, but I can't do much for those here other than plugging them with my gift to avoid more blood loss.

Gathering the air around us, I push the water from his body until he's dry, then do the same for myself. It further depletes the reserves of my gift and means we'll have to cruise back to shore slower, but I can't have either of us dying of hypothermia. Aiden's too exhausted to so much as grumble at me when I dress him in my pants and hoodie to warm him up.

"The others?" His voice is brittle from the seawater, but the tone is just as commanding and in control as always.

A small smile tugs on my lips. I lean on my fist as I watch him lying there, eyes closed, chest moving in normal rhythm.

"Safe."

He cracks an eye open to look at me. I'm sure he's noticed we're still adrift. I haven't put him on my back and started flying anywhere. "What's next?"

I look in the direction we need to go. "I don't have the energy left to fly both of us. I'll push us on the water, but it'll be slow." His eyes are closed again. "Sleep, but don't die," I warn him.

He grunts in acknowledgment. Now that his immediate questions have been answered, he'll rest. Finding him was only the first step. I don't know what other injuries he sustained besides the bruising on his back, which makes getting us back quickly all the more urgent.

Hopefully, Reid will be waiting with Cassandra by the time we arrive.

With that in mind, I whip the air behind us to start the long cruise to the beach.

"I see them!" Dane shouts as we sail toward the shore. He and Kellan dash into the water waist-deep to meet us. Dane's brow wrinkles, and he shoots me a pained look when he sees how pale and motionless Aiden is.

"He's alive." I don't blame them. I'd continuously checked for a pulse during the long ride because of how still he was. "Where's Cassandra?"

Kellan presses two fingers to Aiden's neck anyway as if needing the physical reassurance that he's still with us. "She's with Reid, Tinsley, and Raegan." He frowns, then lifts Aiden.

"Careful of his back," I warn while standing. I'd rather ride the door to shore than return to the water.

"His pulse is weak. Let's go." Kellan wades through the water, keeping Aiden above it in his arms. Once we're on land, I ditch the door and stroll behind them as they run around the curve of the shoreline to the others.

Cassandra's head snaps up where she's sitting against the boulder hiding Raegan. "Aiden!" She scrambles to her hands and knees and pats the sand. "Put him down here."

Reid steps around the boulder into view. One of his twin blades is in his hand, and he's scanning the cliff. "We need to leave. We've been here too long already."

"He could be too weak to survive the teleport," Cassandra snaps. "Give me a second to at least make sure he'll stay with us until I can do the full healing."

Kellan stops in front of Cassandra but doesn't move to put Aiden down. "Check him here and heal what you need to, and then we'll go."

Dane moves next to Kell to watch, but I keep walking around them to where I left Raegan. I've done my part for Aiden. It's up to Cassandra from here.

Now, all I want is to see her. To hold her in my arms, even if she burns me, because I almost lost her.

I almost *lost her*.

Blood pounds in my ears, drowning out everything but the hammering beat that calls on my demons. A haze of numbness seeps through my skin, settling in my chest as the need to spill blood becomes a driving force within me, making my muscles twitch and tremble to act on it. To kill anyone who threatens her. To seek out Charles and burn him alive. Even if he heals, I'll do it over and over again. I won't stop until he's so tired from the pain that he purges Kell's gift so he can finally end the suffering.

As soon as she's in my view, my vision tunnels until all I see is her. Her expression is peaceful as she lies half in and half out of the tide pool. I crouch beside her, scooping her into my arms and holding her so tightly that her heat sears through her clothing and my shirt to scald my chest and arms. I don't have my hoodie to protect me this time, but I welcome the pain. It cuts through the apathy and pins me to the present moment.

I have her.

She's safe.

Lifting her, I bury my face into the crook of her neck where her pulse thumps steadily, then breathe her in on a long inhale.

The crunch of boots snaps my attention up. I tighten my hold on Raegan as a small burst of wind curls and spins protectively around us, stirring her hair and mine.

Reid pauses when he notices the breeze, his steely gaze taking us in before meeting mine. "Ready?"

I release the surrounding air and nod just as the others round the boulder to join us.

"Bring us straight to the Loft," Kellan directs, still holding Aiden whose face has color and is breathing more noticeably. Good.

"Unless you have a picture of it, we'll have to land in the elevator,"

Reid replies.

"Close enough."

"I'll call Cibrina to meet us there," Dane offers, lifting his already-ringing phone to his ear. "We got them. Meet us in the Loft."

Reid holds out both arms. "Grab on."

A second later, the elevator bounces beneath our sudden weight as the world tilts. I use my gift to keep myself upright while Kellan shoulder-checks the wall to avoid falling with Aiden. Dane and Cassandra each manage to right themselves without falling and then Dane shifts to the control panel to bring us to the Loft floor. He handles the security measures to open the doors until we file inside.

Kell lays Aiden down on one side of the U-shaped couch while Cassandra kneels on the floor next to him. "I'll heal the rest now," she says, placing her hands on his chest and closing her eyes.

I sit with Raegan curled in my lap, refusing to let her go. Holding her is the only thing keeping me from losing control.

Dane opens the door for Cibrina once she arrives.

"I'm glad they're both safe. How are they?" she asks, approaching the back of the couch.

"Cassandra said she would be able to heal all of his injuries," Dane answers. "Rae's weren't nearly as bad, but she overdid it with her gift again. They'll both need time to recover."

"It isn't safe in the Tower now that Charles has been here," Reid remarks, reminding us that Charles can teleport anywhere he's been before.

Kellan crosses his arms. "He gave the Guild until the end of the month. As far as he's concerned, Aiden and Raegan are dead. They should be safe up here."

"I'll send out a search party for them on the beach. It should buy us more time," Cibrina adds.

"The safety for the Guild doesn't extend to Dane," Reid argues. "He could come back for him."

Dane makes a sound of frustration and drags his hand through his hair.

Cibrina pinches her chin in thought. "What if we found a way to block his teleportation? And those portals?"

Kellan's brows raise. "That'd make things a helluva lot easier."

She nods. "I'll get to work looking into that as well."

"We'll help you," Tinsley offers, volunteering Reid with her hand on his. He looks less than thrilled but doesn't say anything to counter her. She's only just returned from being with GE—and Vera. Raegan knows more about what happened with her, but we haven't had the time to catch up on those details before the Tower had been attacked. Only Raegan's apparent trust in her after their private conversation is keeping me from reaching for a knife.

Just as Cibrina turns to leave, Dane steps between her and the door. "Wait." He shifts uncomfortably, gripping his hair in one hand and staring at the floor. "Is Vera... I mean... where..."

Cibrina places her hand on his arm. "She's covered on a bed in the infirmary. Next to Harvey," she adds, looking across the room at Kellan.

The room grows quiet at the reminder of a fallen Guild member.

"I'll come downstairs to help finish cleaning up," Kell offers, breaking the silence.

Dane fists his hands. "Cremate both of them. So no one like Royce can use them after death."

Cibrina gives him a curt nod.

Cassandra stands, pushing red curls from her face with a soft sigh.

"Aiden should make a full recovery with rest. I'll be in the infirmary if you need anything."

"Make sure you get some rest, too," Cibrina tells her, and Cassandra smiles.

"I could say the same for all of you. It's the middle of the night." Kellan looks at me.

"I'll keep them safe," I promise, standing and jerking my chin at Aiden. "Get him in bed." I'm not letting either of them out of my sight.

The others leave while Kellan and Dane help get Aiden partially undressed and into his bed. I do the same for Raegan on the other side, placing her next to Aiden before sliding under the sheets beside her.

No one will disturb them so long as I'm here.

Chapter Five

RAEGAN

I wake up to being pulled into a warm body, a breath hot on my neck. Soft, lazy circles tickle up my thigh, clueing me in to who's behind me.

Jackson is the one obsessed with tracing his fingertips over my skin.

It takes another second for me to remember what happened last, and I grab his hand to stop him.

Aiden.

My heart convulses in my chest, a gaping hole widening to consume it. I snap my eyes open—a demand perched on my lips—when Aiden's face fills my view. My breathing stalls. A well of emotions crashes and flails through me like a dam breaking, and my grip on Jack's hand tightens and shakes.

"How?" I croak, fighting back tears.

Jack kisses my nape. "He's a stubborn one," he teases lightly, and I choke on the emotion clogging my throat.

"You got him back?"

He hums into my skin, and it reverberates from my neck down

my spine. "He refused to give up."

My eyes are glued to Aiden lying in bed beside me, still not quite believing it. I watched him get shot—multiple times—then thrown from the headland to the ocean and left there for fuck knows how long. I reach out to him, but hesitate right before I touch his sleeping face and accidentally wake him. "He's really okay?" I whisper, my voice coming out thin and raspy.

Jackson chuckles softly. "Do you think I'd put a corpse in bed with you?"

"Jack!" I gasp, smacking his hand at my thigh.

He moves said hand between my legs and slides it up. "Shh... he needs his rest." His fingers graze over my pussy, the fabric there so thin it's almost nonexistent, and my breath hitches. "And I need to feel you. Taste you. Fuck you," he adds, his voice so low and dark that it makes me shiver.

"Don't even think about it," Aiden threatens in a deadly croon.

My heart squeezes at the sound of his voice.

"Mm. Were you waiting for something else, then?" Jackson taunts.

"Aiden!" I lunge, throwing my arm around him and burying my face against his chest. I sob with relief and clutch at his back. He smells like saltwater rather than cinnamon, and the pain doubles as the full memory resurfaces. Of his blood on my hands when I'd held him. And how still he'd been. Even as much as I'd yelled and tried to get him to open his eyes, he hadn't. And I'd thought... I really thought...

And then he was gone, ripped from my arms in an instant.

"You're here. You're really here."

"Careful," he warns, his knuckle angling my tear-streaked face to his. "It almost sounds as though you have feelings for me."

I grab the back of his head and force his lips to mine before he says anything else stupid. My kiss is hard and demanding, needing to feel him and have that physical connection to prove that this isn't some dream. He survived. He's here. I push my tongue past his lips, taking him with unhinged desperation until the pain in my chest slowly ebbs.

More.

Molding myself to his body, I absorb his warmth and further proof of his life, stroking my hands over the hard muscles of his arms and back. My nails break skin in my avarice, and the next second, his hand circles my throat, and he slams me to my back. Before he can say anything about it, I yell at him, "How can you say that?! I fucking love you, Aiden! And seeing you like that... *losing you...*" The stupid tears are back, clogging my throat with a vulnerability that makes my chest burn for him and Jack to witness.

"Say it again," he commands, his dark stare intense, pinning me in place just as much as his hand.

My lungs deflate, realizing the one time I'd ever admitted how I felt about him was after he'd thrown himself between me and half a dozen bullets and he'd been unconscious. I draw a steadying breath, then lock my gaze with his.

"I love you."

His eyes shutter closed, some emotion crossing his features too quickly for me to identify before his forehead touches mine.

"Aiden?"

"You never cease to amaze me." He withdraws, pulling me upright by one arm while Jack helps with the other.

"She doesn't realize how special she is," Jack adds as they adjust me between them on our knees.

"We'll have to show her then, won't we?"

My heart hammers in my chest, the air in the room suddenly feeling charged with an energy that buzzes through my veins. That heats my blood and makes my pulse race.

I press my hand to Aiden's chest. "Wait. You're still healing—"

"It's been days since the cliff," Jackson informs me as he draws me back against him.

"You were too out of it to remember being up before," Aiden adds, pinching my chin and angling my face to his. "And I'm not so tired that I can't pleasure the woman I love." He slips his hand into my hair and pulls me into a kiss.

I'm still reeling from their words. The immediate counter I want to say is trapped in my throat, forced back as Aiden deepens the kiss. As Jack sucks on my neck from behind. My core pulses with every swipe of tongue. Every suck, every nibble that sets my blood on fire. I run my hands over Aiden's smooth and bullet-free chest, rub the stubble along his jaw and then grip his hair in one hand and reach for Jack's with the other. The words I want to say melt away beneath their touch.

Aiden's alive.

Jackson saved him. Saved me. I owe them everything.

"What about Dane? And Kellan?"

Jack trails his hands up my thighs, catching the hem of my shirt and lifting it upward. I oblige, knowing he wouldn't be continuing this if something was wrong. "Both safe. Here."

I cup his face, turning my head to see him over my shoulder. "Thank you, Jack. Thank you," I breathe, pulling him until our lips meet. My hand slides to his nape, tugging him closer as I willingly drown in him. None of us would be here now if not for him. He's keeping his promise to me, protecting my wishes.

Aiden descends on my breast, swirling his tongue around my nipple. I moan into Jackson as an electric current of pleasure shoots through my body. My aching cunt pulses with the need to be touched. I reach between my legs on autopilot to ease that desire when Aiden snatches my wrist.

He tsks, his breath chilling the slickness covering my nipple and inducing a full-blown shudder. "That's mine."

"Ours," Jackson corrects, then dips a finger into my wet and needy cunt. I gasp at the brief contact before he's spreading my arousal to my clit in slow circles.

Aiden captures my other wrist and guides them over my head, forcing my back to arch. "Do I need to restrain these, or can you hold them here?"

"Yes," I pant in desperate agreement, my hips twitching and rocking into Jackson's touch when he sinks two fingers inside and grinds his palm against my clit.

"Yes, what?" he prompts.

"I'll hold them."

"Good girl." He brushes his knuckles down my sternum, his gaze tracking the movement as if he's devouring me by sight alone. It feels like I'm burning up inside. Like Jackson's stoking a fire within me that Aiden's drawing to the surface with his reverent touch. "Beautiful," Aiden remarks under his breath. I don't know if it was meant for me to hear, but he levels his heated stare on me and says it again. "You're stunning like this, Raegan. Skin flushed, nipples erect, and that look on your face as you ride Jack's fingers to chase your pleasure."

He tweaks one nipple, and a bolt of ecstasy echoes in my pussy.

"Mm." Jackson sucks and nibbles on my earlobe. "She liked that."

Aiden does it again, and I writhe between them.

"Please..."

"Do you want more?" Aiden purrs.

"Yes."

The fingers disappear without warning, and a small whine releases from my throat.

They aren't gone long before another pair joins the first. All four push in at once, slow and together as I'm stretched open more. I groan long and low as Jack and Aiden fill me, then move as one, thrusting into my cunt until my orgasm rips through me.

"Lay her down," Jackson commands. I'm shuffled to my back with my head on the pillows before he crawls between my thighs. He parts my soaked pussy and licks his lips. "So pretty," he murmurs, then lowers his mouth to lick me clean.

"Ah! Jack!" My back bows, hips twisting when his tongue finds my clit.

Jackson wraps his arms around each of my thighs and forces them open, then tugs me back down to his mouth where I'm fed unrelenting pleasure that coils and builds too fast for me to stop. I'm too sensitive still from the last orgasm that I feel the next one creeping up in no time at all. It twists tighter and tighter. Then, it snaps. My climax pulses through me again, and I collapse into the bed, gasping for air.

His dark blue eyes flick up at me, and a wicked smile curls his lips. He dives back in, but this time it's much slower. This time, he drags his tongue over all my sensitive areas until I'm a twitching, boneless mess.

Aiden comes back from wherever he'd been, his briefs gone, revealing his long, hard dick. He strokes it while standing at the side of the bed, and I notice there's some sort of ring at the base of it. "Jack." He tosses something to him.

Jackson catches it, then sits up and removes his briefs as well.

The bed dips beside me as Aiden lies down and pulls me to my side to face him. His fingers test my swollen cunt, and he hums his approval at what he finds. "Such a good girl."

I hike my leg over his, angling my hips toward his cock. "Yes," I pant, desperate to have him inside me. I reach for his cock between us.

"So greedy, too." Aiden grabs my hand, stopping me. "And impatient."

I need him inside of me like I need to breathe right now. I feel incomplete; empty. My throbbing pussy is desperate to have more than what they've been teasing me with. I'm done with foreplay. I squeeze his hard length in return. "I need you to hurry up and fuck me. Now."

Aiden inhales sharply, his jaw locking. His long fingers wrap my throat and squeeze. "Be careful what you ask for," he croons, his tone threatening.

But I've lost all sense to care as the head of his cock notches at my entrance. He drives into me, knocking the breath from my lungs. My cunt pulses, but he's gone before it can grab hold, and then he's slamming into me again.

Aiden groans, his hand tightening on my throat. "How can you act so bad but feel so fucking good? You're. Such. A. Brat," he adds, thrusting with every word and leaving me breathless. "Is this what you wanted? Hurry up and fuck you...Was that it?" My eyes roll to the back of my head. "How do you like it now? Speak up. I can't hear you."

His grip on my neck loosens, and I scream as I'm rocked by another orgasm. But he doesn't stop. He keeps fucking me through it, pushing through the rhythmic clenching that has me seeing stars, and throws me right into another one.

My body goes limp, and Aiden slows. His lips brush against mine. "Any other demands?" he purrs, and I whimper. He smiles, then presses a kiss to my lips. "Good. Next time, I'm going to tie you up and let all of us take turns fucking you until you've had so many orgasms you won't be able to run that mouth of yours. Or should we all fuck your mouth instead and leave your pussy empty so you learn your manners next time?"

Oh, fuck.

"Let's try this again."

Something cold tickles my backside, and I jump. Jackson releases a dark chuckle behind me as he slips a finger into my ass.

I shudder with a heady mixture of anticipation and nerves.

Aiden sinks in until he's fully seated, then stops moving. There's a short click and then a buzzing noise before I feel it. His cock vibrates against my inner walls, and I gasp from the sensation. Then something hits my clit, and it vibrates stronger.

"Oh, fuck!" I moan when he lets it linger there for a few seconds before pulling back.

Jackson glides another finger into me, stretching his fingers wide as he moves them in and out. Pleasure burns at my entrance, but the vibrations and Aiden moving in my cunt overwhelm everything else, and I rock into it.

"Ungh! Yes! Fuckkk, yes!"

"That's it. You're doing so well," Aiden praises. He switches to grinding his hips, holding the vibrating silicone to my clit.

"Oh, god!" I moan, my hips bucking even though my muscles are tight and tired.

Jackson's dick gradually breaches my entrance. He sinks a little deeper, his lubed length coaxing my body to open for him.

Aiden's encouragement continues, "That's my good girl. You look so good taking us both."

Jack steadily rocks in more, stretching me as I cry out from the feeling of them both at once. He reaches around to my front, his fingertips cool and wet as they pinch and tease my nipple.

Aiden swallows my gasp when Jackson's finally in, kissing me softly. I couldn't fight his control even if I wanted to at this point. I'm so lost to the overwhelming sensations that I'm just holding on for dear life when they both begin moving in sync. Now, Aiden fucks me with a slow, sensual drag and thrust as they move in tandem.

I surrender completely to them.

Jackson tugs on my nipple, triggering me to come once more, and I fall apart. They both follow, my body squeezing them in a punishing grip until they're unable to resist joining me.

None of us say a word as we catch our breaths, holding on to each other in this quiet after a storm. In this peaceful moment after we'd almost lost one another. Aiden risked his life for me. Jackson saved us both.

We almost lost.

That realization sinks like a boulder in my gut.

I can't lose them. Any one of them.

I'll do whatever it takes to keep them safe.

CHAPTER SIX

RAEGAN

"Rae! Thank fuck, you're awake! Are you feeling okay?"

I've barely opened the door before I'm swallowed in Dane's arms. "Yeah." I hug him back, relieved that he's here. I'm anxious to learn why, considering how unstoppable Charles had been. What happened after I'd passed out? We're in the Loft, but is it safe here anymore?

"What do you want to eat? I'm sure you're starving." He laces his fingers with mine and walks me to the kitchen. Jack's already sitting on the counter that separates the kitchen from the dining area, eagerly awaiting whatever food is prepared.

"Make whatever's quickest," Aiden answers as he leaves his room. "I need to know what happened and how we're still living here. Where's Kellan?"

Dane kisses my head before releasing me to rummage through the pantry and fridge. "French toast will be quick and easy." He starts pulling out the ingredients and heating up the griddle. "And Kell will be here in a few. Cibrina's been keeping us busy the last few days."

I spot the fresh pot of coffee and pull down four mugs. Jack's the only psycho who doesn't drink it. Dane notices and brings me the creamer as Aiden joins us in the kitchen, leaning against the cabinets with his arms crossed. "Seeing as Kell already knows what happened, do you mind filling the rest of us in?"

Jackson speaks up first. "Raegan fought Charles after he threw you out to sea."

Aiden's gaze swings to me, and I hand him a filled mug.

"I lost. Completely." I take a sip of the hot coffee, hoping it'll warm the sudden chill from the memory of that moment. How I'd given it my all, and he'd still laughed in my face as if it was nothing. All that training, all my confidence in my gift... shredded by that triumphant laugh and the way he easily incapacitated me.

"It was a good test of your gift against his," Jack muses.

"One I clearly failed," I mutter, setting my mug down.

He pokes my forehead, and I frown, rubbing that spot. "No. It showed us more of what he's capable of. How he fights."

"And?" Aiden questions.

Jack shrugs nonchalantly. "Attacking him head-on with power may not be the way to win against him, but I still think her gift can do it."

"How?" I demand, incredulous. "I've never been able to pierce through Kell's gift."

"Charles's gift is an imitation. It's imperfect. There's a weakness to it if we can find it."

"Jack. I threw everything I had at him. *Everything*. I can't beat him."

He smiles, tucking my hair behind one ear. "Don't give up, little one. He wins the second you do."

Fuck. He's right. But I'm not sure what more I can do against him that I didn't already try.

Aiden looks between me and Jack, probably reading my uncertainty. "We'll consider that as a possibility, but we need other plans to try against him—"

The door to the Loft slams open. "Where is she?!" Kellan bellows, charging inside and immediately looking around. The second he sees me, he storms over, lifting my thighs around his waist and crushing me in a kiss. I throw my arms around him, a soft sigh falling from my lips now that we're all together again.

"Get out of the kitchen, Kell!" Dane snaps. "Before you break something or bump one of us into the stove."

He carries me with him to the living room, pressing me back against the wall. Kell grabs my hair and pulls my head to the side, baring my neck to him before he pinches the skin between his teeth. I release a startled shout at the sudden burst of pain before he's sucking it away.

"Kell, what the—"

"You scared the fuck outta me, beautiful," he growls into my neck. "I didn't want to believe anything that bastard said, but seeing him after you'd been fighting... there was a split second when I thought it. When I thought you'd died. And my heart almost gave out right then and there." His chest heaves as if he'd run up here, but the elevator's the only way to the Loft. "And then when I saw you lying unconscious in that puddle..."

I grab his face with both hands. "It's okay. I'm right here. I'm okay."

He yanks me into another bruising kiss that rattles my bones and has me seeing stars. "Kell," I gasp for air before his lips are on mine again.

"Let her breathe, for fuck's sake!" Dane yells. "She's still recovering!"

Kellan smacks his hand against the wall over my head and finally withdraws, his shoulders shaking as he catches his breath. He sets me down, and I lean into him as oxygen refills my lungs, and I wait for strength to return to my legs. He wipes a hand over his face and then strokes a thumb along my cheekbone. "Sorry, beautiful. You alright?"

"Yeah."

"Explain," Aiden demands from the kitchen, and Jack does, updating him on my near-death experience with Charles and how I'd almost drowned. Like him. By the time he's finished, I've returned to my coffee and taken a seat at the dining table with it. Kell leans against the back of the living room couch, and Dane is plating the last of the French toast.

Aiden lifts his hand, opening and then fisting it. "I need more metal."

Dane nods. "The usual source for your titanium is apparently dealing with some other issues right now that have wiped out their stockpile. I've been calling around to see who else has anything in stock to buy whatever we can get."

"That has Charles written all over it." Kellan crosses his arms. "But it's old news. Now that he thinks you're dead, we'll have to get it from somewhere further away and he wouldn't suspect."

"Have the other attacks on the Guild stopped at least?" I ask, realization sinking in that we might actually have an advantage now. He thinks Aiden and I are both dead. We may as well be invisible to him, so long as we don't do anything to draw his attention.

"Cibrina's been keeping up the ruse that you're both missing with a search party that, of course, turned up nothing," Dane explains while taking a seat at the table. "Detective Unger won't be able to try taking Aiden down for Thorne's murder with no Aiden, so we should be getting a break from him. We're waiting on the results of the tax audit, and the offshore account is still frozen."

Kellan points his fork at Dane after swallowing a mouthful. "The shit articles about the Guild were taken down, and there haven't been any reported attacks on Guild members at jobs or while they're out."

Dane scoffs. "Yeah, well, the damage has already been done. Our job options are lower than they've ever been."

"Let the PR company deal with that now," Aiden reasons. "What else? Charles threatened to take the Guild after my death, so I'm surprised we're all sitting here right now."

"Oh, he came here right after his fight with Rae. He was looking for me and trying to convince the members to flip their loyalty to GE."

Aiden thumbs the rim of his mug. "I imagine that didn't go to his liking."

Kellan snorts, but Dane continues, "Nope. I think he'd hoped his charm would win them over without the hassle of brainwashing, but he doesn't understand what the fuck loyalty means. He's still holding out for the Guild to turn to him, though. Once the month ends, he expects us to be out of money and desperate for a leader. And if we still refuse his offer, he said he'll officially declare us enemies. I'm not sure if he'll bother with brainwashing this time around. I think he meant it as a threat to take us out for good."

My stomach turns at the thought, and I swallow the food down before it can stick in my throat. "So, how much time does that give us?"

"Three weeks," Jack answers from the kitchen counter, one foot up and the other dangling.

"How many board members do we have left to find?" Aiden asks Dane, referring to Gifted Enterprise's leaders after Charles.

"Two. But they're just elects."

Aiden frowns. "I still want them. If they know enough to almost be on the board, then they know too much. We'll see if Reid can help us track down the last two so we can move on to them. We'll split our fighters into teams to take out all ten board members and elects at once." He curls his long fingers into a fist on the table. "We'll have to attack Charles immediately after. Regroup in one place and then go after him before he realizes what's happened."

"That the Guild isn't choosing him," Dane fills in, and Aiden dips his chin.

"Everyone in the Guild will be in more danger until we kill Charles."

Kellan chuckles darkly. "No pressure there."

Aiden continues, "Once he's dead, there won't be anyone to step in and take his place with the board gone. The company will fall apart without its leadership, and we can finally get rid of every last trace of Gifted Enterprise."

"As good as that all sounds, we still have to figure out how to kill Charles. *Without* losing anyone," I argue.

Aiden looks at all of us. "We have less than three weeks to come up with a plan—with multiple plans. We're not depending on only one with him. We'll have so many that we'll guarantee our win."

CHAPTER SEVEN

DANE

"I'VE COMPLETELY REDONE OUR network, so if Vera left any trackers or back door access, they're gone with our old one. The cameras and security system have been moved to the new network."

Aiden leans one hand on the desk next to me, peering at my screen. "Good. We can finally use all the measures we'd originally installed to protect the Guild."

Technology we can now use because Vera... she's gone.

Something in my chest twists painfully, squeezing my lungs until there's no air left. I shut my eyes and force myself to breathe in through my nose. To stop the annoying tremble that keeps trying to take control of me. I've kept myself focused on the Guild. On hoping for Raegan and Aiden's recovery. On anything and everything else because I can't lose my shit now. Not when they need me. I'll have all the time in the world to grieve after we've killed Charles.

I can't fall apart—frozen in grief like last time.

I won't. Rae needs me. The others need me.

Aiden squeezes my shoulder. "I'm sorry, Dane."

Swallowing thickly, I nod. "I know. Cibrina cremated

them—Vera and Harvey. Even if Royce is dead, there could be someone else out there like him. And I don't want anyone to fuck with them anymore."

He nods, releasing me. "That's a good call. We can hold a funeral for her here. Where do you want her buried?"

"Close to my parents, so they can visit her after this is all over."

There's a long pause. "What are you going to tell them?"

"The truth." Aiden's face tightens, and I turn in my chair to face him. "They won't tell anyone about it. Or about people like us. I know they'll be happier knowing what happened. They're good people, Aiden."

"It puts them in just as much danger knowing about us. That's why most of the friends and family of the Guild members who know about gifted are working for us. So we can help make sure they aren't targeted, too."

I grip my hair, trying to purge the stress that's building into a headache. "I know, I just..."

Aiden sighs. "Don't worry about it right now. Let's focus on killing Charles and destroying Gifted Enterprise first. What countermeasures do we have for teleporting and portals?"

A few keystrokes bring up the various tabs I have open to research those very gifts. At least, the science fiction and fantasy versions talked about online. "I've been trying to find any useful ideas for how those gifts might work so we can somehow track them or at least identify them to give us a warning, but it's all over the place."

"All the security in the world isn't going to make a difference unless we find a way to block those two gifts."

"Cibrina's been doing her own research and working with Reid and Tinsley."

Aiden taps a message into his phone. A few seconds later, he states, "Cibrina's with them in their apartment. We'll go check on their progress."

The door to Raegan's room opens. I turn to look on instinct, and Aiden does the same. She strolls down the hallway, followed by Kellan and Jack. Aiden had suggested that she empty her bag into the dresser drawers after breakfast. Even though the bathroom's not finished yet, I think he wants to see her feel more at home here with her own space.

"I knew that wouldn't take long," she says, running her fingers through the tangles in her hair now that it's dried.

"She only filled two drawers," Kellan remarks, crossing his arms and giving Aiden a look. "Workout clothes in one, and everything else in the other."

"Don't forget the dresses," she points out. "I had a few of those that went in the closet. I think that's plenty. The rest of my stuff is still in Aiden's bathroom until mine's done." She casts her ocean gaze over my screens, then looks between me and Aiden. "What did we miss?"

"We're going to Reid's apartment to see what we can do about Charles being able to teleport here whenever he wants," I answer first, folding my arms behind my head and leaning back.

Her brow furrows, nose scrunching with displeasure. "I guess it's too easy to hope he'll ignore us for three weeks and we'll kill him before then?"

"Yes," Aiden immediately responds. "Hope all you like, but we'll prepare for the worst. He's already been a step ahead of us with the zombie attack at the beach house and sneaking into the Tower for Harvey." Rae's expression falls at the reminder of her half-brother.

"Keeping him out of the Tower and away from Guild members at this point is our top priority."

"Does the rest of the Guild know? About Harvey?" she asks tentatively.

Kellan clears his throat, shifting on his feet. "Cibrina told them this morning. We've just finished cleaning up from the attack, so everyone's taking a break today to process it all."

Raegan nods slowly. "Can I see his apartment?"

Kell and I share a look as I lower my arms. "Most of it's been cleaned," I tell her softly.

"What are you looking for?" Aiden questions.

"I'm not sure exactly. Maybe something left behind by Charles or Harvey. Didn't his personal things get moved to that apartment? He could have something from his time before the Guild."

She's leaving something out, but none of us pushes for it.

The guilt of his death is sitting with each of us. We'd promised to protect him. He was still a Guild member. Still a part of this family we've been building, even if he had made some wrong choices to spy on the Guild for Charles. Hell, he'd been part of the Guild longer than any of us, coming from Thorne's time.

Aiden swipes his thumb across his phone. "We'll go with you, and then to Reid's after." He types something out—probably letting Cibrina know—then pockets it.

Harvey's temporary apartment is on the thirty-third floor. When we arrive, Aiden plugs in the master key information into his phone to unlock the door.

"Brawn before beauty." Kellan shoves his way to the front, flashing Rae a grin and a wink. He always does that—acts like a clown to distract her. But the way his shoulders tighten tells me he's already slipped into his protective mode for her.

I feel the same way as we walk down the dark corridor toward the living area. Kell and Fabian cleaned it as much as they could with the supplies we have, but... there was no getting the deeper stains out. The smell of blood and death is still here, lurking beneath the harsher chemical scents from the cleaning supplies.

Raegan's sandwiched between Aiden and Jackson as we file down the hallway, and part of me is tempted to take her hand and drag her out. She doesn't need to see this. I'll search the apartment for clues or anything left behind if that's what she wants.

The room opens to the kitchen and living area and, before I can act on that impulse, we all spread out to see the area clearly.

Red stains the carpet in faded blotches, moving in a clear path to the couches, and then to the kitchen, where even the grout is crimson in one area. I look at Raegan. Her gaze follows the evidence of the fight, her face pinched with set determination while her eyes tell a different story. It's that sorrow that has me reaching for her hand to squeeze it.

She turns a sad smile to me, squeezing my hand back and letting go. "I'll start in that room." Rae points to the doorway on the other side of the kitchen and leaves without another word. I debate following her to help, but Jack's already on her heels.

Damn.

"I'll go through the bedroom," Aiden says, striding to another room.

Kell goes into the kitchen, leaving me with the living area.

Great.

I step around the blood spots while moving through the room. I'm not squeamish when it comes to blood. It just seems *wrong* for me to step on it. Disrespectful to Harvey or something like that. Fuck knows why, but I avoid it anyway, moving closer to the entertainment unit. He's got a decent set of video games, but unsurprisingly they're all low stakes or family-friendly types.

One of the games on the other side of the unit falls. Did I bump it?

A random breeze sweeps through the room, and a few more cases drop. Jackson waves his arm toward the open door into the apartment. There's an immediate relief from the stagnant smells in the room, and I take my first large breath since coming inside.

Before I've finished exhaling, something squeezes around my throat—cutting off my air at the same time as something sharp presses along my cheek, ending right below my eye. Another weight pushes into my lower back. I grab at my throat and whatever's there, when an unfamiliar voice whispers in my ear, "Don't. Move."

Fuck.

Did I miss a portal opening somewhere? The voice isn't Charles or anyone else I recognize.

"What are you doing?" Kellan calls from the kitchen. I glare at him, waiting for him to fucking *do something* about this, but he's just looking at me, confused.

The arm around my throat presses harder, and black spots appear in my vision.

Fuck staying still. I pull and shove back, trying to loosen their grip so I can do more than this gasping wheeze.

Kellan finally gets the hint that something's off and leaps over the kitchen island to rush toward me.

"Dane!" Raegan shouts, running into the room before Jackson bands an arm over her chest and yanks her against him. "Jack, what—"

He pulls a handful of throwing knives free and they fly toward us.

"I'll shoot!" a young, feminine voice screeches behind me. The knives and Kell freeze. "Move another step, and I'll shoot him!"

I'm the only one who knows she's bluffing, but her arm's still trapping my throat.

Grabbing the wrist holding the knife, I push and hold it away and then throw all my strength forward, flipping the person over my head. The glass coffee table shatters as she crashes through it to the floor.

I jump on the arm with the knife, pinning it down as I heave oxygen back into my lungs.

"Dane! Are you okay? Who—" Raegan stops.

Ripping the knife from the attacker's hand, I toss it away and turn to look at her.

She's young; probably still a teenager. The rest of her is covered in sweatpants and a hoodie. Her long black hair is wild and unkempt, and her eyes... her ocean blue eyes are angrily locked on Raegan. The girl lunges for her, screaming, "You, bitch!"

We all move at once, either shifting between them like Aiden and Jack, or grabbing the girl like Kell and me. I hold her arm against my chest, even as she flails, still raging at Raegan. "It's all your fault! You did this! You tricked him! He's dead because of you! Because of *you!*"

"That's enough." Aiden's sharp command cuts through her cries. He's stepped directly in front of her, blocking her view of Raegan, as he grabs her face with one hand and forces her to look at him. "Did Charles leave you behind to spy on us?"

She spits in his face. "I'm not telling you shit."

Aiden releases her, wiping his face with his suit jacket sleeve while in the same second, Jackson's suddenly there, squeezing her throat with one hand and wearing a chilling smile. The girl's eyes widen with fear, her mouth opening, but no sound comes out.

"If you've nothing useful to say, then you don't need your tongue." He flips a knife where she can see it, and her body starts to shake.

"...lying..." she croaks through his grip, trying to call his bluff even though a fine tremble overtakes her body.

Unfortunately for her, he's not bluffing.

Jack cocks his head, his smile sharpening.

"Wait! Stop!" Raegan pushes through, grabbing Jackson's arm with the knife. "You're not cutting her tongue out. She's just as much a victim of Charles as Harvey was!"

"Harvey didn't push blame on others for his own failures," he replies coolly.

"She's just a kid," Rae counters. "And she doesn't deserve *that*. She's not our enemy."

"I'm not a kid! I'm sixteen! And we are enemies!"

Fuck's sake.

Kellan slaps his hand over her mouth. "You're not doing yourself any favors. Settle down."

Aiden returns from the kitchen with a set of metal cuffs on a chain—silverware handcuffs. Kell and I each hold her arms in place for him to click them on as she struggles and shouts some more. She tries to disappear, but I mute her gift the second she does. The girl looks around at us, confused when we all stay staring at her. "What's going on?"

"I blocked your gift."

"You don't know who he is?" Raegan asks, and the girl's expression darkens again.

"Of course, I know who he is. The guy Dad wants brought back to him."

"Do you know why your dad wants him?" she presses.

"It's not our business to know why," the girl snaps.

Kellan sighs. "Alright. Have a seat." We walk her to one of the chairs in the room and sit her in it.

"I'm not telling you anything. All of you can go to hell."

"Let's leave her here," I suggest, crossing my arms over my chest. Maybe she'll be more willing to talk after sitting in a timeout for a couple hours.

"She's a threat to us alive," Jackson says, and Raegan shakes her head.

"She's not a threat. She's just angry and confused."

"Aren't we all?" Kell drawls.

"We're not killing or hurting her," Raegan demands, her gaze catching each of ours in turn. "Not in his apartment where he died fighting for us, and not anywhere else. We promised him we would save his siblings. *My* siblings. It doesn't matter how they feel about us. We're keeping our promise."

Her command strikes me in the chest, zinging through my veins like lightning and charging me with a fire to do anything she asks. I nod when she looks my way, as do the others when her eyes land on them.

She turns to face the girl.

"I don't care what you say or do," the girl grinds through her teeth. "You killed Harvey. I know he only would have betrayed Dad because of you. He always thought you were *special*." Her voice chokes with emotion. "Because you got away. But you aren't. You're just like the rest of us. Just as broken and as afraid as we are! And you used him, pretending you could stand a chance against GE, and then got him killed for it! If you hadn't been here, he would still be alive! I hate you! I *hate you*!" She jerks forward and stops short when a metal band circles her chest and the back of the chair.

I clench my fists and snap at her, "He would have died weeks ago at your dear old dad's hands if not for us!"

"You don't know that!"

"We do, actually," Aiden joins, his tone much calmer than ours. "That doesn't excuse our failure or change anything when it comes to what happened here, but Charles no longer needed him after he'd infiltrated the Guild. He considered Harvey and the rest of you expendable. Even if there's the slightest whiff of betrayal, he has you killed. Isn't that what happened to your sister, Wyra?"

I don't remember the name or mention from Harvey, but I'm not surprised Aiden does.

The girl's eyes round as her hands cling together so tightly the chains begin to rattle. "He told you... why? Why would he share that..." She snaps her head up when Raegan crouches in front of her. I tense, ready to jump between them if the girl tries anything.

"What's your name?" Rae asks, her voice soft. The girl's lips whiten as they're pressed together. Raegan smiles with more understanding than I could ever offer this girl who's been nothing but a pain. "I'm sorry about your brother. I'm sorry we didn't protect him enough. But you're directing the blame at the wrong person. Charles killed Harvey. Charles is the one holding you hostage."

"You're wrong," the girl croaks, her eyes swimming.

Raegan continues, "You were here, weren't you? When it happened."

Tears spill over, but she doesn't answer.

"He snuck in using your invisibility. He made you help him come after your brother." Rae pauses. Waits. My chest grows tight as I realize what she's saying. At what this girl must have witnessed. "I've been made to do a lot of horrible things with my gift. I've killed people—innocent people. People whose names I didn't know. I thought that made me a villain and that their blood was on my hands. I still remember their faces to this day. Every. Single. One."

She takes a deep breath. I want to pull her into my arms and hold her tight. Tell her that none of it was her fault. I want to kill Gordon with my own hands and make him beg her for his life. I knew she'd been through a lot... but this...

How much is she still carrying with her? How is she able to smile like she does? Love, as she does?

"But I can't imagine what you must have felt being forced to kill your own brother."

The silence in the room is deafening. My heart pounds in my ears, shock slipping through my limbs like ice.

"The room... it's too messy for Charles. He would have been quick, or it wouldn't have been so bloody unless there was a struggle," Raegan explains, her voice barely more than a whisper. She raises her hands, and a reddish glow encompasses them when she touches the metal band holding the girl back, reducing it to ash.

"Raegan," Aiden warns, stepping closer.

She wraps her arms around the girl who doesn't move, doesn't fight it. "I'm sorry, I'm so, so sorry. No one should ever have to see someone they love be killed. And making you do it was sick and evil. *He's* evil. It wasn't your fault. It wasn't you."

The girl's self-control snaps. She grabs Raegan's arms and breaks down into sobs and cries of anguish. "Harvey! I'm sorry! I'm sorry! I'm sorry!" She curls into Rae, her face bright red and soaked as she clings to her. "I did it! I couldn't say no! H-he was going to kill me, too! I d-didn't want to die! I'm sorry!"

"Dane. I'm sorry I wasn't a better sister to you."

"I'm sorry I wasn't able to save you. I'm so fucking sorry."

The weight in my chest expands, swallowing me in a black hole of sudden despair.

Vera!

I clutch at my chest, stumbling from the apartment and falling to my hands and knees as I gasp for air. The grief twists like a corkscrew, tighter and tighter as I battle to breathe through the shaking that's consumed my entire body.

What if there was another way?

Did I give up too soon?

Could I have saved her from Royce without her dying?

Why did this happen?

How could I let my sister die twice?

Fuck, I'm going to be sick.

My stomach rolls, burning my throat as I force it back down. I tuck my forehead against my arm, breathing in the hardwood floor of the hallway—the rich mahogany smell that proves it's real hardwood and not the fake stuff. I absorb the coolness of the wood through my cheek, closing my eyes.

This was what she wanted. She said it herself.

Because she thought it was the only answer. What if I'd found another way?

And how many more years would she have been used and tortured by Royce before I finally accepted that this was the only way for it to end?

The constriction in my chest eases, filling in with a steadier ache instead. I push myself upright, then fall back against the wall. It still hurts. Still weighs like bricks of loss chained to my heart. But I can breathe. The tension slowly fades from my muscles, and I wipe my face clear of the tears that'd fallen.

I'm not holding on to the grief as I did last time.

I'm sad she's gone.

But I'm happy she's not Royce's puppet anymore.

We did save her, I remind myself. *Just not in the way I wanted.*

Chapter Eight

RAEGAN

Closing the door to the spare room, I take a deep breath. Talking to her, sharing those pieces of my past... it took a lot out of me. I feel disoriented. Weak. Brittle. Each slow breath helps to reinforce my mental and emotional walls, clearing my head so I can focus on what's next. So I can look the others in the eye without shame or guilt.

Once I think I'm safe, I look around the room and notice one of them is missing. "Where's Dane?" I ask, trying not to panic that he's out of sight again.

I'm not losing anyone else.

"Waiting in the hall," Aiden replies, standing at the edge of the corridor to the entry door so he can see both spaces.

"Is she still asleep?" Kell asks, crossing his arms and staring at the closed door.

I nod, walking toward Aiden with Jackson close behind. He'd used his gift to help me carry her into the room, staying with me until we were out before giving me some space. I love he can sense that about me. When I need him, he's right there. When I need time, he's out of sight. I can't say he's completely gone; he probably had been watching me from somewhere close, but as long as I have the illusion of being alone at that time, that's all I need.

"Do you want to return to the Loft? You're still recovering from the fight and your gift," Aiden croons, almost a lulling sound as if to ease me into agreeing with him.

Unfortunately for him, it has the opposite effect, bringing out my disagreeable side to dig in my imaginary heels as I step in close to him. "And you're recovering from near-death. If anyone's going back to the Loft to rest, it should be you."

"I'll sleep after the Tower's secure. We're lucky we found her. There could be others."

"And how the heck am I supposed to relax when you say something like that? No, I'm coming with you. We're doing this together. When you rest, I'll rest."

Aiden slides his hand around my neck, lifting my chin with his thumb. He leans in close. "You're always testing my patience. Especially when I try to look after your well-being," he murmurs, an edge to his tone.

"Pot calling the kettle black?" I challenge and catch the ghost of a smile before he releases me and heads to the door.

"Let's go."

"Did I just win that one?" I ask in shock to Kell.

He laughs and catches me with an arm to bring me out of the apartment with him. "That's what I heard."

Dane's waiting with his back to the opposite wall, his head down and face shadowed.

"Dane?" I trot out of Kell's arm to reach him, and he swings his head up at the sound of my voice. Whatever expression was there clears to a smile.

"Hey. All good in there?"

Jack closes the door as the last to leave while Aiden taps his phone several times. There are a couple of clicks and booms that tell me he's locking up.

"Yeah. What are you doing out here?"

"I forgot my laptop," he says casually, lifting it in one hand. I don't buy it. There's something off about him. I can't see anything specifically to call him out on it, but I can feel it.

Is it Harvey? Harvey's sister?

Fuck.

His sister.

Vera.

How? How could I have forgotten? I was so worried about Aiden, about what's happening next with GE, that she didn't even cross my mind until now.

Every time he's looked at me since I woke up, his smile has been so tender. So comforting.

Guilt eats at my chest. "Dane..."

"Elevator's here," he says at the same time, taking my hand and pulling me inside. "Did you say something?" He looks at me, his amber gaze warm, and the tufts of hair at the top of his head sticking out haphazardly as usual. Or maybe a bit more. The blond is fading at the roots, filling in with his natural brown, so more than half of its length is brown. He's wearing a loose shirt and jeans, exposing the sleeve of tattoos on his left arm and crawling up the side and back of his neck.

"You eye-fucking him, beautiful?" Kellan calls me out. "As much as I've been waiting for my time to shine against these three, I can't say I'll perform my best crammed in an elevator with them unless we all get real comfortable with each other's dicks real quick."

Dane scoffs, rolling his eyes. "Shut the fuck up, man."

Kell throws him a wink with a smirk. "Not you, Rapunzel. I know you're already familiar with the sight of mine."

The elevator dings just in time as Dane curses at him, and I drag him away before they start a fight in that cramped space.

"I'll get it!" Tinsley calls from the apartment following Aiden's knock. The door swings open a millisecond later, and Reid fills the doorway instead, his back to us.

Seeing his protectiveness for her makes me smile. I'm happy he has someone he cares about so fiercely, like how the guys and I feel about each other. It's a relief that she's back from GE, unharmed. Maybe he'll be less grumpy all the time.

Tinsley smiles at him and shrugs. "We knew they were coming. It was safe." She stretches to her toes to kiss his cheek. "Love you!"

He grabs the back of her head and pulls her mouth to his long enough for Tinsley to melt against him. Aiden clears his throat, and Kell chuckles, squeezing my hip. They separate, Tinsley wearing a dazed expression and smile. "Mm, okay." She turns and happily strolls back into the apartment while Reid spins to us.

"Come in," he offers, ignoring Kellan's wide grin and the fact that we'd just watched him kiss Tinsley into submission. His blue gaze lands on me, and he gives me a small nod. I'm not completely fluent in Reid gestures yet, but I think he's telling me he's glad I'm okay. Just like I've become accustomed to him always seeking me out, looking for me within the group to make sure I'm there and okay. I think we'd be hugging right now if either of us were hugging people, but since we're not, I return his nod with one of my own.

He leads us into the living room where Tinsley's sprawled in one chair and Cibrina is standing before a wall of information from her gift. Shimmering, golden lines and text fill the length of one wall. She glances down at her laptop, scrolls with the mouse, and I catch more text appearing in one of the columns the more she reads.

"I see you're still deep in research," Aiden remarks, and Cibrina's head pops up. She smiles warmly and straightens.

"Yes. Reid shared fascinating information about his gift. It's not just teleporting like we thought. His gift allows him to connect one space to another, then slingshot himself across a void dimension to get there—"

"Slingshot is a stretch," Reid corrects.

"Oh, I'll fix that." She poises her hands in front of her as a golden keyboard appears and then starts typing away. Some of the text along the wall changes as she works.

"How does that help us block it from being used?" Dane asks, taking a seat and flipping open his laptop.

I walk to the wall. Ever since I first saw her gift, I've been wanting to touch it and see what happens. The letters smudge when I run my hand over them, then fix themselves a second later. "Cibrina, have I ever told you how cool your gift is?" Now that I know I'm not actually messing anything up by touching it, I play with it some more and watch it rearrange, shift, or sharpen.

"Thank you, Raegan. I do enjoy it."

The glowing text suddenly changes to outline an image of something. I step back to see it better. Two circles and some wavy lines?

"Reid's gift is quite similar to Bea's portal magic. We're dealing with dimensional-type gifts for both. While there's limited information on dimensions, there have been studies on string theory and M-Theory, which is the closest I've found to what we're looking for. This is all theoretical physics, of course, but I think there's something here. I've analyzed all the published studies as well as some scientific journal articles, and there are a few tests I'd like to try."

"You did all that this morning?" I ask, amazed.

"No." Oh. "I started last night."

...Oh.

Kellan laughs, throwing his arm around my shoulders and pushing my slack jaw back in place. "I'll bet she's an expert physicist by the time this is over."

Cibrina laughs. "I wouldn't go that far."

"We also need a way to identify anyone at the Tower who's invisible," Aiden adds.

Reid shoots a look at Tinsley, who shrugs, then turns to Aiden. "As a precaution, or did something happen?"

"We met one of Harvey's sisters in the locked-down apartment. She's still there, and I've re-secured it."

"Her name is Alice," I tell Reid, sharing the name she'd given me before falling asleep. "Looks like you have another younger sister." And I have a younger sister. My chest tightens at the realization that I've gone from no family to a dozen half-siblings. Maybe even more out there.

It's... exciting. And terrifying.

They could all hate me like Alice. They might not want anything to do with me.

But they might also want to get to know me, too. Just like I'm becoming more curious about them.

Reid slices through my train of thought. "You're the only sibling who matters to me."

I stare at him, shocked. "What? Why?"

He looks away, his face giving away nothing.

Tinsley smiles warmly at him. There's so much love and understanding in her hazel eyes that I almost feel the need to look away to give them privacy. She touches his thigh. "I can answer that." Tinsley faces me. "Charles started using and training Reid more around the time he watched you."

If I was a baby then, that would make Reid still a kid. We're only five years apart in age.

She continues, "When he was forced to witness and participate in some of the horrible things that Charles did, you were the only good thing in his life. You showed him that the world wasn't all dark and bloody as it was when he was with Charles. That there was good in it. You helped keep him grounded in the real world, not Charles's world, and—"

Reid grasps her hand on his thigh, and she stops. His cool gaze returns to mine. "I wouldn't be here today, or with Tinsley, if not for you. You also escaped his influence. The others didn't. They could be just as cruel and manipulative as him. I don't owe every spawn of Charles any loyalty."

I think of how Alice had blindly tried kidnapping Dane for Charles and attacked me. But then I remember how she cried for Harvey and what she'd done. "I think it's still worth trying to help them. I promised Harvey we would save them from Charles."

He gives me a sharp nod but doesn't say anything further as if he's acknowledging my choice, even if he doesn't agree with it.

When no one else chimes in on that topic, Cibrina responds to Aiden's original request. "Thermal scans should be able to detect any other invisible... guests."

Dane starts typing and clicking on his laptop. "I think we have that option on these cameras. I'd gotten the ones with all the bells and whistles when we had them installed."

"Good. Let's find a way to compare the thermal readings with what the camera actually sees for body count. If there's a discrepancy, flag security and notify each of us for a manual review," Aiden orders, and Dane nods.

"I'll stay here to work on that and the tests with Cibrina and Reid."

"Before you go, we received Harvey and Vera back this morning." Cibrina looks between Aiden and Dane. "When and where should we have the service? There are a lot of members who wish to say goodbye to Harvey."

My heart sinks like a weighted balloon.

Aiden slants his gaze to Dane, who's staring hard at his screen. "Tomorrow. We'll have Harvey's in the Hall and Vera's in the unused office, as it'll just be the five of us."

Cibrina nods. "Understood. I'll have Penn and Quinn get everything prepared."

"Thank you."

Chapter Nine

DANE

"You realize you won't be able to teleport around the Tower or in and out of it with this, right?" I ask Reid, who's now standing with crossed arms and staring at the wall of glowing golden text. We've put together a general concept of how we might block inter-dimensional or Void travel into the Tower, and now Cibrina's out picking up the parts we need with her assistants.

Reid answers, deadpan, with his back still to me. "I could use the exercise."

I release a small puff of laughter. That might be the first time I've ever heard the guy make something close to a joke.

Tinsley swivels her elbow on the couch to casually lift her hand. "I can still get him somewhere fast if I need to."

There's nothing else to do now but wait, so I slap my laptop shut and set it aside so I can relax against the upholstered chair. "You never did tell the rest of us what happened with you while you were with GE. You told Rae, but we've been distracted today with an invisible guest and Tower security."

Tinsley leans into her fist, seeming unbothered by my question, while Reid does a one-eighty to stare me down as if daring me to say anything negative or push her. I raise my brows.

"Vera needed me for her plan against Royce—and to protect you—so I made her a deal. She had to fix what was done to me two years ago for her plan to work, but I also demanded she protect the other Guild members who'd been taken. She would pretend she was torturing us for information or using her special brainwashing technique against them, and no one else at GE would question it or bother us. You guys showed up at Royce's house and Vera said it was time for the plan anyway, so she let us go. Or, let you rescue us, I suppose."

Imaginary bricks pile onto my chest until it's a struggle to breathe.

How long had she been planning that? When did something change for her to switch from trying to get me to join her to protecting me from them instead?

Why, Vera? Why did it have to end like this when you were starting to help?

I grip the armrest. "Do you know why"—I clear my throat when it starts to thicken— "why she was doing it?"

Tinsley offers me a kind smile. "She told me she learned their plans for you, and it changed everything. At least when it came to you. She still hated the rest of us," she adds with a soft laugh.

Reid grunts and goes back to reading the hovering text.

A knock on his apartment door interrupts our conversation. Fabian calls through it, "Pizza's here."

"I'll get it," I volunteer, pushing to my feet. I need to move. To shake out the grief that's trying to latch on again by distracting myself with a new—even if temporary—purpose. Fabian's already shoveled half a slice into his mouth while he holds a stack of boxes in his other hand. "Are these all for us?" Aiden probably ordered them since I haven't come back yet.

"All but one," he answers once his mouth is clear. "The bottom one I'm bringing to the girl in Harvey's apartment."

He doesn't bother asking me who she is or why she's there. Aiden could have filled him in already—he is one of the Guild's most trusted members—but he's also the kind of guy to trust us enough that he'll wait for us to tell him when we're ready.

The mention of Alice while Vera's still fresh on my mind makes my heart squeeze. I'll be saying goodbye to Vera at the funeral to-morrow, but what about her?

"I'll take it to her," I offer before the idea is fully formed, taking the stack.

Fabian nods, finishing off his slice. "Thanks, man. Let me know if you need anything."

I set the boxes on the kitchen island and pull out my phone to text Aiden my idea. Or... more like my request. He's usually quick to respond since his phone is practically glued to his hand, so the fact that I wait for almost a minute means he's taking more time to consider it first.

Finally, his reply comes through.

"I'll be back," I tell Reid and Tinsley as I slide the bottom box out. "Call me if Cibrina gets here before me."

Once the elevator doors open, I call Aiden and wait for it to connect, unlock Harvey's apartment door with the app, then slip the phone into my pocket. He'll be muting it on his end and keeping an ear on us to make sure she doesn't try anything stupid with me.

I quickly slip inside and shut the door behind me, locking it so she doesn't try to escape while I'm here.

"Alice?" I call out from the dark hallway. "It's Dane. I've got dinner."

I give her a minute to respond before I stride to the kitchen. She's sitting in one of the sofa chairs in the living room with her knees pulled up to her chest and her chin resting on her arms while she stares at the TV. The broken table is gone, cleaned up by the others probably while Raegan was comforting Alice, and the bloodied furniture has also been removed. A rug covers most of the living room carpet.

At least Aiden made the effort to better tidy up the reminders of Harvey's death here while he prepares another equally locked-down apartment for her.

The volume is barely a whisper, so I know she heard me.

"I've got pizza." I flip open the top. "It's cheese and pepperoni. Is that what you like?"

She whips her head around to glare at me. "Is that what I *like*? What the hell would you care? I'm your prisoner. Or are you looking for me to thank you for bothering to feed me? Because if you are, you're wasting your time."

"For fuck's sake," I mutter, dropping the cardboard top. I lean against the kitchen counter and cross my arms over my chest. "I'll just get to the fucking point, then. We're having a funeral for Harvey tomorrow."

All the vitriol melts from her expression, and her eyes widen.

"If you want to say goodbye... I can make that happen."

Her gaze hardens. "And what will I have to do for you to *make it happen*?"

I hold her stare. "Nothing. This isn't a tit for tat."

Alice's brows knit with confusion, the anger once again leeching from her to something I recognize. Something vulnerable. "Why? Why would you let me—" Her lip quivers, and she bites it.

My own grief aches and echoes hers.

"Because I know some of what you're going through. I lost my sister the same day you lost your brother. There's going to be a smaller funeral for her first with just a few people because she didn't have friends. She was obsessed with her work for GE and that's all she knew." I swallow the knot in my throat, dropping my hands to grip the counter behind me on either side instead. "No matter what you're here for or which side you're on, I don't think you should miss your brother's funeral. You deserve to say goodbye to him and see how much he meant to the friends and people who were around him."

Her eyes water and her lip wobbles before she turns away from me.

"We'll send someone up to escort you to the funeral. You can talk about him to the others if you want or not. But if you ever need to talk to someone... if you don't want to be alone when you're having a rough time... I can be here."

She sniffs, still turned away from me.

I'm not sure what sort of response I expected from her, but I don't know what I should do next. Leaving seems like the best thing if she doesn't have anything else she wants to say to me. I'll give her some space. "Just think about what I said. Make sure you eat and put the leftovers in the fridge."

As I exit the apartment and lock it down, I feel a little bit lighter.

Chapter Ten

RAEGAN

Do dresses carry bad luck?

I pick at the black fabric of the skater dress I'd worn to the Guild party that feels like forever ago. The one that was interrupted by Thorne's untimely fake death and Gordon's real death, which led to Harvey's betrayal and Charles's attack.

The only other black dress I have is the one Kellan got me for dancing at a nightclub, and it doesn't seem appropriate.

Like Vera gives a shit what you wear to see her.

Three sharp knocks at the bathroom door precede Aiden's voice. "Are you ready?"

I check myself in the mirror one last time. The dress covers my arms and hugs the curve of my shoulders before cutting to a V-shape in the front, and an even deeper one in the back. The skirt flows and moves with me, and between its shorter length and my heels, showcases my legs. My hair is pulled to one side over my shoulder, and I stuck with simple eyeliner and mascara.

Trying to look nice does nothing to ease the knots in my stomach.

I've hardly seen Dane since we left him at Reid's apartment. He'd stayed there all night working with them to get the enhanced security features in place. The last thing we'd need is GE catching us off guard during Harvey's service.

They were able to make some sort of quantum field that blocks dimensional travel on each floor of the Tower. There are gaps, but Dane says they're tiny and tucked into places that don't matter. As soon as they'd finished, he crashed into his bed. Aiden was going to wake him up while I got ready.

The bathroom door opens. "Oh! Yeah. I'm read—" The words die on my lips when I see him. I'm expecting a suit as he usually wears, but instead, he's dressed *down* from his standard. Black slacks and a black cashmere sweater with a loose V-neck, teasing his smooth chest and lining the swell of his biceps. His hair is still styled back with a single strand falling to his forehead.

His dark gaze drags up my legs, heating me where it lands as it continues upward.

"You're underdressed," I scold him, but it's diminished by the breathiness of my voice when he swiftly closes the distance between us.

His fingers graze down my back, his touch gentle over my exposed scars. "You're perfect," he purrs, and a shiver curls at the base of my spine. Aiden kisses the side of my neck, sending a parade of goosebumps across my skin. I close my eyes, my mouth popping open as I inhale sharply, and my body comes alive at his touch.

Suddenly, I'm pressed against the vanity, his mouth devouring mine, his hand sliding up my thigh beneath my skirt to grab my ass. He kicks my feet apart,guiding my thigh to his hip, while his hard length rubs against my core.

I moan, wrapping my leg around him to pull him closer and

grinding my hips to increase the friction between us.

"What's taking so long?" Kellan shouts from the living room, and I nearly jump out of my skin and shove Aiden back.

He releases me but doesn't move away. He grips the counter on either side of me and pants, his intense stare drilling into me as if I'm his greatest vice and he's given up fighting it. "I almost dragged you out of the crowd that night," he eventually says. "You thought you were safe being a brat with the Guild around, but you should know that I don't care about that." His hand curls over my throat. He squeezes lightly. A soft but no less real threat.

"Everything goes out the window when it comes to you. I'd have no problem throwing you over my lap and spanking your ass in front of the others if it teaches you a lesson. Remember that." He gives me a peck on the lips and leaves.

My heart races from what just happened, flooding my veins with heat as his words replay in my mind.

As they finally sink in past the lust.

He wouldn't *dare*.

I rush to the living room, ready to throw him a retort, until I see the somber expression on Dane's face. The rush of anger instantly fizzles out.

Fuck.

Dane smiles when he sees me, then stands. "I like that dress."

"Thanks."

He nods and turns to the door that Aiden's holding open.

Right.

Time to see Vera.

The office is overflowing with flowers of all colors, shapes, and sizes. There are stands with flower wreaths, massive vases of bouquets, and even hanging garlands with flowers interwoven in them. The single desk is pushed against the back wall, and an ornately carved box sits at its center. A champagne bucket and stand of white roses are off to the side of it.

I've never been to a funeral or wake before, but I've seen enough movies and shows with them. No loved ones or friends of Vera sent these flowers. There are no pictures, no memories of her displayed anywhere in the room, because we have none.

For all the beauty in this small space, it's also a harsh reminder of Vera's life.

And I wonder how lonely she's been all these years, hiding behind anger and her wish to be a part of something. Only for that wish to be twisted and abused.

Aiden goes first, picking a white rose from the bucket and speaking softly to Vera. The rest of us are on the opposite side of the room to give him privacy. I keep sneaking glances at Dane to check on him, but his face is carefully calm.

Too calm.

Kellan is next. His time up there is shorter than Aiden's before he lays the rose over the box. Jackson takes a rose and then sets it beside the others before walking back.

Kell nudges me forward.

I use that push to propel my feet across the room as much as I'm dreading it. I move on autopilot, letting my body mimic the moves I'd watched the others take. Stop in front of the desk. Take a rose.

Breathe.

The box is simple on the front and sides, but the lid has carved flowers, vines, and branches surrounding a heart in the center. It's beautiful.

But one of the vines, snaking down and then splitting into two... it reminds me of the scar I'd given her when she'd died the first time. The one that ran into her eyebrow and continued to her cheekbone.

"I'm sorry. I don't think I have anything nice to say. I already grieved for the girl who'd been like a sister to me a long time ago. I can't mourn your death this time like before." I tighten my grip on the rose stem. "I guess... I'm sorry for everything that happened after. You didn't deserve to be used and controlled like that. And I'm sorry that I was the one to kill you again, but I understand why you wanted it to be me." I think of Harvey's sister and what she's going through, what she'll have to live with. "You didn't want Dane forced to kill his sister. At least you gave him that.

"But," I continue, my throat thickening, "more than anything, I'm relieved that you're gone. That you won't put Dane in any more danger. I'm happy, but I'm also terrified of what this is going to do to him. To us. I killed you again, and I know he swore what happened to you wouldn't change anything between us, but—"

My breath catches when Dane steps up next to me. I place my flower on her urn and start to leave to give him privacy, but he takes my hand and holds me there.

"Hey, Ver," he greets, his voice soft. "I didn't mean to interrupt you two, but I felt like it couldn't wait." He squeezes my hand like a silent plea to stay.

So, I do.

"Thank you for giving me whatever kept Royce's gift from controlling me. For thinking of me at all when you were with them. I know we stopped seeing eye to eye a long time ago, but seeing that you still cared about me... it meant a lot." He swallows hard. "I never stopped caring about you. Even when you did and said shitty things. Even when you refused to read my letters. There were times I think I hated you, too. But because I cared so much and you seemed not to care at all."

A tear slips past my defenses. I don't look at him. I can't. I know I'll lose it if I do. I stare at Vera and listen to his voice. I hold on to his hand as much as he's holding on to mine, grounding ourselves in each other as his words rip me apart piece by piece.

"I wish I could have saved you. I wish this had been a second chance for us to start over. I wish I had seen what you were going through on the island before they got to you. Sometimes, I wish so hard that I think my chest is going to cave in, Ver. And there's a hole at the bottom, waiting for me if I let it, just like I had last time, when I couldn't let you go or let go of my wishes. Where I could stay with the good memories of you. But... I can't this time. I hate who I was then. I never want to be him again. Don't be mad, okay?"

He draws a shuddering breath. "When all this is over, I'll bring our parents to see you so you won't be lonely." He lifts the lid of the urn with his notebook, sliding it into a slot at the back, as if it'd been made for it. "Here. I wrote you one last letter. Read it for me?"

I break, a sob slipping free. Dane presses a tender kiss to my cheek, then releases my hand and leaves the room. I drop to my knees as the emotion crashes through me like a storm at sea, raging in my chest and spilling over. Anger and sadness thrash and collide within me, and I feel my gift churning in my gut.

GE did this. They made Dane go through her death all over again. They use us like tools. Like test rats to get what they want, then toss us aside when they're done. Like Vera. Like Harvey.

Heat flashes through me, searing my veins and glowing red.

I'm pulled into a broad chest and thick arms. "I've got you, beautiful."

I'm too emotional, my thoughts so rampant that some of my gift cracks his skin. I try to push away when I see it, but he embraces me tighter. "It's okay. Let it all out. I won't let go."

"Kell, I'm hurting you," I choke, still struggling.

"I can take it." He pulls me into his lap, separating my body from touching anything but him. Some of his skin is already healed over, scales emerging along his sides and neck.

I bury my face there, releasing the anger and sadness as he holds me like that. As I let go, cocooned in his warmth.

The funeral for Harvey later is a complete turnaround from Vera's. Guild members show up wearing whatever black clothes they could find in their closets, whether it was jeans, leggings, sweats, or tops. I'm the one overdressed compared to the others, and I almost chew Aiden out for not telling me until I remember the way he'd looked at me in the dress.

Fabian and Evie escort Alice to the front row and sit on either side of her like guards. She has a plain black dress on, and her face is tight as she takes in the Hall, the decorations, and the people in it. Once she spots the urn, though, she doesn't look away the entire service.

When members take to the stage to talk about Harvey, they share silly stories that make everyone laugh at what they'd done together or something Harvey had said or done. After eating a buffet of his favorite foods—which were mostly snacks and tacos—everyone splits to various tables to play some of his favorite games. The Guild Hall is loud and rowdy, laughing as they play and continue to share stories of Harvey when another one comes to them.

I learn more about Harvey tonight than I knew when he was alive.

Eventually, members retire to their apartments for the night. Alice approaches us with Evie and Fabian at her sides. Her face is still red and splotchy as if she'd just finished wiping away a fresh set of tears. They'd been bouncing between tables to hear more stories all evening, but I hadn't seen her speak to anyone. She's been soaking in everyone's stories of Harvey without a word.

She looks at me, then Dane. "Thank you for this," she murmurs, then spins on her heel and walks away.

We migrate to one of the lounge areas under the glass half-dome. The lights in the Hall are dimmed, allowing some of the brighter stars to shine through the windows. A tiny gas fire dances over colored beads at the center of the low table we're sitting around.

"How many siblings did he have?" Silas asks, pinching a bit of lint from the couch he's lying on and tossing it in the fire.

Evie smacks his hand. "Stop that."

A sly smile stretches across his face as he looks up at her, his fingers going back for another one. She grabs his hand.

"Ten," Aiden answers absentmindedly, swirling the bourbon in his glass.

"And another on the way," I add, remembering when Charles

told Harvey he could have time off when his newest sibling was born.

Gabe leans back against Zedd, who's strumming softly on his guitar, and claps. "Eleven, wow! That man sure gets busy. You hear that, Zeddy? We've a lot of cleaning to do."

Zedd's hand freezes over the strings. "Why?"

"They'll need *somewhere* to go after we rescue them. You can be the stern no-nonsense figure, and I'll be the cool, keeping-it-hip one."

"No."

Kellan laughs, stretching his arm behind me on the couch. "You think you can handle that many kids and teenagers who can turn invisible and were trained to stay hidden?"

Gabriel pushes off Zedd, balancing on the chair arm. "Can I? You should have seen the way I single-handedly turned a group of bloodthirsty fans into a gaggle of giggling besties by the end of one night!"

"You bribed them with stolen jewelry and snacks," Zedd deadpans.

Tinsley titters with laughter, and Silas snickers in the ensuing silence.

"They always say the best way to someone's heart is through their stomach," Gabe presses on, unperturbed.

"Accurate," Fabian chimes in, a bag of chips in his lap.

Aiden sighs.

"We have bigger things to worry about before that," Dane cuts in, running his fingers through his hair on the other side of Kell. "Taking down the board members and elects, for starters. Charles, on his own, is going to be difficult, and then there's the rest of Gifted Enterprise operating all over the world, handing out gift-blocking jewelry to the highest bidder."

Wait. Gift-blocking jewelry. Something wiggles at the back of my mind, trying to remind me of something.

"Damn. When you say it like that..." Silas grumbles.

The machine Vera made. She said it could mass-produce those, but also...

"Oh!" I exclaim, the memory coming back in a rush. All eyes turn to me. "Vera." My gaze inadvertently slides to Dane. His face tightens. "She told me they're weaponizing gifts. Dane's, of course, but others' too if they have their blood. And they made her program a machine that can synthesize gifts from blood samples into objects." I seek out Tinsley to confirm what I've said, and she nods.

"We should have killed her sooner," Reid remarks, his tone bitter.

Dane stands abruptly. I start to rise, too, but he's already walking across the room without slowing down.

"Give him a minute," Kell murmurs just for me, his hand guiding me to sink back onto the couch.

"He shouldn't be alone," I argue.

"Jack's in the Loft. He won't be completely alone."

I nod, still worried, but look back to the others and catch Tinsley smacking Reid's chest.

"That's still his sister, Reid. Have some compassion. Or *tact*. Besides, she was trying to do good when I was with her last." Tinsley wraps her hand around his. "She fixed me."

"There would have been nothing to fix if not for her," he replies coldly.

Tinsley stands, bringing him with her by his hand. She smiles apologetically to the rest of us, waving goodbye. "Sorry about that! We're going to call it a night."

The rest of us don't say a word until the elevator doors close.

It's Silas who speaks up first. "So, what got fixed?"

The others give varying sounds and gestures of having no idea before looking at Aiden, who takes another drink. "No."

"No, you don't know, or no, you won't say?" Silas questions.

"What kinds of blood samples does GE have?" Evie asks, redirecting the conversation.

I chime in, "Anyone who was on an island or captured by them, and anyone who works for them. At minimum. But Vera and Tinsley said they'd tried destroying as many of the samples as they could, like ours."

"With all those samples, Daddy Psycho could have had his pick of gifts," Kellan drawls.

"Unlikely," Aiden says. "Based on what Reid's said and what we know about him, I think he has to get it directly from the source. Otherwise, he could have had your gift a long time ago."

Kellan shrugs. "Or he didn't know about me until he saw me. Maybe I don't look as good on paper."

"Regardless, we need to add finding and destroying that machine to the list. Even if we kill Charles, that gives too much power to any other agents who have access to it," Aiden adds.

As if our list isn't already big enough. But he has a point. We're taking down the board members to avoid someone else picking up GE and running with it. The scientists and agents are too separated from the management level to know the first thing about leading the shadow organization. But with the ability to mass produce gift-blocking cuffs or other gift-imbued objects, it would only be a matter of time before things spiral out of control.

We continue discussing other possible gifts and how they could be—or might not be—applied to objects. Jackson's gift, for example. He controls air, but could an object with no brain or real body be able to control air? Or is it only property-based gifts that could be used?

After it feels like we debate it for an hour and there's still no sign of Dane, I decide to say goodnight and return to the Loft.

Jackson's there waiting at the door when I open it. He gives me an enigmatic smile. "Here for Dane?"

"Yeah. Is he in his room?"

Jack nods. "Don't stay up late. We're training in the morning."

Oof. It's already after midnight. Maybe Dane went straight to bed, and I'll just go snuggle in his arms.

But I hope he's awake. I want to know what was on his mind after the funeral and what Reid said. He didn't and hasn't sounded like he blames me at all, but... I have to know.

"Good night," I whisper, pushing to my toes to give him a kiss, but he somehow sneaks around me to kiss my cheek instead.

He chuckles softly. "If you kiss me now, little one, I won't stop. Go."

Oh.

Warmth floods my face. As tempting as that is, I need to see how Dane's doing, and I hurry around him to Dane's room.

I tap on his door a couple of times with my knuckles. "Dane? Can I come in?"

No answer.

I turn the knob and poke my head through. "Hello?" The bedroom's dark. And empty. But the bathroom door is cracked, and light shines into the room in a bold line along the floor. I close the door behind me and approach the bathroom. "Dane?" I gently push the door open.

He snaps his head up, looking at me through the mirror and then over his shoulder. There are two boxes of hair dye on the sink in front of him. One blond. One brown.

"What are you doing?"

"Staring at hair dye, apparently." He looks back at his reflection. He runs his fingers through the longer hair at the top of his head. "The blond is almost gone," he says, almost wistfully. "And I don't know what I should do. If I dye it, does that mean I'm still stuck in the past? But this guy with brown hair... I don't know who that is."

I move to his side, my gaze on his through the mirror. "Dye your hair whatever you're comfortable with. Don't worry about if it means something or not."

His brows pinch and his lips thin to a line as he looks between the two boxes with uncertainty.

"You don't have to force her out of your life, you know. It's okay if you take some time to let certain things go. And it's also okay if you've just grown to like the color."

He turns, settling his hands on my waist and tugging me a step closer. "Which color do you like?"

I gaze into his warm amber eyes, drawing me in and trapping me like honey. "I'd like you in any color if that's what makes you happy."

Dane raises an incredulous brow. "Any color? Even if I dye it blue?"

I shrug, a small smirk pulling at my lips. "If that makes you happy."

He chuckles, pressing a chaste kiss to my forehead. "*You* make me happy."

I tilt my head back without thinking, my lips seeking his on instinct. His eyelids droop as he leans in, our mouths fusing as one. Clutching his shirt in my hands, I pull myself against him. His heart hammers, matching mine as if they've somehow synced. He wraps an arm around my waist, tucking me even closer as his other hand cradles my face so he can deepen the kiss, melting me from the inside out.

Eventually, we part, our eyes locked. As much as I want to stay in this warm feeling, it's eating me alive to know what he's thinking.

"Dane... I'm sorry. I'm so sorry. I promised to—"

He kisses me. It's a short press of lips. A sweet stop to my words.

He strokes his thumb over my cheek. "Thank you. For doing what I couldn't." His eyes turn glassy. "I wish we could have saved her some other way, but I think you did the right thing. She's free from them now. So... thanks." His throat bobs with the effort it's taking to hold himself back.

I throw my arms around his neck, pulling his head to my shoulder and holding him tight. He wraps himself around me, exhaling a shuddering breath against my skin. "Thank you," he repeats, his voice strained.

Tears prick my eyes as I squeeze him tighter. Hold him, as if I can somehow transfer my strength to him. "I'm sorry she's gone," I whisper.

It's one thing to lose his sister the first time. But to then have hope that he could have her back, only for it to be crushed again...

He draws back, kissing my cheek. My lips. "Me too." Dane somehow manages a soft smile. "Want to help me dye my hair? I've decided on a color."

I share a watery smile in return.

"Sure... Is it blue?"

Chapter Eleven

RAEGAN

WE'RE IN AIDEN'S OFFICE, discussing board member details, when multiple phones ring like an alarm.

"Pull up security footage," Aiden orders before he's even read whatever message is on his phone.

Dane—with his re-dyed blond hair—turns to the keyboard. Individual camera feeds pop up one after another in boxes across the screens on the wall as Cibrina recalls her gift, and the golden text of information we'd been reviewing fades.

Kellan moves in front of the door as a barrier, crossing his arms, his gaze scanning the camera views with a fierce expression. Jackson pushes off the wall, his hands automatically going to his hoodie pocket to start pulling knives.

I call on my gift, readying myself for a fight.

"Is it Charles?" I ask, looking to Aiden.

"No." Reid takes Tinsley's hand, as if in preparation to get her away, if needed. "I'd be able to tell if it was."

"We've blocked his ability to teleport here anyway, so unless he came through the front door—" Dane adds, then stops himself when Aiden's head snaps up, his dark eyes pinning mine. His jaw tics.

"It's a false alarm," he begins, lifting the phone to his ear. The tension in the room eases a fraction. "What happened?" He listens to the person's reply, then pinches the bridge of his nose, his eyes closed. "No. Clear the alert and let them through. We'll be right there." He shoves the phone into his pocket. "It's Elias," he finally elaborates, his tone edged with distaste as he says the name. I can tell because it's no longer there when he continues, "And Portia. They apparently forced their way past the initial security checkpoint and set off our alarms."

I'm only half-listening as I practically leap to the door, pushing at Kellan to make room so I can leave the office.

"Watch out! I need to go see her!" I shout when he doesn't *immediately* shift aside.

"Who're they?" Reid asks, his brow scrunched as he stands and watches me.

Kellan laughs and grabs the doorknob. "Slow down, beautiful. We're going with you."

The others gather at my back as Cibrina explains my friendship with Portia and Elias before I started working with the guys, which leads Reid to ask why I wasn't on the best of terms with them when I'd first arrived in this city.

Thankfully, Kell's opened the door, and I'm out before I have to worry about Reid's reaction to that whole story. The five of us take the elevator to the first floor.

I'm brimming with excitement and nerves. Excitement, because I really freaking missed Portia and her contagious energy. And nerves, because we'd only known each other for a short time before she was taken and then ran away. What if I've over-fantasized our friendship in the last few months? What if it meant more to me than to her?

The doors open, and I make myself push past that doubt as I race down the hallway to the large open area that's just beyond the security checkpoint and a wall of translucent glass. The murky glass blocks this side of the first level from being visible to the entrance, so Aiden and I don't have to hide.

Security guards form a line a few yards in, blocking a small group of people. It's more than just Elias and Portia. I don't recognize the others, and the surprise of seeing more people slows my steps.

"Oh my god, she's here! Rae!" Portia shouts when she sees me, then runs at me at full speed.

Shit, she's not slowing down.

I brace myself, then feel Kellan at my back just before she crashes into me, her arms squeezing me against her full chest. We bump into Kell, but he helps steady us so we don't fall.

"You're alive! They kept saying you died, and Aiden died, and I knew it couldn't be true! But then these guys wouldn't let us through, and I had to see you no matter what!"

I can't help but laugh, wrapping my arms around her. "We're okay. Thanks to Jack, we made it. But we have everyone still pretending we died."

Portia pulls back, her forest green eyes bright. "I have a gazillion questions for you and so much to tell you, too."

"Me too." I glance over my shoulder at the guys and notice Aiden and Elias eyeing each other, their postures stiff.

"Thorton."

"Adams."

"It's still appropriate to provide notice of a visit. Or at least follow the security protocols a business has in place rather than forcing your way in," Aiden remarks in a smooth yet threatening tone.

Elias smiles. "A landlord doesn't require giving advance notice to check on his tenants. It's polite, of course, but not mandatory." Aiden's eyes narrow, but Elias continues, "The forced entry was out of concern for Raegan's well-being. Security confirmed with my source that you'd both died, and it was necessary that we press through to verify it for ourselves by someone with a first-hand account. Portia wouldn't have been satisfied with anything less. And it appears it's a good thing we did."

He turns to me, his smile softening. "Raegan. I'm relieved to see the rumor is false. Have they been treating you well since I've been gone?"

I open my mouth to respond, but Dane steps forward and snaps, "Says the guy who kicked her out of his apartment the second things got rough."

Portia jabs a finger at Dane. "Hey! Don't talk to Elias like that! You weren't so great to Rae when we were here before, either."

Dane's jaw snaps shut.

Kellan bursts out laughing.

But Portia isn't finished. "That's right! I remember you. And now that I'm back, just try saying mean things to Rae again and I'll make you regret it!"

Dane takes another step toward her, and I jump between them. "Guys, stop—"

"Good!" Dane retorts, his fist raised. "Do it. If I ever say anything like that to Rae again, then you'd better follow through on that threat. Because I'd rather die than ever hurt her again."

Portia mirrors him. "I will! I'll—Wait." She looks at me, confused.

"What?"

I offer her a small smile and shrug. "How soon are we catching up?"

Elias clears his throat. "That aside, he was right in his accusation." He bows his head at me. "I shouldn't have done that or said those words to you. Regardless of what I was feeling at the time, it's no excuse. I hope you'll forgive me."

"Oh, I never—I didn't—"

"Apology accepted," Aiden says, suddenly at my side. He leans in close, crooning softly in my ear, "You could have been back on the streets with what he did. You deserve the apology for his selfishness."

His warm breath and voice send a pleasurable shiver through me.

"Now! We're catching up now!" Portia grabs my wrist and pulls me away, only to pause three steps in. "Oh. Which way?"

A quick check over my shoulder reveals seven pairs of watching eyes. I turn my wrist to take her hand. "The snack bar. This way."

I guide her to the gym in the back, scanning the tattoo on my wrist to gain entry, and then pulling us inside. Training for the day is over, but there are still some Guild members putting in extra time. Portia watches them with wide eyes, and I casually wave to Evie and Silas as we pass by to the snack and shake bar.

"Uh, Rae?"

"Yeah?"

Portia points behind me. Jackson follows within arm's reach, his hood up and hands tucked in his kangaroo pocket as he strolls behind us. He smiles at me when our eyes meet.

"Don't worry about him."

Portia loops her arm through mine and leans in, whispering, "He knows I'm not a bad guy, right? He's not here to kill me if I sneeze wrong?"

"He wouldn't *dare* touch you without my permission, Porsh," I reassure her, throwing a swift *look* over my shoulder to drive home that fact.

Jackson's smile curves to a smirk.

Opening the door to the mini cafeteria, Portia walks in first. Jack leans against the gym wall outside the door, settling in as our guard, before I close it.

She tackles me into another hug. "I'm so glad you're okay! Elias has ears everywhere, and when he heard that you died, we rushed here as soon as we could! I'm sorry I left when I did. I'm sorry I wasn't here to help with GE."

"Don't be. I was relieved you were out of harm's way. I just wish we'd kept in contact more so I knew you were okay."

She withdraws, a guilty expression on her face, before she looks away. "Well, actually..."

"*Elias* did that?!" I gasp, mind blown.

Portia giggles, swaying in her seat as if the act of laughing throws her off-balance. A loud *slurp* sounds between us as she sucks on the straw for the last drop of spiked smoothie. "Mhm... it was—it was *so* hot, Rae. Like... I wouldn't have thought that'd be something I'm into, but *seeing* him do it?" She swoons and falls in her chair, which thankfully has a back rest.

I drink my own alcohol-infused smoothie through a straw straight from the blender. Warmth cocoons me as armor between deep feelings and the stories we've been swapping back and forth. I didn't hold anything back, giving her the details of some things I haven't yet shared with anyone else. Everything that happened when I was back with Gordon. How I felt. How I'm still battling the memory of him in the dark or my nightmares. My self-doubt.

I've gotten better. I can see it now, looking back, that I've changed. While it doesn't always feel like it in the moment, it's comforting to go through my past and see, in hindsight, that I am moving forward, bit by bit.

Between sharing scars and new tattoos, we've both stripped our shirts off and haven't bothered putting them back on. Kellan told me no one outside would be able to see us through the windows, so it's just us.

We've been sharing bombshell after bombshell of information all afternoon. While the Guild has been fighting off Gifted Enterprise, who deals with experimentation, brainwashing, and control of world governments from the shadows, Portia's group has been tackling trafficking rings of gifted using the very jewelry Charles has been producing from Danc's gift. I think we've spent half of it gaping at one another, and we're finally through the darkest truths that we can turn to more lighthearted moments. I'm both shocked and amused that Portia is also in a relationship with multiple men like me.

"If you weren't the one telling me, I wouldn't believe it!" I laugh, finishing off my drink and setting it down on the table between us a bit harder than I intended.

"Well, believe it! And we're here to help you now. All of us!"

"Thanks, Porsh." I clench my hands. "When I thought I'd lost Aiden... I can't do that again. I can't lose any of us. If I could confront Charles alone right now to keep everyone else safe, I would."

Portia grabs one of my hands. "But none of us want that! I know your guys wouldn't, and I don't, and Elias wouldn't, either. Or your half-brother, or anyone else in this Guild! We're all here, and we'll fight him together. You're not alone."

Smiling, I nod.

Portia's stomach growls loudly, interrupting our moment as we devolve into laughter.

"Let's find something to eat. This is a shake and snack bar, after all," I muse with a grin, pushing unsteadily to my feet.

"It's Elias!" Portia shouts. She points at the window where Elias is standing outside on the phone, his back turned. She runs over to the glass separating them and flashes him with a cackle, wiggling her ass and making faces at him.

I burst out laughing. Something dark suddenly covers my face, and my heart stops. The warm fabric is tugged down, and my head pops through an opening.

Jackson stands between me and the windows, his sapphire gaze wild and dark.

Immediately, I think something's happened with GE. "What is it?" I demand, flailing beneath his hoodie to get my arms through the sleeves, when it hits me. He stuffed me in his hoodie. He's blocking me from the windows. "Kellan said no one can see in here."

"It's tinted to block the sun," he replies. "And the sun's going down."

Oh.

Oh.

"Portia—!"

Elias stares at Portia for a beat, and I realize I'm too late.

"He can see you!" I whisper-shout, leaning around Jackson.

Portia freezes, then looks at me. "I thought you said…"

Elias steps up to the glass, pointing his finger at Portia in a silent threat. He says something that we can't hear, and then a flurry of those strangers who'd arrived with them start herding people away, creating a bubble on this side of the Tower.

Elias's gray-blue eyes slide my way, then return to Portia. He mouths, "Don't move," and stalks toward the entrance.

I grab her shirt and shove it into her hand. "Put it on."

She hurriedly yanks her top on. "Whoopsie! Where's the back door?"

"There isn't one in here. But he can't get in without access—"

The door opens. Elias enters with Aiden close behind.

Aiden quirks a brow at me. "What's this I hear about flashing pedestrians outside the Tower?"

Jackson ushers me toward Aiden and the door as Elias beelines for Portia.

"If you were looking for an excuse to get my attention, you have it," he continues, his voice smooth as velvet. He grasps my elbow when I'm in reach. "But someone who's supposedly no longer on this Earth shouldn't be spotted through our windows, let alone so *much* of you."

I pull away from him, knocking into Jackson when I sway off-balance. Jack pins my hips against him so I'm facing Aiden. "I thought it was one-way glass," I mumble, knowing it sounds as dumb as it feels to admit.

Aiden's thumb drags across my lower lip, his imposing presence dwarfing me between them. "Do I need to lock you away in the Loft?"

Jackson slips his hands under the hoodie. His icy fingertips press into my hips, making me gasp. It feels amazing against my hot skin, and I squirm beneath his touch. "She's been drinking," he snitches. My traitorous body clenches at the sound of his husky voice as if he'd whispered a sensual secret in my ear instead of outing me to Aiden.

"Traitor," I mutter, then stop breathing entirely when he shifts his cool fingers lower. The movement's hidden by his large hoodie, but the simmering heat in Aiden's gaze tells me he noticed anyway.

"If you'll excuse us," Elias interjects. A couple of others have joined us, and Portia is now dangling over the shoulder of someone else before they disappear through the door. "We'll be taking our leave for today and will you see tomorrow, as discussed." His gaze lands on me. "Raegan. Your apartment is always open if you want it." He looks between Aiden and Jack, then offers me a polite smile. "Have a good evening."

Aiden gives him a curt nod before he exits, leaving the three of us alone. "Well, then," he starts in a seductive croon. "Let's take her to the Loft and find a fitting punishment."

Chapter Twelve

RAEGAN

A door crashes open, followed by Dane exclaiming, "What the fuck? Is that Rae?"

I kick my feet again, struggling to get free of Aiden, even if it means falling on my ass. My attempts at cussing him out are muted by the gag and the shirt they'd used to cover my head, and my hands are cuffed behind my back.

Aiden doesn't stop moving. I haven't heard Jackson since he blinded me with my shirt, giving me a final smirk as my last view before covering me in darkness, but I'm sure he's still here.

I'm tossed backward and land with a soft bounce.

Knuckles crack. "What've we got here?" Kellan.

My shirt is removed, and my hair flies wildly around me in that swift motion. Rocking my body to the side and onto my knees to face them, I bite down on the cloth gag and seek out Aiden, teeth bared in a snarl. All four men stand at the foot of my bed, watching me with different expressions.

Jackson cocks his head and smirks at me as if this is exactly the result he'd hoped for when ratting me out to Aiden. Like he's seeing a plan in his mind come to fruition at last.

Aiden is next to him, his jacket removed, and sleeves rolled to his elbows. He's wearing a look of firm disapproval that would make me smile if I wasn't so pissed at the way he'd restrained and kidnapped me.

Kellan grins at me wide enough to see the sharp points of his canines. He looks like a man about to feast on me—his favorite dish.

Dane's at the end, worry in his amber gaze as if he might dive between me and the others if he thinks I'm in trouble.

"Someone with complete disregard for her own safety," Aiden replies smoothly. He tugs the gag free to drop around my neck. "Care to share what you did?"

"Get fucked, Aiden," I snap.

His smile is dripping with arrogance when he pinches my chin. "That's exactly what we're here for. You told me you could handle all four of us, isn't that right?"

I gawk at him. "This is your punishment? Sex?"

"Are you holding to that sentiment?" he fires another question instead.

My eyes narrow suspiciously. "Yes."

He releases me. "Jack. Her clothes."

Aiden moves to the head of the bed and out of sight while Jackson steps forward with a knife and a smile that would be terrifying to anyone else on the receiving end of it. For me, that dangerous light in his eyes makes me tremble with anticipation rather than fear. He pinches the neckline of the hoodie and holds his knife there—the tip hovering at the base of my throat.

His gaze goes from his knife to my eyes, holding me captive and breathless in that instant as if time stands still.

I don't move; don't flinch or look away when his blade cuts through the fabric a hairsbreadth away from my skin. I hold his dark stare with defiance as he strips away the hoodie and my bra.

Aiden tugs the sleeve and strap off one arm, then replaces it with something smooth and tight around my wrist before I realize the cuffs are gone. I yank on my other hand, but Aiden's grip on my arm doesn't budge when he repeats the steps on that side. The material around my wrists is cool and soft, unlike the hard metal of before. Silk. Attached to a metal loop and then black paracord rope that ties to hooks protruding from the corner posts at the head of the bed.

"Arms up, and lie back," he instructs—to me, I think—even though he and Jack move my body on either side to do it anyway. The sound of a small motor clicks on, and the rope tied to my silk cuffs pulls taut. Slowly, I'm dragged up the bed. Aiden stops me at its center.

"Her pants," Aiden directs next. This time, Kellan obliges, unbuttoning and then hooking my underwear to pull them down until I'm completely naked before them.

I tug at the ropes, testing the slight give they still allow me. It isn't enough to reach anything, but comfortable enough that my hands rest on the pillows above me. "You know these can't hold me," I comment mildly. I'm still unconvinced this is a punishment. Curiosity has replaced the initial sweep of anger; lust and alcohol fusing a flush of warmth in my veins.

Aiden squeezes a pea-sized drop of liquid onto his index finger from a small bottle. "Of course not," he agrees with equal composure. He leisurely spreads the liquid over and around one nipple. "You could have freed yourself the second I restrained you downstairs, yet you didn't." The liquid warms, then tingles when he stops to add more to his finger. Gasping, I clench my thighs as the sensation spreads to a resounding throb in my cunt. He applies it to the other nipple before continuing, "Because you know what you did was wrong. You know you deserve a little punishment."

"I didn't see you stop me from going there if you were so worried," I grit out. The other nipple pulses and tingles with pleasure. I yank harder on my restraints.

"Jackson did," Aiden counters. "Once you were at risk of being seen, he made sure to hide you. You had the chance to prove you'd be careful, and yet you stripped before the windows and consumed alcohol when left alone."

Dane swears, swiping his hand through his hair. Kellan's grin disappears as he clenches his fists.

Fuck.

He's right.

I fucked up. I hadn't realized it was a test, but that shouldn't matter. Even though we're safe inside, that doesn't mean GE isn't watching us from the outside. I mentally curse my recklessness for being so excited to see Portia that I'd possibly put us both in danger. That was the old Raegan—the one who ran around on her own and acted impulsively without considering the consequences.

Aiden nods as if he can read my sudden regret. He reaches for me. My muscles instantly tense, and my hips buck on the bed out of desperation to be touched. The warm tingle on my nipples hasn't subsided. It's getting stronger; an incessant tease that demands more. He flips me onto my front instead, putting me on my knees and my ass in the air. The rope crosses above my hands, and my weight falls over them.

A single, slick finger glides into my pussy, followed by a second.

I moan into the pillow, my thighs quivering. It feels like he coated them in lube even though I'm sure I'm wet. "You wanted to have all of us, Raegan. This is what it means." I rock back, matching my timing with the unhurried slide of his fingers, urging him to pick up the pace. He doesn't. "We belong to you, but you also belong to us. Your body, your life... they're ours. So when you put yourself in danger, that is a grave offense to us, and we will demand retribution."

I'm struggling to pay attention while his fingers work me over, and my breasts are on fire with need. It feels so fucking good and not enough. I need him to curl his fingers. Touch my clit. Pinch my nipple. My hands clench as my movements become more frenzied, trying to take more from him than he's giving me.

His fingers disappear and then something swats my backside. I hiss into my arm at the flare of pain. He rubs the tender spot until the pain fades. "Repeat what I just said."

"You four belong to me..."—I pant—"...and I... belong... to all of you."

"And?" His hand caresses my other ass cheek in warning.

I scramble to remember what else he'd said. Something about being in danger. "And... and..." I breathe, trying to buy myself more time.

The bite of his palm finds my ass, and I cry out.

"You will be punished for putting yourself in harm's way unnecessarily." This time, he doesn't follow up the slap with a gentle hand. He brushes his lips across the tender mark and purrs, "We are each going to fuck you, Raegan. And you will not come. Do you understand?"

My heart trips and catches in my throat. "Wait. What?"

"Kellan."

I crane my neck to look at him over my shoulder. His blue-green eyes are smoldering as they meet mine. There's an edge to him that warns me his playful mood is long gone. He's here for my punishment.

"I watched you falling toward the ocean with Charles. Saw you fighting him alone before Reid grabbed me and took me to the Guild, where I couldn't see you. Couldn't reach you." He unbuckles his belt and slides it free. "And then he appeared at the Guild, and you were nowhere in sight." His jeans and briefs are gone next, kicked out of the way as he grips his hard dick in one hand. Aiden hands him the bottle of lube, and Kellan squirts it along his length from base to tip. He tosses it back, then twists and pumps his hand to spread it over every inch of him.

"You scared the living shit outta me, beautiful. You shouldn't have tried taking him on alone. We're a team, and you should have come to the rest of us for backup."

"You think I—"

Aiden pulls the gag over my chin and back into my mouth. "Just listen."

I shoot him a glare, then shudder when Kellan's cock glides over my pussy and clit. "Let me protect you. Use me. I don't care how, so long as it keeps you safe." He notches at my core, and my body clenches in anticipation. His large hands dwarf my hips, locking me in place, before he pushes inside.

A low moan is drawn from my throat and muffled by the fabric between my teeth. I drop my head, unable to hold it up as he starts to move. Once he's inside, he doesn't hold back. Kellan fucks me like a punishment. He slams into me in violent thrusts that knock the air from my lungs and shove me forward. Kell wraps my hair in one hand and pulls back, forcing me to arch my back and hold steady for every punishing stroke.

There's something animalistic in the way he takes me. Like all reasoning and thought have flown out the window, and he's giving in to his more primal nature. We are nothing but sweating bodies and desire, joining together in one of the three base needs of fucking, fighting, and feasting.

Every time his dick strikes the deepest part of me, a shot of ecstasy bursts through me. My scalp tingles from his grip, adding to the electric pleasure still pulsing through my nipples and echoing in my pussy. I close my eyes, reveling in the building euphoria as I near the peak.

Kellan comes with a loud groan, his hands holding my hair and hip firmly in place as he empties himself inside me, and my orgasm slips out of reach.

I'm gasping around the gag, my heart galloping at how close I'd gotten. Kell releases my hair and carefully pushes it over one shoulder. He bites between my neck and shoulder. I shout at the sudden pain, then shudder as he sucks at that spot, caressing it with his tongue. "I hope you remember this, beautiful." He extracts himself too fast for me to gain pleasure from, and I whimper.

"Jackson," Aiden commands.

The bed dips behind me. A cool hand strokes down my spine, its bold contrast to the heat of my skin making me shiver. His hand travels back up, then wraps around my throat. He guides the head of his cock to my swollen cunt. He doesn't need lube as Kellan had. There's enough from before and Kell's cum to give him smooth entry.

He waits until he's fully seated before the hand at my neck drags me upright. My hands are trapped a foot off the bed in front of me, the rope taut where he holds me back against him. When he speaks, his lips graze the shell of my ear. "I had to watch the water swallow you whole while you were unconscious. Then wait for Charles to leave before I could go after you. It was our best chance for survival." His fingers tighten, cutting off my air. "I died a little every second I was forced to wait. Every second you weren't breathing. Your air is my air."

Jackson oozes violence. His voice, his grip, his energy; it's like a dark swirling storm has descended on me and I'm trapped in the eye of it. One false move, one step out of line, and it'll rip me to shreds.

He withdraws slowly, then drives his cock back in so hard I nearly blackout from the lack of oxygen. My hands are restricted midair, my body completely pinned by Jack, so that I'm helpless to fight it. And I don't. I surrender to him. My body. My oxygen. My life. It's all his in this moment.

My body goes limp.

Jack releases a sigh of relief. "You're perfect, little one." He loosens his grip on my throat, and I suck in as much air as I can without choking on it. The sudden headrush as he fucks me has an orgasm rushing up on me. It spreads through my limbs in warning, ready to break through and shatter me, when Jackson twists my nipple. Hard.

"Ah!" I cry out from the pain and loss of my climax as I come tumbling down.

Jackson finishes with another thrust. He releases a low groan in my ear that makes my pussy throb. "Aiden's rules," he reminds me, his husky voice deeper than usual from his recent release.

I cuss at him through the gag, and Jackson chuckles. "Keep that fire for his turn," he whispers for me alone. Then he's gone, and I collapse to my forearms.

"Dane."

Of course, Aiden is saving himself for the end. Maybe he thinks he's saving the best for last, but I'll make him regret that position. I've had two missed orgasms now, and each one is doubling my frustration and anger for this punishment.

I get why he's doing it. And I hear what they're all saying. I felt the same way about Aiden. *So why aren't we all fucking* him *with no orgasm for what he did,* the petulant brat in me snarks. *Because I'm the one who almost blew the secret that I'm not dead.*

"Rae."

I look to the side, surprised to find Dane standing there instead of behind the bed. He kneels on the edge to get closer, then peels the gag from my mouth. He slides his hand into my hair and draws me into a kiss. His lips are soft across mine, tasting my bottom lip with the gentle press of his. Then his mouth coaxes mine open. His tongue tangles with mine, and it's like I can taste his love and heartbreak. Feel the desperation as he sucks me deeper. Dane's hand curls to my nape, kissing me with his heart and soul poured into it and settling in my chest as a deep ache.

I struggle against the silk, trying to reach him. I want to wrap myself around him. Hold him and kiss him. Then sink onto his dick and ride him until we're both blissed out.

Dane separates slowly; his honeyed gaze locked on mine when they open. My lips thrum from the pressure of his as he returns the gag to my mouth and then moves to the spot behind me. He reaches over his head to yank his shirt free, exposing the sleeve of tattoos on his left arm and continuing up his neck. The rest of his clothes follow, shoved to the floor, and then he climbs on the bed.

His touch is reverent as it grazes my ass. He leans over me, sliding one hand to my front to cup one breast. He kneads it in his grasp, spurring a shock of pleasure to my cunt when his finger flicks my throbbing nipple. Dane's cock rubs into the cum leaking from me, covering himself as he slowly grinds over my core and spreads the slickness to my clit.

A shudder rocks through me, pleasure unfurling like a flower in bloom with every stroke. Dane kisses my spine. "I love you." Another kiss. "I *need* you." Kiss. "I know how far you'll go to protect those you care about." Kiss. "I love you for it." Kiss. "I'm alive because of it." He draws back for a second, and then his cock easily slides into my aching cunt.

I moan, the building pleasure making my legs quake.

"So I'll do anything if it'll keep you safe." He pulls out, then gradually pushes back in, drawing a garbled noise from my throat. "Even if it means punishing you for taking an unnecessary risk." Thrust. "I'll do it." He picks up speed with his next thrust. "Until you can swear it won't happen again." Thrust. Thrust. "Until you take your life as seriously as you take ours." He drives into me again and again, all talking done.

Even as he holds on to my hips, his grip is softer than the others. Firm enough to keep from slipping and act as an anchor, but not so rough to risk bruising me.

I lean into my arm, closing my eyes and focusing on the ecstasy that feels like it's mere seconds away. If only I could reach my clit. Even just rub it against the bedding...

Dane's groan echoes through the room as he comes without holding back.

I want to sob in frustration.

"I'm sorry," Dane whispers, slipping free and kissing my lower back.

Chapter Thirteen

RAEGAN

All I want to do is wait for Aiden to step into position so I can kick him in the balls. The asshole didn't tie up my legs, so as long as he's within range, there's nothing stopping me.

Nothing... except my weak, shaking body.

I can't even muster the strength to raise my head to glare at him.

The room is quiet, so I can't tell what's happening until hands circle my ankles. A short tug drops my knees under me, and I collapse to the bed. I breathe a sigh of relief, my body sinking into the bedding that's soft and comforting. In another swift motion, I'm flipped to my back.

Aiden straightens at my feet. He reaches for his tie, pulling it back and forth to loosen it in a move that shouldn't look as sexy as it does. It fuels my anger, and I gather the energy to kick at him and curse him out.

"Ah-th-ah uh-g-ng ah-ohe!"

He steps back to strip the rest of his clothes off, dodging my kick in the process as if it never happened. "Have you reached your limit?" he inquires, a challenge in his tone. He doesn't touch me, doesn't move to do anything as he waits for my answer.

I glare at him, biting the fabric between my teeth hard enough to make my jaw ache.

"Tell me right now that you're done, and I'll walk out of here. You just have to blink three times."

The problem is, as tired as I am, I'm not done. I want more. I want to hear what he has to say. I want to fulfill my word of having all of them. And I want him to slip up and make me come. We're not ending the night until I have.

Staring him down, I shake my head.

He huffs with a small smile. "I didn't think so." Aiden spreads my legs, holding them open as he positions himself between them. "You've done so well tonight. But I don't think we're there yet." He takes his time to enter me, giving my body the time to stretch and lubricate his cock as he rocks the first couple of inches in and out. "I'm not trying to control what you do. But I do want you to run things by me first. Let me worry about the risks and best course of action." His dick hits that deep spot in me that has my toes curling, and I gasp. "My primary goal in this life is to see that you and the others survive."

Aiden lifts one leg, and his cock drives into my cunt, striking that spot with more force. My hips lift on their own, meeting him with every stroke as pleasure curls at the base of my spine. He may be fucking me, but I'm fucking him right back, throwing everything I have into it. The silk digs into my skin as I use it as leverage to move my hips.

My climax flutters in my abdomen.

So close.

So. Close!

My movements are frantic, chasing an orgasm as if my life depends on it. Even though I can hardly breathe and my muscles scream and tighten, I keep going.

And Aiden stops.

He freezes, buried inside of me, holding himself still as if he could feel my quivering pussy about to grip him tight.

I scream into the gag with frustration before it changes to a whimper. "Hee-z. Ai-yen. Hee-hee-hee-sh."

Aiden chuckles. "Good girl. I think that's enough. We'll give you what you need, now." He motions to the others, who surround the bed on either side. "Remove her gag."

Jackson cuts the cloth and frees my mouth before taking it for himself. He kisses me with dark possession at the same time as Aiden starts to move again, his hands on my breasts, my clit. I'm overwhelmed with sensations that pool at my core. One nipple is sucked, tugged, and nibbled, while the other is massaged and teased with fingers. The attention to my clit reduces me to nothing more than trembling, needy nerve endings.

My body erupts with pleasure, my orgasm hitting me in uncontrollable waves. I barely register Aiden groaning as he finishes with me before everything goes dark.

I come to feeling like I'm trapped inside my own body. It's too heavy to move. Sated and warm. And somehow, my body is moving. It takes a few seconds for me to realize I'm being carried to a bathroom when the squeal of a shower sounds. Multiple hands are on me, holding me upright and guiding me. Some are on my hair, holding it up and out of the way, while others wash my body clean. I'm in there for only a couple of minutes before the water's gone and I'm bundled into a soft towel and dried.

I'm carried again. I try to peel open my eyes, but they're laden with exhaustion. Soft, cool sheets greet my naked body as I'm laid down. Bodies surround me, tucking me in against them as hands rest on any exposed skin.

I don't bother trying to wake now as I'm cocooned by their warmth.

This is exactly where I want to be.

"I want to try talking to Alice again," I blurt out over breakfast.

Dane nearly snaps his neck to look at me from where he's working at his computer desk. "What? Why?"

Kellan and Jack keep eating, unbothered, while Aiden sits back in his chair at the head of the table to regard me with an unreadable expression. He doesn't say anything immediately, waiting for me to answer Dane's questions first.

"She's been alone in that apartment for a few days now. I think she might want some company. Maybe she's more willing to talk to someone."

Fabian was picked to bring her food or anything she needed these past few days. He's a big teddy bear with the impulsivity of a sloth unless it comes to food. Any potential temper or anger she throws his way won't bother him in the slightest. And if she refused to eat anything he brought, he'd have no problem sitting and eating it in front of her to prove it wasn't poison. She'd have to fight him for whatever's left by the time she changes her mind.

"Besides"—I redirect my attention to Aiden—"we can't just leave her there forever. Maybe if she sees the Guild, she'll want to join. Or what if she has information to share about Charles?"

"Or board members," Kellan adds with his mouth full.

Dane shakes his head. "Let someone else go, then. Kellan. Or, hell, Fabian could do it with his next food delivery."

"No. It has to be me. And... Portia wants to help." I'd told her about Alice yesterday, and Portia jumped at the chance. She's already planning on being here for it later this afternoon.

"She attacked you last time," he argues.

"At first, but—"

"Who knows what she's thinking now? What if she's changed her mind and wants to try hurting you again?" Dane clenches his hands.

"I don't think she will. Besides, Portia and I can handle it."

Aiden finally speaks up. "Okay."

Dane's eyes widen as he whips his head over to him. "Okay? Aiden—"

"But you'll take Jack and Dane with you," Aiden finishes.

I frown. "She's not going to open up to us then."

"I can't tell if I'm relieved or annoyed I don't get the invite," Kellan drawls.

"If she uses her gift, then Jackson can find her, and Dane can mute it. I don't know enough about how Portia's gift works and if she has to see the person to use it on them. And I'm sure you don't intend on destroying the apartment or hurting her with your gift, so the other two are the safest option," Aiden explains. "I can't help it if that makes her uncomfortable. Your safety—and those of the Guild if you're offering her a trip to the Hall—are non-negotiable. Considering she tried to kidnap Dane, then attack you, she shouldn't be surprised we're taking extra precautions."

Dane looks as thrilled as I am with the decision. Kellan chuckles and drops his fork to lean back, spreading his legs and arms wide behind him. "What's the matter, Rapunzel? Afraid of a feral teenage girl?"

"Of course not," he heatedly counters. "I'm more worried I'll strangle her if she spouts crap at Rae again."

"No one is strangling anyone," I cut in, then swing my gaze to Jack. "Or threatening, stabbing, cutting, or otherwise maiming her."

The person I'm most concerned about being in the same apartment with her again is him. He'd almost stabbed Ethan—my friend and the bar manager at Hype—for trying to take my hand. He's already threatened to cut her tongue out for what she'd said to me.

Jackson balances the tip of one of his throwing knives on the table with a finger. I don't know when or how he'd pulled one of those out so quickly during this conversation, but now he's smirking and toying with it.

"Jack." I know he heard me, but he doesn't say anything. "*Jack.*"

"As you wish, little one." I almost breathe a sigh of relief, but stop short when he continues, "Unless she threatens you again." The knife twirls between his fingertip and the table.

I give Aiden a look that clearly shows how much I *don't* think their presence is going to help her warm up to me and Portia. He stares at me head-on when he says, "I agree with Jackson. We're not taking any more chances." With that, he stands and excuses himself as I stare after him in disbelief.

It's dinnertime when we arrive outside the apartment where Alice has been staying. Aiden had moved her from Harvey's apartment to one on a different floor. To separate her from the bad memories and because he'd had all the flowers and gifts from his funeral moved there. The apartment remains open now for Guild members to visit Harvey whenever they want.

I knock three times. "It's Raegan and a couple others. Can we come in?"

"Go away!"

Dane scoffs behind me.

Portia cups her hands around her mouth and then holds them against the door. "Knock, knock! It's just a couple gal pals and some delicious food to eat! And two guys we can ignore who're going to sit in the corner because you attacked Rae and they're worrywarts!"

The plastic bags rustle as Dane drags a hand down his face. Portia had instantly handed him the Chinese food when she'd arrived, declaring that he could hold them for us. Shockingly, he hadn't argued and took them.

Jack's been silent as usual, his hood up to hide his face, and his hands tucked into his kangaroo pocket while following our little group as our shadow.

"I already unlocked it when we came out of the elevator," Dane reminds me as if we hadn't all seen him do it. I'd hoped to get her consent to enter, but maybe that was being overly optimistic.

I open the door and peek inside. She's nowhere to be seen in the hallway or from what I can see of the living room. "We're coming in, okay?"

Portia wraps her arm around mine and tugs me inside. "Come on! I'm *starving*, and I'm sure she will be too when she smells it."

We stride down the hallway until it opens to a kitchen and living area. It's a carbon copy of Harvey's and Reid's except with fewer doors. There are two on the left wall and one on the right corner of the living space. There are no doors or windows that open outside like Harvey's old apartment, but the windows on either side of the entertainment unit are floor to ceiling. Even with a thin shade covering them, the light from the setting sun filters through as a soft, orange glow over the beige carpet and furniture.

"Who the heck are you?"

Alice is standing at the counter with a glass of water. She's eyeing Portia up and down with her brows pinched as if she can't figure out what to make of her, which is fair. I'd done my own double-take of glitter girl when I'd first met her. She's not wearing her usual getup for the nightclub, but she's still in a thigh-length skirt with tulle that swishes around her legs as she walks. It's black velvet and covered in glitter and sequins, so even the apartment lighting catches and reflects the sparkles every time she moves. A fitted sleeveless turtleneck at least contains her chest. Her hair is half up in two space buns and laced with glittering ribbons, while her face is bejeweled and shimmering to highlight her cheekbones and make her vibrant green eyes pop.

I'm convinced Elias made her wear something with more coverage before allowing her to join us. He isn't far; he'd stayed behind with Aiden to work through some details of the Tower and costs. I'm a bit worried how they'll do together, but at least Cibrina was walking into the office as I left. Hopefully, she was there to stay and could act as a peaceful mediator when needed.

Portia isn't the least bit deterred by Alice's demand. She bounces forward and grabs her hand. "Alice! It's nice to meet you! I'm Portia: Raegan's bestie, partner-in-crime, and now a badass too. Maybe not as end-of-the-world badass as Rae is, but definitely close."

Dane moves next to me and sets the bags of food on the counter. He leans and whispers in my ear, "I thought Kell was your partner-in-crime."

I cringe. Maybe he'll welcome another partner instead of taking it as her trying to replace him. Right. Because Kellan would definitely not see it as a challenge and try to duke it out with Portia. My cheek grazes his when I whisper back, "Not a word to Kellan."

He smirks and straightens, silently retrieving the containers of food to stack on the counter.

Alice pulls her hand back, still staring at Portia like she's struggling to figure out how to respond. I'll bet she wants to be mean to push us away, but Portia completely derailed her anger with her excitement and smile.

Jackson strolls past us and disappears into the nearest attached room. He reappears a few seconds later and heads to the next one. Alice stiffens when she notices him exiting the first room. "Making yourselves at home already," she comments, sarcasm dripping from her tone. She sets her glass down hard on the counter.

Dane's arm tenses where it's pressed against me. He's eyeing the glass like a possible weapon. When he drags his stare to Alice, she's glaring back, no sign of the humbled girl who thanked him at the funeral.

"What? You think I'm stupid enough to try breaking a piece to attack her? I know I'd be dead the second the glass breaks."

"Sounds like you've thought about it," he accuses.

I nudge his arm with mine. "Dane."

This is why I didn't want them coming. Between the two of them, her guard is up. She couldn't keep her anger on Portia, so she redirected it to the guys.

"Are you hungry?" I ask her, trying to restart the conversation.

Alice looks at me but doesn't answer.

Portia starts pulling the containers of food in front of her. "What's your favorite? I got a little of everything... well, maybe not *everything*, but close enough since we weren't sure what you liked. Do you want some soup? Pork fried rice? Or lo mein? Maybe beef and broccoli or orange chicken? Oh! And egg rolls! Lots and lots of egg rolls!"

Damn. No wonder there were so many bags.

"Did you buy all their food for the night?" Dane questions in disbelief.

Portia shrugs. "Just a bit of everything."

"I'm not hungry." Alice avoids looking at the food and Portia. "So you can take it and leave."

"Don't be silly. Here." Portia snaps a pair of chopsticks apart and stabs them into an open container of lo mein noodles. She takes Alice's hand and shoves it around the food. "Start with this, and you can decide later what else you want. Rae, let's dig in and then eat in the bedroom. The boys can stay out here."

Jackson is suddenly behind me, his cool fingertips sliding beneath my shirt to find my hips as if he needs the skin-on-skin contact. "The apartment's safe," he breathes quietly into my nape. "I've confiscated anything that might be dangerous and checked the rooms. Call out if you need me."

Everyone's eyes are on us. Only Dane was close enough to hear, and the tension in his body eases with Jackson's words. I give Jack a short nod. He presses his lips to my hair, holding himself there longer than normal. Alice's eyes widen a fraction with fear, and I realize he must be looking at her over my head in warning. I lean forward to break his contact, then glance at him over my shoulder. There's just enough lighting in the kitchen to see the quirk of his lips and the dangerous depths of his blue eyes within his hood.

He reaches toward me. I hold my ground, waiting to see what he's going to do, but his hand continues past me. Jack withdraws with a skewer of meat in his hand. He bites the first piece off, still smirking, then stalks to a chair in the corner of the living room. An array of kitchen knives and anything else with a point hover behind him. He jumps, effortlessly reaching the height needed to squat on the back of the chair so he can see the whole apartment from his perch. The floating objects spread throughout the room like metal sentries as he bites off another piece of meat.

Portia sidles up to me, wrapping her arms around one of mine. "Sooooo... what do I need to do to stay on his good side? I know what you told me before, and I believe you, it's just... he looks stab-happy."

I pat and squeeze her hand. "I promise, you're safe."

Alice huffs irritably and pokes her chopsticks into the noodles. "Not me, though, right? He's here because of me."

"Come on." Rather than lie to her, I detangle from Portia and start filling my arms with food while Portia does the same. "Let's go eat and relax. We'll even close the door, and you can pretend they aren't here." I usher Alice to lead the way.

She makes a face but turns and complies, probably just to escape Jackson's critical gaze. The bedroom is a decent size with a bed, a simple desk, and a sofa chair. There aren't any knick-knacks or personal items, of course. Still, I see clothes on the floor and hanging in the closet, so at least she's been given enough basic amenities to be comfortable.

Portia empties her armful of food onto the desk, grabbing a container and a pair of chopsticks before hopping onto the bed. "Finally!" She crosses her legs and digs in with a small groan. "Mmmygawd! I missed this. The chicken is so much better here." She points her chopsticks at Alice, who's still standing awkwardly in the middle of the room with her noodles. "Did you know they make the chicken different depending on which coast you're on?"

Dragging the desk chair to the side of the bed, I sit and set in to consume my food as if it's been days since I've eaten last.

"What is this?" Alice asks, ignoring Portia's commentary on the food.

"What's what?" Portia responds through a mouthful and stuffed cheeks. "Chinese food?" She swallows, then gasps, eyes growing wide. "Is this your first time?"

Alice rolls her eyes. "Not the food. This. You two. Is this some sort of interrogation technique to get me to open up and tell you what I know? Because if it is, you can leave right now. I'm not making the same mistake as Harvey. I'm not dying for you people." Her face almost flinches as the words fall from her lips. She sucks them in and looks away.

I keep quiet, letting Portia take the lead since this is more her thing.

She laughs, and it's such a bright and bubbly sound that I can't help but smile. "Oh, this is just girls' night! I heard you were in here all alone and thought you might like some female company."

The girl frowns. "Company to do what?"

Portia chews on her next bite and waves at us and the room. "This. Eat and talk about stuff." When she sees Alice's annoyed expression, she shakes her head. "We don't have to talk about any of *that* stuff. You know, dumb, silly things. Like how one time I replaced Ethan's body wash with latex-based glow paint on Wear White Night, and apparently, he'd layered it on thick enough that you could see his dick through his shorts all night. The worst part was that it wouldn't wash off like I thought it would. He had to scrub a lot of it off, and even then, it took a few days. He had a date the next night, and I told him he should tell her that he had fallen into a pool of nuclear waste and now had glowing superpowers. Which wasn't wrong!"

"Oh my god, Porsh!" I cackle.

"What?" She giggles. "How was I supposed to know he uses body wash on his dick?"

"You're a savage. Remind me to never get in a prank war with you."

She beams. "He and I have been at this for two years now, and I still think all mine have been winners." She swings her arm at Alice and the open sofa chair. "Sit! Sit!"

Surprisingly, she does. "I don't have any stories like that," she admits softly.

Portia smiles. "That's okay; they don't have to be like that one."

Alice grips her food. "No. I mean... I don't have stories... at all," she grits out like it's painful to admit.

I nod, shifting my food around with the chopsticks. "I don't have many, either. The ones I do have are actually from my time on the island where we'd been kidnapped to. But I'm starting to make more here."

"I just have my siblings. And Mom and Dad." Her cheek indents. "They're the only ones who know I exist."

Portia stretches her leg out and pokes Alice's knee with her toe. "Not anymore." She draws it back and leans forward. "Let's make lots of fun memories, Alice! We could go dancing together, go shopping, or just hang out eating and watching movies all day. Oh, and I could introduce you to everyone at the club, too! You'll have loads of friends!"

"Or you could join the Guild," I offer, and when Alice appears unconvinced, I shrug. "It's just an option. You don't have to be isolated anymore, not in here, and not by Charles. You could live here, pick the jobs you want, work with friends. I know they'd all be happy to have you. They welcomed me, after all, and it's like I've been here all along with how they treat me. Once you're in, you're family."

CHAPTER FOURTEEN

RAEGAN

PORTIA KEEPS THE MOOD light with endless stories that have me gasping for air from laughing so hard. Even Alice caves, smiling and chuckling as much as she tries to hide it, while finally eating and then finishing her food.

"I have one memory..." Alice chimes in tentatively. Portia and I both perk up. She chews her lip and tucks a black strand of hair behind her ear. "It's nothing funny, but... I remember playing hide and seek with Harvey and some of my brothers and sisters on the island. I must've been only seven or eight. Harvey was home for a bit and got all of us to play it together to practice with our gifts." She smiles to herself. "We would have to be invisible, and he would try to find us. It was to make sure we could be quiet and not bump into things to give ourselves away.

"I went to the cliffs and to a small hole. Even though we weren't supposed to hide like that, I really wanted to win. The rocks were slippery because it had rained earlier, and I fell in too deep. The sound of the ocean echoed in the hole, so no one could hear me cry for help. But Harvey didn't stop looking for me." She sniffs. "He was covered in dirt and scratches like he'd been checking every bush and tree for me. When he found me that night, he didn't yell or get upset with me. He smiled and helped me out of the hole, then told me I was too good at hiding."

A tear slips down her face. "He loved us more than our parents ever will."

I reach for her hand and squeeze. "The first thing Harvey asked us to do when we found out he was working for Charles was to save his brothers and sisters. And I swear to you we will keep that promise."

She nods, swiping the fallen tears from her cheeks and clearing her throat. "Just don't get us killed for it." Her voice is raspy yet hard, like she's trying to put strength back into it after being so vulnerable.

"I won't let that happen again, and I'm so sorry that it did. We all cared about Harvey."

"I know," she chokes out. "I could see how much he meant to you guys at the funeral. He would have loved it." More tears fall, but she doesn't bother to catch them as she twists her hands in her lap. "I never knew... I just thought..." She closes her eyes and takes a breath. "I'm so happy he had this place." Alice grabs a pillow and buries her face in it. "So, what's next?" Her muffled voice asks through the pillow. "Is this girls' night over?"

Portia cocks her head, her finger to her lips. "Do you want it to be?"

Alice withdraws from the pillow, scrubbing her face dry with her shirt. "No, I don't think so. But I don't want to sit around and talk anymore."

"Want to meet some of the Guild?" I suggest.

"Ooh! I do!" Portia exclaims and claps.

"It's not too late?"

I bark out a short laugh. "There's almost always someone up. But no, it's not too late. I'm sure most of the members are hanging out in the Hall still. I can show you around a bit, and you can consider my offer of joining after you see it and meet some people."

She doesn't say anything to that, which I take as a positive sign. If she still hated the idea of joining or helping us, she would have said something. Alice doesn't seem like the kind of person to keep her negative opinions to herself. It's when she's not angry that she seems less sure of herself and more timid. As if being shown simple kindness is foreign to her, and she doesn't know what to say or do anymore.

Jackson and Dane are already standing expectantly in the living room. Alice stops short in the doorway when she sees the guys. "Don't tell me they're coming too."

Dane rolls his eyes. "Why? Because we're men? Don't tell me you're young enough to still believe in cooties."

"What the hell are cooties?"

He shakes his head. "Not knowing is even worse."

"You're not making any sense!"

Sighing, I head to the exit while they bicker. The only reason I don't put a stop to it is because Dane's getting her to talk to him, even if it is by poking at her temper. It takes her attention away from Jack, who looms in the corner of the elevator like a specter of death. Portia is wiggling beside me in her excitement to see more of the Guild.

As soon as we step out of the elevator, Jackson leaves.

"The hallway to the left is offices and storage rooms. Up ahead is what we call the Guild Hall, which has a bar and access to the kitchen behind it." I point as we approach the Hall, and the echo of conversation grows louder. Dane casually slows, shifting himself to walk behind us as I give Portia and Alice the two-second tour of this floor.

We're officially in the Hall when the ceiling opens three stories above us to wide wooden beams. Tables and members fill the space with rowdy games and conversation.

"Son of a sea biscuit," Portia breathes with wonder. "Are we in the same building?"

"REGGIE!"

I huff a laugh at Gabriel. He waves both arms over his head to get my attention as if the out-of-place top hat on his head didn't already grab my focus.

Alice and Portia ignore it, assuming he's shouting for someone else. "Come on." I urge them to follow me when I go to him.

Alice looks at me. "Wait, you're Reggie? Why—"

Dane chuckles behind us. "It's easier not to ask that question when it comes to Gabe."

Gabriel hangs over the back of his chair. "Are you here to play with me?" A glance at the table shows one of the card games we play—one that I still don't have much luck with.

"Sorry, not tonight."

He pushes himself up in a rush when he sees the two new faces. "Oh! Who are these lovely ladies?" Gabe hops to his feet and bows. "Gabriel, at your service. Are these new Guild members?"

"This is Portia and Alice... my half-sister. She's one of Harvey's invisible siblings."

The discussion at the table stops abruptly.

"What is she doing here?" Reid demands, standing from a table over. Tinsley's up and by his side in a blink, tugging on his arm as he stalks over.

"Reid," she whispers loudly.

"What's it matter to you?" Alice snaps defensively.

"It matters to me that you snuck in here to kill your own brother and then attacked Raegan."

Damn it, Reid.

Dane mutters something under his breath.

"You know she was forced to do it," I reason. "I brought her here as my guest."

"She had a choice. She just chose herself over the brother who died trying to save her and the rest of her siblings."

"How *dare* you?!" Alice screams. "You don't know anything about me or what I've been through! You have no idea what it's like—"

Reid's voice is hard when he interrupts. "I know more than you think. I heard you refused to help us even after 'all you've been through'. That you blamed Raegan for your brother's choice and for what *you* did." His eyes narrow. "I'll never trust someone who shoves blame onto everyone else and then uses that as an excuse to attack them."

Alice freezes.

"Wow!" Gabriel interjects, cutting through the thick tension. "She looks just like a mini-Reid, doesn't she? You know... without the sharp jawline, chiseled body, and that perfected state of brood-iness."

"Reid, leave her be," Tinsley urges softly. "If Raegan says she's fine to be here, then you can trust her, right?"

His gaze pins Alice for another beat and then snaps to mine. I drop my chin in a small nod of agreement. I'm grateful Tinsley's here since it seems she's the only one he really listens to when he's heated about something. She and Aiden. Sometimes me... unless he gets into big-brother mode, where he thinks he knows best.

Thankfully, he gives me an acknowledging nod. He takes Tinsley's hand and walks away.

"Asshole," Alice scathes, her body still trembling and hands clenched.

"I'm sorry about Reid," I offer softly. "He has trust issues. Especially for anyone tied to Charles."

"As if I had any choice in being born by him," Alice argues hotly, then storms off.

I move to follow her, but Portia puts a hand on my arm. "I'll go after her. We'll go sit by that garden-looking area, okay?" She smiles and hurries after her. "Alice, wait up!"

Silas is the first to break the silence at the table. "Sooo, she seems like a real peach."

Evie elbows him. "Don't be a dick."

Gabe hums. "I see her more as a lemon." We all look at him for further explanation. "A bit sour at first but with the right amount of sugar sprinkled on top"—he motions sprinkling something over his other hand in a fist—"voilá! Citrusy sweetness."

"No one eats lemons with sugar," Silas counters. "Anyone who does must be a serial killer."

Gabriel tuts. "So negative. I'll bet you enjoy a fresh glass of lemonade on a hot summer day."

"You didn't say lemonade."

Dane sighs, rubbing his hands over his face. "Don't you all have something better to be doing?"

"Like kicking everyone's asses at this game?" Silas jokes.

"Fabian's the only one claiming that right now," Evie muses as she picks up her cards.

Fabian shrugs and chews on his Twizzler.

"Where's Cassandra?" I ask.

I found Zedd sleeping on the table behind Gabriel, so aside from Cibrina, who is most likely with Aiden, Cassandra is the only one missing.

"Fabian was able to convince her to go to bed early," Evie explains. "She's been doing a lot this week, even with Holly from the Pits here to help."

My brows shoot up in surprise that Fabian can convince anyone to do anything. He's so chill.

"So, are you joining the game, Reg?" Gabriel asks me, plopping back in his seat.

I look over to where Portia said they'd be and find them talking on one of the couches. "Maybe next time. I should check on Alice."

"I'll give you guys some space and keep an eye on you from here. Just let me know when we're heading back," Dane says, leaning to kiss my cheek.

Smiling, I nod and wave goodbye to the others.

Alice is staring at her clasped hands in her lap when I get there. Portia sits sideways on the couch next to her, an arm up on the back cushion and her legs folded under her.

"I'm not helping you fight or putting myself in danger like Harvey did," Alice suddenly says without looking at me. "But I can at least tell you what I know about the board members." She raises her head, her blue eyes catching mine. "And how to find my siblings."

Chapter Fifteen

RAEGAN

The size of the group working on the GE attack plan has nearly doubled. We could all fit in one of the conference rooms, but for security and privacy's sake, Aiden agreed to have us meet in the Loft.

As soon as we'd dropped Alice off in her apartment, we reported to Aiden about the information she'd shared. We almost started planning then and there until a few of us started yawning, and he decided to postpone it until this morning, when we would all be more alert.

Now the Loft is a full house with Dane and Kellan sitting at the dining table, Aiden and Cibrina standing in front of the television where we can all see them, and Elias, Portia, Reid, Tinsley, Jackson, and I sitting on the U-shaped couch. I'm leaning back against Jack's side with his arm wrapped around my front as he teases small circles across my skin. Tinsley is cuddled against Reid near one of the couch arms, while Elias is relaxed into the cushions near the opposite end of the couch with one arm out and another in his lap. Portia sits cross-legged between us.

Aiden begins, "With the last board members, we need to plan our attack. There's a week until Charles's deadline for the Guild, but I want to move as quickly as we can before that."

Portia rocks forward. "We have some news, too." She looks expectantly at Elias, who raises a brow. Was it something he hadn't planned to share?

With all our attention on him now, he sighs. "There have been rumors circulating in the gifted trafficking circles we've been... monitoring." Portia slides me a look that confirms it's one of the ones nearby they're trying to take down. "One of the big money-makers for them is throwing a bunch of gifted into a locked down area—a cage, an arena, you name it—and betting on the one to survive. Use of gifts is expected, and lack of participation will get you killed within the first few minutes." Disgusted, he describes the cruel and inhumane event.

"There's a heavy buy-in, so only the wealthiest of people or other traffickers are usually in attendance. And sometimes there's a special guest. A VIP." He pauses, and dread pools in my gut. "It sounds like there's going to be a very big event in one week. And this time, the very special VIP is actually hosting all the others."

"While that all sounds terrible, what's it got to do with us?" Kellan quips.

Portia shrugs one shoulder. "We just thought the timing was odd being the same as the Guild's deadline with the GE Prez."

Elias elaborates further. "There are a few things different with these rumors than the normal ones. The date, the secretive VIP, the VIP hosting, and the word that this event is going to be bigger than the rest. It's a lot of hype that's sure to draw more than the usual crowd."

"I'll bet some board members participate in shit like that," Dane snarks.

"Are you trying to insinuate that our Guild members might be the planned participants of this upcoming event?" Aiden inquires.

Elias dips his chin. "It crossed my mind."

Kellan and Dane both curse. The former speaks up first. "We'd better take them down first, then."

Dane nods. "Give me an hour and I'll have every house address, home security plan, and residents for the last two board members. It might take more time to figure out their gifts. And we're still missing the gifts for four members, if they have any."

"Joe, the congressman and board elect member I killed, didn't have a gift," I remind the others.

"He was an exception," Reid states, matter of fact. "Charles hates anyone who's non-gifted. The fact that he made it to an elect status means he must have given Charles something he couldn't have gotten elsewhere. But I'm sure my father would have had him killed long before he ever made it to officially joining the board."

Aiden continues with the plan. "We'll have to take the risk of facing them without that knowledge." His gaze swings toward Kell at the table. "We'll decide on the ten strike teams and match them to one board member per team based on their strengths and the member's weaknesses." Kellan nods, and Aiden resumes regarding the rest of the room. "The teams will attack their assigned board member simultaneously. I want them to train together over the next two days."

"These guys are all over the country. How is everyone getting to their assigned target?" Dane asks.

"Your report showed a majority within a twelve-hour drive. The teams with those members will drive. Reid's team can teleport—"

Portia excitedly throws her hand up. "Oh! We can fly and drop off the others on our way to ours. Elias has his own plane."

Aiden's expression turns to stone.

I touch her knee to get her attention. "You're sure? Even just dropping the others off would be a huge help. You don't have to volunteer to take a board member, too."

She grabs my hand and pulls it up between us. "We've got a lot of strong people on our team too, remember? We're helping you end this, Rae."

Elias angles his head, his eyes focused on Aiden when he muses aloud, "Last night you mentioned attacking these people in their sleep." There's a slight edge to his tone that hints at disapproval of Aiden's method. "Why undergo so much effort in research and training if that's your plan?"

Aiden's dark stare levels with Elias's pale one. If Elias hadn't been in the office with Aiden last night, he wouldn't be here now. As soon as he heard what information we'd gotten from Alice, he insisted that he and Portia be included in the plans. They offered their resources to assist, and surprisingly, Aiden didn't refuse.

We're at the point now where we'll do anything to win, even if it means putting aside differences to accept help from outside the Guild's resources.

Jackson releases a dark chuckle that sends shivers down my spine. "You underestimate them."

Elias turns his gaze to Jack. "I disagree. I have experience with Gifted Enterprise and am well aware of their abilities. As well as their numbers."

This time, Aiden replies, "Then you should understand that we have to be prepared regardless of the plan. And if you're too squeamish to get the job done, then you're free to leave. This isn't a fight where we wait until the enemy is ready before we attack. This is a war. Every board member has blood on their hands for what's been done to gifted and ungifted alike. They kill without conscience, brainwash and torture for their gain, and imprison others for their research. Leaving even one alive risks the resurrection of GE after Charles's death."

"It's also going to be a huge blow to his ego and operations when his board is gone," Reid tags in.

Dane scoffs. "Maybe the smiling psycho will finally make some mistakes."

Aiden nods in agreement. "Every target will have an invisible spy with them—one of Harvey's siblings. The teams will bring them back to the Tower. Our team and Reid's team will meet back here, and after confirmation that the entire board is dead, we'll go after the GE president."

"I'll be on standby here with the rest of the Guild members should we need to evacuate," Cibrina chimes in. If we fail or we don't act soon enough, the Tower is the first place Charles will strike to retaliate.

"What *is* the plan for Charles?" Reid questions.

"We have a few ideas," Cibrina answers, and Dane scoffs, running his hand through his blond hair.

"All of them have weaknesses. The guy's too powerful with all his gifts. Even if we try something, one of his gifts will somehow get him out of it."

Reid nods. "He curated the gifts he has for that reason. At least until he finds immortality."

"Wait. You said *all* his gifts. He has more than one?" Portia asks, confused. "How is that possible?"

"He can copy gifts from people with the same blood type as him. By licking it," I add with distaste, and her face scrunches with disgust. "So far, he can teleport, put people to sleep through touch, use telekinesis, and he copied Kell's gift."

"You forgot frequency manipulation," Reid adds.

"Oh, right. I haven't seen him use that one yet."

"It's not anything you can see."

"What does it do?" I prompt, and Tinsley squirms closer to Reid. A bad memory?

"The simplest usage is to block or manipulate communications." Okay. That's not... terrible compared to his other abilities.

Reid goes on, "He can also use it to alter the speed of an object or person. Usually, he uses it on himself. He hasn't mastered using it on more than one thing at a time. Or maybe that's one of the copy's flaws. But the reason I've never been able to beat him is that he's found a way to use frequency to affect my gift. He can block spatial travel, like mine and Bea's. It affects him too, but he has enough other gifts to still put me at a disadvantage. I also believe it's a combination of this gift and Dane's that enables the gift-blocking jewelry to work," he finishes.

Superpowered freak.

"Sausage and rice!" Portia exclaims, and everyone pauses.

It takes me a second before it clicks. "Did you mean *cheese* and rice?"

She frowns. "No. I meant what I said."

Dane chimes in, "It's cheese and rice because it sounds like Jesus Christ."

"No, it doesn't," she counters, chest puffed in her confidence.

"And I really like sausage."

Dane spews orange juice across the table and chokes on the rest. Kellan whoops with laughter and slams his fist on the table, making the dishes rattle. I check on Elias, who's sitting motionless on the couch with a blank expression. I'm sure he heard her, but it looks like his mind has chosen to go elsewhere rather than join or react to the conversation. Cibrina hides a smile behind her hand while Aiden frowns.

"What am I missing?" Tinsley murmurs to Reid. He drops his chin to whisper in her ear. She slaps both hands over her mouth, and her face heats from zero to one hundred in three seconds until she's as bright as a firetruck. I'm waiting for the steam to spout from her ears with how red she's become, and when Reid withdraws with a smirk, she has nothing further to add to the conversation.

"As Cibrina was saying," Aiden continues, his tone stern to get everyone back on task. "We have a few ideas. The best-case scenario would be getting him to purge one of his gifts for a dud, but that involves risking letting him copy someone's gift." He lifts his hand, revealing the cuffs we'd last used on Thorne before he killed Gordon. "We also have these, but with his gifts of teleportation and telekinesis, getting close enough to get them on will be difficult."

"It'll be easier for me to grab him," Dane offers, but Kellan snorts and speaks up.

"So he can teleport away with you? How did that work out last time?"

"If you remember anything at all, he couldn't teleport because of my gift. He had to drag me through a portal," Dane argues.

"Bea is another problem if she's around," I mutter. She's a backup escape route for Charles, and worse, her portals tend to appear with legions of GE agents pouring through them.

"I've got her," Reid says. "She escaped on me at Royce's place, but I think I know how to get to her now. Leave her to me."

"What is the plan if you're unable to block his gifts?" Elias inquires.

"Crush him," I volunteer. "If he's too crushed to move, then his body won't regenerate. And if it knocks him out, then we can kill him."

There are still flaws in that plan and too many what-ifs, but it's the best we have at this point. Pin him down, block his gifts with the cuffs or Dane, then kill him.

Hopefully, it will be enough.

Chapter Sixteen

RAEGAN

The two days of training drag. I feel every minute that passes like a looming countdown that has my nerves buzzing and heart racing. After we take out our assigned board member, our group is going after Charles.

We're going to defeat GE.

Dane gathered as much information as he could on the final board members before switching his time to hunting down Charles. We need to know where he is or will be tonight so we can move on him before he has time to hear about his board. Finding him is easier said than done, considering how well he hides himself and never has any recorded travel logs. When I'd last seen Dane after lunch, he'd been so stressed that he snapped at me for asking how it was going. His face paled when he looked up and realized it was me.

After an apology, I kissed him good luck and left him to it.

He didn't need to say anything for me to understand how important this piece is. If we don't have Charles, then this gives him a clear statement that the Guild is against him, and I'm sure he'll attack us in full force. We don't have the numbers compared to his to survive if it comes down to that.

Aiden offered Dane one more day, as much as he wasn't thrilled with it, but Dane told him to fuck off so he could focus.

Alice has been released from her apartment to hang out in the Guild Hall and watch the training. She's still restricted to the Tower and without access to a phone or the internet, but I'm hoping she'll see hope for a new life. Mostly, she stands in the background and watches on in silence. It's probably what she's used to... quietly observing rather than getting involved. It's better than her getting angry with others or arguing with them, at least. Instead, she looks more nervous to talk to anyone than anything, like a new kid at school trying to figure out how to fit in.

I invited Portia and Elias to our training, but they'd politely declined and said they'd prepare for their assigned guild member with their team.

On the last day, Jack takes me to an abandoned beach to test more of my strengthened gift. He keeps the tests to a minimum to avoid wearing me out while we learn more about what I can do now. Then he takes me back to the Loft for a quick fuck and some rest.

Until the alarm sounds.

The salty ocean air stings my nose and sours my mood. Too many memories claw at me the second I'm this close to the water, and unease settles deep in my gut. I hadn't expected our board member to live in a mansion on a rock cliff with private beach access. If I had, I would have asked Aiden to assign us to someone else.

I'll take the city or Old Red in the woods any day over a beach-front property.

Jackson slips his fingers through mine as if he can sense my anxiety. The leather of his fingerless gloves blocks my palm from his. Normally, I don't mind it. Tonight, it bothers me. I need the skin-on-skin contact to put me at ease, even if I know there's no logical reason for it.

I scratch my thumbnail over the leather, pushing at it. Jack smirks, immediately removing his gloves and returning his hand to mine. His lips graze my ear when he murmurs, "Let me go alone. I'll slit his throat, and we can leave."

His dark, blood-soaked promise has me clenching my thighs.

Dane continues typing on his laptop on the other side of me in the backseat of the car. We're in a five-seater this time with Kell and Aiden up front. It was a two-hour drive to get here from the Tower. Others rode with Portia's group on Elias's private jet to their destinations, while Reid's team has the board member on the opposite coast.

Squeezing Jack's hand, I shake my head. As tempting as his offer is, we have a board member whose gift is unknown. I'm not risking him going alone as much as he believes he can handle it. If killing the man is going to be so simple, then there's no reason why the rest of us can't be there as well to watch his back.

"I'm in," Dane remarks quietly. His fingers fly over the keyboard as he disables the security systems. He never found Charles, but he came up with the idea of using our target's phone to find him. All it will take is a call to Charles for Dane to find out exactly where he is.

"Are there cameras inside?" Aiden questions from the passenger seat.

"Just outside."

Which means we don't know where he is or if anyone else is there. From Dane's research, he lives alone with no family. And considering it's two in the morning, he should be asleep in bed.

Jack draws a throwing knife free, spinning the loop around his finger before catching the handle. He kisses the back of my hand in his. "See you inside." He slips out of the car, disappearing like a shadow in the night. He'll come in from the back while we enter through the front.

"Let's go," Aiden directs.

The rest of us exit the vehicle. The ocean breeze sweeps over us, inciting a cool chill and another wave of unease. Something moves out of the corner of my eye, but when I turn to look at the car, there's nothing there. Dane reaches for my hand with a look of concern. "You okay?"

Damn. I need to get my shit together if everyone's noticing.

"Yeah," I lie, more to myself than him. If I say it aloud, maybe it'll become true. "Let's just get this over with." We run down the street from where we parked to the house and Aiden works his magic to unlock the front door. Once we're inside, I activate my gift. The reddish glow gives us away, but it should be okay now that we're not on the street. I'd rather have it ready to use than not, so it's worth the risk even if he is awake to see it.

Kellan takes point through the first floor. When there are no bedrooms to be found, he leads us up the creaking stairs. I mentally curse them for always being noisy.

Jackson crouches behind the wall next to an open doorway on the second floor. His fingers undulate a few inches off the ground. He must've sent his origami creatures into the room to check for Harvey's sibling. Alice said she would sleep in the member's room on the floor so she would wake up when they did. We expect the same thing from her siblings. That also means that while they've been told not to interfere with anything—including a threat to the board member's life—they are required to report any updates to Charles. We need to restrain or incapacitate them before that happens.

Jack motions to Kellan, pointing in the room. I peek with him. A single white crane sits in the air a foot off the ground at the end of the bed. Dane and Kell go in first. While Dane uses his gift to make them visible, Kellan covers their mouth and restrains them. Aiden fashions a set of cuffs and retrieves a small roll of duct tape from his jacket.

The boy panics when he wakes up enough to realize what's happening, thrashing in Kellan's hold yet barely moving at all.

I step in front of him to try calming him down with a finger to my lips, a prayer position, and then pointing at the board member.

His eyes widen when he sees me, and I realize then that the reddish glow likely makes me look terrifying in the dead of night.

Fuck.

I turn it off to see if that helps, but now that he's seen it, he stares at me like I'm a nightmare. At least I'm able to distract him so that Aiden can get everything on him. Jackson hops onto the bed, landing soft as a feather as he squats over the sleeping board member. Once he's in position, he grips the guy's hair and shoves his head to the side into the pillow. Jack swipes his blade across his carotid artery as soon as it's exposed, before the board member even opens his eyes. Blood spurts from the wound, spraying Jack in the chest and face as he holds him there.

The boy screams into the gag, terror reflecting in his wide eyes as he watches on in horror.

Probably not a good first impression on our part.

I would try to soothe him, but I'd only make things worse at this point.

At least this part is done. Now we need to find his phone and Charles.

Jackson whips around to the door, his arm flying out and the bloody blade sailing through the air. He blinks in surprise just as something stings my neck.

"Ow! What the fuck?!" Dane cries out, echoing my thoughts aloud.

I reach for my neck and find a dart stuck there.

Fuck.

It pulls free without a problem, but that only means whatever was in it is already entering my bloodstream.

A thud sounds in the doorway. A stranger lies there, a knife in his heart and a gun in his hand. The one who darted us, then.

"Raegan!" Aiden shouts.

I turn to see what's wrong just as the floor vanishes, and I drop. Jackson dives after me, and we disappear into a portal.

Chapter Seventeen

AIDEN

Concrete rushes toward us. I reach for my gift and instinctively seek out Raegan. But Jackson's already wrapped around her instead of slowing our fall, and the truth hits me like a punch—we're giftless. My gut hollows out, the power that was flooding my veins a heartbeat ago gone. Completely.

We slam to the ground before I can do anything more than cover my head. Pain shoots through my left arm, and my head bounces and smacks the concrete. Another burst of pain erupts in my head, ricocheting through my body as the injuries begin to register.

"Jack! Jack!"

I crack my eyes open at the sound of her voice. She's on her hands and knees over Jack, whose eyes are closed. I roll to my side, biting back a groan and forcing myself to stand. Severe throbbing nags at my left temple, momentarily blinding me before I attempt moving again. Kellan's sitting up and rolling his wrist.

Dane's not here.

Neither is Harvey's sibling nor the two dead men who'd been in the bedroom with us. It was a targeted attack, exactly where we'd been standing, to make sure only we fell through.

"Jack! Wake up!" she begs, stroking his face and running her hand through his hair. She freezes, lifting her hand and staring at it in horror. I move behind her to see it.

Blood.

Raegan dives forward and angles his head to one side, lifting his hair and stroking her fingers along his scalp to find the source. I drop to his other side to help her until we find it.

"It's just a scrape," I reassure her, checking its size and depth. It's what we can't see beneath the surface injury that worries me. I'm sure he angled himself to avoid his head hitting first, but it clearly got him anyway, as it had me.

Kellan walks around us to a wall of thick metal bars, cursing under his breath. "They dropped us in a prison cell."

"Where's Dane?" Raegan asks breathlessly, her gaze scanning the ten-by-ten concrete box we're in and coming to the same realization as me.

They've taken him.

Kell cups his hands over his mouth as he presses his forehead against the bars. "Dane!"

Nothing.

I leave Jack with Raegan and join Kellan, walking under the sets of chains and shackles dangling ominously from the ceiling. I reach for one of the bars separating us from what looks like a narrow, rectangular office. The metal is cool in my grip. So familiar, so comforting, and yet it betrays me. It doesn't bend, doesn't even flicker with a response when I try to force my will over it. What usually feels so alive, so *right*, is now cold and rigid.

"The darts we were hit with must be what shut down our gifts,"

I muse aloud. Vera told Raegan they were weaponizing gifts. This is just one terrifying application of that. They don't even have to be within reach and holding still to get jewelry on. They can fire from a distance, from a hiding place, and immediately get the advantage over any gifted person, regardless of what they can do.

"Do either of you still have yours?" It's wishful thinking to hope one of us got missed, but it's worth asking the question. Both shake their heads, and I already know the answer about Jack. If he'd had his gift, he would have caught all of us before we hit the ground.

"What if it's permanent?" Raegan holds one of Jack's hands in hers, her other hand cradling his face and trying to wake him. "The collar and cuffs are on all the time. If we got injected with it, does that mean...?"

Jackson's hand twitches, then twists and snatches her hand as his eyes fly open.

"Jack!" Raegan gasps with relief, but it's short-lived when he pushes himself upright and her brow furrows with concern. "Wait. You could have a concussion."

His eyes do a quick sweep around us, taking account of our situation in a single glance, then focus on Raegan. "Are you hurt?"

She shakes her head. "No. But your head—"

"It's fine." He looks at me, ready for my assessment of our predicament since he'd been unconscious.

I pick up where we left off, knowing Jack will fill in what he missed easily enough. "There's no telling how long the effects will last or if it'll be permanent. If it's temporary, then I'd assume the effects will wear off either by fluids flushing it out of our system or by time lessening its strength." I don't bother going into what it'll mean for us if it'll be permanent.

At the very least, we'd no longer be a threat to Charles. A more optimistic person might hope he'd let us go, but the realist in me says otherwise. We know about Gifted Enterprise and what they're really doing. We're a liability.

But then, why drop us in a cell unless he's planning on holding us for some reason? Why not just kill us immediately after making our gifts inert?

It's that thought that tells me our gifts will be coming back.

And Charles has plans for us.

I lift my phone from my pocket, checking for service. As expected, there is none. We're either too remote for our phones to pick anything up, or it's being blocked by something. That removes the option of calling Dane or others for their whereabouts.

It's highly unlikely the tracking app will be able to pinpoint our location, let alone Dane's, but I open it anyway to make sure. After Vera stuck Dane with something and I'd brought him to the infirmary, we'd decided it was best that he receive a tracker, too. And then we did the same with Kellan, Jack, and me.

A warning window pops up on the screen:

No service.

Jackson and Raegan stand when I return my attention to the cell, and Kellan runs his hand down her spine where he'd moved to her other side.

"Dane and the others who went after board members could be here," I finally continue. "We can't leave until we know where they are."

Jack nods, his hands toying with something in his kangaroo pocket. His lock-picking kit, I suspect. He never goes anywhere without it. Which means we can leave here whenever we want, but will we get information faster by waiting for Charles or his agents to tip us off on the others as an attempt to scare or upset us?

"There's a camera in the corner there"—he tilts his head toward the office-looking room outside of these bars—"and another on this side there." Jack indicates the opposite side of the room, but on the same wall as us. Both are small and the same color as the concrete walls, blending in to hardly more than what would appear to be a mark or chip at first glance. It takes concentrated effort to identify them. Only one of them points into our cell while the other covers the rest of the room and the single door.

If the cameras obtain audio, we'll have to be careful with our planning.

Kellan stiffens, then shifts himself between Raegan and the bars so he's blocking her from sight. "Someone's coming," he growls.

I widen my stance in preparation, but there's only so much I can do without my gift or a weapon in hand. The metal I'd molded to gauntlets or weapons wrapped around me had dropped back to their original form once the dart struck and didn't come through with us.

I can hear the heavy clomp of boots behind the door draw closer and count at least two sets. Jackson passes Raegan a small throwing knife out of the corner of my eye. She relaxes her hand around it and holds it at her side just behind her leg to keep the blade hidden.

Good girl.

The heavy door swings open and bangs into the wall as two agents dressed in typical black GE gear stroll in.

"There she is," the taller one with a brown military cut drawls, his thumbs tucked into his vest as he leers through the bars and stomps down the three steps to the room.

Heat burns in my chest when he says *she* and looks her way. I clench and release a fist at my side, my body tense and at the ready. My mind turns a mile a minute, running through scenarios and trying to figure out what to say to swing this to our advantage.

"Where? I don't see her," the other one gripes, his beady eyes scanning the cell and likely only finding three men.

"You blind, Stephens? Behind the big one."

"How the hell am I supposed to see anything behind him? I'm not tall like you."

"Fuck, you idiot. Can't you see her legs there? Never mind. Just go and grab her, will ya?"

Stephens mutters to himself, stalking over to the lock. I go there without thought, adding another barrier between them and her. The agent startles when he notices me there suddenly and yanks his pistol free to aim it at me.

My heart thrashes at the memory of Charles shooting me. At the pain I'd felt. The fear that I'd failed her. Failed everyone. My lungs seize as my body remembers being unable to breathe underwater.

"No!" Raegan cries out, wrenching me back to the present.

I take a deep breath. Exhale. Then raise my hands nonthreateningly. "I'm unarmed and giftless," I remind him slowly, like speaking to a frightened animal. He seems like the weaker of the two, but that means he might act more rashly. I'd prefer not being shot again if I can help it. "I'm just wondering what you need her for and not the rest of us. Aren't we all your prisoners?" I keep my voice a calming croon.

He doesn't lower his gun, but the tremble of fear in his arms eases. It's a small consolation that I won't get shot from a twitching finger, but one I'll take, nonetheless. "You are," he affirms a bit harder than would be normal. Like he's still convincing himself that he's the one in control.

I nod, keeping my focus on him as much as instinct tells me to watch the other one. There was something off about his smile when he'd peered into the cell as if he could see through Kellan to Raegan. Something twisted. He won't be so easily manipulated. Fortunately, he's busy staring at his phone. This agent seems less self-confident; more likely to go overboard to prove himself to others. "Then why her? Or are you gathering all the women from the Guild for some reason?"

"No, just her," he answers automatically, confirming that the others are here, too. Dane's the only question left. I have a sinking feeling that he's not here, though. We've escaped Charles too many times for him to trust putting Dane too close to us and risk us taking him back again.

"May I ask why? Or is that not something you're privy to?" I challenge softly, just a nudge to his ego.

"The president requested her personally," Stephens counters heatedly, then flicks his wrist with the gun. "Now, move it. She's the only one we're here for, but we have permission to shoot if we have to."

"What are you going on about with the prisoners?" The taller agent pockets his phone and narrows his gaze on me and his partner. His thumb strokes the grip of his gun still at his hip. When he sees where his associate's gun is pointed, his eyes flash, and the smirk on his lips curls tighter. "Someone looking for a fight?"

I step aside, but only to be closer to Kellan.

Stephens seems satisfied I'm no longer waiting just behind where the bars will swing open and stuffs his gun away after clicking the safety back on. "It's all good, Creighton. I've got it." He shoves the key into the lock, and the rest of us still.

None of us need to say a word to the other to know that they're not walking out of here with Raegan.

We just have to wait for the bars to open before we make our move.

The lock clunks, the sound bouncing off the concrete walls, followed by screeching metal when the door drags open. It's so loud that I don't hear Jackson move. Stephens doesn't either, because he still has two hands on the door to get it open when Jackson drives one knife through his eye and another into his chest.

The sound of a gunshot plants my feet before I can charge the opening. Jackson drops to one knee, yanking his knives free as he goes and freeing Stephens' body to crash to the ground. When he looks up, the second agent has his pistol trained at his forehead.

Creighton grins like a madman, his crazed eyes flicking to Kellan—and Raegan—and back to Jack. "What a loyal dog you are. So willing to die for one girl." He laughs under his breath. "She must be something special. *Real* special, for the president to ask for her, too." He licks his lips.

Jackson stands abruptly, and the agent jabs him back down with the muzzle. "Ah-ah! Down, boy. I'd love to give you a chance to fight me when your bite's not muzzled, but you can't do that if you're dead, right?"

I rack my brain for a way out without Jackson being shot. Again. I can't tell where exactly because of his damn clothes, but a trail of blood leaks down the side of his boot to a small but growing puddle on the floor.

"No, stay back," Kellan rumbles. I turn on them and grasp Raegan's arm as she tries to go around him.

"Wait. Let me think," I caution her. "Giving yourself up isn't the answer."

She stares at me with fierce resolve. Even though he's planning to bring her to Charles, and it could mean her death, she holds my gaze, and a soft smile tugs at her lips. "You'll find me. You always do."

My chest contracts painfully, stealing my breath away. I tighten my grip. "No." I'm not letting her be taken from us again.

Raegan puts her hand on mine. "Any of you dying right now isn't the answer, either. You have to let me go." She squeezes my hand, lowering her voice to a whisper. "We just need to stall for time, right?"

Until our gifts return. Until she can reduce whatever place we're being held in to ash.

But what will happen to her until then? How long will it take?

I can't risk it. I can't risk *her*.

"If we rush him together, maybe we can catch him off guard," Kellan murmurs between us, equally defiant at the thought of them taking her.

"Do you hear that? They're plotting against me," Creighton feigns a whisper, then chuckles. "I guess they don't care much for your life."

Everything next happens in an instant.

Jackson swipes one of his blades over the agent's arm holding the gun. Instead of dropping it, he fires, and my heart lodges in my throat.

"Jackson!" Raegan screams.

Kellan and I rush at the agent.

Creighton swings again, his fist slicing toward Jack's face.

Jack barely dodges, and it grazes his ear with no new bullet injury in sight. He thrusts his knife upward toward Creighton's gut.

Creighton catches his wrist and twists, then crack's Jack's elbow with the butt of his gun.

Jack's other hand arcs toward his throat while his hands are occupied, and Creighton lowers his face, taking the slice from ear to jaw over his nose instead. He pistol-whips Jackson and knocks him back, dropping in time to miss Kellan's swing. He twirls up, kicking Kellan in the chest, and sending him flying to the middle of the cell.

I kick the back of his knee, then throw an elbow at the side of his head. The second my foot connects, something feels off. Creighton turns his head, a manic grin on his lips as my elbow slides past him, and he lands a solid punch to my kidney. It feels like a wrecking ball drove a knife into my side, and the force of it has me airborne.

I hit the wall, and all the air is knocked out of me before I collapse to the floor.

Chapter Eighteen

RAEGAN

Kellan and Aiden join the fight with Creighton, and I use their bodies as a shield to dash past and behind them to the dead agent. His gun isn't even snapped properly into his holster, so it slides free with ease, and I hurriedly flick off the safety and turn, aiming for Creighton's head.

"Drop it, or I'll blow a hole through his skull."

Kellan's halfway across the floor, Jackson's still on the ground a few steps into the cell, and Aiden's eyes are closed where he's hunched over against the wall.

And Creighton's gun is pointed at Aiden's temple.

Fuck.

If I shoot him in the head, will that be fast enough? How much time is there between when he hears the shot or sees my finger move for him to react? Considering all three of them are down, I can't underestimate him.

Creighton's hand snaps out, capturing my wrist and dropping my aim. I fire, trying to hit him first, but it sinks into the concrete. The gun heavies in my hand, weighing it down more and more until I can't hold it anymore, and my grip loosens on its own. It clatters to the ground. He drags me to my feet easily, and I struggle to escape his hold even though my wrist aches and twinges.

"What did you do to my hand?" I demand, biting back the pain when I try to twist away from him. "I didn't drop it."

Blood trickles down his face to his lips, and he licks them clean. "Oh, but you did. It was too heavy, and your body had to let it go." I almost gasp with relief when he finally releases my wrist, but then his fingers grip the hair at my scalp as he drags me back against him and holds his other arm to my throat. The more I fight him, the more tired my body feels. The more sluggish and weak I become.

He laughs. "I didn't think I'd have to resort to using my gift on some powerless prisoners. What a fucking treat. I can only imagine what fighting you all will be like when you're at full strength." Creighton smushes his nose into my cheekbone, then takes a long breath. "Mm... and what a pretty prize you are. I wonder if you're worth three strong dogs and GE's president."

My pulse accelerates at the unspoken threat, and he chuckles as if he can hear it. Or maybe he feels it.

"Charles will kill you himself if you don't get your fucking hands off me."

Creighton throws his head back and laughs. "That's cute. His actual order was to bring you to him dead or alive, so... you know... your life is in my hands, Babycakes." Dread slips through my veins like ice. "Though it'd be a shame to see any of you dead before your gifts return. Can't say that's the ending I'm hoping for."

"Your gift," Jackson grunts, his injured leg shaking as he tries to put weight on it to stand. "You steal our strength by touch. Even if it's while we're hitting you."

Of course. And he's *still* touching me.

I mentally thank Jack for telling me without *telling* me. I need to separate from him and then try attacking without touching him directly. Considering how long he's held me compared to making contact with Jack during their fight, it seems like he can control how much to take. I'm just weak enough to make holding me easy for him, but not so weak that I can't move or stand.

Creighton smirks. "Figured me out, did ya? See why it's no fun when you don't really have a chance to fight back?" He kicks the door to the cell closed in a single strike. The heavy door that had taken two hands and a strong effort by his partner to finally drag open. "Now"—he presses his lips to my ear, and I shiver with disgust—"be a doll and wait for me while I lock your dogs in their cage." He shoves me forward. I slam into the unforgiving concrete from his borrowed strength, barely protecting my head.

Aiden stands slowly. Jackson staggers forward, and I worry about the gunshot wound and how much of his strength Creighton's stolen. Kellan runs at the door, coming seemingly out of nowhere until he crosses my field of vision. My eyes catch on a glint of silver in the lighting, and I find the knives Jackson had dropped earlier. One is within reach.

The door clangs when Kellan rams it, but it doesn't budge from where Creighton leans against it and fits the key into the lock.

I reach for the first blade, touching my fingertips to the smooth metal and encouraging it closer to me without drawing too much attention.

"Careful now," the agent teases in a singsong voice. I freeze, my heart sledgehammering as I slide my gaze up. But he's looking at Kellan, not me. "I've hardly tasted your strength, but I'd be happy to siphon more that I can use against your girl." Creighton sticks one hand through the bars, and Kellan angles out of reach. He laughs and withdraws his hand. "Mm… maybe later. I have a feeling you'll be a bigger meal, then."

The first knife fits under my palm, and I pull it back to me. I slowly rise to my feet with the knife clutched in my right hand. I think Creighton's about to look at me when Kellan smacks his fist into the bars to grab his attention.

"Keep your filthy hands off her," Kellan snarls.

Creighton chuckles. "Or what?"

I lift the knife and run at him, throwing my arm down with as much strength as I can muster to stab it into the back of his neck. He turns at the last second, his eyes widening when my arm flies down and the blade plunges above his collarbone.

He gasps. Blood pours from the wound, and before I can rip it out, he snatches my arm in a death grip. My strength leeches from me fast and hard. My legs collapse, and whatever damage I'd done to him seems inconsequential to the strength he absorbs from me. The others are yelling and banging on the bars, calling my name and cursing him if he hurts me, but they're background noise as I sink backward to the ground, my limbs feeling heavy and useless.

Once I'm on my back, Creighton straddles me, tossing my arm away and squeezing my neck instead, cutting off my air. But he's not sucking my strength anymore. "I think I know what I'll do with you now. I'm going to leave you with just enough strength to believe you can fight back, although it won't be enough to actually hurt me. Let you struggle a little, ya know? Because I'm going to fuck you in front of them. It'll make the fight with them later that much sweeter when they have something to avenge. And I think the president will be happy if I deliver you in rough shape instead of just dead."

"Don't you fucking dare! I'm going to kill you, you piece of shit!" Kellan roars over the clanging of metal.

"Raegan! Fuck! Creighton, I'll give you whatever the fuck you want. Leave her alone, and we can talk." Aiden's smooth cadence cracks.

Jackson's trying to pick the lock, his face ashen. How much blood has he lost? We need to get him to a healer.

I drag my tired hand over cold concrete. It's like moving a bar of pure lead. It takes all my remaining strength and concentration to bring my hand to my side, under my shirt, and to the band of my bra.

Black spots speckle my vision, and I mouth something to Creighton.

"What's that? I couldn't hear you."

I move my lips again, air barely passing through them until he loosens his grip and leans closer.

I grip the knife Jackson had slipped me earlier and shove it through his throat, using his forward motion and whatever strength I have left to do this one act. Thankfully, Jack keeps his blades honed to perfection, so even with my minimally available effort, it slides into him with ease. His fingers dig into my neck, choking me as he gurgles on his own blood. As we both fight to survive.

His grip finally loosens. I force my head to the side to gasp for air through the layer of blood.

"Fuck, beautiful! You did so good! Tell me you're okay. Talk to me."

"Hurry up, Jackson. I don't think she can breathe," Aiden presses, urgency sharpening his tone.

"Where did he put the key? This lock isn't the usual kind," Jackson grunts.

I don't move. I'm still catching my breath. Still feeling weak and filled with bags of sand, that the very idea of trying to push this body off me sounds exhausting.

"Raegan. Say something. Give us a sign you're okay, beautiful. I'm losing my mind over here."

I stretch my hand open. Then close it.

Huh. That wasn't so bad. I do it again. Then raise my forearm.

My strength's returning.

I offer them a thumbs up. I'm not ready to talk until after I wipe this bastard's blood off my face.

"We may not have much time before others come to see what's taken so long. I know you must be exhausted, but we have to keep moving. See if you can find his key and give it to Jackson. We'll take the rest from there." Aiden's voice is pure velvet. I'd really love to fall asleep to it right now.

But he needs me to do something.

Key.

Right.

I push at Creighton's body and try to roll myself at the same time. Let gravity finish the job of getting him off me. He slides to the floor, and I take a deeper breath through parted lips. The overwhelming scent and taste of copper chokes my lungs, and I hack and spit. It doesn't help that my shirt is soaked in his blood. And my face and hair.

"Here." Something soft smacks me in the face. "Wipe the blood off." I do as Kellan instructs, clearing the blood from my face and neck as much as I can with his shirt. Even squeezing chunks of hair until I think I've gotten what I can until I'm under a hot shower.

Now that I can see and talk again, I begin searching for the key, starting with his vest pockets. Velcro scratches open as I dig my fingers into each one, hurrying to the next one and then just feeling the outside for a key outline. My strength is gradually returning to me, which is a huge fucking relief for me and the others. I dip into one of his cargo pants pockets, pinching something hard and narrow. "I think I f—"

The words die on my lips when the door opens, and Charles walks in.

I grasp the metal object and slowly retract my hand to my lap, trying to avoid his attention as he surveys the room. Two armed agents position themselves behind him. Creighton's gun is closest to me, but it's re-holstered and will waste precious time and sound getting it free. Stephens's gun is on the floor, maybe six feet from me. If I get a foot under me and jump, I could make it. The safety's off. I just have to grab it, point, and shoot.

And then what, Raegan? He'll heal.

Fuck.

Charles's stare lands briefly on Stephens's and Creighton's bodies before touching on each of the guys and finally landing on me.

He smiles and addresses all of us.

"I'd been expecting an attack from the Guild on my board if they were going to reject my offer. They're low-hanging fruit, so to speak. The easy targets because of their public statuses. I had Bea prepare portals at their homes and workplaces, ready to adjust and activate should she see anyone of alarm. It was one of many plans I had in place should the Guild be arrogant enough to fight back. Your predictability has become your downfall once again.

"It's almost disappointing you fell for one of the simplest traps. And yet, you've somehow still managed to surprise me." His eyes settle on me. "How did you survive?"

I press my lips together, running through my options. The guys are still locked up. If I throw them the key, would they be able to unlock it in time? Or should I hold onto it and slip it to them when he's not looking, so they can escape later?

But I'm no match for him without my gift.

His eyes slide to the other three in the cell. Jackson and Aiden aren't in great shape. Even if their strength has returned like mine, their injuries are still dangerous if they don't get help. Kellan is the only one mostly unharmed.

"I presume one of them helped you. You *and* the Guild Master I'd killed." He holds his hand out, and Stephens's gun flies into his hand to aim at me. I freeze, fear wrapping me in immobilizing vines as I stare down death.

What do I do? Is this it?

"We'll do it execution style this time, I think. I got carried away before with all the bells and whistles in my fun."

"No! Raegan!" Kellan bellows, yanking and beating the bars in his attempt to get to me.

Jackson rams his shoulder into the bars, running through the pool of blood he's accumulated.

I swallow thickly, unsure of what words I could say to change his mind.

"Wait!" Aiden shouts. "You don't want to kill her. If you let her live, you can have the Guild."

What?

"They've already made their decision," Charles counters Aiden without looking away from me.

"Because of me. They'll follow me. And I'll work for you. I'll do whatever you want. If you have me leading them, then you'll have the Guild, too. Just don't hurt her. If she dies, then any chance of us or the Guild working for you dies with her."

Charles stares at me. He takes in my blood-soaked appearance, his arm holding the gun steadily on me as he debates Aiden's offer.

I fight to get my heart rate and breathing under control.

"And you?" Charles directs to Jack and Kell, turning his face to them. "Would you do anything to ensure she lives?"

"Yes," they both answer without hesitation.

"Prove it." Charles smiles at them. "See those dangling chains? Cuff yourselves. Show me how well you listen with her life in the balance."

All three of them move to do it, raising their arms over their heads to clasp the metal cuffs to each wrist. My chest tightens at the sight of them like that, knowing it's because of me. If Charles wasn't such a superpowered psycho, I'd give it my all to take him down right here and now.

"Hm..." Charles scratches his jaw and looks past the barrel of his gun at me again. "Perhaps you do have some usefulness left. Do the other Guild members care about you this much?"

I don't answer.

"It's no matter." Charles turns to the guys, finally lowering the gun. "I'll consider your offer, Guild Master, and what you bring to the table in exchange for her life."

"For her safety!" Kellan shouts, his arms rattling the chains. "Swear that she won't be hurt!"

Charles gives him a polite, businessman smile. "I'll take your notes into consideration as well."

While he's busy watching them, I slip the key between my boot and the floor.

"Take her," the GE president orders the two agents who'd arrived with him. He leaves first.

Standing, I pretend my leg is injured and drag my foot and hop over to the cell, gripping the bars and wishing I was in there with them. But this is for the best. I'll find a way out and then come rescue them this time. "I'll see you guys soon, okay?" I slide my boot to the edge of the cell as I talk, leaving the key against the wall just behind the thick edge of the cell wall before the bars begin.

I'm not sure what good it'll do while they're restrained as they are, but if there's any chance they can get out of those and I can remove one more obstacle, then it's worth it.

"Hurry up," one of the agents grunts, grabbing my elbow and pulling me away.

"Don't touch her," Aiden demands.

"We're killing anyone who lays a finger on you, beautiful. Let everyone know that."

I yank my elbow from the agent, and he doesn't try to touch it again. I walk awkwardly with them to the door, keeping up the charade of my injured leg, then look one last time over my shoulder.

Jackson's blue eyes are as dark as the deepest ocean, a terrifying gleam in them as he watches me leave.

The agents lead me down hallway after hallway lined with concrete walls and fluorescent lighting. I try to keep track of every turn, counting my steps and the hallways, but they all look identical.

We go down a couple flights of stairs and the hallway changes to tile flooring and white walls. There's an odd smell here, some sort of chemical that reminds me of the hospital. They unlock the fifth door on the right and stand back for me to enter.

The room reminds me of solitary back on the island when I was little.

A single cot, toilet, and a six-by-six area of hard walls and floors. The only upside is that there's light in here. The downside is that there's no switch on the wall for me to control it.

Please don't leave me in the dark.

Just looking at this room has my skin crawling with the suffocating need to get out. To turn and run, even if it means he kills me for doing it. My chest grows tight, oxygen suddenly feeling limited in this small space while I try—and fail—to convince myself it's all in my head.

Knowing it isn't real doesn't stop my body from reacting like it is.

I linger in the doorway, too scared to take the final steps in and commit to being here.

Charles appears out of nowhere behind me, startling me forward the last steps into the room and reminding me he can teleport anywhere he wants in whatever hellhole this is.

"Welcome to your new home. It has all the amenities you need. And privacy, of course. An upgrade from the last room, wouldn't you say?" He chuckles softly to himself as if he's enjoying his own joke. Then he lifts his hand, and pressure shoves me up against the wall. "You really are like a cockroach, Raegan. I'd love nothing more than to snuff out your life here and now to be done with you, but your Guild Master's Hail Mary has promise. Even with the Guild aside, I've seen what he and the other two in that cell can do, and they'd be great assets to GE. All I have to do is keep you alive, brush you off every now and then, and show you to them. That said..."

He smiles, and his hand twitches. The pressure increases, and I'm squished against the wall, the force making my head throb and my body ache like I'll pop if pushed much more. "I'm a businessman first. And we don't like to waste resources by letting them stand around. You and your friends have cost me too much with all the facilities you've destroyed, dead employees, and stolen assets. You and the others are all going to earn your keep until that debt has been repaid."

Charles stretches his other arm to draw his sleeve back, then peers at the watch. "You're ahead of schedule, but I can be flexible. We'll put some of the Guild members to work right away once I've brought the rest of them here. Maybe I'll be kind enough to let you watch."

I don't know if it's the threat of *watching* something happen to the others I've grown to care about or that his gift is making it hard to breathe, but the room begins to spin, and I squeeze my eyes shut, feeling woozy.

He laughs as if he's enjoying seeing me this way. "Fight me again, and you won't just watch. You and those boys will be participants.

Don't test me, Raegan."

Slowly, I force my eyes open.

"As for you…" He scratches his chin. "I was unable to try again with your mother, but perhaps I could hand pick some agents who could be a good match with your gift. You can make me grand-children who actually listen. Little terrors of destruction, can you imagine?"

Charles chuckles. "In any case, don't cause trouble, and I'll main-tain my word of keeping you alive and well." He drops me, and I crash onto the cold tile floor. Pain flares in my left arm and knees as something cool snaps around my wrist. "Your shackle, daughter. To keep that dangerous gift of yours contained."

His heeled dress shoes click on the tile floor as he walks out.

The door shuts—no knob or handle on my side—and a lock thunks into place.

Panic rises like bile from my gut, choking me as I squeeze my hands and eyes shut.

"Whatever you need, I'm here. I've got you."

Dane's voice echoes in my head from memory, and I latch on to it, pretending he's right next to me, holding my hand and talking me through it.

And I pray he's okay, wherever he is.

CHAPTER NINETEEN

DANE

I'M FALLING.

Darkness surrounds me with no end in sight. I open my mouth to scream, to shout for the others, but nothing comes out. My arms and legs won't move. I'm a prisoner in my body, plummeting deeper into pitch-black.

A faint beep echoes in the distance. Another follows, steady and slow.

Then a motor hums, and something clamps around my upper left arm. Before I understand what's happening, I hit solid ground.

I jerk my arm, but it still doesn't move. The buzz now shifts into a slow chug as the stranglehold eases.

I inhale sharply, peeling my eyes open. Drop ceiling tiles and recessed lighting stare back at me. The unexpected brightness spikes my headache, and I groan.

"Oh, you're awake," a woman says nearby. "Good, you should drink some water." Something pokes my left cheek. "Turn your head."

Where the fuck am I?

I force myself to blink and squint through the lighting. I try to lift my hand, but my arm doesn't budge. My wrist and elbow are pinned by restraints.

The beeps increase as realization sinks in.

No.

I struggle to move both arms and legs. A strap catches my throat, giving me barely two inches before it stops me.

"I'd advise you get yourself under control before you pass out," the woman states casually.

Whipping my head around is a baaaad move on my part. Everything spins. Pain jackhammers in my head like a demolition frenzy, and nausea rolls in my gut.

Fuck.

There's a short huff, then heels click away from me. "You're almost finished with your session. I'd stay still if I were you. I'll be back in an hour for your transfusion."

Transfusion.

Shit.

Fuck.

When I open my eyes again, a straw stares me down—three straws linked together, dipping into a jug of water. Machines crowd the space beyond it. Wires trail to electrodes, to a blood pressure cuff, to an IV of fluids, and an another filled with blood. My blood.

No wonder I feel like shit.

I lean as much as I can to reach the straw, and wrap my lips around it.

After several chugs, I finally feel sated and slowly roll my head onto the pillow and assess my situation.

I'm alone in a tiny room with a curtain for a door.

There's a toilet and sink in the corner—no privacy—but I take that to mean at some point they'll let me out of this bed for bathroom breaks.

Considering how tightly I'm locked to this bed, it's my only opportunity for escape. I could be anywhere, though.

I close my eyes, trying to ignore the pounding headache and failing miserably as it consumes most of my attention. Fear snakes up my limbs and wraps my chest in tight coils at the direness of my situation. Even if I did escape, I wouldn't make it off this place against everyone here.

What about the others? Are they okay? Are they together, at least?

Damn it! I can't give up. What if Charles tries to kill Rae again?

I thrash, straining and throwing everything I have at the restraints, even though the pain in my head screams at me to stop moving, I push through it, desperate to find a weak point to help me out. I yell and grunt and try to kick or twist, but I'm granted no wiggle room or even a sign of anything loosening.

The machines are beeping like crazy until I collapse, panting for air and absorbing the repercussions of those attempts as they hit my body like a train. I'm too worn out from the blood loss. Too weak to fight back, even if there was an opening.

The world spins again, and I close my eyes, unable to resist my body pulling me back to oblivion.

"Wake up!" someone hisses in my ear, followed by a tap on my cheek.

"Come onnn," she groans in a whisper. A whole hand starts patting my face. "We don't have much time."

As I come to, a grunt escapes my chest involuntarily at the tightness in my muscles from a bed that's no longer comfortable. It also doesn't help that I can't move or stretch my limbs at all, aside from the brief bathroom break I was allowed earlier between exchanging the blood draw and the transfusion.

Something smacks over my mouth. "Shhh!"

I recognize the voice but am too out of it still to place who it belongs to.

Cracking my eyes open, I turn my head toward it.

No one's there.

I blink, confused. I swear I felt something on my face.

Was I imagining it?

"Hello?"

This time, whatever it is squeezes my cheeks. "It's Alice."

"How—" The words come out funny with her hand still squishing my face, and her hold tightens before I can continue.

"I followed you guys because I was worried. I'm obviously an expert spy, so I hitched a ride in the trunk and held onto you when we fell in the portal."

"If you've been here the whole time, you could have rescued me sooner," I gripe. When she doesn't say anything, I release a small huff. She was probably too scared to do anything until now. "Never mind that. What's the plan?"

"The scientist monitoring you went to the bathroom."

Great. And we've been wasting time chatting.

A hand grips mine and tugs. Only now do I realize my arm is free. I bend my knees and test the other arm.

Another groan crawls up my throat, but I bite it back with gritted teeth.

It feels so fucking good to move again.

I push myself upright and throw my legs over the bed, testing my leg strength. I have no idea how long it's been. Has it even been a day?

Thankfully, I'm still having the blood transfusion, so my body's almost back to normal once I stretch a bit.

I go to each machine and start powering them down. If they're anything like the ones in our infirmary, they'll beep or set off alarms if I disconnect first. Hopefully, being off won't trigger their own alarm to whoever's watching my vitals remotely. Then, I start ripping wires and the cuff off, then remove the two IVs and needle from my arm and slap my hand over it to put pressure there.

"Alright. Make me invisible," I tell her. It's quiet, and for a second, I think she's bailed on me. "Alice?"

"Um... right. Let me see."

She pokes my arm.

"What the fuck are you doing?" I guess where her arm is from that poke, grabbing her and directing her hand to my forearm. "Take my arm."

"Oh. Yeah."

I narrow my eyes at her. At least, where I think she is. "Have you done this before?"

"I've made objects invisible. Same thing, right?"

"We don't have time for this," I growl, pulling her with me to the curtained door. "Keep trying and don't let go. I need to find that scientist before he realizes I'm gone and tells everyone. Which way?"

"Three curtains and then a door on the left."

I nod, covering her hand on my arm to make sure I don't lose her while running. The door's cracked open, so I slip us inside and close it. A guy with buzzed black hair and a lab coat jumps around in his office chair to look at me, his hand hovering over the phone.

There's a heartbeat of silence as we both stare at each other, and then we move, him grabbing the phone and opening his mouth to yell, and me wrapping my arm around his throat and dragging him out of his chair. I use my other arm against my wrist to help add more pressure, cutting off his air. His hands scratch and beat at my arm, but I refuse to let him go and miss this chance.

I kick the backs of his knees to make him drop and give me a better angle, squeezing with all my strength.

Finally, he falls limp. I drop him to the floor and search his lab coat and pockets for anything that might be useful. There's not much other than some gum, a paperclip, and a pen, but I'll bet his ID will come in handy.

Slipping off his lab coat, I pull it on. He and I look nothing alike, but at first glance, all anyone will see is another scientist in their coat with a clipped-on badge.

I plop into the office chair and spin to the computer. "See if you can find any weapons nearby."

"A gun?"

"If that's an option, then yeah. If not, then maybe a kitchen knife or something sharp will do."

"Got it. I'll be right back."

"Oh, and Alice?"

"Yeah?"

"Thanks."

It's quiet. Then, "You thought of me for Harvey's funeral even after I attacked you." Another pause. "I want to be a part of the family he made. I want people to share stories about me like they did for him." She sniffs. "I also need you guys to kill Dad. I really don't wanna die."

I nod, offering her a soft smile. "We'll kill him," I promise. "And I won't let you die. Just stay close to me or stay hidden."

The door opens slightly and closes again.

I get to work clearing the monitors from my chart. The scientist was already logged in, giving me access, but it won't be a high enough clearance to get me all the information I'm looking for. But I can start with checking other active patient charts.

When those only show subject code names and their vitals, I flip to their cameras.

It doesn't take long for me to find them.

Or, some of them, at least.

There's no sign of Raegan or my brothers, but I do find a room filled with some of the Guild members who'd been on this mission with us. They're in narrow hospital beds and hooked up to their own machines, like I'd been. I notice Fabian first, considering his football player size, and then Zedd and Gabriel are a few beds away, followed by over half of the others from our mission.

But where are the rest?

I don't see Raegan's friend Portia and her group or Reid and his team.

This time, I hack into the network to get full access, sweeping through every security camera angle I can find. I start mapping out the island—which I confirmed from outside camera feeds—and where I am in relation to the others while searching.

The door creaks, and I snatch a pen from the desk, my body

tensing for a fight. It closes without a soul in sight, and I breathe a sigh of relief.

"A warning next time would be nice," I mutter to Alice, who appears and rolls her eyes.

"Here." A scalpel and a pair of scissors drop to the desk by my hand. "It was the best I could find."

I keep flipping through cameras and adding to my rough sketch until I think I've been through them all.

The others aren't here.

But I can at least get the rest of the Guild free. I counted a few boats along a dock that would fit all of us. That leaves freeing them and fighting off the numerous scientists and patrolling agents.

With a scalpel and scissors.

I run my hand back and forth over my hair, scowling at the stupidity of that plan.

Think.

Think.

What would Jack do?

Scratch that. Jackson would just walk out there and start killing people. Aiden, then.

"We need a distraction," I murmur. Something to keep their attention elsewhere while I get everyone free and able to fight. "A fire."

"Uh, are you crazy? We're in this building, too."

"Look." I push my sketched map over for her to see, and she peers over my shoulder. "We're on the far end of the building. If we start a fire in the break room here, that'll draw anyone around to try putting it out while we sneak over here"—I draw my finger along the hallway lines to a larger rectangle where the others are being held—"to free the others. Their vitals all looked good, so once we unhook them, they should be able to move and fight." I slide my finger across the hallways that lead to an exit, then tap the docks. "We run and grab a boat, fighting anyone who gets in our way."

Alice shakes her head, crossing her arms. "I'm not fighting anyone."

"What?" I ask, frowning, unsure if I'd heard her right.

"What?" she demands back. "I freed you. You get us off this island. That's the deal."

"You realize there is no getting off the island without fighting some people. And you, being invisible, have the biggest advantage."

She shrugs and gives me a look that says she's not going to budge on this.

It's a fucking waste, but I stop trying to argue it. There are enough strong fighters here that we should be fine without her help. Raegan wants me to keep her safe, for her and Harvey, and—fuck, I owe him that, too. We'll need to talk about her invisible stalking habits when we get home, but at least this time it worked out.

"Fine, no fighting. But you're going to start the fire." She opens her mouth, but I keep going. "Start it here, in the break room. I'm sure you'll find something to get it going. Make sure enough things catch fire that it can't be put out easily. Then get out of there and meet me in my old room."

"Why can't you do it?"

"Because I'm going to be setting this guy"—I kick the scientist at my feet while pocketing my two weapons—"up in that bed and covering him up so no one thinks I'm missing. Unless you want to drag him back to that room, lift him on the bed, and put all the monitors and IVs on him."

She makes a face.

I continue, "Good. It's settled. Get going. And obviously don't make it too big and get yourself trapped in there."

Alice rolls her eyes. "Obviously." She vanishes from her head down to her feet, and the door cracks open. I fold my sketch and shove it in my pocket, then push the chair out of my way to lift the scientist under his arms. "It's clear," she reports.

The door opens all the way, and I hurriedly drag the unconscious man backward, pausing at the doorway for a quick check of my own, before I beeline it to the room where they'd had me. Pushing through the curtains, I get him on my bed and work the straps over him. All the monitors, and lastly, the IVs.

I can't say if I did those right, but at this point, I couldn't care less. This guy was watching me suffer from his office and did nothing about it. So, if I jab him a bit harder than necessary when sticking it in, then it is what it is.

The smell of something burning enters the room.

I finish up, tossing a sheet over him and turning his head away from the doorway and camera, then stand at the curtain. Something taps my arm.

Alice.

"Do you smell that?" I hear down the hallway.

A door opens.

"What's going on?"

"Did someone burn something in the break room again?"

"Oh my god! Fire! Get the fire extinguisher! Hurry!"

A flock of white lab coats run down the hallway to the break room. I wait until they've all passed, giving another few seconds to make sure no others are going to follow, before slipping out of the room. "Keep up," I whisper to Alice, then run in the opposite direction.

The scent continues even after we turn a couple of hallways. "How big did you—"

An explosion cuts me off, the sound deafening as a wave of heat rolls down the corridor. I reach for Alice, grabbing whatever I touch first and shoving her into the nearest room, then slamming the door behind us. "What the fuck did you use?" I demand.

"It wasn't me! Maybe they had something in the next room that did that!"

I curse, hoping it didn't cause the fire to spread to other areas of the building. The hallway's back to normal when I poke my hand out. Maybe a couple degrees warmer than usual, but nothing to worry about. "Come on."

The hallway isn't as quiet this time around with more scientists running around. I keep my head down or to the side, blending in with the lab coat and pretending I'm looking for someone in all the chaos. When we reach the room with the Guild members, I rush to the connecting office first and launch myself at one of the two scientists with the scalpel.

The first one is easy to take out with the element of surprise on my side. The second one jumps on my back and starts choking me out. I cut his arm, pressing deep with the precision blade. He releases me with a scream.

Fuck.

I slap my hand over his mouth and slam him to the wall, finishing the kill.

The *click-clack* of a bullet being chambered makes me freeze.

"Don't move."

Chapter Twenty

RAEGAN

The door latch cranks and echoes through my tiny room. I jump up from the cot, keeping to the back wall to wait and see what's in store for me next.

I've hardly slept in the hours I've been here. Even with the lights staying on, nightmares crept easily into my dreams without the others around. There are too many similarities with this room and solitary that it's impossible not to be reminded of the memories I'd tried to lock away. I gave up after the second one and paced the room instead.

My stomach growls angrily. It has to be past morning. They haven't opened the door since Charles left, which means I've had no food or water.

I hope they've at least taken care of the guys with a healer. Or some sort of medical attention. Did their gifts come back? If they escaped, I'm sure the agent wouldn't be as calm as he is standing there. I try to tell myself it's not because of their injuries. They're okay. They have to be.

"You've been requested," the agent announces at the door. His arm rests casually over the gun hanging in front of his chest—a warning.

I'm all out of knives anyway, and the thin silver bracelet around my wrist continues to block my gift. Every once in a while, I feel an odd pulse. Or something I can sense but not physically feel, because the hair on my arm rises, and I feel the urge to itch and rub the area beneath the bracelet.

If only I could break it somehow. It's too small for me to remove, even if I dislocated my thumb. My best chance is to find something hard to hit it with.

"Let's go," he grunts when I don't move right away.

Another rumble echoes from my stomach. Loud enough that I know he can hear it.

"Are we going to breakfast?" I ask, my tone teasing and breathless. I try not to let him see how nervous I am at being "requested".

"I could hand pick some agents..."

He wouldn't go through with that plan already, would he?

My blood chills.

Of course, he would.

The agent doesn't react at all to my words or apparent hunger. He strides into the room and grips my arm.

I jerk away from him on instinct, and he slaps me hard across the face. My head whips to the side, and my ear rings. He pulls me with him while I'm distracted by the pulsing heat in my cheek. Pressing my cooler fingers to it, I scowl at him. "You can let go of me. I'll walk."

Thankfully, he does, though he keeps pace beside me with little space between us.

The door we stop in front of has a small square window offering a glimpse inside. When I see multiple lab coats, relief rushes through me, making my limbs weak.

Thank fuck.

The agent knocks twice.

"Come in."

Hatred bubbles in my chest at Charles's voice. What new threat has he thought up this time?

We walk into the room, and I freeze.

"Kellan!" I shout, lurching toward him and being tugged back as he roars and yanks on the chains that are keeping his arms stretched out. He's kneeling shirtless in the middle of the room, shackled and chained to the walls on either side of him so there's no give for him to relax his arms. Scientists stand around him, poking him with knives to trigger his gift, while others try to peel the scales from his skin. Another scientist is trying to hammer a nail into his protected skin where there are no scales.

Kell bellows as a knife is pushed into his back, and I realize he has a slew of them sticking out of him like a pincushion. His arms bulge and shake as he tries to rip free of the chains.

I shout his name again, but he doesn't hear me. He doesn't see me. He's lost in a haze of pain and anger.

There's a sharp crack from the wall by one of his chains, and the scientists startle back. Kellan falls back on his calves, leaning forward as his chest heaves. His dark hair is no longer tied, running free to his shoulders and covering his face in a curtain. I twist out of the agent's grip and run to him, wrapping his head in my arms and glaring over my shoulder at the man responsible.

"Stop! Just because he heals doesn't mean that he feels no pain!"

Charles hums. "Does he? He's handled more than anyone I've

ever seen. I need to understand where his limit lies, and therefore, my own."

While he's talking, I let one hand slide down Kell's back, carefully plucking the knives free so he can heal. "You're a monster."

The GE president smiles. "To you, perhaps."

"Beautiful? That you?" His voice is rough. He sounds exhausted.

Anger sparks through my nerves like a live wire. If I had my gift...

I fish another blade free, and he grunts.

"It's me. I'm here," I whisper soothingly.

His head leans more heavily against me.

"She's removing the knives!" someone yells.

I'm ripped away from Kellan before I can finish, but I swing around and slash at the agent with the knife still in my hand. He blocks it with his arm, taking the cut before grabbing me by the front of my shirt, spinning, and trapping my back to his chest. He knocks the knife from my hand and pins my arms to my sides with a painful one-armed bear hug.

I throw my head back to break his nose, but he dodges and pinches my jaw to hold me still.

Charles looks over my shoulder to the agent and nods. His gaze drops to mine. "You're only here to watch. So, watch quietly, or I'll have you bound and gagged for these visits in the future." He turns to Kellan, who's now staring down the agent touching me with a look of pure malice. "You promised cooperation if I kept her alive. And here she is. Alive. If you can't keep your promise to do as we ask, then our deal is over. Fight your chains again, and I'll personally deliver the bullet to her brain. Do you understand?"

Kellan's pupils have consumed the blue-green color of his eyes when he slowly drags his gaze from the agent to Charles. His jaw rolls from clenching his teeth so hard I'm waiting to hear a tooth snap. "Yes," he growls.

"Sir, he's—his gift," a scientist speaks up. "It's fully active again."

Charles sighs. "Give him another microdose." One of them hurries to do exactly that. Charles smiles pleasantly at me, even though I know that's the furthest thing he's feeling for me right now. "There's a bottle of water and a sandwich on the table." He indicates a metal table on the other side of him. "You can eat it yourself or give it to him. I'll leave it up to you to decide which of you will have the advantage."

The advantage?

He leaves the room, and everyone, including the agent, follows him. Leaving me alone with Kellan.

As soon as the door clicks shut, I run to him. "Kell!" He drops his face on my shoulder, his body still trembling from the strain on his arms. Or is it residual pain from what they were doing earlier? His scales are fading, which means his extra strength is leaving with them.

He may be healed from the earlier injuries, but his body must be exhausted.

"How long have they been doing this?" I ask, stroking my hands through his hair and along the back of his neck.

"Not long after he took you," he admits.

Fuck.

Hours and hours of this. Of torturing him until his gift takes over fully, then muting it so they can start over again.

I cradle his face and rest my forehead against his. The unrelenting quiver of his muscles breaks my heart. His eyes remain closed. He hasn't slept then, either.

"I'm getting you out of this." I press my lips to his, trying to draw him back to me. He barely reciprocates, but his lips part ever so slightly to invite me in. "You have to keep fighting."

"Not with your life on the line, beautiful. I'll face this a thousand times if it means you'll be safe."

"Well, I can't." I stand, leaving to grab the sandwich and water and then kneel before him. "Here." I offer the water to his lips first, using my other hand to guide his chin up.

"Wait." When he says that, I pause. "Have you had any?"

"Of course," I lie. "I've got my own room and everything. Now, drink it."

He guzzles half of it down, his throat working as some of it trickles to his beard and down his neck. His lips press together to block the remaining water, and I pull it away.

He refuses the sandwich.

I huff. "I already told you, I'm fine. Eat it."

"Your stomach hasn't stopped growling. There's no fucking way I'm taking a bite until I see you eat some of it."

Damn it. "I'm still in better shape than you," I mutter, taking a single bite of the sandwich to make him happy, then hold it out for him again.

"More."

"I ate some."

"Eat. More."

"Stubborn prick." I take two more bites, then show him.

Kellan finally takes a piece the size of my three, and I could hug him. "Your turn," he rumbles with his mouth full.

Sighing, I eat more until he's satisfied, and we go back and forth until it's gone. He makes me drink some water, too, before he finishes it off.

It wasn't a lot, but it was something, and I'm already feeling a bit better than before. I gently stroke his beard. "How do you feel?"

"Never better," he teases, finally shooting me a smile. It's not his playful grin, but I still take it as a good sign.

"I mean it, Kell. We're getting out of here. I need to know if I have to find a way to carry or drag your ass out, or if you can walk."

His smile vanishes. "Unless it's a sure bet, I'm not risking your life. Leaving this room isn't it."

I give him my own soft smile. "We're together, Kell. Of course, it's a sure bet. And I thought you were always up for a challenge." His eyes widen, and some of the spark returns to them. Before he can reply, I walk to the door and peek through the window. "I don't see any guards..." Gripping the handle for shits and giggles, I pull it down, waiting for the inevitable click as it hits the lock.

It doesn't.

It turns without resistance, and when I tug gently on the door, it cracks open.

Holy shit.

"Kell..." I murmur, checking the crack and spotting a single guard. I carefully close the door.

It's a trap, right? There's no way that Charles just left the door unlocked with only one agent to guard us. That's too careless.

But he wasn't the last one in the room. It was one of the scientists. Did they forget?

"...which of you will have the advantage."

No.

He was being cryptic about something again. There's a nagging in my head that I should know what he's talking about. He'd mentioned I could either watch or participate in something depending if I fought back. It's safe to assume that trying to escape counts as fighting back.

This is probably a test.

I look over at Kellan. At his hunched over frame. His spread and chained arms.

I can't let this continue. I don't care if it is a test and I fail. If I can break him free and we can find the others, then we'll fight our way out.

The only problem is getting him out of those chains. But I'd heard the crack when he'd been pulling on them. I just need to find it and chip away at it.

I start searching the room for anything hard or heavy, pushing things aside and checking drawers. Kellan doesn't say a word through any of it, and I'm convinced he's fallen asleep. It makes me try not to make too much noise so he can get some rest now.

Maybe it's selfish and reckless of me to force us into this situation while he's so worn out, but I can't wait for the perfect opportunity. I don't think things will get better with time. They'll only get worse.

I pick up some of the knives on the floor around Kell and hide one in each boot and one at my back under my bra. The hammer that one of the scientists had been using is also still on the floor.

Perfect.

Kellan stirs when he hears the hammer striking the concrete where the metal loop for the chain is mounted. "What are you doing?"

"The door's unlocked with only one agent out there. We're getting out of here."

He doesn't say anything for a few swings. "You go. They could come back before you can get me free."

"I'm not leaving without you."

Clink. Clink. Clink.

The metal loop doesn't budge.

"Pull on this side," I tell him without stopping.

"Raegan..."

When I look up, he isn't trying at all. I storm over to him, getting in his face. "If we stay here, I'll become a breeding mare for Charles to build a mini army of destruction. Are you going to stay on your knees and let that happen? Or are you going to help me break you free so we can rescue the others and get the fuck out of here?"

That lights a fire in his eyes and he snaps his teeth together. He starts jerking the chain on the side where I was working, and I rush back to hammer at it at the same time. The loop starts to angle down, and I throw my strength behind every swing to keep it up.

Come on.

Come *on*.

It flies free, ripping from the already-damaged concrete. I jump back to avoid it and then grin at Kell. "One to go."

CHAPTER TWENTY-ONE

DANE

A BLUR OF COLOR flies between me and the scientist. The gun disappears from his hand, and then he flies off his feet, crashing hard against the wall and collapsing unconscious to the floor.

"There you are!" Tinsley exclaims, breathless, from where the scientist had been standing. "Okay, stay right there." She starts to turn, then whips back. "Oh, you can have this." She clicks the safety on the gun and tosses it to me. She's gone before I catch it.

"Did some of your friends already escape?" Alice appears beside me.

Tucking the gun in the back of my jeans, I sit at the nearest computer and set up an upload of all their files to my private cloud of GE data. It'll keep running during our escape until it's done, or someone notices and stops it early. "No. She wasn't one of the members in the room," I reply absently, finishing up and then turning off the monitor.

If she wasn't in one of the rooms, was she somewhere else on the island without a camera view? More likely, Reid brought her. I have no clue how he found me, but it's a relief to know I had another rescue team if Alice hadn't been here.

Are Rae and the others with him?

"See?" Tinsley's voice returns. "He's already gotten himself out. I saved him from being shot, though."

I turn just as Reid drops someone on the ground. "Good. Activate your gift and carry her," he directs at me, pointing to the girl. His gaze flicks to Alice. A small tightening appears around his mouth, but he returns his attention to me.

Annoyance pricks my temper at the demand. "Why the fuck—"

Wait. Is that the portal chick?

I notice the bleeding wound from hip to shoulder across her front. "You took her out?"

Reid doesn't answer.

Her chest rises imperceptibly. She's alive.

"You didn't kill her?" I ask next, realizing she could wake up and portal away back to Charles.

"Be my guest," Reid states flatly, and I scowl at him.

I can't kill her when she's unconscious like this. It's one thing if she's coming after us or trying to hurt one of us, but lying defenseless on the floor?

Reid nods, as if he expected I'd refuse. "Keep her gift inert so she doesn't escape on us."

Kneeling by her side, I call my gift forward. "Put her on my back, then."

Tinsley helps Reid place her over my back. I grab the gun and shift it to my front, then wrap my arms under her legs. "Why didn't you kill her during your fight?" I grumble, standing and adjusting to her weight.

"We failed to kill the board members last night," he says. I'd figured as much, but it confirms that the other teams not here were also unsuccessful. "We can use her gift against them next time."

I doubt we'll convince her to do it willingly. But I leave it at that. Aiden can decide what he wants to do when he sees her. "Since my hands are full now, go into the room there and unhook everyone. Turn off the machines first so we don't alert anyone walking by when they get detached."

Alice opens the door to the large room of Guild members in narrow hospital beds, and Tinsley races through. "On it!"

Machine after machine powers down as she speeds through the room too fast to see clearly.

"Hurray! We're saved!" Gabriel cheers from his bed, his voice weak and strained.

Before I can check on him, Fabian groans. Fuck. He's going to need to eat something. "You didn't happen to bring any food, did you?" I ask Reid, who shakes his head.

Damn.

"She's got something in her pockets," Alice speaks up. I check over my shoulder, and she pokes at Bea.

"See what it is," I tell her. She pinches something and pulls it out. A candy bar. "Let me see it." I hold my hand out, careful to keep myself angled where Bea won't slip off. Carrying her around like this is going to be annoying as fuck. "At least go and check if this place has any gift-blocking crap," I tell Reid while Alice hands me the bar. "I don't care if it's a cuff, collar, or something else."

Reid's mouth turns down, his eyes locked on Tinsley's quick movements. "I'll see what I can find." He teleports away, and I walk to Fabian's side.

"Ungh, Dane. I'm gonna be sick."

"I know, buddy. I need you to hold on a bit longer until we can get out of here." I remove his straps with one hand, helping him sit up. He yanks off the rest, IVs included, and his stomach sounds like a cavern of thunder. "Here's a candy bar to take the edge off."

He grabs it from my palm with more speed than one would expect from a man his size, ripping the plastic off and devouring a third of it in one bite. Fabian stares at Bea on my back as he chews. "Who's she?"

"The GE agent who can open portals and got us all in this mess."

He grunts and focuses back on the candy bar.

"No. No, no, no. Not again."

I snap my head around at Gabe's voice. "What's wrong?" He's staring at the ceiling, his head shaking back and forth as he continues to mumble to himself. His body tenses as if struck by lightning. "Hey!" I run and find Zedd jerking violently at his restraints, his gaze caught on Gabriel, and a gag in his mouth.

I reach for Gabe's restraints first, but Zedd's muffled voice raises and brings my attention to him. Once he has it, he motions with his head for me to go to him. Trusting that he knows Gabriel best, I jog to him instead and untie the gag first.

"Hurry," he urges, stilling his arms while I work them free and then flying upright to undo the strap on his ankle opposite the one I'm doing.

The second he's free, he throws himself off the bed and flies to Gabe's side in a few long strides. Rather than touch the straps, Zedd takes Gabe's face in his hands and leans over him. "Look at me. At me, disaster. Eyes on me," he commands.

I move to the other side of Gabe, remembering the seizure he'd had after helping Raegan. "I can mute his gift."

"That won't do anything. This is a side effect of his gift, but it's not active. He's stuck in someone's memory," he replies curtly.

Gabriel's body is shaking now, a full-blown case of tremors rocking through him. He sucks in a breath, blinking rapidly. The distant look in his stare fades, and recognition takes its place as he finally sees Zedd. A shaky smile stretches his lips. "They took my drugs, Zedd. I can't—"

"You can," Zedd cuts him off. He starts removing the restraints on his side, so I do the same on mine. He helps Gabe sit up slowly, then grips the back of his neck. "I know you can. So, let's give them hell for it."

"I do love a little mayhem in the morning," Gabe teases weakly, his upbeat demeanor poking through the exhaustion.

Tinsley speeds to my side. "Everyone's unhooked and free," she reports, smiling breathlessly. "Where's Reid?"

I heft Bea further up my back again, trying not to get queasy at the slickness of her blood that's now soaked the back of my shirt. "Looking for something to block her gift. I needed my hands to help you, but I guess you didn't need it."

The rest of the Guild members are all on their feet, either stretching and looking around or leaning on the beds for support. Fabian's rummaging through the cabinets on the wall—looking for food most likely—and Alice stands awkwardly to the side, watching everyone with a nervous expression.

"What's going on?" a man questions behind me.

Gabe stumbles over to the scientist. "Hey there, doc." He waves with a worn smile, his face glistening with sweat as he moves. "Whaddya have here that can help me out? Where's your medicine cabinet? The good stuff, though. The things you keep locked away."

The GE worker lifts something in his hand.

Gabe grabs his wrist.

His thumb depresses, and a blaring alarm rings through the room. I'll bet it continues throughout the entire building, if not the whole damn island.

Considering the shape the Guild members are in, we're fucked.

Gabe's smile stretches, and I think he chuckles. When he speaks next, his voice is raised to carry over the siren. "I hope you don't have any traumatic memories, or this isn't going to go well for the both of us."

The scientist flinches. Again. And again. He starts to scream. Red bleeds through his white lab coat at his arm, and a scrape appears at his temple.

Gabe continues, "Oh, dear. Your brother did that?"

There's a snapping sound, and the scientist falls to the ground. But Gabe doesn't release his wrist.

"Oh! Ooooh, that had to hurt. The first time and this time, I mean. Leg breaks are hard, you know?"

"We have to go." Reid's suddenly at my side, clicking a bracelet around Bea's dangling wrist. "All the GE agents are heading this way."

"Let them come." Zedd steps up beside me, his arms crossed and staring intensely at Gabriel. "Is there an intercom?"

I set Bea down on the nearest bed with a grunt and roll my shoulders. "The phones have access. Why?"

"Show me."

I nod, leading the way to the previous room as I hear Gabriel still talking to the scientist.

"So, all your past fun times aside, where are your drugs? Or mine?

I know they're somewhere, and I'm not letting you go until I have them."

I give Zedd the rundown of the phone intercom button, expecting it to work like any other.

"Let me know when most or all the agents are in the building. I'll use my gift to put them to sleep through the intercom. Find something everyone can use to plug their ears before that happens. Using your hands or fingers alone won't work."

Dragging the office chair back, I sit and turn to Reid. "I'll keep an eye on the agents."

"I'll find the ear plugs," Tinsley volunteers, disappearing the next second.

"We'll block the doors to hold out until they're all in," Reid adds, then leaves the small attached office.

There's a window the size of the wall into the room, so we can keep an eye on things in there while we wait. Zedd closes the door from the hallway into this room, and I help him drag the dead scientists behind it.

Once that's secure, I check my upload and confirm it's complete, then flip to the cameras in a grid view. Armed agents are swarming into the building from different doors.

Something drops on the desk. "Here you go!" Tinsley chirps, gone again before I can see her.

A small pile of cotton balls litter the desk. I pinch one and look at Zedd. "Will these work?"

He nods, once again focused on Gabriel, who's pressing buttons on a safe in the corner. The scientist he'd been with is on the floor in a pool of blood.

Damn. Maybe I underestimated Gabe as a fighter.

The door handle jiggles, then something slams against it.

My heart jackhammers, and I reach for the gun at my waist. The cool metal grip in my hand adds a small comfort. I release the mag, count the bullets, then click it back in place.

Seven.

That's not going to get me very far. There are at least three dozen agents, including the last stragglers running inside.

"Get ready," I warn Zedd, tracking the last agent coming this way. Moving to the doorway, I poke my head in to check with Reid, tapping my ear. He gives the OK, and I sink back to my seat and stuff my own ears. The final agent clears the door, and I don't see anyone else outside. "Now."

Zedd holds the intercom button and starts singing.

His words and tone are muted, and I try not to focus on them just in case. Instead, I train my gaze on the cameras. Someone yawns. Someone else rubs their eyes. The fists swinging at the doors slow, then stop altogether.

And one by one, they slump down or just fall, eyes closed.

A tap at my shoulder brings me back to Zedd. He motions to pull the cotton ball from my ear, and I do. "That's it?" I question, disbelief coloring my tone.

He shrugs. "It has its weaknesses. Friendly fire is one of them. Enemies knowing how to block it is another." Zedd gives me a look, and I nod.

We won't tell anyone. He's part of the Guild now. His secret is our secret.

We stroll back into the room with the others. Gabe's lying back on one of the beds, belting one of Zedd's songs until the man himself sits at the edge of the bed. Gabriel tosses his cotton balls away and sits up. "I thought if I couldn't listen to your voice, I'd sing one of your songs instead."

"You found them?" Zedd asks, and he grins, holding up his bag of pills.

"I'm starting to feel so much better. But I also think I could use a long nap. How far in my future do I get one of those?"

"I'll drop everyone off at the meeting point, then destroy this place," Reid speaks up. "Cibrina's already moved members to a safe location now that Charles knows we won't be joining him and the mission failed."

"Did any other teams make it back?" Fabian asks, and Reid nods.

"Elias's team is the only one that returned. They're helping Cibrina move everyone."

There are only four teams here. Add in Reid's, Elias's, and mine, that means we're still missing three teams—twelve members. Hopefully, they're in the same location as Aiden.

I grab Reid's arm. "I need to get to Rae and the others. The last three teams could be with them, too. Where are they?"

His expression darkens. "With Charles."

Fuck.

"Stay with Cibrina. I'll get Raegan and the rest of the captured members," Reid argues before I've even said anything.

"Like fuck," I snap. "I'm helping rescue them, too. Drop the others off, but I'm coming with you."

"You're a liability," he counters, his voice flat.

I grab him by the shirt and yank him close. "Think whatever the fuck you want about me, but I have to be there. Use me as a bargaining chip for Raegan's life if you have to. Whatever it takes to make sure she gets out of there safe."

Reid's gaze pierces mine, holding steady for who-the-fuck-knows what's going on in his head. Finally, he nods. "Alright."

"Then, let's go."

Chapter Twenty-Two

RAEGAN

I DRIVE THE KNIFE into the next agent, ripping the blade through his neck. Another one runs at me, and I spin to meet his attack. My arm is already mid-motion in the swing when the agent I'm attacking suddenly changes to Kell.

Shit!

I let go of the knife and hit him with my empty fist.

Kellan yanks me to his chest just as a bite of pain strikes my hip. He punches the agent who'd attacked me from behind, knocking him back.

Touching my hip, my fingers come back red from a slice that could've been a lot worse if Kell hadn't pulled me away in time.

"Down!" he barks, and I drop. Another agent's power-imbued disc shoots overhead. I recover my knife from the floor as Kellan leaps after the disc, knocking it down with the length of chain still attached to his wrists.

I take off after the agent while his disc is occupied. He blocks my slash with his arm, and I release the blade to my other hand to thrust it into his gut.

Kellan appears in the agent's place, taking my knife into his side instead.

"Fuck! Kell!"

He clenches his jaw and wraps his hand around mine, jerking it free with a grunt. "It's just a scratch," he reassures me, even as blood drains from the open wound. His gift still hasn't returned, and he's exhausted. I need to end this fight before it leaves us too injured to escape. We'd made it out of the room just fine, but we've been bumping into agents left and right since getting to the floor where Aiden and Jackson are.

Kell puts the knife back in my hand. I grip it tight. "Can you hold that guy for me?"

He gives me a wolfish grin. "Anything for you, beautiful."

We run toward the two remaining agents. Kellan throws his chain at the one who keeps switching us around, and it curves and then wraps around his neck. I pivot toward them, where Kell now holds him. The hairs on my neck and arms rise, sensing the powered disc behind me, but Kell bats it down again with the chain on his other wrist.

I raise my hand with the knife, and just as expected, when I'm mid-swing, the guy switches with Kellan. I'd already prepared for it, though, and stretch my arm past Kell to stab the agent before he gets a chance to switch again.

The agent screams. I twist the knife, pushing it deeper.

He swaps with the other agent, who then joins his screams when I pierce him as well. I drag my arm up at an angle, then kick him to the ground.

Kellan's already rushed the swapping agent, throwing his arms to whip the chains back and forth.

And then I'm there in the crossfire as a chain comes flying toward me.

I duck and run toward him, under his arms, and away from the attack.

"You up for a game of chicken?" Kellan drawls, the chains now dangling at his sides and curled on the floor.

Turning with my back to his chest, I seek out the last agent. He's holding his side, blood escaping past his hand. I know I did some damage there, but if I'd been a few inches higher, I might've hit something more fatal, and we could be done with this already.

"Yeah. I'll get behind him," I answer.

We separate at once, and I run wide to get around him before curving so we're coming at him from either side of the hallway. The agent's head swivels between us. I pull out a second knife, readying for a switch. There's only me and Kellan left, so as long as we're ready to swap with each other or him, we can keep fighting with a small adjustment.

He tries to run to the side, but Kell and I follow and close off any route of escape.

The agent switches with me at the last second. I spin on my next step, then strike. My knife finds its target just as Kellan slams his fist into his jaw. He falls to the ground, knocked out.

Kell throws his head back, his chest working as he catches his breath.

"I'll go scout up ahead—"

His large hand falls gently on my head. "Not a chance. Let's go."

Sighing, I wipe the blood from my knives on my pants. It was worth a shot. I nod, and we run down the hallway to the end.

The moment I clear the corner, something dark knocks into me, sending me flying. I hit a soft cushion between me and the wall, saving me from a concussion, before lips crash into mine and the smell of blood burns my nose.

I know it's Jackson before my eyes can register the black blur. I can feel it in his touch; in the way he holds me both reverently and firmly at the same time. Like I'm someone precious, and he'll never let me go. His kiss is dark and possessive, feeding off my lips with an insatiable hunger that makes me weak in the knees. I grip his hoodie and curl my other hand around the back of his neck as I kiss him back with the same fervor, then slide my hand up into his hair until I find long enough length to latch onto. I tug him back, breaking the kiss.

"Where—" I breathlessly start, then stop when I see Aiden using his gift to remove Kellan's cuffs and chains and transforming them into his whip sword. Now that I know he's also safe, I return my focus to Jack. His eyes shine with a wild look, and blood streaks his face. Judging by the smell, his clothes are soaked in it, too. "Your knee...?"

"Healed," he answers, and I exhale in relief.

"Partially healed," Aiden corrects from behind Jackson, who finally loosens his hold. "The healer only did enough to prevent him from bleeding out. It's still there, and there's still the risk of infection."

Jackson shrugs, as if the details are inconsequential, and I shoot him a look. He flashes me an adoring smile.

Aiden pushes past Jack and pulls me against him, wrapping me in his arms. "Are you hurt?" He releases me enough to grasp my chin and study my face, as if preparing to read past any possible lie. His eyes narrow, and he strokes one cheek. The flicker of pain there is brief. I'd forgotten all about the slap, and it's hardly something compared to a gunshot wound.

"I'm fine. I can fight, although I'd do a hell of a lot better if you could get this thing off." I hold up the bracelet between us. "It's been blocking my gift. He didn't make you guys wear anything?"

Aiden pinches the small band of metal. "The cuffs we were in did. Once Jackson was able to pick our locks to free us, our gifts returned." The bracelet morphs into a tiny blade. He presses it to his whip sword at his side, and it joins the other metal. His brows pinch as he inspects the blade with a slight frown, but I'm distracted when warmth floods my veins in a rush.

I close my eyes and go to that place in my mind, touching my gift and sighing with relief to feel it there, alive and thriving. When I open my eyes, I smile.

Aiden raises a brow, the corner of his lips quirked in amusement. "Your gift's returned?" he asks for confirmation, and I nod.

"Mm. And I feel much better."

"Mine should be back any minute now," Kellan adds. He runs a hand over the back of his arm, as if waiting for the feel of cool scales to appear beneath his fingertips.

"How did you escape?" Aiden asks us, turning to see all of us with a hand curving around my waist to keep me close.

Kellan and I look at each other. "They left the door unlocked," I reply. "We've run into some agents since then, but..."

Aiden nods and finishes my thought aloud, "But not as many as you would've expected. We've also run into a fair number of agents, but if we're at a stronghold or a large enough compound of theirs, then it's too small of a response. I haven't heard any sort of alarm going off that we've escaped, either."

"So, it's a trap," I reason. "How do we avoid it?"

Kell scratches his beard. "Do what he'd least expect, right?"

What would I normally try next now that we've found each other?

"Has anyone seen or heard any news on Dane?" I ask, my chest tightening at the thought of him being captured and alone.

Aiden answers, "No, but the smart thing to do would be to separate us from him. I doubt he's here, but that doesn't mean we shouldn't check. We would need to find their security room to review all the cameras, rather than fighting with every agent here and Charles by running around to search each room. There could be other Guild members here, too."

We'll find you, Dane. I have a promise to keep. But I can't destroy wherever we are until we know where the others are first. "If Charles is expecting that, then what's our next option for finding them?"

"We don't," Jack offers. "We escape instead. Come back with a stronger force."

Aiden's brow pinches in thought. The idea of leaving everyone else behind *is* the last thing we'd think of.

"What if he kills them because we leave?" Kellan demands, his hands clenching into fists.

Jackson cocks his head. "What if he's killing them right now?"

Fuck. "Don't say that, Jack!" I snap, that very thought now taking root in my mind and inciting a small panic. "We can't just stand around talking. Let's go." I move to pull away from Aiden, but he tugs me back to him.

"Don't go running off," he warns.

I give him a wicked smile. "Don't fall behind."

Kellan curses, throwing the stairwell door open and revealing a wall of concrete. "How much do we wanna bet that wasn't there before?"

Fuck.

"Jack," Aiden says, and Jackson's already on the move, checking the other doors in this hallway. Kellan jogs the hallway he and I came from, disappearing around the corner.

While they're busy with that, I pull free of Aiden, which he reluctantly relents to, and place my palm against the concrete wall blocking our way to the stairs. I close my eyes, dipping into my gift and sending a thread of it into the cool cement.

A small crack appears beneath my hand, but it doesn't do more than that as I push it further out, sending it deeper to where the concrete runs out.

It doesn't.

Kellan huffs when he returns and I draw my gift back before turning around.

"There's a wall blocking the entire hallway now," Kellan reports, and Jackson, who's also back, nods.

"The way we came is also blocked. The hallway meeting in the middle of this one is open until two doors, but both are also like this." Jackson tilts his head to indicate this stairwell door.

Aiden looks at me next.

"I couldn't feel an end to it. It's not just blocking the doorway. It's filling the entire stairwell," I admit. "But I can break it. I'll have to be careful it doesn't wreck the rest of the building with it, but I can do it."

His dark stare trails over my body, then returns to my face. "Did you sleep at all? Have you had anything to eat or drink?"

"Kell and I split a sandwich about an hour ago. And we had some water."

Aiden frowns, unimpressed. "Test the walls and the other two doors for the thinnest escape. This could all be an effort to wear us down."

I do as he instructs, checking the other escape routes and then giving them my findings after the last one. "These two doors don't have as much behind them. It would be easy to break through them." The walls blocking the corridors were almost as deep and thick as the stairwell.

He nods. "We'll try one of these, then."

I press my hand against the concrete at one of the doorways, sending my gift through its shape until I've reached the boundaries, and then triggering a burst of power. It disintegrates, falling to dust at my feet.

Kellan steps into the room first. "It's a dead end," he calls out before we can follow him inside. He returns to the doorway. "It's a storage room. No other doors and no windows."

Damn.

"I'll try the other one," I mutter, turning to the last available door to us other than the stairwell. I use my gift on the concrete there as well. It dusts, disappearing into a floor made of sand.

The wild roar of a crowd echoes so loudly it shakes my bones.

"It looks like round two is here at last!"

Fuck.

We picked the wrong door.

Chapter Twenty-Three

RAEGAN

The room isn't a room at all. It opens to a massive cavern, as large as a football field, covered with sand. An eight-foot wall borders the ground in an oval shape, and stacked levels with tables and chairs circle around it so every seat has a clear view. People in suits and dresses fill the stadium, cheering, shouting, drinking, talking...

"One of the big money-makers for them is throwing a bunch of gifted into a locked down area—a cage, an arena, you name it—and betting on the one to survive."

"Fight me again, and you won't just watch. You and those boys will be participants."

"I'll leave it up to you to decide which of you will have the advantage."

So, that was it. If we'd stayed put, he might have agreed to our deal. And if not, we'd end up here.

I wasn't a fan of the last deal anyway.

"It's the fight Elias was talking about," I share, now that I've realized what's happened. "Because we escaped."

Kellan holds my arm, tugging me back. "We'll go another way."

There are dark shapes scattered about the arena, and movement off to the right catches my attention. I step forward, pulling against Kell. "Wait."

Aiden moves around us to look further in. He curses. "They're ours." Pits fighters and Guild members.

They're already here.

Fuck. Did he capture the members at the Tower with Cibrina? Was this his plan all along, to use our deaths to regain whatever money we've lost him?

I recognize Knight and a few others who fought in the Pits grouped together, watching each other's backs. Trinity and Parker—Guild members—are the only ones from their team still standing. Both were strike teams like us. I don't see any members who stayed behind. And then...

A vine lashes out at someone still moving out there. The agent dodges. A flower blooms on the vine, and then shoots something at him, and he drops.

I try to follow the vine, but there are already so many out there, either motionless in the sand or poised in the air, ready to strike. A green ball draws my stare, and I see Silas crouched and panting in front of it, one arm out protectively.

Another agent creeps up behind him, targeting whoever must be within Silas's makeshift barrier. "Aiden," I gasp when I see them, taking another step into the room. We won't make it in time. Not unless... I snap my head around to find Jackson. "Jack!" I shout.

He nods once, then throws a knife at that agent. They fall. He pulls out three more knives, sending them around the ring to strike any remaining agents.

Silas's expression melts to relief when he sees us running toward him. "'Bout time," he pants, leaning into his ball of vines for support. His other arm hangs limply at his side, and his face and arms are covered in scratches and bruises.

"What happened?" I ask him, even though I have a sinking feeling I know the answer. Kell and Aiden check the nearest fallen members while Jackson retrieves his knives.

A bell rings. Doors around the arena drag open, and the audience cheers. A loud click sounds overhead where a black box blinks to life, its digital scoreboard updating with our names and numbers.

Silas grips his arm and taps his temple against the vine ball, closing his eyes. "Portals appeared under us at the board member's house. We fell into cages, and then we were dragged out here an hour ago after a day with no food or water." He swallows hard, and I wish I still had some of that water left for him. "It's a fight between us and them. For their entertainment," he spits out. His eyes flip open, pinning to the scoreboard above us. "Charles said we made our choice, so he made his. They're betting on how long we'll last, and the fighting agents get rewards for killing us."

The half a sandwich I ate now churns in my gut. Maybe eating that wasn't a good idea.

When I look at Aiden, he's checking the pulse of a Guild member. He drops his hand, his face tight and hard. He surveys the arena, the agents striding from the doors and then standing to the side, as if they're all waiting for a signal. Aiden stands, his whip sword stretching and sharpening around his feet.

A bright light and buzzing snaps my attention to the left. Jackson's blade is stuck in some sort of electrified force field above the bordering wall. There's a flicker of energy that runs through the air, revealing a dome over us. The door we came through is already blocked by a wall of concrete.

Even if I had the time to break through it, could we all escape together in time?

I peek through a break in the vines. There's a body in there, but the vines are so dense I can't make them out. "Who's in there?"

"Evie," Silas answers. "She got thrown into that fucking electrical field and stopped breathing. I got her back, but…" He clenches his jaw and stares at the ground.

Kellan walks up behind him and squeezes his uninjured shoulder.

Aiden and Jackson join us.

"Just stay here and protect Evie. We'll take care of the rest," Aiden says.

"Are any of the others…?" I start, but he shakes his head, and another wave of nausea rolls through me.

Closing my eyes, I take a slow breath and reach for my gift. It responds eagerly, permeating my body with a soft burn that I revel in now. It floods my veins, burning away the nausea and replacing it with anger. Resolve.

Another bell rings.

The dozens of agents surrounding us break into a run.

"Cover me," I shout, sprinting far enough away from Silas to try drawing their fire toward us instead of him, and then crouch. The guys circle me without question, blocking any attacks that come our way so I can concentrate. I push my fingers into the gritty sand and send my gift down. Down, and out.

My gift runs deep beneath the surface, hidden as it stretches in every direction. The arena echoes with grunts, screams, and the clash of metal. But I keep my focus on my gift as I keep it going, on and on until it's beneath the entire arena.

And then beyond it.

I don't know who the people dining at the tables are. All I know is that they're betting on our lives, finding entertainment in the bloodshed, eating and drinking while our members were murdered in front of them.

I mark them all.

If I'm lucky, there might be board members in the crowd as well.

I don't even feel the strain of spreading my gift so far and wide. It fills the massive room from end to end like an invisible trap.

Now.

I draw my gift to the surface, seeking out the bodies above and spreading destruction like a disease. Agents and spectators alike scream when my gift touches them. Stone cracks and shifts under our feet. The attacks stop as people try to run. Or they fall from the pain, and my gift attacks more of them at once, eating away at them until they're nothing but husks.

Aiden, Jackson, and Kellan suddenly fly off their feet, thrown halfway across the arena.

I whip around to see what caused it, preparing for an attack, just as Charles raises a gun at me from only a few feet away.

Fuck.

A gunshot fires before I can think of what to do next. I'm frozen in place, staring at the gun when the sound registers.

Charles lands face-first at my feet, a hole blown through the back of his head.

My heart thrashes, shock seizing my lungs as I try to work out what the fuck just happened.

I'm not dead.

Is Charles?

How?

"Rae!"

Dane stands on the wall bordering the arena with a gun in his hand. Our eyes connect for a heartbeat, and then hands outside the arena yank him off the wall, and he disappears.

"Dane!"

A grunt at my feet reminds me of Charles.

Lifting my boot, I slam it down with my gift.

He vanishes just before my attack hits, the ground cracking instead.

Damn it.

I draw more of my gift out. It's going to take everything I have to kill him. More than last time. More than I ever had before. I call on all of it. Even when my body's thrumming with magic, overflowing with my gift as it scalds my nerves and red lightning crawls up my limbs and strikes the area around me.

The sheer force of my gift brings my feet off the ground. I hold my hands out, building it up, feeding it with everything I am.

Charles watches me rise, the bullet hole through the side of his face already closed in and a patch of hardened skin in its place. He aims his gun.

Bullets fly at me one after another. My gift seeks them out, red lightning flashing in jagged arcs to disintegrate anything they touch. The bullets are dust before they can reach me. Agents in the arena are struck at random, held captive by my gift as it eats away at them, before releasing them to the sand. Lightning hits the people in the audience as well, destroying without thought.

Only the Guild members remain unaffected.

I aim it at Charles. I don't have to physically touch him now, not as long as my lightning can reach him.

He starts cutting his own skin in shallow swipes, forcing Kellan's gift to activate. My gift skates over his scales, burrowing into any areas he'd missed but not dealing nearly as much damage as I'd hoped.

I catch Kellan hopping the wall after Dane from the corner of my eye, no sign of the electrified barrier there. More agents have swarmed the room, and I realize a group of them is trying to throw their attacks at me, but Aiden and Jackson are fighting them back.

Aiden's whip sword sails through the air, cutting through agents as far as it can reach and swinging in a half-circle. Jackson's using his gift to cut the agents on his side with slashes of air.

Something shoots around the arena, taking down one agent after another. Reid appears by another agent, cutting him down with one of his twin blades.

A large block of cement slams to the ground between me and Charles. Another smaller one falls from the ceiling. The lightning scours the ceiling, creating fissures of heat and destruction.

Right above Charles.

One of our plans to kill him was to bury him alive. We don't have the board members yet, but I'm not missing this opportunity.

I double down on my gift there, my heart racing with the hope that we can end this right here. He may heal from damage, but not if he's crushed. Like when Kellan had been stuck in the car accident, if Charles is so pinned that he can't move, then he can't heal, either.

More concrete crashes around him.

Charles teleports before being crushed by a massive chunk of debris, reappearing closer to me. He raises his hand, and I'm hurled backward. "Don't be foolish. This is an underground facility. You'll be dead by rubble long before me."

Before I hit the wall, a cushion of air catches me from behind.

The pressure from Charles's gift intensifies, pinning me between the two forces. A gasp wrenches from my lips as pain lances through me.

The GE president laughs.

I catch Jackson's hand shaking, his face pinched in concentration as he slowly releases the air, and I glide backward.

Charles flashes to his side and punches Jack in the gut. The added strength of Kell's gift has Jackson doubled over, and I strike the wall the last few feet before tumbling to the ground.

The fall does more damage than anything else, pain ringing through my head like alarm bells as I choke on sand and struggle to my hands and knees. My gift is still active, but the lightning and power I'd been harnessing earlier have retreated.

When I check on Jack, his hand is fisted as if he's trying to cut off Charles's air. The GE President smiles and flicks his wrist, sending Jackson at me at high speed.

I scramble to my feet, unsure if I'll even make it in time, before Kellan is suddenly in front of me and catches Jack.

"Are you okay?" Dane steadies me with his hands on my forearms, unbothered by the soft glow of my gift running through them. There's dried blood on his face and neck. It's caked in his blond hair and soaked through his shirt. Yet there's an overpowering smell of gasoline coming from him instead.

Even with all the blood, I don't spot anything fresh.

Tinsley and Reid attack Charles, pushing him back before he can land a hit on either of them, while Aiden and Kell check on Jackson.

Dane's gaze sweeps over me for his own inspection, and once our eyes meet again, I nod. "Yeah." I grip his arms. "You?"

He starts to say something, but Aiden cuts him off. "We need to hold him off so Reid can get the others out."

"Then what?" Kellan asks. Golden scales are spread along the backs of his arms and up the sides of his neck and torso. The impenetrable skin fills in the rest of what I can see. His gift is fully active, but there's a slight tremble to his arms where he stands, and exhaustion lines his face. His gift may be back, but for how long?

"Then I bury this place with Charles in it," I answer first, stepping around Dane so I can see them all. "Have Reid get you out with the others."

Aiden's speckled with blood and sporting a few shallow cuts and torn clothing, but otherwise looks okay. Jackson offers me a smile when I check on him next, playing off his own injuries as nothing, even though I'm sure his knee is in a lot of pain.

"He'll teleport before you get the chance," Aiden counters, but I'm undeterred.

"Then I'll destroy his facility and crush anyone left. I'm tired of running away. Even if he runs, it's a small win for us." And hopefully a blow to his confidence. "Are there any other prisoners here?" I continue, looking at Dane.

He shakes his head. "Not anymore."

Perfect.

Tinsley sails through the air. Reid appears midair to catch her, vanishes, then teleports to us. "What's the plan?" he demands, breathless.

"Get Silas and the rest of our people," Aiden answers. "We'll take it from here."

Reid nods.

Tinsley gasps, "Wait—" and then they're gone, revealing a barrage of ceiling debris flying toward us.

Jackson blows the first round to the side. Aiden uses his whip sword to knock them down, and Kellan hits whatever's left with his fists.

Those seconds are all I need to reignite the full strength of my gift. Charles teleports beside Dane, and I don't hesitate. I strike him in the chest with my gift and shove myself between them. Red lightning zaps over his skin and scales before dissipating into the sand.

Kellan grabs him by the throat and squeezes.

Charles smiles at him, unaffected. He grips Kell's arm in return. "You and I are a poor match-up at the best of times. But I've had more sleep. More food. I'm at my peak, and your gift is waning. I can see it. In a battle of stamina, you don't have a chance." He breaks Kellan's hold and knocks him back with a telekinetic blast.

I send my gift back to the ceiling. To whatever structure is between us and above-ground, spreading it as I had beneath us at the start of this fight.

Aiden shouts directions behind me. "Jack, clear this area of sand. Dane, keep Kell's gift active." He starts attacking Charles. Even though his blade can't cut the scales, he blunts and thickens it instead to hammer him hard enough to send him flying. "Kell, break through the concrete until you reach rebar. I need more metal." He stabs his sharpened sword into the concrete beneath the sand. It pierces the cement by a couple of inches, cracking the surrounding area.

I'm grateful he's realized I can't do it myself while I'm concentrated above us. One misstep, and I'll trigger my gift too early and have everything falling down over us, too.

Kellan beats his scaled knuckles into the cracked area that Aiden started for him. Dane holds his hand on Kell's shoulder as he works while Jack and Aiden position themselves between us and Charles, who's dusting himself off.

The president eyes the fissures of stone above us, noisily snapping and popping, as my gift continues to expand through it.

He lifts his hand, but instead of propelling me back, I'm drawn toward him.

Jackson's air slows me down.

Aiden's blunted sword swings at Charles, who lifts his arm to block it. He slides some feet back, but he doesn't lose control over his telekinesis.

"Aiden!" Kellan shouts.

A large block of concrete suddenly hovers over Charles, then falls.

I'm no longer being pulled forward, and Jackson quickly shoots me back to the group while Charles is preoccupied with dodging the stone.

"Now, Raegan," Aiden commands, and I realize thick walls of metal are surrounding us. Only the space above me remains open.

I unleash my gift.

Sharp cracks and a deep rumble roll through the arena. The sound drowns out shouts of my name before I'm roughly yanked down, and the world darkens.

We're pressed together in the cramped space as booms like thunder and the pounding of stone against metal echo around us. My heart jumps into my throat at the incursion of sound that's so loud I can feel it echoing in my bones.

I fight against the panic that threatens to take over as we all hold
on to each other.

It feels like a lifetime.

It's maybe minutes.

And then it ends.

Chapter Twenty-Four

AIDEN

It doesn't take long before I realize the metal I'd gathered won't be enough to hold back the onslaught of rock and concrete. The unrelenting, hammering force jolts through the smooth alloy and vibrates down my arms as I brace it, working to strengthen it where it's weakest. The small amount of metal I'd accumulated and the rebar beneath the arena had been enough to create the shell, but it's beginning to dent.

I need more.

Pushing deeper into my gift, I give it everything I have. Thicker. Stronger. Fix the dents. Find more. There has to be more.

As if in response to my silent demand, something flickers in my senses. Metal. I don't know how I know that's what I'm sensing, but I use a thin strand of steel to seek it out. Touch it. Fortify the shield surrounding us.

I sense more metal.

There.

I do the same as before. Link metal to it and draw it in.

It's when my senses overwhelm with alerts of metal above us that

I realize a building must have been on top of us and joined the destruction.

By the time it all ends, I don't think anything would be able to penetrate the barrier of metal between us and the rubble. Every muscle burns and aches. My chest heaves, taking in too much oxygen when we're limited. Sweat trickles down my face—from the exertion and being trapped in a metal box with the others.

Individual pebbles and rocks sprinkle over the metal in sharp *tinks* as everything above us settles. The sound reminds me to stay conscious. We aren't done yet.

"Give me an opening," Raegan rasps like she's on her own last bit of strength.

We're all dead if she and I don't finish this before we pass out. I'm sure my barrier will hold, but we'll die from lack of oxygen.

Dane's gift is a soft glow where his hand still presses to Kellan, allowing us to see where the opening will be. It feels like I'm already empty. I scrape the bottom of my gift for this last task, scrounging whatever remnants I can find, and expose a small hole in the metal above us. It's just large enough for her hand but too small for the larger concrete to fall through.

Raegan reaches for the rubble and activates her gift. Red cracks appear in the stone before they disappear. She's finding our exit. Her body trembles as she works, and I fear what might happen if we're all in this state and Charles surprises us at the surface.

The stone and debris above are a chorus of thunderous cracks, and then it's gone. I widen the opening and find a five-foot diameter tunnel directly above us to the surface. Raegan slumps into Jackson's waiting arms. "There," she gasps, eyes closed.

A soft wind tickles my sweat-soaked skin, and I relish the fresh air

Jackson must have drawn in. Metal groans overhead, and I stiffen, flexing my hand even though I don't think I could curve a spoon, much less fight.

Boots crunch on sand next to me, and Reid is suddenly standing beside Jackson and Raegan. Now that her job's done, it looks like she's passed out. "Is she hurt?"

"She's exhausted," I reply. "Is Charles up there?"

"He's gone." Reid places his hand on Raegan's shoulder. "Grab on. I'll take you to the others."

We claim a spot on his arm, and then the hole of dirt and metal vanish.

Everything spins, and then slams to a halt.

I take a firm step from practice with these jumps, catching and steadying myself before my face meets the glittery black floor. Jackson has Raegan in his arms, while Kellan and Dane are both on the floor. Kell grimaces when he heaves to his feet after landing facedown. Dane's no longer keeping his gift active, so he's returned to his usual state.

A quick glance around the room tells me exactly where we are.

Black bench seat tables line the back wall up to a stage. A bar is on the opposite wall, and large glass boxes dangle over our heads for dancers to make some cash in a touch-free setting.

The Hype bar and nightclub.

Dane struggles to his feet with a groan.

"Why are we here?" I demand, mustering the strength from pride alone.

"Where else were you planning to go?" Elias asks, strolling from the hallway behind the bar. "You can't return to the Tower now that you've shown your hand to Gifted Enterprise."

He's one of the last people I'd like to see when I'm feeling this rundown, and it spikes a bit of temper that I don't have the energy to control. "I'm merely surprised you'd accept us into your home when we all have targets on our backs. You'd kicked Raegan out for that very reason, after all," I counter with smooth vehemence.

Elias's smile doesn't falter. "Yes, and that was a mistake I've since learned from."

Kellan throws his arm around my neck, leaning on me in what might look playful, but is actually seconds away from flooring me. I don't have the strength to hold up his full weight on a good day, let alone now. Thankfully, a cushion of air catches me before we both collapse.

"Alright, you two," Kell drawls. "Let's get past the posturing bullshit and move to the part where you tell us where the beds are so I can crash. Or else I'll park it right here on your dance floor, then good luck moving me."

"The rest of your Guild is already here and settled. I've put aside apartments 367 and 368 for you," Elias says, holding out two cards. "Once you've scanned those cards, you can enter a code to use moving forward. Raegan can return to her apartment."

No one steps forward to take the cards.

I answer instead, "You can give those to someone else. We'll stay with Raegan in her apartment."

Elias doesn't look surprised by that admission. He tucks the cards into his inner jacket pocket and nods. "There's a spare futon in the closet. We'll talk after you've had time to rest."

Dane slips under my other arm, and with Jackson's gift also helping with some of Kell's weight, we somehow manage to trek upstairs. After getting Raegan and Kellan in bed, I call Cassandra to stop by for a quick healing, and then finally allow myself to sleep.

Habit dictates that I wake up after only four hours of rest, despite my body needing far more. My head throbs mercilessly while simultaneously feeling stuffed with cotton. And I'm parched.

Forcing myself upright, I hold my head as if that might help stabilize it. Sunlight peeks through the drapes in a thin sliver, and even that small burst of light makes me cringe and turn away from it.

Something nags in my periphery. Drawn behind me, I stare at Jackson's hoodie.

Metal.

It's not much. Maybe a throwing knife or two. I tell myself it wouldn't have made a difference in protection even though a small part of me is annoyed he'd withheld any metal when I needed it. But one small blade he'd given Raegan saved her life from Creighton, so I should be grateful he always keeps a stash for emergencies.

Another flicker.

I'm drawn to Kellan's belt on the floor.

More flickers.

There's metal in the walls. Pipes. Wires.

It's every-fucking-where.

All of it calls to me, softly begging to be touched. To bend to my will. To turn into something more.

Goddamn it.

I pushed my gift too far, and now I have to figure out how to ignore or quiet these signals so I'm not driven mad by them. It was useful when I needed to find more metal in a time of need.

I don't need it just to get up for a glass of water.

I skip the bathroom and water, heading for the living room instead. Coffee it is.

"You should still be sleeping." Jackson's voice stops me at the doorway.

"I'll sleep when I'm dead," I counter grumpily.

"Says the man I saved from death."

I pause, then admit slowly, "I don't think I could fall asleep right now if I tried."

Jack studies me with a cocked head and observant eyes. "You strengthened your gift."

I nod. "Aside from the new sixth sense of metal I've acquired, I need to see how the Guild members have settled in and prepare for their stay here."

He smirks, then lies back down.

I don't know why he backed off, but I don't wait to find out.

Cibrina answers on the second ring. "Aiden? I thought you'd still be sleeping."

"How many injured members are there and what're their statuses?"

"Most of the strike teams were restrained and only had blood drawn. They'll be better with food, water, and rest. The ones in the arena who were injured have all been through their first round of healing between Cassandra and Holly. There were broken bones, internal bleeding, stab wounds, abrasions, and electrical burns. It'll take another session or two for a few of them as well as time to rest, the healers included. Evie is in that group, and we're waiting for her to wake up."

She takes an audible breath. "Greg and Skylar—both Pits fighters—Parker and Lyla didn't make it. Reid brought them back."

I close my eyes and scrub a hand over my face. Four dead.

It's unrealistic to think we could take down Gifted Enterprise without losses, but that doesn't make it easier. Not when I'm supposed to protect them.

Skipping the cream and sugar, I let the scalding coffee burn my mouth and throat to see if I can cut through the headache and loss with a hit of caffeine. "What do we still need for the Guild? Has a hold been put on any job requests?"

"Yes, Quinn updated our website and the automated phone message if anyone tries to call. The official word is that the company is temporarily closed while the unofficial word Penn has spread online is that the company took its employees on a long vacation."

"Great. Are there adequate kitchens downstairs for Miranda and her staff to work in?"

Cibrina hesitates.

"What is it?"

"There is no kitchen downstairs. Just a break room."

I close my eyes, breathing through the pounding headache and incessant flickers telling me about all the metal nearby.

"Aiden. You should really get more rest. We can discuss this tomorrow or the next day," Cibrina coaxes.

"What are we going to do about food? Income? Bills? Security? I'll sleep when I know the Guild is taken care of."

"Should we meet with Elias? He might have more insight on what's available here for security." And the financial concerns, but thankfully she doesn't voice that admission.

I can't stand how much we've had to lean on him for that aspect, but defeating Gifted Enterprise is more important than my pride. Making sure the Guild members are taken care of is more important. Without any income, they won't be able to afford food. We also can't have them walking around the city and being grabbed by GE agents. We have to hunker down until Charles is dead.

The clock on the cable box shows it's mid-afternoon.

It feels like four in the morning.

"Yes. Let's meet downstairs and we can go to his office to discuss the plan for the Guild while we're here."

"I'll see you shortly."

CHAPTER TWENTY-FIVE

RAEGAN

It takes a full day and a half for me to wake up. Thankfully, I didn't overdo my gift this time. The same can't be said for Kellan. It's the first time he's ever pushed his limit, and he's still recovering in bed when I finally rise. Dane and Aiden are coordinating grocery deliveries downstairs for Guild members, according to Jack.

"I'm going to go see Portia," I tell him, pointing to the shared wall so he knows I'll be just next door. He gave me a simple "Yes" when I'd asked if her team was okay. That could mean anything from 'she's alive with no injuries' to 'she's in serious condition, but not on her deathbed'. That thought decided it.

He taps his thumb multiple times over his phone screen—and I wonder for a second who he's messaging—before he glances at the open bedroom door where Kellan's sleeping. I'm sure he's annoyed he can't come with me, but if the brute wakes up for a piss, there's no way I can help carry him to the bathroom. "Go see Aiden after." When I give him a questioning look, he elaborates, "Make him get more sleep. He won't listen to me."

"When has that man ever listened to me?"

Jackson smirks. "He listens." I scoff, incredulous and ready to refute it when he adds in a more serious tone, "He pushed his limit, too. But he's only slept eight hours in the last two days."

Eight hours. I didn't push my body and gift to the limit this time and still slept for thirty-six hours.

Fuck, Aiden!

"Alright, I'll track him down after checking on Portia." And see if he does actually listen to me for anything when it comes to his health.

I take the two steps to Portia's apartment door before knocking.

"Porsh? It's Rae. Can I come in?"

There's a scuffle behind the door that sends my heart into my throat. Is she being kidnapped again? I jam her code into the keypad to unlock it. "I'm coming in!" I shout, throwing the door open just as Portia shoves someone into her bedroom.

"I told you, my *best friend* is here. Take a cold shower!" Portia yanks the door closed and beams at me over her shoulder. "You're awake!" she screeches excitedly, running and tackling me in a hug. "I was worried when I tried to visit yesterday, and Jackson said you were still sleeping. Are you okay?"

I release a sigh of relief with a small laugh. "Was that who I think it was? You could have told me you were busy. I thought you were in danger when you didn't answer."

She laughs, and it's such a sweet sound that I'm still in awe every time I hear it. "He knew how worried I was about you and that you were coming. Serves him right for trying to start something anyway."

"You knew I was coming?"

Portia gives me a wicked smile and taps on her phone, then shows me the screen.

> **Rae's Scary Stalker Assassin:** She's coming.

I blink, stunned. "Is that Jackson?"

She cackles and tugs me onto her couch with her. "When I said I tried to visit yesterday, it *may* have been multiple times. And I *may* have slipped my number under the door when he stopped answering with a note requesting that he update me as soon as you woke up."

Laughing, I shake my head trying to imagine Jackson dealing with Portia.

"You haven't answered my question, though. *Are* you okay?" Her expression sobers when she looks at me, and I'm immediately compelled to smile to ease that worry.

"Yeah. Everything that happened, well... it was bad, but... we're—I'm okay." I need to check on Aiden and wait for Kell to wake up before I can claim that for all of us.

Instead of relaxing, her eyes round with concern. "What happened?"

I don't sugarcoat things for Portia. I explain what happened with Creighton and his strength-sucking gift. Then the threats Charles made against me and the others; her face bleaches at the mention of me producing offspring for him to manipulate and use against the world. Followed by Kellan's torture, the arena where we found other Guild members and reunited with Dane, Reid, and Tinsley, and then how we'd tried to crush Charles and escape.

"Holy shit balls," she breathes when I finish. "Is Kellan okay? I know he heals and all that, but still..."

My chest aches when I remember what they'd been doing to him. And then it burns hot with anger. I clench my fists in my lap. "He hasn't woken up yet, so I don't know."

She sniffs with anger and crosses her arms. "At least you know everyone who touched him is dead and buried now."

True. That does help a little.

Everyone except Charles.

"What happened with you guys?" I ask next.

"Oh, Noah went through the memories of the staff before we went near our target," she answers, reminding me of how Noah had once gone through my memories to vet I wasn't involved with GE or Portia's kidnapping. I'm still pissed at Joe for going after Portia even though he's dead. "He found out about the guard hanging out with the gift-blocking darts, so we took him out first. We tried calling about the trap, but I think everyone was already taken because no one answered. Probably because we were dropping other teams off and got to our target later than the rest."

All that makes sense as much as it sucks.

"Then I got the spy—Sam—to reveal himself and come with us. Elias shot the target from outside of the room, and we bolted out of there." She shrugs, as if what they did wasn't as incredible as it was. First off, her gift and Noah's are both amazing and terrifying. Then to hear Elias shooting a gun and taking a life—even if she told me about it happening before—still shocks the shit out of me. Then, how easily they were able to get in and out even with all the traps set for them. They made it seem effortless. Even if I didn't know about how they'd taken down a trafficking empire, it's obvious they've worked as a team on missions like this before.

"That's seriously incredible, Porsh. We're lucky to have you guys on our side."

Her cheeks flush, and she ducks her head, tucking hair behind her ear. "Yeah, I guess we're pretty cool."

I laugh at her sudden humility, showing me more how she feels about her men rather than their flawless mission. Otherwise, she'd have no problem boasting about their success.

The apartment door opens, and Elias enters. His brow peaks when he sees us together on the couch. "Is this a private conversation or should I wait patiently in my office for the chance to join you both?"

I look at Portia, and she shrugs. Even if we hadn't already caught up on everything, I would have shared that information with him if he'd asked.

"You can join us," she relays once we've both agreed through body language and expressions.

Elias smiles and dips his chin, ever the gentleman, then gracefully sits in one of the single upholstered chairs facing us. He reclines into the seat back, his forearms covering most of the armrests on either side, and leans into his fist. "It's hard to believe you're the same girl who walked into my club trying to take down Gifted Enterprise by yourself."

"What do you mean?"

"Now you have the support of the Guild, underground gifted fighters, my team and Hype, and apparently half-siblings of yours continue to pop-up. Not to mention the four men who look ready to take a bullet for you at any moment." His smile is warm. "I'm pleased to see you open up and let so many people in. The world is too dark and unforgiving for those who walk in it alone."

Portia shifts the slightest amount. I wouldn't have even noticed if

Elias's gaze didn't snap to her immediately.

"Thank you," I mumble, embarrassed. But he's right. I was a lone wolf on a mission of vengeance.

But now... there are so many people I'd call friends in the Guild and with Portia. I have Aiden, Kellan, Jackson, and Dane.

"Thanks for taking a chance on a reckless girl. And for still helping her and her friends even though it's putting all our lives in danger."

Elias nods once. "I could see your potential when we met. And I have to say, you did not disappoint. Your gift is stronger than anyone's I've ever met. Did you know one of Gifted Enterprise's headquarters was directly above you when you destroyed it?"

"Above the arena? I'd only been trying to destroy the underground facility."

"By our research, you decimated his nonprofit front that managed all the donations and finances for the company. As well as whatever dark secrets he'd had in that underground facility. It's a major win against him."

Oh. Wow.

My body tenses as I realize what that could mean. How I could have put us all in danger. "And the public? What are they saying about the randomly destroyed building?"

Elias gives me a reassuring smile. "Charles already intervened, it seems. They're passing it off as a freak sink hole that appeared beneath the building. Because of its potential to expand, the area has been blocked off from anyone going in. I'm sure only the government agents in his pocket will clear it before someone sees something they shouldn't."

Well, then.

"It was a remarkable feat, Raegan. I can easily say I'm honored to be part of your team and helping you finally accomplish your goal."

Damn it, I will not get emotional.

I swallow the sudden knot in my throat, and Portia giggles and wraps her arms around one of mine, knocking into me in the process and helping me get out of my head. "He says the sweetest things, doesn't he?" She turns to him. "How are things downstairs?" she prompts, her tone casual even as her eyes slide to mine and shimmer with mischief.

I'm relieved that the attention has been pulled away from me. It's tempting to retreat inward to get my shit together, but I'm too curious to see what Portia's up to that I stay focused on their conversation.

"Ah, well. This is my reprieve while the Guild Master is preoccupied questioning a prisoner. My assistance was not needed for that task."

That piques my attention. "Prisoner?"

Portia releases me and collapses into the cushions behind her. "Someone from GE. Dee? Bee?"

"Bea?" I repeat, realizing who she must mean. The portal girl. "Where is she?"

Elias sighs. "As we are not as... *accustomed* to having prisoners, we've locked her in the storage room for office supplies in the basement."

"I should go see if they need any help." Especially if Aiden is as tired as Jackson claimed and he's now alone with Bea. *Dane should be with him, but still...*

They both wave me off, promising to catch up more on next steps once all of our crew are rested and awake, and I head to Hype's basement.

The hallway at the foot of the stairs is a hallucinogenic experience. The lighting is a soft purple over white walls and a reflective tile. But it's the bright neon lights steaking along the walls like thick waves that makes me feel like I'm traveling through time or something. It's disorienting.

A raised voice draws me to a cracked door a few feet down the neon tunnel to the left.

"And when he comes for me, he'll kill all of you!" a female voice shrieks.

"I destroyed your tracker before we left your space. He's not coming," Reid replies evenly.

"He'll find me! He *needs* me!"

"He doesn't need anyone but himself. You're delusional if you think otherwise."

I draw the door open enough to see the room. Bea's pacing at the back wall while Reid stands in the middle of the room facing her. Aiden leans against one of the shelving units of office supplies, his eyes closed. Dane looks pissed beside him, but he relaxes when he sees me.

"You're awake." He sounds relieved as he approaches.

Aiden opens his eyes, and Reid looks over his shoulder.

"We're done for now," Aiden says, pushing off the shelves and striding toward us and the door. Reid follows without a word, and I make room for everyone to exit. Once the door's locked, I throw my arms around Dane. Even though he'd reunited with us in the arena,

I'm still fucking relieved he's okay.

"How did you escape?" I ask, slowly withdrawing.

He kisses my cheek. "Alice followed us. And me, when we fell through the portal." Dane jerks his chin at Reid. "He and Tinsley showed up, too. We destroyed the island and got everyone to Cibrina. Then we went to rescue you."

"And Bea?"

Reid glances at the door. "I was able to tether to one of her portals and use it to get into her space."

"Her space?"

He nods. "It's a pocket in space-time where she manages most of her portals for GE."

"We found a cuff on the island and put it on her before locking her up here," Dane adds.

Aiden's eyes are closed again when I check on him. I place my palm to the side of his face, then gasp.

"Aiden, you're burning up."

He opens his eyes, and they immediately lock onto me. It feels like I'm his anchor, holding him steady now that he's latched on. I grab his arm.

"Dane, take his other side. We're bringing him to the room."

Aiden grunts. "Ibuprofen must've worn off," he mutters. "I'll take more."

Tucking myself under his arm, I grab his wrist and start pulling him toward the stairs.

"I'll watch her," Reid murmurs, stepping in front of the door with his arms crossed to guard Bea.

"I'll call Elias. Get security," Aiden continues, determined to keep on top of everything.

Dane curses from under his other arm where it looks like Aiden's leaning most of his weight. "How much fucking metal is *on* you right now?"

"*I'll* call Elias. You're going to bed," I argue through gritted teeth. "But if you could pick up your feet more, that would be great."

Thank fuck, he does.

The stairs are still a bitch.

Up from the basement. Then up to the second floor.

At least we're not on the top floor.

"How is he rich as fuck but doesn't bother with an elevator in this fucking place," Dane rages aloud when we finally make it off the stairs.

Aiden's so overtired and feverish that I think he's barely conscious enough to move his feet for us. The rest of his mental faculties have checked out as he rambles some nonsense that I think he thinks are commands for things that still need to be done.

Dane shoots me a look and eye roll, and I smirk back.

Once Jackson answers the door, his gift relieves us of his weight so we can get him to take more medicine, undress him, and lay him on the futon since Kellan is sprawled across the bed. Aiden drags me down with him, locking me against his heated bare chest with both arms and mumbling into my hair. "Nagging metal... bend it... quiet... shhh..."

I stroke my fingers over his skin. "Go to sleep."

Dane snorts and pulls a sheet over us. "I'll come get you when food's here."

"Call Elias so someone can swap out with Reid," I add before he leaves, and he nods with a smirk.

"Sleep tight."

Chapter Twenty-Six

RAEGAN

Aiden's surprisingly better after only a full day's rest, and Kellan wakes up with him, starving. When I update Portia on our group finally being awake and coherent, we receive a group text from Elias less than five minutes later that he's ordered a breakfast buffet to be set up on Hype's dance floor.

"I don't understand how you and Elias don't get along," I remark to Aiden while shimmying out of my shorts and one of his soft shirts in the bedroom. The others are waiting in the living area while Aiden and I dress in our regular clothes before we head downstairs to eat. "He's such a nice guy. I really like him. He's letting us stay here, he's feeding us, he's—"

A hand covers my mouth and shoves me into the wall. "Tell me again how much you *really like* another man and see what happens," Aiden croons, his voice smooth and dangerous. I clench my thighs as his voice makes my core throb. I don't know how he does it. The sound of it alone, whispered in my ear, feels like he's stroking my pussy. I struggle to move my head, and his grip tightens to hold me in place.

"We've already established that I'm a jealous man with the others." He rubs his fingers over my underwear in taunting strokes. My legs twitch as pleasure blooms from his touch. "How do you think I'll be if I hear you talking about someone else? If I hear you talking up another man outside of your existing harem?" He shifts the underwear aside and coats a finger in the arousal he's already drawn from me.

I whimper behind his other hand.

"Shall I fuck you until the only name on your lips is mine? Make you come until you forget his name and everyone else's?" He sinks two fingers into me, and they're welcomed with slick passage. I moan, my eyes shuttering as those fingers curl and spark a current of need.

His hand shifts from my mouth to my throat, and he kisses me. I'm expecting it to be rough with his current mood. Teeth and tongue, and the demand for submission. Instead, it's smooth and languorous. I arch into him, desire burgeoning through me with every soft stroke of his tongue. Every press of his mouth that lights me on fire, coaxing my soul from my body as his fingers pick up the pace, fucking my cunt and sucking my essence through my lips.

Pushing to my toes, I wrap a leg around his hips to grant him deeper access, my hands clawing at his shoulders, his nape, into his hair to remove any distance between us. The reason why he's doing this has completely left my thoughts as I zero in on the pleasure building between my thighs. As I rock against his fingers to chase the orgasm that's curling at the base of my spine.

My pussy flutters around his fingers, and my body stiffens.

He retracts his fingers and breaks the kiss, pinning me to the wall by my neck.

"No!" I cry, gasping and pulling both sides of his untied tie to try to bring him closer.

"Next time you want to come, you'll have to beg me for it."

Anger replaces lust, growing hot in my chest. I shove at him, but he doesn't budge. "Good thing I have three others who'd be happy to help," I snarl.

His smirk is nothing short of devious. "Go ahead and try. I'll tell them what you said about Elias." Aiden's lips graze my ear. "What do you think Jackson will do to him?"

Fuck.

This time, when I push him back, he releases me. Aiden brings the fingers he'd been fucking me with to his mouth and sucks them clean without breaking eye contact.

My breath hitches, and a resounding throb echoes in my cunt, desperate for more.

"I'm looking forward to your begging." He pinches my chin and runs his thumb over my bottom lip. "And the name on your lips better be mine."

I smack his hand away, and he chuckles, picking up his jacket from the bed and leaving the room.

Asshole.

I'm half tempted to get myself off while I'm alone, but with my luck, he'd fucking sense it and storm in with an even greater punishment. I keep my shaking hands to myself, roughly yanking clothes on to try erasing his teasing touch that still lingers.

When I leave the bedroom, Kellan's sitting on the couch with one arm up and his legs spread wide. He gives me a wolfish grin like he knows an embarrassing secret of mine. Dane is in one of the upholstered chairs and looks at me with heat in his molten amber eyes. It's a look that says he's fully on board with teasing the shit out of me until I beg. Aiden stands when I enter, fixing the cuff of one sleeve as he appraises me from head to toe.

Jackson is missing.

"Where's Jack?" I ask.

"Reid stopped by while we were getting dressed. Jackson left with him," Aiden replies.

I breathe a sigh of relief. Aiden cocks a brow, as if he can sense there's more than just my recent compliment of Elias that I'm worried over, and I beeline to the door before my face gives anything away. "Should we see where he went?"

Kellan's arm wraps around my shoulder, and he tugs me against him while my hand is on the doorknob. I'm annoyingly aware of the firm press of muscle and heat radiating from him. "Don't run or else be prepared for the consequences, beautiful."

Smiling wickedly at him, I purr, "Maybe that's exactly what I want."

He grins. "Oh, I'm sure it is. But you might not like the ending." Kellan's teeth scrape my earlobe, and I shiver. "Seeing as you've been banned from orgasms."

Growling, I push him away and shoot daggers at Aiden.

He's completely unapologetic as he returns my glare with nothing more than a tiny smirk of victory. "I'm sure he'll join us when he's finished," he says, answering my original question.

Dane captures my hand in his, linking our fingers together. "Come on. Let's eat before the rest of the Guild gets there and there's nothing left. As soon as Fabian shows up, it'll be over."

I laugh now that I know Fabian and how true it is. I think it's a superpower of Dane's to be able to comfort me and make me laugh even when I'm in the thick of a bad mood. He smiles at me with that boyish I'm-so-in-love-with-you look that makes the world feel like it could be filled with rainbows and butterflies if I stare at him too long.

It's dangerous.

Hype's dance floor is filled with circular tables and folding chairs. Long tables bordering either side are packed with food. I take back my earlier sentiment. There should be enough food for us *and* Fabian, by the looks of it. The platters are heaping with food and filled with every breakfast dish one could think of.

There are a few Guild members here so far, but we're still early enough to have first pick of seats. Dane guides me to one of them. "What can I get for you?"

I almost refuse—I can get my own food—but his look of pure excitement to bring me something has me hold my tongue. "All of it looks good," I answer honestly. I'm not sure if there's anything here I wouldn't like. "I'll be happy with whatever you grab."

Metal screeches behind me, and I turn to see Kellan sprawled in the folding chair next to me. "If you're taking orders, Rapunzel, I'll take whatever she's having. Then double it."

Dane glares at him. "Get it yourself."

"I'll get it," I offer, moving to stand. Dane puts his hand on my shoulder to keep me in my seat.

"No. I'll do it." He shoots a look over at Kell. "But I'm getting hers first."

Kellan grins, and Dane rolls his eyes and stalks off to the tables.

"Well played, beautiful," Kell drawls, leaning an elbow on the table to shift closer to me.

I shrug, scanning the room and finding Aiden speaking to Elias by the bar. No sign of Jackson yet. "You're just starting to feel better. I would've gotten the food for you whether Dane did or not."

He growls, grabbing my face and forcing my full attention to him. "I don't think it's possible for me to love you more than I do. It makes me feral. Makes me want to rut you into the table while everyone watches so they know you're mine."

Wings flutter in my abdomen. As hot as that sounds, I know the others might gouge some eyes out if that were to happen. And I like all the people here. Instead of leaning into that train of conversation, I tease him instead. "Like how you asked me to pet your rooster?"

His eyebrows lift. "My rooster?"

"I'm assuming you meant your cock. You asked me several times if I was there to pet your rooster while you were still out of it."

"What else did I say?"

"Something about a wet whistle and another comment involving sloths," I recount with a smile.

Dane sets a plate in front of me with a scoff. "I'm not repeating the shit you told me when I helped you to the bathroom. I was traumatized enough the first time." He returns to the buffet tables with a fresh plate before we can question him further.

I jab my fork into scrambled eggs. "Geez, Kell. What did you say to him?"

Kellan snorts. "Hell if I know."

The chair on my other side slides back. Aiden sits with a mug of coffee.

"There's been no word from Charles and no sign of GE activity. I'd expected something to happen at the Tower, but security footage hasn't shown anything."

"Elias told me we destroyed one of his headquarters. Maybe he's too busy cleaning that up?" I guess between bites.

"Or he's waiting for one of us to show before he attacks it," Kellan adds. "Either way, I'm not complaining it's been left alone."

Aiden rubs the rim of the mug in an almost self-soothing motion as he becomes lost in internal debate.

Dane returns with a plate for Kellan and himself. He frowns at Aiden in the seat next to me as if he'd been planning to sit there. He takes the chair on Aiden's other side with a grunt, then digs into his food.

Aiden finishes whatever line of thought in his head and continues, "I spoke to Elias. We're going to regroup in his apartment after breakfast—"

"Lunch," Kellan interrupts, but Aiden presses on as if he hadn't said anything.

"—to discuss the plan moving forward. I've gotten the reports from the other strike team leads to see who was able to eliminate their board member and who was not. We were able to take out three of the ten."

"That's not even half," Dane grumps.

Gasps and whispers erupt around us, and I realize how full the room is now with Guild members, Pits fighters, and Hype staff combined. The crowd standing around or waiting for the line to move parts, and Jackson strolls through the center.

With fresh blood speckling his face.

Chapter Twenty-Seven

RAEGAN

Aiden and I stand at once, our metal chairs scraping the floor and cutting through the hushed voices. It's then that I notice Reid following behind him, expressionless as usual. There are a few flecks of red on his jaw and cheek as if he'd been close enough to receive some of the spray. But the one who dealt whatever damage was definitely Jack.

"What happened?" Aiden demands. "Where were you?"

Jackson stops a couple of feet from us, his sapphire gaze eyeing the crowd gathering around us. Some move back when he looks at them, and a small smile forms on his lips. "In the basement," he replies coolly. "Taking care of a loose end."

"Excuse me." Elias taps on a couple shoulders to grab their attention that's pinned on Jack before they realize who's speaking and hurriedly move aside. "What's all this about?" He freezes when Jackson glances over his shoulder at him.

"He killed Bea," Reid supplies.

Dane curses. "Dammit, Jack!"

"Let's take this upstairs," Aiden says in a tone that brooks no arguments.

"My apartment," Elias adds, garnering a look from Aiden, who'd probably wanted us to handle this between the five of us.

Aiden begrudgingly nods, and Elias leads the way. I grab my napkin and go to Jack. He immediately takes my free hand while I wipe some of the blood from his face.

It doesn't bother me. The crimson color he wears is a reminder of what he'll do to keep me protected. I do it out of respect for Elias and his home to make sure he's not leaving evidence of what he's done behind.

Jackson grabs the back of my head and pulls me into a kiss before I can finish. He kisses me like the God of Death as he takes my breath away. Takes my mouth with a ruthlessness that has my knees trembling. Violence radiates from him like a dark energy that prickles along my skin. It demands more blood, more death.

I push back, meeting his savagery with my own. I dig my nails into the back of his neck. Bite his lip so hard he groans, and that bloodlust shifts to desire.

Hold my leash, the words he once told me whisper through my head.

Gripping his hair, I yank him back. "Upstairs. Now," I command, trying to keep my voice firm even though I'm breathless.

Kellan and Dane stand behind me, blocking others from watching the show. I grip Jack's hand and lead the rest of us to Elias's apartment on the top floor. It takes up the entire floor, which means there will be plenty of room for us without being on top of one another.

Which is for the best.

I knock at the door, and Aiden opens it for us.

As soon as the door closes, Elias sighs and pinches the bridge of his nose. "Please explain what happened."

Reid looks at Jack, and when he doesn't offer up an explanation, replies, "Bea was causing trouble in the basement."

"The girl you'd taken prisoner?" Elias clarifies, and Reid nods once. "How does someone who is locked up and giftless cause trouble?"

Jackson cocks his head, regarding Elias with a dark stare and a smile. He looks dangerous and unpredictable right now. "By trying to cut her hand off to get free."

Elias blanches.

My stomach curls. I've dislocated my thumb to get out of cuffs, but I'm not sure I could do something as terrible as that.

"How did she even get something to do that?" I ask.

"Aside from the cuffs, she wasn't restrained in the basement. I had Cassandra heal her injury. I wanted to see what she would do with that little bit of freedom," Aiden explains.

"A normal person would've tried picking the lock or breaking the door down," Dane mutters.

"She's brainwashed by Charles," Reid says. "She'll do anything to get back to him."

"Then why did you have me carrying her around?" Dane snaps at him. "You should have just killed her then."

Reid levels him with an unbothered stare. "It was worth a try to use her gift against them."

"Portia could have convinced her," I murmur softly.

"We don't need Bea," Jack counters mildly. "The plan was always to kill her." He locks his blue eyes on mine. "Alive, she was a threat. And I'll kill anyone who threatens you."

Fuck, I should be worried. Concerned, at least. I shouldn't stare obsessively into the eyes of a man who says something as unhinged as that and feel heat swimming through my veins. Or feel the need to wrap myself around him and kiss him until I've robbed us both of air.

Elias's brow cinches. "That's not how we do things—"

Jackson's eyes snap to him with a look that would have any normal person shitting their pants. He wraps his arm around my chest, pulling me against him protectively with his cheek pressed to my temple. "I do. If someone is a threat to her, I'll kill them. No questions. No mercy."

I can't help but lean into him, drawn to the calm confidence in his husky voice even as he promises death on my behalf. I've never felt safer or more at ease than when he's wrapped around me.

Elias looks at Aiden, who doesn't refute Jack's statement.

"There's no need for you to be concerned, Thorton. So long as you and those at Hype don't wish her harm, we can continue working together to take down Gifted Enterprise."

"Of course, I don't."

Aiden nods. "Then, there's no problem."

Elias sighs, rubbing the back of his neck. "Your body, your clean-up," he finally says, which honestly shocks the shit out of me. I'd expected him to be more... disgusted? Angry and upset? Then again, I shouldn't be surprised after what Portia told me. "Hype opens in one hour, so that takes priority. We'll reconvene once you've finished."

Once the dance floor has been thoroughly bleached and washed as per Elias's standards—and the body removed and the basement cleaned—we return to his apartment to figure out our next move.

"There are still seven board members alive," Aiden reminds the group. Cibrina, Reid, and Tinsley have joined us, spread out across the large living area and kitchen.

"A few have gone into hiding after our last attempt," Dane reports. Which was exactly what we were afraid of and why we'd gone after them all at once. Kill them before they get skittish and disappear.

"But that doesn't matter now, right?" I ask, shifting between them. "Alice gave us private cell phone numbers of her siblings. We didn't need them for our last plan, but now..."

"Even if we know where they are, there's a high probability they're somewhere more secure or with agents protecting them. It won't be as easy to get to them," Aiden counters.

Elias nods in agreement. He's sitting in one of the living room chairs opposite Aiden with an ankle resting over one knee and his hands gently clasped and resting on top. "Have you made contact with these half-siblings yet? Are they on our side?"

I sink into the couch, chewing my lip. He has a point. Look how long it took Alice to come around. How can we expect the others to go against Charles when Alice had been—and still is—adamant she doesn't have to fight him? None of them want to be on the receiving end of his fury if he realizes any one of them betrayed him.

Dane squeezes my hand. "Alice can convince them."

I frown, doubtful.

"She's seen the Guild and the people in it. She wants to be a part of it, and I'm sure she wants that for her siblings, too. If anyone is going to persuade them to help us, it's her. She was in the same position as them not that long ago," he presses.

"Our last failed attempt isn't going to look good to them," Kellan remarks, his arm thrown over the back of the couch behind me.

"No, but the destruction of one of their headquarters and the underground facility will," Dane retorts.

Kell grins at me, and my neck crawls with heat. "That's right. They'd be fools to not see the winning side now."

Aiden taps his fingers on the armrest, a sign of his mind working in overdrive. "We'll offer them our protection as well. Regardless of the outcome, if they can get us to the board member, we'll ensure their escape and protection." His hand stops. "That can give us the intel we need on where they are and what protections are in place, but it's still messy to deal with. It would be easier if—"

An idea hits me.

"If they're all in one place?" I breathe, a rush of adrenaline surging through me as the idea solidifies.

All eyes are on me.

"What if we could draw them out? Get them all in one place? Maybe another HQ like the last one just as a big eff you to Charles?" I rush out.

Aiden frowns. "Slow down. How would we draw them out?"

"I'm not sure yet. Maybe lure them out with Charles somehow? Make them think he wants them to meet him at a specific location? And then I destroy it like I had the last one. Charles didn't hesitate to cover it up, so I'm sure he'd do the same for another GE building." He can't have officials sniffing around and finding evidence of Gifted Enterprise's true nature.

"If we have the invisible spy network on our side, I just need information from one of the board member's phones," Dane tags in. "I can spoof Charles's number to the board members' phones so they think it's him texting them to meet." He glances at Reid. "Reid can help me write the message so it sounds like him."

Reid nods. "He usually makes the board meet him wherever he is. It wouldn't be out of the ordinary."

Kellan scratches his beard. "How are you going to bring the building down without being seen, beautiful? I'm all for the plan up to that point. The building could fall on you, and people might see you."

"I'll cover her," Jackson calmly interjects.

I nod, then answer the second concern. "We'll have to rely on Alice again."

Dane shakes his head. "She doesn't know how to make other people invisible."

Damn.

But I'm not giving up. "Then we train her. Or maybe one of her siblings. I'm sure between them, someone can do it."

"We're putting a lot of hope in the girl who killed her own brother out of fear of Charles," Kellan drawls.

"She saved me, and she didn't have to," Dane argues, surprising me.

"We need to see if she can make others invisible first. The rest of the plan falls apart if she can't do that," Aiden intervenes. "Dane, you and Jackson will help her figure out how to do it. Kellan and

Raegan will focus on training and stamina to prepare for the building's demolition. The rest of us will put together the full plan on how we'll execute this trap for the board while minimizing risks."

Chapter Twenty-Eight
RAEGAN

It's later in the evening when I find myself grinding over Dane's hard dick, straddling his lap while Kellan and Jackson watch us from the couch. We're still fully clothed—something I plan to rectify shortly—as I grip Dane's nape and shoulder and reignite the desire that Aiden had started this afternoon.

Dane and Kellan have been teasing me all night once we got back to our apartment. Jackson hasn't touched me yet, but I can feel his eyes on me. The intensity of his stare has me shivering with excitement.

Even with Aiden's order hanging over us, I'm confident I can make them cave. I'll tease them and wind them up just as much as me until they're helpless to resist. I'll fuck all three of them, and Aiden can listen from where he's working in the bedroom.

Dane throws his head back into the couch, releasing a moan as his hands twitch and grip my hips. I'm in control, though, gyrating my hips and pressing my cunt over his length in rolling strokes. "Fuck, babe. Ungh, that feels so fucking good. Don't stop."

Kellan chuckles. "Careful you don't make him nut in his pants," he teases, and I smirk at him. He rubs a hand over the bulge in his jeans, then squeezes it. "You want some of this too, beautiful?"

"Shut the fuck up," Dane growls through a gasp of pleasure. "Have her ride your dick like this and see how long you last."

"Oh, I'll last," Kellan drawls with a grin. "It's her I'm worried about. What with her no orgasm rule still in place."

"Fuck that rule," I snap. "I'm not begging that asshole."

Kell leans forward, his forearms resting on his knees. "Oh really? He said if you refused, he'd tell us all what you did to earn that. I'm really curious now. What was it?"

Dane slips his hand beneath my shirt and pops my bra. He pushes it out of the way and squeezes my breast. "Fuck, do you two always talk during foreplay?" He kneads my breast with his fingers, then drops his mouth to the nipple, nibbling on it through my shirt.

Pleasure strikes my core with every scrape of his teeth and swipe of his tongue. My shirt dampens and sticks to my stiff peak, warming it until I'm squirming and rubbing my pussy over him with desperation.

Clothes. Get rid of the clothes.

I stop moving, scrambling at his jeans to yank the button free and rip the zipper down.

Kellan chuckles and stands. "What did you do? Flip a switch somewhere?"

"Hurry up and grab her hands before I lose it." I scoot back and reach into his briefs. My cooler hands wrap around his cock, and Dane groans like it's the best thing he's ever felt.

"Fucking hell!" he moans again, and it turns me on just as much as the feel of his rock-hard dick in my hand.

There's precum collecting at the tip, and my thumb swipes

through it, spreading it over the head.

I lean forward, pressing my lips to his in a brief kiss, then whisper against them, "Dane... fuck me."

"Fuck! Go apologize to Aiden or do whatever the fuck he wants so that shit's lifted. *I'll* fucking do it if I have to. Whatever it is, it can't be worse than this."

"I'm not begging him."

"Babe. *I'm* begging you. I don't want to have sex with you again without making you come, but I'll do it if you push me."

I shift off him to work on my pants with one hand while I pump his dick with the other. "I don't think you will," I challenge.

A large hand grips my throat. "And what about me?" Kellan growls in my ear, his beard tickling the side of my face. He pushes his hand into my pants I'd just undone and slides his fingers through my arousal. I gasp, my legs quivering at the touch and my hand convulsing over Dane's cock.

He hisses through his teeth and then curses, throwing his head back.

"You think I can't control myself?" Kellan thrusts his fingers into my cunt, and I cry out. He pumps them in and out a few times, then drags the slickness to my clit and circles it.

"Yes! Kell!"

He pushes back into my pussy, and I practically sit on his hand to drive them deeper. Twist my hips to get him to touch that spot inside.

Kellan chuckles, pressing his thumb to my clit but not moving it. "I can do this all night, beautiful. Either give Aiden what he wants, or you can tell me what you did. It's your choice."

Fuck.

I slide my gaze to Jackson. He cocks his head when he sees me looking at him, a dangerous smile curling his lips.

No. I can't say it, especially not after what happened earlier today.

Kell's fingers are relentless, giving me just enough to increase the pleasure without pushing me over the edge. His thumb is a constant pressure that I try to grind into, but it doesn't budge.

I stroke Dane's dick at the speed and pressure I'm desperate for, as if I can somehow get that pleasure for myself. It isn't long before he hits his limit.

"I'm going to come, babe," he grits out, ready to catch it with his hand. But I knock it aside and dive forward to deep throat his dick. Dane's slewing a string of curses as cum drains down the back of my throat.

My own orgasm creeps up my spine as I swallow him down, setting off another round of groans from Dane that make my pussy clench around Kell's fingers.

"Oh no, you don't," Kellan warns. He pulls his hand free and chokes me until I release Dane's dick.

My climax slips out of reach.

Frustration wells in my chest and floods my veins in a rush of heat. I reach around to beat a fist into his chest. "Let me go, asshole!"

Kell laughs and releases me. "Ready to get this shit fixed with Aiden? Or should we go again?"

"Prick!" I snarl, then whip my head around to Jackson.

He smoothly shifts forward.

Yes.

Jackson won't deny me. He crooks a finger at me, and I bend down at his instruction. He places two fingers under my chin, guiding my lips toward his. I think he's about to kiss me, but the second his lips graze mine, his smirk deepens. "Come to me after Aiden's fucked the good girl out of you."

Fuck's sake.

I flip all three of them off and storm into the bedroom, slamming the door behind me.

Aiden looks up from the small desk and the papers in front of him. His deep chocolate eyes take in my disheveled appearance. My unbuttoned pants. My unclasped bra is making my shirt stick out comically above my chest. The way my chest moves in rapid succession.

He carefully sets his pen down.

Then turns to face me fully, his fingers loosely linked in his lap.

And he waits without a word.

All the words I want to call him rise up in me at once.

But I know that'll only make things worse. Instead, I plead my case.

"It was a compliment! I didn't say I want to marry or fuck the guy!"

"That doesn't sound like begging to me," he replies.

"Fuck you, Aiden! I'll do it myself." I shove my pants and underwear down, kicking them off after my shoes, and then removing my shirt and bra too because they're annoying me.

He's suddenly standing in front of me and grabs my wrist. "You touch yourself, and this punishment will seem like a breeze compared to what I'll do to you," he croons. "You want to come? Beg me for it. Tell me what you need, Raegan, and you'll have it."

I grind my teeth, glaring at him while I debate my options. Push this further—where I'm sure he'll stop me before I can get any relief—and risk a bigger punishment, or give him what he wants this time to finally get what I want.

"Please," I bite out through clenched teeth. "Let me come."

"You can do better than that."

Fucker.

"What more do you want? Me to crawl to you?" I snap without thinking.

His brows rise, and his impossibly dark eyes seem black now. "Mm, I like that idea. But let's save it for another time when I have that collar and leash we talked about prepared."

Aiden steps into me, and I back up. He does it again, and this time, the back of my knees hit the bed, and I drop onto it. He looms over me, stretching and loosening his tie before dragging the silk free. He thumbs the first few buttons of his dress shirt apart, then kneels before me at the foot of the bed.

Wait. Did I somehow pass?

His eyes never leave mine as he moves, and I'm captured by them, trapped in their endless depths as they suck me in. Aiden shuffles my legs over his shoulders, and he tugs my dripping pussy to his face. "Maybe I've been going about this the wrong way," he begins, and I think, maybe, I've won.

"Oh?" I ask breathily as I feel the heat of his breath on my core.

"Let's see if this method helps you find the right words to say." He drags his tongue up my center, and my body convulses around him. I fall back on the bed as he eats me out, and I lose control of my body. All my strength is sucked out of me by his mouth as he devours me until my mind goes numb. I'm a shaking, quivering heap of over-sensitive nerve-endings as he brings me just short of a climax again and again. I curse him and cry each time he denies me. Then hold my breath when I'm brought within seconds of an orgasm as if this time might be different.

When I can't take it anymore, I break.

"Please, Aiden, I need it. I need to come so bad. I can be a good girl. I'll do whatever you want, so please, please don't stop again. I'm begging you. Whatever you want."

Aiden hums. "That's a good girl. Was that so hard?"

I'm at the point where the brat is long gone. "No. Please, Aiden. Please."

Thank fuck he doesn't take his time. He returns his tongue to my clit and gives me the added reward of his fingers. I explode before I have time to enjoy the build-up, but I don't give a fuck. The delayed release is like a bomb of pleasure has gone off inside me, and I'm screaming as I come tumbling down.

It feels so fucking good.

But I want more. My pussy aches for more than his fingers.

As if he can read my mind, he drawls, "Do you want more?"

"Yes," I beg, but he doesn't move. "Yes, please, Aiden," I try again. "I want more. I want your cock inside me. Please fuck me, Aiden."

"Such a good girl."

He climbs over me on the bed, pinning my wrists over my head and driving into me in a single thrust. Aiden doesn't bother trying to wind me up. He fucks me into the bed like he's been just as desperate for this as I've been. There's no room for breathing, no room for thought as he brings me to ruin once again. He flips me to my front and thrusts back into my aching cunt, gripping my hips and holding my shoulders down so his dick hits deeper.

"Ah! Nngh! Aiden! I-I can't take anymore!" My whole body's shaking, exhaustion weighing me down as he sparks my pleasure back to life. As it grips me again in an iron fist, and all I can do is breathe and hold on.

"You're doing so well. I know you can take it. Give me one more, Raegan." He slides his fingers through my cum and circles my clit. "Come for me like a good girl."

He pulls another orgasm from me, demolishing me from the inside out. It burns through me like a wildfire and leaves nothing behind. Aiden finishes right after me, then collapses over my back. He holds his weight off me with one hand and brushes his lips over my shoulder. "Stay here. I'll clean you up."

I'm asleep before I even feel him leave.

Chapter Twenty-Nine

RAEGAN

Training at Hype starts at sunrise and ends two hours before the nightclub opens. The dance floor is unfortunately the biggest space in the building, so when people pile into booths and stand behind the bar to watch, I feel more like I'm putting on a performance than actually training.

"Focus," Kellan barks, grabbing my wrist and throwing me to the ground.

I lean into that momentum and roll across the glittery black floor instead, then push to my feet. "I'm trying," I growl, frustrated by the audience. At least when we'd trained in the gym at the Tower, the other members were too busy with their own training to stand and stare. But there isn't room here for others to train.

Not while Kell and my gifts are active.

I throw punches and jabs anywhere I think he's open, but the prick blocks them all. Gathering more of my gift in one fist, I launch it at his face.

Kellan snatches my hand and grunts. I'd bet it felt like more than a tickle that time. "Make an opening." He tosses my hand aside and kicks my feet out from under me. "Come at me from all sides." His boot slams down, and I catch it instead of dodging, bolstering my gift there until it eats away at it.

"Like here?"

His grin turns feral. "I liked these boots."

"My bad," I taunt, holding his leg and rolling to drag him off-balance.

He jumps and twists out of my grip, landing with one foot bare. Kell unlaces and casts his remaining boot aside.

"You go, Reggie!" Gabriel cheers from the sidelines.

"Yeah! You got 'im, Rae!" Portia hollers behind the bar.

Others join them in shouting my name, bringing a flush of heat to my face that has nothing to do with my gift.

Kellan laughs and shakes his head. "You've got some fans, beautiful. You think they're hoping you'll get me naked?"

Now that he mentions it, I need to be more careful with my gift. That's not the result I'm going for. This training is about control and stamina with our gifts. Keep them active all day, fight with them, and not break anything.

Which is easier said than done when that's *all my gift does*.

"Maybe they're hoping to see someone win against the mighty Dragon."

"Hate to disappoint them, but I call bullshit on that happening here. So let's at least give them a good show, yeah?"

I clench my fists, heat pulsing in my chest at the challenge. "Bullshit, huh? You don't think I can actually beat you, even with my gift?"

His grin sharpens, that arrogant look that says he's about to stick his middle finger in some shit and stir it. "Not a chance."

Oh. Game fucking on.

Reaching for my gift, I draw more out. I pull it through my limbs until the reddish glow electrifies and dances like lightning over my skin. It burns and tingles where it makes contact, but not in a painful way. Before it expands beyond myself, I stop it.

This is a good exercise in control, keeping the balance of power between where I was before and releasing it completely.

Kellan shifts his stance, the golden scales along the backs of his arms and up the side of his neck almost blinding when they catch the lighting right. I think he's just preparing for my attack since his gift is already active when his body suddenly shifts to something *more*.

His blue-green eyes are pitch-black, and two horns protrude from his head and curve back. His fingers are elongated to sharp claws, and a line of scales are raised to razor points along the backs of his arms to his elbows. His feet have shifted to something inhuman.

Like the feet of a Dragon.

I'm waiting for wings and a tail to burst from him any moment.

Someone screams.

The room becomes a mad scramble of people fighting to leave and others trying not to be swept away.

"Kell?" I shout over the chaos to make sure it's still him.

His usual grin is gone, and there's a darker, deadlier energy radiating from him. When he hears my voice, he cocks his head at me like a beast eyeing its prey.

"Is that still you?" I approach him slowly, instinct warning me to make no sudden movements. Nothing that could be perceived as an attack. Raising my hand, red lightning still jolts and dances over it.

He captures my hand, then brings it to his lips. Kell licks my palm like he's enjoying the taste of my gift. His blackened gaze fixates on me like he's preparing to devour me next.

Something wet sprinkles the side of my face.

"Hey! Change back before everyone panics!" Portia sprays Kellan with water. "I don't want to use my gift on you, but I will!" She sprays him again.

Kellan turns his head and just stares at her.

I covertly slide myself a bit in front of her. "It's okay, Porsh. He's not going to hurt anyone." At least, I don't think he will.

Aiden pushes through the crowd of people and runs to our side. "Kellan. What…"

Kell closes his eyes and releases a slow, long breath. His gift recedes, fading to his golden-brown skin and no horns or talons in sight. When he opens his eyes, he grins. "That's only the second time I've tested out the increase in my gift, so I'm still getting the hang of it. What do you think, beautiful?" His blue-green gaze twinkles with excitement.

I release my gift too, now that I think the match is over, and run my hand over his smooth and muscular arm. "That was amazing," I breathe, still waiting for it all to sink in. "I thought you were going to shift into an actual dragon for a second."

"Not quite, but it's pretty damn close." He chuckles.

"Wow," Portia commends, and Kell's attention zeros in on the spray bottle in her hands. He snatches it and sprays her in the face. "Hey! Wait!" she sputters.

He sprays her again, his arm maneuvering out of reach whenever she tries to grab it. "Payback." He does it one more time. "And for threatening to use your gift on me. I'll do more than spray you with water if you ever try that."

Portia squeals each time the water hits her in the face, her arms flailing in front of her to try to grab it blindly. He finally returns it, and she wipes her face with her arm and hand. "How was I supposed to know you were fine when you looked like that? What if you breathed fire and we needed to put you out?"

I'm not sure how a spray bottle would combat a fire-breathing dragon, but I don't mention that. Instead, I focus on the possibility she raised. "Can you do that?"

"No. At least, I don't think I can. But I have more than that. I just held back so I wouldn't break the rule of not damaging anything."

Aiden scans the room. "You may not have broken anything, but you certainly scared some people away." Surprisingly, only a quarter of the bystanders are gone. The rest are watching on in awe or whispering amongst themselves and pointing our way.

"Not nearly enough," I mumble more to myself, but Aiden looks at me and lifts his brows. "Sorry, it was just a lot."

"It's good the training ended, then. Especially before the two of you actually tried to fight like that. I doubt the nightclub would still be standing if you had." He glances over his shoulder as Elias approaches. "I'll explain what happened. You head upstairs and out of sight for a bit."

"I'll help smooth things over, too," Portia offers, following Aiden.

Kellan throws his arm around my shoulder as if to give me a hug, but some of his weight presses down, and I plant my feet. "Sorry, beautiful. It wears me out pretty fast still. I'll be fine after a nap."

I grip his wrist over my shoulder and wrap my arm around his waist, though I can't reach his other side. "Come on. I'll see if Dane's finished with Alice and can make you something to eat, too." Once we're at the top of the stairs, I tell him, "Next time, show me all of it."

He chuckles. "You just want to see if I have a dragon dick."

I gently shove him with my hip. "Shut up."

Raised voices behind the door are a bad sign of how Alice's training is going. I knock three times, knowing Jackson will still hear me through the noise. "It's Raegan," I call out.

The door opens before I've even finished. Jackson holds it open for me as I walk inside Alice's apartment, where they've been trying to teach her how to make others invisible.

"Why are you even here if you're not going to help me?!" Alice shout-whines.

Dane scoffs. "And what else do you want me to do? I can't do it for you, Alice. You have to actually fucking try."

"I *am* trying, asshole!"

"Are you? Because all I hear is complaining. You want me to leave, but the second I do, you'll be begging me to come back so you're not alone with Jack."

"You're supposed to protect me from him if he threatens me again—"

Dane cuts her off with a mocking laugh. "I couldn't do shit to stop him if that's what he wants to do. I'm just here to make you feel better."

"Well, you're doing a terrible fucking job of that!"

"Heyyyy, guys..." I slowly cut in.

Dane's eyes widen when he sees me. He looks away, rubbing the back of his head. "I need a minute to cool down," he mutters, storming into the bathroom and closing the door behind him.

Alice glares after him. "Jerk." She faces me, still looking annoyed. "If you're here to see how it's going, it's not. I can't do it!"

I offer her a comforting smile. "I wasn't expecting you to get it like that." I snap my fingers. "But that doesn't mean we give up. Let's take a short break and try again when you're feeling up to it again." Looking around her apartment, I don't see the other person I'd been expecting. "Elias said your brother is staying here with you, too? I heard he doesn't do well with a lot of people, which is why you wanted to train in here."

She makes a face and plops into the nearest seat. "Sam's in his bedroom. He's been spying on the same board member for a long freaking time. I'm not sure he even remembers *how* to talk. And he's fine with other people as long as they're not talking to him or looking at him."

Right. Just that.

Dane rejoins us. He comes up behind me, sliding his hands around my waist and tucking his chin over my shoulder in a backward hug. "Somehow, Harvey is looking like the most well-adjusted sibling," he remarks, earning a middle finger and sour face from Alice. He lowers his voice for only me. "Sorry about before."

I hold his arms over my stomach and kiss his cheek. "It's okay. You guys have been at this for a while. Maybe I can help change things up."

"How'd your training go?"

When I spin in his arms, he effortlessly adjusts to holding my hips while I settle my hands on his chest and share a wicked smirk. "Oh, well enough to almost cause a mass panic in the crowd."

His eyebrows lift.

"Because Kellan almost turned into a fucking dragon," I continue, laying that bombshell down.

Dane's mouth pops open. I peek around him and find even Jackson looking a bit surprised. "He, what?!"

"No wings or tail popped out, but he looked like he was right there. Horns and claws and all."

"Fuck." He cranes his head to peer over his shoulder at Jack. "What's the death rate for leveling up again?"

Jackson smirks. "Sixty percent, according to Thorne."

"That's a forty percent chance of surviving and getting stronger," Dane muses when he turns back around.

I smack his chest. "That's still too high a risk, Dane."

"What if I could do more, though? More people. Or make it stronger some other way."

Alice snorts. "I bet it'd just glow brighter."

"Says the girl whose idea of trying is just squeezing my arm to death," Dane retorts.

"Can Sam turn others invisible?" I ask before another squabble breaks out.

"Yeah, but he won't spit out how," Alice grumps.

"If he won't teach her, we should just ask him to do it. At least he'll be quiet," Dane murmurs. He grabs and spins us. A shoe slaps to the floor.

"I heard that, asshole!"

"Dane," I admonish, pushing away from him. "Stop antagonizing her. Alice, can I try talking to Sam?"

She shrugs, flapping her hand at the door. "You can try."

A quick glance at Jackson shows he's still sitting on the stool at the kitchen counter, one foot up and the other dangling while he leans into his fist and watches the room. The amount of patience he must have had working with these two all day is astonishing. I'm glad I didn't walk in to find bodies instead. Unless letting them fight it out is somehow part of his training plan.

The corner of his lips lifts in a secretive smirk, and I realize I'd been staring.

I head to the bedroom door and knock lightly. "Sam? Can I come in?"

There's no answer.

"You'll be standing there all day if you wait for him to give you permission," Alice remarks.

Right.

Turning the handle, I poke my head in. He's not at all what I expected. Alice did say he'd been spying for a long time, but I still pictured a kid. This is a grown man—maybe mid-twenties—based on his size. His hair is a shaggy white-blond, as if he chops it off himself without a mirror every few months. It covers most of his eyes like a curtain, so he has to look through the small slits where his hair isn't. He's skinny, too, making me wonder how often he ate while undercover.

Sam sits against the headboard with his knees to his chest, his eyes staring at the television, reminding me of a child. He doesn't look up when I enter.

"Sam?"

Nothing.

I move inside slowly, then sit on the corner of the bed furthest from him. Dane follows quietly and stops just inside the doorway. Glancing at the screen, I recognize the movie and smile. "Oh, this is a good one. Have you seen it before?"

He blinks at me suddenly, as if just now realizing I've been talking to him. His cheeks flush, and he nods once, casting his ocean blue eyes downward.

It's then I notice there's no other sound in the room. The movie is quiet. "Do you want me to turn the sound on?"

No reply.

Dane and I look at each other.

Did he mute it on purpose?

"I heard you haven't left your room much. You know it's okay for you to leave it, right? We could go with you downstairs to meet some people, if you want. Or maybe with Alice if that'd make you more comfortable."

He gives a tiny shake of his head.

"Okay. We can stay here, too."

Sam stays frozen. Like a frightened animal hiding from a predator. It makes my chest ache.

"I'm Raegan. I don't know if Alice told you, but I'm your half-sister."

His gaze slides to mine. Or, my nose, maybe. It's not quite eye contact, but it feels like this is as close as I'll get right now.

"Do you know sign language?"

Sam shakes his head at the same time as Dane scoffs and goes, "Do you?"

I shoot him a look, catching his teasing smirk. "No, but I could learn it, asshole."

The bedroom door crashes open as Alice waltzes inside. She stands on the opposite side of the bed with her hands on her hips. "Talk, would you? Or are you going to sit there until you melt into the bed?"

His shoulders hunch as he leans away from her.

She throws her hands up and sighs in exasperation. "Look, I know it's probably been a while since you talked to people. But your job is over now. Your assignment is dead. You're *free*, Sam. You can make noise"—she knocks her fist into the headboard, then shakes it—"you can be *seen*. Be loud! Tell us what you want, for fuck's sake! Because none of us know you well enough yet to figure it out."

"How come you're not afraid to speak up?" I ask her, genuinely curious.

Alice's eyes narrow on Sam, waiting for something from him. When he doesn't give her anything, she huffs and responds, "My assignment didn't require as much supervision, so Dad would pick me up a lot to help him with other things. And anytime I was with the guy, he'd be doing boring stuff. So I'd go in the den to watch TV. Made his staff think the room was haunted," she adds with a snicker.

Dane scoffs, crossing his arms over his chest. "So even then, you slacked off. When's the last time you pushed yourself? I'm not trying to be a dick this time. I'm serious."

She flips her hair and sits on the bed with a bounce. "Look. Not all of us can do the same exact thing as the others. Maybe it skipped me. Maybe only my brothers can do it."

He gives me a look, like, *see what I've been dealing with?*

"Can you try again with me?" I ask her softly. She frowns, and I lift a shoulder. "It can't hurt. Maybe trying with a different person will help."

"Fine." She scoots to the middle of the bed and places her hand on my arm.

Sam looks up, watching us.

Alice closes her eyes, her face tightening like she's straining to get something out, then gasps and lets me go. "See? Nothing."

I mean... I saw something, but I'm not sure if that was real or not.

"How do you make objects invisible?"

She leans past Sam to a pillow, touching her hand to it as she had to me. It vanishes almost as soon as she makes contact. "Like that. That's what I tried to do with you."

Sam shakes his head.

"What is it?" I ask.

He disappears at the same time as Alice.

I look at Dane. He shrugs, but gently nudges the door closed and stands in front of the smaller opening.

They both reappear a few seconds later.

Sam taps the sides of his index fingers together.

"What does that mean?" Alice prompts.

I mirror him, as if that might help me understand. Then think about how they'd both disappeared together. "Together? Do you mean at the same time?"

He nods.

Holding my hand out to Alice, I offer her a short head bob of encouragement. "Try it. Make me invisible at the same time as you."

She frowns, her brow pinching with concentration before she takes my hand.

I give it a second before looking around. Nothing looks different...

"I still see both of you," Dane answers my unspoken question. Alice releases me with a dramatic sigh. "But," he presses before she can say anything negative, "I started to see you fading away. It was only a little, but it was there."

She perks up. "Really?"

"Yup." He smirks. "Looks like you have a lot more to practice now."

Chapter Thirty

JACKSON

The smooth slide of steel on whetstone soothes something in me. The sound of it, the gritty texture that vibrates into my fingers as I drag the blade along the stone, strokes my soul. If I were a feline, I'd probably be purring.

Water runs from the kitchen sink as I work through each of my knives and spread them out on the counter.

We're getting close to Raegan's plan being put into action. Alice finally managed to make another person invisible two days ago. Now, she and Reid are teleporting around the country to find and convince her siblings to help us.

Considering Harvey's and Alice's initial refusal to go against Charles, I don't expect it to be easy. Reid's been instructed to grab and bring back anyone who can't be convinced, so they don't squeal to Daddy President. It's up to Alice to avoid that outcome. If we lose eyes on a board member, it puts the whole plan at risk.

They're trying to reach all of them in one day, which means they'll be gone all day and likely won't return until later this evening.

Then, it'll be our turn.

I angle the current blade into my arm, and a line of red blooms with minimal pressure. I swipe it clean with a cloth and place it beside the others.

The small creak of a door opening tells me Raegan's exiting the bedroom. "Hey," she greets, strolling up to the counter while squeezing the ends of her wet hair with a towel. "Cassandra invited a bunch of us to her apartment. Evie still hasn't woken up yet, so she and Silas think she might if she hears us playing cards."

Cassandra and Evie are sharing one of Elias's apartments, as all of the Guild members are. There aren't enough for everyone to have their own, but this combination in particular was chosen when Evie didn't wake up even after being healed.

She's in a coma.

"I'm going to join them for a bit since Kell and I finished training."

I don't share my annoyance again that he let her walk up here on her own. She'd defended him, saying that he'd gotten caught up talking with one of Elias's crew, and she was too impatient for a shower to wait for him.

Doesn't matter.

This isn't home.

Though Aiden believes Elias and his people are allies, that doesn't mean we can trust them like our people. Raegan shouldn't be out of our sight for even a second until Charles and Gifted Enterprise are wiped from the board.

And maybe not even then.

"I'll come with you," I tell her before she can rush out the door on her own. I have one knife left to sharpen before my backup set is ready for use.

Raegan nods, settling in to watch my process with interest. A smile curls my lips at her concentration on what I do and how I move the blade along the stone. I know she's memorizing all of it, even if she doesn't know why I do something. She trusts that I know, and for her, that's enough.

"Do you want to try?" I offer, extending my hand to her.

She bites her lip to hide her smile, but I see it anyway. I can see it in the way her eyes light up or widen a fraction. I can hear it when her breath catches. Feel it when her quiet, reserved strength vibrates the very air around us. She's not just strong when she's using her gift to bring the world to heel at her fingertips. It's in the moments of calm, like this, when I feel it just as much. Her desire to learn more, know more. To push herself beyond complacency.

Her hand falls in mine, and I tug her to the small space I've made between me and the counter. With my arms capturing her on either side, I take her hands and guide them to the blade. "Keep it at an angle—like this. Then drag it back from heel to tip down the stone. Mm... good."

She shivers. It's barely more than a tightening of her muscles as if she tried to hide it. But she should know by now there is no hiding from me.

Releasing her hands, I settle mine on her hips, grazing my thumbs along her skin beneath her shirt. "Keep going, little one. Ten times per side should do." I pull her hair around one shoulder, revealing the perfect curve of her neck that begs to be tasted.

"Jack," she pants.

"Focus on the knife," I warn without stopping. The sound of steel on whetstone paired with her intoxicating vanilla-cinnamon scent from a fresh shower is stirring my desire faster than I can keep it leashed. My lips descend onto her skin, and an unmistakable shudder rolls through her.

She presses her ass against me, finding my hard dick and releasing a tiny gasp as if she's surprised. She shouldn't be. I'm hard the moment she deigns to lay her eyes upon me. The second her skin meets mine. Or her scent overwhelms the air I breathe.

"Turn it over," I remind her after I've counted ten strokes of the blade, even though my eyes are closed. It feels like she's touching me with that knife when I block my sight. Like she's the one stroking my soul with that blade in a way that sends ripples of pleasure straight to my cock.

Shhhhhhnk. Shhhhhhnk.

Her breathing is shallow, but her pulse beats excitedly against my tongue.

Shhhhhhnk. Shhhhhhnk.

Her body wash smells sweet, but its taste isn't the same as hers. And now that's all I want—to taste her.

"Use the black stone next," I direct huskily, tapping the shallow tub of water beside it. "Ten strokes on each side again."

Hooking my fingers into her waistband, I push her pants to the floor and drop to my knees, twisting to sink my tongue into her core without delay. Raegan cries out and almost drops on my face if not for my gift pushing her upright.

"Oh fuck! Jack!"

I don't stop. I'm not sure I could now that I'm here. I'm dying for her taste, starved for her to coat my face until it buries into my skin, and everyone knows I belong to her, that I would do anything for her.

Her strength calls to mine as it always has. Even before she knew her full potential, I was drawn to her. Drawn to the only person whose strength could put me in my place if she wanted to.

She rocks her pussy onto my mouth, wanting this just as much as me and only feeding my own hunger to give it to her. Once I add my fingers, she detonates. Her sweetness is everything I'd been hoping for as I lap it up and hold her steady. She quivers with every stroke of tongue. Squirms when I graze an overly sensitive spot. It's tempting to give her another orgasm, but I know she's worried about Evie. If I keep her here too long and our Guild member happens to wake up to everyone's rowdiness, as they hope, then she'll be unhappy with me.

I can wait to finish this later.

This was just a taste.

An appetizer.

Once I've cleaned her up, I pull her clothes over her hips and pick up the throwing blade to study it over her shoulder while she catches her breath. I test the edge of one side on my arm like the others, and Raegan gasps.

"Jack! What are you—How many are there?!" She grabs my arm once I've pulled the knife away to stare at the myriad of thin red lines. They're all shallow cuts. Nothing to bleed out by, and they won't scar. It's how I always test them.

"They'll heal," I reassure her, unbothered. Swiping the cloth over the blade to remove the blood, I place it with the rest.

"We'll have Cassandra heal you when we get there," she says with a bit of bite to her tone. As if to say, *I don't care if you think this is fine; I'm not fine with this.* A soft reprimand.

Smiling, I don't reply.

It's obvious I'll do exactly that if it's what she wishes me to do.

She turns in my arms to face me. "I'm going to use the bathroom quick and then we can go. You can clean up while I'm in there."

I tilt my head, my smile still in place.

Raegan motions her hand in front of her face, then sighs when I still don't give her anything. "Your face. Me. Off your face."

"I want it there."

Her mouth pops open. "What? No. Absolutely not." She snatches the nearest dish towel and swipes it over my face. "Wipe it off, or you're not escorting me anywhere," she threatens while handing me the towel to finish what she started.

I'm helpless to disobey a direct command from her. I do as she says, and she smiles at me. "I'll be two minutes." Then she's off to the bathroom.

I tuck the towel in my pocket.

For safekeeping.

Raegan knocks eagerly on Cassandra's apartment door. The laughter and excited chatter are loud enough to be heard through the door even without my gift. The fun's already started, and it doesn't sound as if anyone heard her knocks.

Before she wastes her effort knocking again, I pinch the key card in my back pocket. I'd had Dane program it to unlock every door in the building. It's not something Elias would be happy to learn about, but I don't care how he feels. I need to know that I'll have direct and easy access to any room where Raegan may be. Whether it's with another Guild member or Portia or Elias doesn't matter.

Picking these locks with their electronics would be a pain and take too long. This was the easiest solution by using Raegan's old card and some tech.

I hold the card against the door lock and—to Raegan's surprise—it clicks and the door pops open.

"How did you—" she starts, but cuts herself off when the door swings open to a just-as-shocked Silas.

His dark eyes freeze on mine. "Well, that's terrifying."

"Oh my god. Does that work on all our rooms?" Cassandra whispers not-so-quietly.

Raegan enters the room, and I follow. Silas closes the door behind us.

"It does," I confirm coolly.

"Wowee!" Gabe laughs from the floor around the coffee table since the seats are filled. "But my guess is it's just for Reggie's benefit and not ours," he concludes cheekily.

"Oh. Right." Cassandra shakes her head, her red curls bouncing with the motion. "Thanks for coming. We think Evie's finger twitched earlier when a few of us were getting loud in there. Hopefully, she'll be so mad at missing out on a game that she'll come running in here," she says with a chuckle.

"We should be playing on the bed," Fabian remarks, nonchalant.

"We're not playing on top of her," Silas snaps. He's not usually so short-tempered, but I'm not surprised. He cares a lot about Evie.

"Says the guy who practically sleeps in her bed," Cassandra counters conspiratorially, and he recoils.

Fabian gently nudges his foot. "Relax. We know you've been talking to her a lot and fell asleep once. Evie likes it. I'm sure of it. Don't let what Sondra says bother you."

"Zeddy, can you move please? My Reggie needs a place to sit." Gabriel pats Zedd's leg on one side of him. He's sitting behind him on the couch with his head back and eyes closed. But his breathing changed when tensions rose with the conversation.

"It's okay. I can join you on the floor. It looks like he's sleeping." Raegan moves to sit across from him on the floor.

"He's not," I calmly snitch, staring Zedd down. He pops one annoyed eye open at me. I smile back.

"I'm fine here, Jack." Raegan gives me a look over her shoulder. I maintain my smile. "Oh, Cassandra. Would you mind healing his arm? He has some cuts on it. They aren't bad, they're just... there's a lot. Jack." She motions for me to move closer to her. And them.

I do. Reluctantly.

"Sure." She stands and moves around everyone as Raegan twists and reaches for me.

I squat by her side. She pulls the sleeve back to reveal the wounds and slips her hand in mine at the same time. It helps settle the instinct to stab Cassandra when she touches me. I grip Raegan's hand back, needing her to keep me grounded and focused on her as Cassandra assesses the injuries.

She places her palms over my arm and closes her eyes. Warmth spreads from her touch through my skin, encouraging it to heal and put itself back together. It tingles and heats, and then her hands are gone.

"There."

Raegan smiles. "Thank you."

Gabe smacks his hands together. "Now that that's done. Let's play!"

It's hours later when my cell phone buzzes in my pocket. I pull it out and read the text on it. It's Briar. And Mallory.

She wants to see Raegan.

It's not the first time she's asked. She wasn't ready then. She was still scared of the idea of seeing her. Initially, it was the fear of Raegan herself and her gift. Then it turned to a mixture of fear and shame of what Raegan might think of her for what she'd been forced to do because of her.

But now, she might be ready.

The time shows it's just after seven in the evening.

Tossing my latest slice of pizza to the cardboard box, I stand.

Raegan smacks her hand down on the pile and drags it in front of her. "Yes! I got it!"

The others laugh or playfully boo her victory.

"Mallory wants to see you," I tell her, carrying my voice to whisper in her ear.

She blinks when it reaches her, then looks over her shoulder at me with raised eyebrows. But there's hidden pain in her eyes at the mention of the girl's name. As I've seen any time she's been mentioned.

It's time to fix those broken pieces and turn them into something new.

She doesn't move or respond immediately, and I don't rush her. She's likely running through a wild flurry of imaginary reasons Mallory might want to see her and is mentally preparing herself for it, or debating if she'll be able to keep her cool around the young girl.

I let her process it all while holding her gaze, keeping still and silent so I'm not a distraction. I'm here. And I'll be here when she returns from the swirling thoughts that cloud her mind.

"Raegan! It's your turn," Cassandra prompts her when she doesn't throw a card down with the others.

That snaps her out of it. Raegan gives me a short nod, then puts her cards on the table. "Sorry, I need to run out for a little bit."

"Are you coming back?" Tinsley asks, her head angled with curiosity.

Raegan hesitates. I answer for her. "No."

Either she's too emotionally raw from her meeting with Mallory, or I'm going to finish what I'd started this afternoon until she passes out.

"Okay. See you tomorrow, then!" Tinsley waves, and the others follow suit.

Once we've closed the door behind us, Raegan tilts her head back so she can see me. "Did she say why? Or, what it's about?"

I lace my fingers with hers and walk us to where Briar and the kids are staying. "No." I catch her frown from the corner of my eye. "But she's wanted to see you for a while now."

"Why?"

"I helped her understand you were only doing those things to protect her." Even if Mallory had gone along with it, that didn't make her life any less in danger. Gordon still may have hurt or killed her if it got him what he wanted. Raegan understood that. "You didn't want to hurt anyone. GE did."

I don't tell her that Mallory told me everything. Every "training" she had to endure. Every life she'd been forced to take. There are still holes missing in her story when she'd been returned to her room and had no idea what happened to Raegan then. Missing pieces I'll need to coax from her, since the only other people who I think have that information are dead already.

Holt's death should have lasted longer. I'd have gladly taken him back with us to do what Raegan had threatened him with.

And Gordon—I'm still dealing with that failure every day.

We stop in front of the door, and I turn to her, pinching her chin and lifting her gaze to mine. "Tell me you don't want to see her, and we'll go back to our apartment, little one. This is your choice."

Her ocean eyes harden with determination. "No, I need to do this."

Smiling, I nod and release her to knock.

Briar answers within seconds, with a bright smile and glittery tattoos on her face. "Oh, thank goodness you both could make it! Mallory was pretty insistent she see you before she went to bed. Oh, I don't think we've actually met. I'm Briar. You must be Raegan." She offers her hand to Raegan, who takes it.

"Yeah. It's nice to meet you, Briar."

"Please! Come in." She holds the door for us to enter and then closes it. "The others are going through their bedtime routines. We don't have the extra room here, so why don't you use my bedroom to talk? Mallory doesn't like to talk about her time with GE in front of the others."

It's a two-bedroom apartment, similar to what most Guild members were given. Fortunately for Briar, since moving in here, Elias has sped up the process of getting kids into homes. There are only four left—plus Mallory, who will be staying here.

Briar beams at Raegan. "She's come a long way from the shy, quiet girl when she first showed up. Her confidence has really grown since she started training with Jackson. Oh! The bedroom is this one over here," Briar continues, indicating the bedroom to the left. "Mallory! Your guests are here." She turns to us. "I'll send her in once she's ready. Thank you again for coming on such short notice."

Briar leaves us in the bedroom with the door partially open. I find a spot in the back of the room to lean against the wall and keep out of the way of this interaction.

Raegan starts to pace, then stops herself when she realizes she's doing it and shakes her hands. She's tense. It's as if she's about to step onto a battlefield rather than talk to a six-year-old, which only shows me how much she's been suppressing since she came back from her time with Gordon.

The door creaks. "Hello?" Mallory's voice is small and shy. She finds me first, smiling nervously and then peeking around the door to Raegan. Her eyes widen, and she grips the door.

"Hi." Raegan gives her a small smile, trying to hide her own nerves behind it.

Mallory is stiff as if—now that Raegan is standing in front of her—all her confidence has fled somewhere else.

I don't intervene... yet. If she can't handle this encounter, I'll end it early. But I give them both time to adjust to one another before I insert myself into the conversation.

I do retrieve a small square of paper from my pants to fold an origami creature to life.

Mallory notices, and a tiny smile appears.

"Do you want to sit?" Raegan offers, patting the bed.

Mallory nods. "Yeah." She climbs up on the bed while Raegan leans more than sits a foot or so next to her.

They're both quiet.

The girl plays with her foot, arching it back and forth against the bedding. "Um…" Her voice is soft and thready. "I wanted… I mean… I wanted to ask if… um… you know…" she rambles, struggling to get the words out. Raegan waits patiently for the words to finally come. "… if we're safe… here, I mean."

Raegan peeks over at me. I shrug. I don't know what Briar told the kids about why we'd moved from the Tower to Hype. Or if they even know where *here* is. No one is supposed to leave the building.

"Yes, we're safe." Raegan comforts her with a gentle hand on hers, which is balled up on her leg.

"Why'd we leave? I liked it there."

"Because it wasn't as safe as here."

"From GE?"

"Yes."

"I thought Gordon and Holt… Jack told me they were… dead."

"They are. But the company they worked for is still around."

"Did you…Did you kill them?"

Raegan hesitates. "Holt… I did."

"Not Gordon?"

"No. His company did that to him."

Mallory's eyes round to saucers, her confidence slowly growing the more back and forth they have. "Why? Aren't they on the same team?"

"They're bad guys," Raegan simplifies.

"Oh. Yeah." A pause. "You're still fighting them?"

"Yes. I won't stop until they can't hurt anyone else."

The girl nods slowly, her hands fidgeting. "Then what?"

"What do you mean?"

"What happens to me? My friends... they keep going away. Briar says it's to nice families. But I have a family. Why can't I go home?"

Raegan's face pinches before she looks at her own lap. "You're not sick, Mallory. You're special. You have an amazing gift, one your parents didn't understand. If you go back, they might send you away again. And we don't want that."

"But—but if I told them that, they'd know I wasn't sick anymore." Her voice cracks. "They could keep me."

Raegan wraps her arm around Mallory's shoulders, and she collapses against her chest with a sob. She rubs her back. "I'm sorry. I'm so sorry."

"I want to go home!" she cries, clinging to Raegan, who holds her tight.

"I know. Maybe... after we've gotten rid of GE, you could try it. Especially now that you can control it better. But if there's anything that they try or say or do that hurts you, you can come back with us. You can stay with the Guild, and we'll take care of you, okay? Maybe we can even convince Aiden to let you get a dog since you love them so much."

Mallory sniffles and nods her head. "I'm sorry for everything. I'm sorry he hurt you so bad because of me. I was so scared..."

"Shhh..." Raegan strokes her hair that's so similar to her own. "It's okay. It's not your fault. Nothing that happened there is your fault."

She cranes her head back, tears soaking her face. "You, too. Jack said it wasn't either of our faults."

Raegan blanches, but she still forces a smile and nods. "Yeah. Jack's usually right about things." She pats her back a while longer until Mallory starts to slide down her front. "Mal? I think she's asleep," she murmurs to me.

I push off the wall and crouch in front of them, peeling Mallory from her arms and holding her to my chest. Raegan opens the door for me, and I carry her into the living room. Briar stands from the couch with a hand to her chest.

"I'll show you to her bed." She brings me into the other bedroom of bunk beds and sleeping children, pointing to the top bunk.

Stepping up the ladder, I lay her down and pull the blankets over her, then leave the room.

"Thank you so much again," Briar whispers, leading us to the door.

"Do you like dogs, Briar?" Raegan asks on our way out.

Briar looks confused for a moment, then smiles when she realizes what she means. "I do. I think that's a wonderful idea."

Later, after we've returned to our apartment and I convince Raegan into bed, I wrap my arm under her neck and draw small circles over her skin. The others aren't in yet, meaning it's just the two of us. She hasn't spoken much since leaving Mallory, so I know those spinning thoughts are fit to burst.

All it takes is a little quiet and patience.

At long last, I'm rewarded.

"Most days, after Gordon pushed me to my limit, I'd be too tired to stand. Holt would have to carry me. And on those days, he'd take me to this room in the basement. It was pitch-black. No lights, no windows. No sound. It reminded me of solitary." She swallows. "There was a water pod in the center of the room where he would put me. He'd stuff little headphones in my ears and then strap me inside so I couldn't move. I'd float in that tank and feel nothing."

I take her hand in mine and press it to my lips, reminding her that I'm here. She's here. Not in that memory.

She blinks a few times, swallows again, and continues, "And then, he would talk to me. I don't know if it was a recording or him, but he would talk. And talk. Saying horrible things. Repeating my own doubts back to me. Telling me how to think. How to feel." She squeezes her eyes shut, her voice thick with emotion. "It would go on forever... until I wouldn't know if he was saying it, or I was."

It's a struggle to keep myself composed right now. But I do. For her. I am her rock in this tempest of bad memories. Her lifeline. I won't let go. I won't sink into the realm of death and darkness that calls for blood. For retribution. There's nothing I can do about Gordon anymore, and that fact burns me alive inside. I'll have to take it out on the rest of Gifted Enterprise. I don't care who they are or their role. I want blood. Pain. Death by my hands.

But she will always come first.

"Sometimes..." she continues softly. Her words are getting harder to understand, but I focus on them like my life depends on it. "I can still hear him in my head when it's dark. Or when I'm afraid."

I brush my lips across her knuckles when she's quiet for a long time. "I'm here, little one. Whatever you need. Tell me, and it's yours."

She curls into my chest and releases a shuddering breath. "Just... hold me. And don't let go."

I bundle her in my arms and rest my head on hers. "Never."

Chapter Thirty-One

KELLAN

"I don't like this," Dane argues, clutching the longer blond hair at the top of his head. "Most of Harvey's brothers and sisters didn't seem thrilled by this plan, according to Reid."

Aiden's the only one standing where the five of us are gathered in our small apartment living room. It's been over a day since they got back from meeting with each spying sibling. None had to be kidnapped, thankfully, but that was probably the best news they had to report. Aiden slides his hands into the pockets of his slacks. "We don't need them to be thrilled. We just need them as our eyes on the board members and to report in."

The muscle in Dane's jaw feathers. He turns his face to the rest of us on the couch. "Am I the only one worried we're going to fall into another one of Charles's traps?"

I shrug, relaxed into the back cushions with my arms spread on either side. Raegan's sitting to my left, her arms crossed and face tight, while Jack lies along the back of the couch, sharing the space behind her with my hand. "That's just your fear talking. Look, this whole thing involving the invisible spies was your idea. Just because none of them jumped for joy at the chance to go against Psycho Dad doesn't mean we back out. It's still a good plan."

As much as I want to poke at him for arguing his own damn plan, I also don't blame him for it. We've fallen for enough of Charles's attacks to have developed a minor complex over it. Particularly him.

Raegan moves while he's talking, plopping herself sideways in Dane's lap. "Can I sit here?"

The immediate flip of emotions on his face is comical, and I snicker into my shoulder.

Dane drags her ass further against him, his attention completely locked on her. "Babe, you can sit on me whenever and wherever the fuck you want. I'll be your permanent seat. My face is a bit chilly, actually, if you'd like to sit there."

An adorable pink flush colors her cheeks. "What about Charles?"

"What about him?" He picks her up, shifting her legs around his waist. He's clearly conceded this fight between the promise of Raegan and none of us backing down on the plan. It's happening.

"Pussy-whipped," I fake-cough into my fist.

Dane pauses in the doorway to smirk over his shoulder. "You can call it whatever the fuck you want, but all I know is that I'm head over fucking heels, falling off a cliff without wings, in love with her."

With a roar of laughter, I call after him as he disappears into the bedroom, "Damn, Rapunzel. Way to ruin the joke with honesty."

Aiden sighs, rubbing his temples. "We're meeting with the rest of the team to go over the exact plan in an hour. Make sure you're ready." The door to the apartment closes behind him, and Jack and I look at each other.

We move in unison to the bedroom.

Don't mind if we do.

Raegan's soft moan beckons behind the closed door, and my cock thickens. I'm more excited than I thought I'd be at the foursome that's about to happen, but maybe it's because we're about to make another one of my girl's dreams come true.

Last time was hot, but it was one at a time.

Now, there's no line. No waiting our turn.

Throwing the door open, I saunter inside with a lazy grin stretching my face as I slide my belt free and let it fall to the floor. Raegan and Dane wasted no time in stripping their clothes off, as evidenced by the scattered articles on the floor or hanging on the lamp and nightstand.

Raegan tears away from their kiss to look at me and Jack, her face flushed in a sexy pink shade and her lips plump and wet from their heavy make-out session.

Dane smirks at my entrance, almost as if he expected my arrival and had been waiting for it, before he lies on the bed. He's lying sideways at the foot of it with his head on the edge and his knees hooked over the other side. "Sit on my face, babe. I'm fucking starving."

She crawls over him, and he grips her ass to pull her pussy to his mouth.

Goddamn, that's sexy.

I don't know what Jack's planning on doing, but I beeline to the right side of the bed first. While her eyes are rolled back in her head and her lips are slightly parted, I steal a nipple with my mouth. She gasps, her hips gyrating over Dane and her hands burying into my hair.

Chuckling, I release her nipple following a stiff tug and drawl, "You think you can take three of us together, beautiful?"

"Yes!" she pants, then inhales sharply. A quick glance behind her reveals Jackson spreading lube between her cheeks, where Dane's already got them spread wide for him.

"That's my filthy girl. I made a promise about us filling your pretty holes, didn't I? Are you ready to be dicked out of your mind? Because I can't wait to see you taking all of us at once."

Raegan mewls, tightening her grip in my hair as she chases her pleasure from Dane. She rocks and grinds mercilessly against his face, and I'd worry she might suffocate him if I didn't see his fingers grip her ass tighter, crushing and pulling her closer as if he can't get enough. She leans into me suddenly, panting hard, and I notice Jack's already finger-fucking her ass.

Wrapping a hand around her throat, I push her upright and capture her mouth with mine. She drops her hands to my chest, her nails digging into my skin in stinging, sharp crescents that I can feel running straight to my dick. Her nails drag down, breaking my skin in bloody lines that have me groaning.

Her body shakes, convulses. Then it locks, and a sob rips from her lungs.

I hold her through her orgasm as she shudders and quakes, then catch her when it releases her before she can smother Dane.

"Fuck," he gasps, chest heaving and face soaked in her cum. "I need you on my cock, babe. Right-the-fuck-now."

Raegan nods while catching her breath, and Jack and I help her shift until she's positioned over Dane's dick. She's fucking gushing down her thighs, and my cock pulses at the sight of it.

Her pussy devours Dane's dick in a single, smooth stroke.

Fuck.

Dane lets out a garbled mixture of a groan and curses.

My dick strains uncomfortably against my unforgiving jeans, and

I'm forced to let her go so I can free it. Her ocean blue eyes light up when she sees my hard length, like her gaze was inexorably drawn to it. Raegan licks her lips, and I groan, pumping it beneath her heated stare.

"Fuck, beautiful. I'm taking those lips as soon as Jackson's seated in your tight ass."

Jackson smirks behind her, whispering against the shell of her ear, "Lean forward, little one. And open up for me."

Raegan practically purrs for him, her eyes shuttering closed.

His hand guides her to Dane's chest, where Dane pulls her into a heated kiss. Jack notches at her core, caressing her lower back and then holding her cheeks apart. He pushes the head of his dick in and stops, rocking his hips and working little by little to sink in further. Jackson moans—a husky, dark sound I've never heard from him before—as he gains another inch.

"Yes, little one. Relax for me. Breathe. I'm almost there."

She bites her lip on Dane's chest, who's drawing his fingers through the top of her head and offering his own murmured encouragement.

Once he's in, we all breathe a sigh of relief.

My turn.

Wrapping her hair around my fist, I drag her up and crush our lips together. I'm so fucking ravenous for her that I don't hold back. I take her mouth in a furor, claiming it with every swipe of my tongue and by the unforgiving press of my lips. She's *mine*. Even when my brothers are buried inside of her, it doesn't make that fact any less true. She belongs to me and to them. *Ours*.

I roughly snap us apart, then guide her head to my cock.

Raegan opens her mouth with the edges of a smile on her lips, then uses those wicked lips and tongue to suck the soul from my body.

Sweet fucking hell!

My grip on her hair tightens as I thrust into her perfect mouth, and Dane begins driving into her pussy. Jackson rolls his hips to match Dane, and Raegan cries out, shooting powerful vibrations through my dick until I'm cursing viciously.

Her firm lips grip my cock like they were made for it. I shove myself harder down her throat, and her echoing moans intensify like she's getting off on the roughness just as much as I am. She's perfect. Fucking perfect in every way.

I pump furiously into her mouth, taking that pleasure until there's so much that it bursts. The ecstasy that floods my veins and fills my lungs when I come is like a dam breaking, surging through me until all I can do is roar it out into the world. Raegan eagerly drinks my cum, swallowing it with a wanton moan and sucking me clean. Shuddering, I pull her up and kiss her.

"Hold her still," Dane grunts. He picks up his pace, fucking her pussy like it's his mission to send her over the edge next.

Reaching for the puddle she's created between her and Dane, I rub it around her clit, circling it as I devour her mouth. Her body quakes between us on the brink of destruction. Jackson pulls back to the tip, then slowly pushes back into her tight ass.

Raegan screams, her body erupting with pleasure. Dane and Jackson each curse and moan, then follow her orgasm with their own.

Jackson pulls her back against him, pinching her chin to draw her lips to his. She moves like a rag doll, soft and pliant as we each take turns kissing and touching her. Running our hands down her curves. Fingering her nipples and grasping her breasts.

Like we can never get enough.

Once Jack extracts himself from her, I strip the rest of my clothes off and lift her from Dane to bring her to the shower. Her smile is warm and satisfied as I get the water to temperature and the other two enter the bathroom. Smirking, I drawl, "Feeling good, beautiful?"

Raegan looks damn sexy with that smile on her swollen lips, her hair wild around her. "Mm... I'm feeling much better." She scratches her nails through my beard, and a resounding throb echoes in my cock. I growl in warning before she starts something I'm going to have to finish.

Damn rookie move on my part, thinking to challenge her.

She pinches what facial hair she can grab on both sides of my face and yanks me into a kiss. The jolt of pleasure that hits my dick has me moaning into her lips. Her arms wrap around my neck, and then she's flipping her legs around my waist and deepening the kiss, trying to get me to submit to her.

It's adorable.

"Fuck..." Dane mutters behind us.

Remembering the others are with us, I open my eyes and find Jackson already washing himself in the shower, his dark blue gaze glued on Raegan.

Guess we're not finished.

Oh darn.

Fisting her hair, I tug her head back and drag the pad of my tongue along the length of her neck while walking us into the shower. Her pulse jackhammers beneath my tongue, and I suck on it, running my tongue over it obsessively.

She grabs my shoulders, her hips rocking into my chest, and I chuckle.

There's not a whole lot of room in this shower for four people, let alone with me. I turn her against Jackson on the back wall, my own back mere inches from the glass, while Dane stands in front of the bench. Leaning her into Jack, I guide her now-slick body down his front until she's on her feet, then sprinkle her with kisses and bites on the way to my knees. Even in the hot steam and spray, she shivers at my touch, and it heats my blood in a way that nothing else can.

Jack brings her arms up to wrap around his neck, arching her pretty cunt toward me like a meal on a fucking platter. I lift her thigh over my shoulder and spread her pussy lips. I've wanted a taste ever since Dane nearly drowned by her. Since I saw her gushing arousal weeping from her pussy, just waiting to be devoured by me.

And that's exactly what I do. I bury my face between her thighs and groan at her sweet taste. Licking, sucking, nibbling, running my tongue along every surface. My lips, my beard tickling her as I move. She writhes in Jackson's arms, partly pushing for more and also pulling away when it's too much. I grab her ass, wrenching her as close as can be until all I can breathe is her. There's no escaping this, no escaping me until I've had my fill.

She's an aphrodisiac. The more I taste, the more of her I consume. I want to eat her out until she's driven insane with ecstasy. Until I've made a complete mess of her. I press my fingers harder into her plump ass cheeks, my mission turning fanatical as I carve out her pleasure with my tongue. Her quivering voice echoes through the shower, the bathroom, sending me to another level of fucking need to hear her screaming for me.

Jackson lifts her by her thighs, spreading them for me and holding her prisoner against him. She tries to reach for my hair, but Dane grabs her hands and brings them back up in one hand, stretching her torso. He takes her tit in his mouth, and I can almost feel the ripple of her pussy clench, seeking something there.

Smirking, I watch the pleasure overtake her face as I swirl my tongue around her clit. Her thighs tense in Jackson's grip, desperate to close around me, but forced to take every sensation, every flick and stroke of my tongue. I latch around her clit, sucking and licking furiously, my eyes turned upward to watch her break for me.

Her spine bows, a scream shattering the room as she falls apart. I don't stop. I suck and lick and rub until her arousal runs down her thighs. Begging me to fill her pussy with my dick. Just as I break away, sucking down a lungful of oxygen to catch my breath, Jackson impales her on his cock.

Son of a bitch.

He pounds into her at an unforgiving pace, and she sobs as he brings her back to the brink without reprieve. I grab her thighs, holding her still as I return to her swollen clit and he fucks her from behind. She's already so over-sensitized that she comes again with hardly a break in between. Jackson drives into her one last time and holds himself there, emptying himself.

Once he pulls himself free, she collapses over me, then reaches for Dane. He steps closer, holding his hand out for whatever she's looking for. She takes it, then wraps her other hand around the base of his cock and buries it in her mouth.

"Fuuuuuck!" Dane throws his head back, hissing his surprise and widening his stance.

She moans around his dick, and he smacks his hand on the tile to keep himself upright, his chest heaving while she sucks him down.

"Jack," I bark while he's busy washing himself. He looks to them and back to me, smirking. There's no way I can angle myself behind her on the floor. Thankfully, he gets it without any explanation needed, and he uses his gift to raise her so she's level with Dane's dick. And high enough for me to fuck.

There's absolutely no resistance when I slide into her pussy. Her walls hug my cock in her warm embrace, and I release a shuddering sigh of relief. I'm not in a rush to fuck her now that I'm here. I let her focus on Dane, on taking care of him, while I content myself with slow, languid strokes of my cock. In. And out. In. And... out. Fucking hell, it's obscene how good this feels. How *right* she feels. I'd love to stay here and fuck her long and slow like this all day. Build her up slowly, nudge her over the edge, and then start all over from the bottom again.

Over and over until we're both wrung dry.

Dane curses. "I'm gonna come, babe," he warns her, but it only provokes her to take him deeper. His moans ricochet off the walls, especially when she licks him clean after he's finished.

I push her shoulders down now that it's just us, angling my hips to hit that spot that drives her wild. She pushes against me with a low whimper. "More," she begs, rocking her hips to meet me and encourage me faster. I grit my teeth, forcing myself to continue this unhurried pace even when I'm tempted to break at the sound of her begging.

"You're going to take it slow this time. I want to feel every flicker, every squeeze of your perfect pussy on my dick. I want to feel your cum dripping down my cock until it's drenched. Think you can do that for me, beautiful?"

Raegan gasps when my shaft rubs over that spot, then again,

drawing out the pleasure with every languorous stroke.

The slow rhythm becomes torturous for me as well. Every other thrust has her pussy gripping my dick in a stranglehold, and it takes everything in me not to up my pace. The pleasure swells with every slide of my cock, every mewl and whimper that falls from her lips. Jack and Dane join us when they've finished washing themselves, with Dane teasing her clit with his fingers and Jackson giving her a kiss that's just as slow and erotic as what she and I are doing.

When I think I'm about to snap, she crests. Her pussy clamps my cock in a vise, triggering my orgasm in an instant as her body grips and releases me in rhythmic pulses. Groaning, I let her sweet cunt milk me dry, shuddering as the pleasure continues to roll through me like aftershocks.

Pounding knocks at the bathroom door draw my attention unwillingly to it, my relaxed muscles tensing immediately in case of trouble.

"It's been over an hour," Aiden shouts. "You have one minute to get out here—dressed—or else there'll be a sex ban on the three of you for a week, and you'll be forced to watch me fuck her for the four of us."

Oh. Hell no.

I don't think I've ever washed and dressed so fast in my life.

CHAPTER THIRTY-TWO

RAEGAN

WE'RE THE LAST ONES to arrive at Elias's apartment for the final meeting. Portia lets us in, waggling her eyebrows at me as if she knows *exactly* why we're all late, then giggles and drags me inside. Alice and Sam are sitting on the kitchen island stools.

I offer them a smile. "Hey. Thanks for coming."

Sam gives me a slight nod and types into a cell phone. He lifts the screen so I can read it.

> I want to help you.

Smiling wider, my gaze switches from the message to his face. "Thank you." The texts are a great way to communicate for now, but I hope one day I'll be able to hear his voice, too.

Alice scoffs. "You don't really need me now that he's coming. All that training was for nothing."

"Don't be a jelly Nelly!" Portia waves her hand and grins. "We need you, too. It's an all-hands-on-deck situation. You just upped your skill on your path to badassery like the rest of us. Be proud of that."

Alice's sour expression softens, and she looks away.

Portia tosses me a wink when she's not looking, and pulls me to the couch where the others are already settled around or near it.

"I'm sorry we kept you waiting." Aiden's smooth tone doesn't hide the undercurrent of annoyance aimed at me and the other three at fault. It's hard to say if it's because we made Elias wait on us or because he's jealous he didn't have the time to join us.

I'm betting on the latter.

As if hearing my thoughts, his dark brown eyes lock on mine with so much intensity it takes my breath away.

Portia snickers, and I bump her with my elbow.

"We were just discussing the West Coast Gifted Enterprise head-quarters," Elias dives right in. He's relaxed in his usual seat while Noah sits in a folding chair beside him with a laptop. "Raegan took care of the one on the East coast, but they have one other major location if you're looking to cause the most damage to Charles."

Taking down another primary office with the last of his board would be a double fuck you.

It's perfect.

Dane opens his laptop next to me. "What's the address?"

Noah shares it, and Dane pulls it up on the screen. Reid leans over the couch with a furrowed brow.

"Do you recognize it?" I ask him.

He nods. "It's an admin building. Legal, HR, accounts payable... all the paperwork to make Gifted Enterprise look like it's a legitimate business." Reid straightens. "It's not useful for information on its illegal activities, but losing it will make future moves difficult for

Charles."

"One HQ is a tragedy. Two is a target," Noah shares softly, and Elias dips his chin.

"People will start asking questions. Some may pass it off as a coincidence, but others will realize they're being targeted. And then they'll try to figure out why anyone would go after a nonprofit for children with learning disabilities."

Kellan chuckles. "I'm sure the psycho will love the sudden attention."

"Serves him right after the smear campaign he put us through," Dane grumbles.

Glancing back at Reid, I ask another question. "Are the workers innocent?"

He shakes his head. "They know. They help cover it up." He turns to Aiden. "How many?" I assume he's asking for the number of people he'll be teleporting there.

"We're going to drive," Aiden replies.

Dane types on the keyboard and then supplies, "It's a six-hour drive from here. Seven with fuel stops." He passes the laptop to Aiden.

I frown. "Why would we drive?"

Aiden starts clicking and focuses on the screen. "First, because it'll provide us with a secure and hidden location to work from. Mostly, I don't want to wear out Reid if we need to escape. It will be a large group of us once your half-siblings join us and we won't have Evie to shrink the group's size and reduce that burden."

My mood sobers at the reminder of Evie's condition.

His face tightens with concentration, and then he faces Elias. "We'll need a discreet vehicle that fits eleven with dark tinted windows." Aiden surveys the rest of the room. "After we arrive, Sam will go to the coffee shop across the street."

Sam's eyes widen when he hears his name, his attention now locked on Aiden.

"He'll text his siblings to meet him there once they arrive with their board member. After all seven are there, Sam will give the okay for us to proceed with the plan."

Sam nods once, acknowledging his role.

"Tinsley, Reid, Portia, and Noah will ensure the area is clear of bystanders. If we plan for the meeting to take place at ten, that time should have the least amount of traffic outside during business hours. Kellan and Dane will stay in the vehicle for back-up. Dane needs to keep up the ruse as Charles for any additional messages from the board as well as hack into any security cameras with views of the headquarters and surrounding streets to make sure they stop working while we're there.

"Then, Alice will hide herself and Raegan so she can take the building down. Tinsley and Reid will knock back or move any lower debris to keep it from going too far, as long as you can do it without being seen. Portia and Noah will be on standby to direct innocent civilians away or erase their memories if they see something they shouldn't. Jackson and I will help with anything higher up from a nearby building roof so any strays land with the rest of the building."

Aiden pauses to take a breath. "With the building destroyed and the board dead, Reid will teleport the rescued invisible crew to Hype with Sam to get settled. Then we'll drive the car back, rest, and put together the final plan to kill Charles once and for all."

Reid makes a low grunt, drawing our attention. "This will destroy a lot of what Charles has built in one hit. The board he's cultivated to support him and the legitimate business to cover his tracks. He'll be exposed and weak." His gaze locks on Aiden's. "I've never seen him lose control before, but this might do it. I've waited a long time for this. I'm glad to be a part of it."

My chest swells with hope. If we pull this off, we might have an advantage against him. The psycho mastermind might make a mistake.

We could win.

Aiden nods, his expression resolute. He scans the rest of the room. "Any questions?"

He returns the laptop to Dane, who murmurs, "We'll need to leave at three in the morning to make that time."

"I'll have the vehicle waiting for you outside at two-thirty," Elias confirms.

Aiden nods, his gaze flicking between Dane and Reid. "Send the message. Then get some sleep. Our mission starts in six hours."

Jackson carefully fits his rolled-up hoodie over my head. He guides it down my sides, then nods for me to seek out the arms. There's a protective layer between me and his knives, but it's better to move slowly than to catch anything accidentally. He's filled this hoodie with his spare knives even though the plan shouldn't involve me fighting anyone directly. It still puts him and the others more at ease since they won't be right beside me.

He pushes the gaiter over my head next, then pulls it up to cover the bottom half of my face. His hood is last, blocking my face from view of any overhead cameras.

The others are dressed similarly with either hoodies or a hat and sunglasses.

"Elias has the car ready. Make sure your face is hidden before you step outside," Aiden directs us. He's wearing a gray zip-up jacket that he probably borrowed from Dane or Kellan. I can't imagine him owning one of those himself.

Dane's in a pale blue and white hoodie and jeans with a cap and sunglasses. Kell stands out the most with his size, but if all goes to plan, he won't be leaving the car anyway. He grins through the dark blue hood and pushes the center of his sunglasses up his nose. "I feel like we're cosplaying at something. And failing." He snickers, nudging Aiden's shoulder.

Aiden definitely looks out of place and uncomfortable. "It's just for the cameras," he reminds Kellan. "You can take them off once we're in the car. Elias has assured me the tint is dark enough that cameras won't be able to see inside."

Portia links her arm through mine. "I can't wait to see your gift in action!" She's dressed in business casual clothes to fit in with the people who might be walking around that area. I thought she'd look sad and dull in monotone and without any colorful flair, but somehow, she looks like a cosplay sexy secretary.

Her smile widens when she catches me eyeing her outfit, and she pushes her fake glasses up her nose. "What? I can be a plain Jane to go undercover."

Scoffing, I shake my head. "Sorry to disappoint you, but there isn't a plain Jane bone in your body."

We join the rest of the group at the front entrance to Hype.

Cibrina greets us with a warm smile. "I've packed sandwiches, water, and snacks in the car for you. Make sure you eat something before the big mission and take care of yourselves."

Alice's brows pinch. "How long are we going to be gone for? I thought this was just a day."

Tinsley shrugs from where she's reading an open textbook. "It takes as long as it takes." She snaps the book shut and smiles at Alice. "Plus, it's always good to stay hydrated when using your gift."

Reid opens the door to reveal the car.

Aiden frowns, turning to Elias. "We didn't want flashy. We're trying to *not* stand out."

Elias slides his hands into his slacks and offers a polite smile. "You asked for something that comfortably seats eleven. Considering the height of some of the group, there needed to be ample space in the back seats as well. This is what's available with those requirements. Unless you'd prefer I find you a short school bus instead."

Kellan howls with laughter, and Dane scoffs, pushing him to the door. "Shut up and get in. You're driving."

Aiden's stone-faced when he appraises Elias with his dark stare. I grab his arm and smile at Elias. "*Thank you,*" I emphasize sweetly, "for everything you've done for us, Elias. We really appreciate it and are in your debt."

He bows with a hand over his heart. "For you, Raegan, it's always a pleasure."

Aiden's arm bulges in my grasp, and Portia giggles behind me. I shove him toward the car while Portia and Noah say their goodbyes to Elias.

Sam keeps shuffling his feet while he waits for the next step. I offer him a warm smile. "Do you want to take the back row?" The further away he is from the crowd, the more comfortable I think he'll be.

"I'll sit in front of you and you can squeeze my arm or shoulder if you need anything."

He nods twice, his arms crossed and gaze locked on the ground.

Cibrina smiles and waves us off as we pile into the massive black vehicle with shining chrome accents that reflect the neon lights of the city in their pre-dawn glow. The interior is just as luxurious with leather seats, plenty of legroom, and air control per seat.

Kellan whistles from the driver's seat, where a screen the length of the dash gives him all the information he could need on the car's stats. "Goddamn. This is *fancy* fancy." He strokes his hands along the curve of the wheel. "Let's hope they didn't waste all the money on looks."

He pushes a button, and the engine roars to life. "Buckle up, buttercups!"

"Who the fuck are you calling buttercup?" Alice snarks from the first row window seat. Reid made Tinsley switch with him, so he's between the two girls. I don't think Alice can or would do anything to Tinsley, but he's nothing if not overprotective of her.

Portia invites Sam to sit with her and Noah in the back row, but Noah stealthily maneuvers himself between them, so Sam's in the window seat and Portia's on the aisle.

Jack, Dane, and I are in the middle row. It's roomy as heck, even sandwiched between the other two rows. There's plenty of room to stretch my legs and between us. The headspace is so far above mine that I can almost stand.

"They're going to think someone famous is in here," Dane mutters as he discovers a hidden tray on one side of his seat.

I don't disagree. It looks like an SUV limo with full tints like people with money and power ride around in.

"If we need to teleport it back, will you be able to move it?" Aiden asks Reid from the passenger seat.

Reid considers quietly, then replies, "Even if I can, it won't be easy. It'll be draining."

Aiden nods. "If it comes to that, we'll abandon it."

Kellan snorts as he drives us away from Hype to the nearest highway. "You just want to come back to Elias without it."

"I would never be so petty."

Dane rolls his eyes and smirks at me. I lean toward him, and he automatically bends so I can whisper in his ear. "Only this group could be so unserious at the start of a big mission."

His smirk spreads to a grin and a low chuckle. "Gotta have some fun between fights of life and death." As soon as the words leave him, his expression darkens. Then, as if catching himself, he forces a small smile for me.

I squeeze his hand. He grazes his thumb over mine.

"You don't have to pretend you're okay with me. I'd rather know exactly what you're feeling."

"I am okay. Sometimes it just creeps up on me. Then I remind myself this was what she wanted. GE isn't hurting her anymore."

I nod, pride and sadness blending in my chest to a warm ache.

He checks the time on his phone. "We've a while until we get there if you want to rest on me and Jack."

It's just before three in the morning—when the Hype bar and nightclub usually closes for the night but Elias had them close an hour earlier because of this.

Dane lifts his arm expectantly, and I lean into him. Jackson removes my boots and holds my feet on his lap so I'm completely horizontal. Considering how much work I have ahead of me, I won't refuse a few more hours of sleep.

CHAPTER THIRTY-THREE

RAEGAN

SOMEONE GENTLY SHAKES MY shoulder. "We're here." Dane's voice draws me from my slumber. He and Jackson help me upright as I stretch.

Aiden directs Kellan on where to park while Dane pulls his laptop out and opens it up. "I need to be within a block to find nearby cameras," he says.

"Doesn't that put us in the boom zone?" Alice inquires.

"Raegan's gift doesn't go boom," Aiden answers smoothly. "She'll control its destruction to land in its own footprint while Jackson contains any dirt and dust within a tight radius. It'll be safe for anyone standing outside so long as they don't breach that radius."

I hope I live up to his expectation of controlling my gift so well. We've done a lot of practice on my control, even testing this on a smaller scale. But replicating it on something so large and with people around is still going to be a novel experience.

Kellan parks along a curb. There's a building between us and the one we want, but we can see it stretching above this one. "This work?"

"Yeah, I think this'll work." His fingers fly over the keyboard at a crazy speed.

Aiden cranes his neck to find Sam in the far back. "Sam. The coffee shop is just up ahead at the corner on the right. Time to be invisible and wait for your siblings."

Sam nods, turning invisible before he's even finished as if he couldn't wait to be hidden away again.

"We'll go get coffee," Portia adds excitedly. That'll be hers and Noah's cover until they hear the word that it's time to bring the building down. It also keeps their eyes on Sam—or at least on where he is since they can't see him—to make sure he's okay.

My heart starts to pound in anticipation as the plan goes into action. What if I accidentally kill innocent people? What if the board members don't show up? What if Charles has another trap somewhere that we didn't think of?

Jackson kisses my cheek, startling me from my thoughts. "Breathe. I always have your back. No one else will get hurt." He shifts in front of me and keeps going toward the door.

"Where are you going?"

His smile is a bit manic. "To find a roost." He leaves, taking to the rooftop in front of us and then moving to a higher one and out of sight.

After a few minutes of silence, my foot starts tapping with restless energy.

"Got ants in your boot, beautiful?" Kellan drawls, reclining his seat to get comfortable. I almost snipe at him for being too relaxed until I notice the shimmer of gold scales at his temple through his dark hair. He's too covered up for me to see more, but he must have activated at least some of it to prepare for whatever might happen.

"I'll feel better once the board members show up." Without them, this whole plan is a bust.

"It's a shame I don't get a part to play in this."

"You're Dane's protection and back-up," I remind him.

He lifts a hand, and I watch it elongate and sharpen to deadly claws.

Tinsley gasps when she sees it.

"Maybe you'll let me get the first round with Charles, then. Let me test out my new strength against his."

"Don't get cocky."

Our phones ding within seconds of one another. Aiden reads the message first. "Sam says they're all there, except for one."

Fuck.

Dane frowns at the laptop screen. "The medical director just replied to last night's message."

I lean over to read it as Aiden asks, "What does it say?"

"Sounds important. Fill me in tonight," Dane reads aloud.

Reid doesn't look surprised—not that I've ever seen him show that emotion before. "Dr. James is closest to Charles. He probably felt comfortable enough to skip the request if they already had plans."

The door opens, and Jackson slips inside to the open back row. He probably read the message of the missing member.

"Now what?" Alice demands, crossing her arms.

"We continue with the plan," Aiden responds evenly. "If the other six are there, there's no time to waste before they become suspicious." He turns to Reid and Tinsley. "Check the area. Make sure Portia and Noah are starting their rounds," he reminds them.

Tinsley fixes her wig and reaches for the door. "It'll just take us a sec." The door opens, and then she's gone. Reid vanishes a second after her.

Aiden's near-obsidian eyes land on mine. "Ready?"

"I think so," Alice answers instead. "Are we sure her gift won't do the same thing to me while I'm touching her?"

I reply first, "I'm sure. Just don't let go."

Tinsley returns within a minute. "There's no one around. I'd hurry and do it now."

"Good. It's up to Portia and Noah to monitor the perimeter and keep anyone new back. You and Reid focus on lower debris falling further than twenty feet from the building," Aiden directs. She gives him a two-finger salute and is gone again.

My turn.

We shuffle around to the door. Alice grabs my shoulder.

At first, I don't think she's done anything. The door looks the same, and I can see my hands. It's when I look at the others that I almost feel as though I'm looking through a pane of glass. It's transparent enough to see through, but something's off... like light catching on a hidden veil between us and them.

"We're good. You can open the door," Alice tells me.

I make sure to keep my movements slow so we don't lose contact. Jackson and Aiden leave, while Kell and Dane remain in the vehicle.

"We're going to walk fast," I warn Alice, then break out into an almost jog. The longer we take, the longer we risk the board members becoming suspicious and calling for backup.

We stop at the nearest side of the building.

"Stand behind me," I whisper. Jackson's going to control any debris from somewhere above, but we're within that radius.

Reaching for my gift, I exhale deeply as it flows eagerly through my veins. Its warmth burns and sizzles beneath my skin, making my body thrum and pulse along with it. I make sure it stays contained and doesn't spread to Alice or get too hot on my shoulder, and then I focus on the building.

On pushing my gift into the hard brick façade and spreading to the steel beam framework. The varying material slows me down as I have to adjust through each transition, pushing harder or slower depending on what's there. It brings me back to my time destroying piles of concrete. Over and under, winding around and through it all until I've mapped out the area with my gift and in my mind.

I keep drawing out more and more, feeding my power into the building with hidden webs of disaster until I can feel it all in my grasp.

I'm gasping by the time it's all there, my body trembling as I hold it all in place. Spreading my power isn't the problem. Holding it back, keeping it from devouring everything it's touching, is. As soon as I let it go, I can breathe again. It's like releasing a leash on a rabid dog. It immediately goes on the attack, consuming whatever it touches.

The building groans and snaps. Metal splits. Entire floors crack and disintegrate as the building caves at the center, its roof collapsing inward. I'd spread my gift in a particular pattern, focusing on the middle of the building and then the lower floors so they'd buckle first.

Wind picks up around us, whipping our hair up like a vacuum. Any debris or dust is swept into this mini tornado, pulled to its core before falling over the building.

I can't hear anything over the destruction; the wind. It drowns out anything else around us as if we're in our own world.

At last, the rest of the building crumbles into a heap, and the wind dies down.

Kellan pulls into an open space in a packed park-n-ride parking lot. Cars sandwich us from all sides, and a train horn bellows nearby.

"Which building is it?" I ask groggily, rising from Jackson's chest once we've stopped.

After completely decimating the Gifted Enterprise headquarters, Reid took Portia, Noah, Alice, Sam, and the six rescued siblings back to Hype. Elias argued on the phone with Aiden that the rest of us should return as well, but we aren't going back until the last one is dead.

Reid returned, and then Kellan started the long drive to the medical director's hospital.

We're going to end this, even if we have to chase him to the end of the world.

I've been eating and taking naps between them to recover my strength. The world outside is dark, which means I've missed sunset and we're now stretching into the night.

"It's behind us," Dane answers, typing something out on an old flip phone. It's the burner phone we have to communicate with Alice's siblings. His mouth is tight, his brows pinched together as he finishes his text.

"What's wrong?"

Aiden responds from the front passenger seat. "The medical director knows he's our target." Damn. But I'm not surprised. When six of your colleagues are called together for a meeting and then the building collapses, killing them, it's not a far stretch to assume it was a planned attack. I'd hoped we might reach him before the news did, though.

Dane flips the phone closed. "He's waiting for us. Karl—Alice's brother—just sent that warning."

Unease curls in my gut. It shouldn't matter if he's waiting for us. It doesn't change anything. Yet, hearing the warning sets off internal alarm bells that there's more to it. "So what's the plan?"

"We get in, make sure he's alone, and kill him," Aiden replies.

I shake my head before he's even finished. "No. The point of all this is to avoid close contact with the board. If he's waiting for us, then it's got to be a trap."

Dane sighs and runs his fingers through his messy blond hair. It looks like he's been doing that a lot. "It's the only way we'll get him. I don't fucking like it, either. But Karl said he didn't go home when his shift ended today. He's staying there indefinitely. Or at least until we confront him. We have to get him here or not at all."

"He's going to use the patients against us," Jackson muses.

We'd worried about this guy the most, and he's already proving we'd been right to be concerned. We can't exactly take down a hospital with sick and injured patients inside. He's also been on the board longer than anyone else and seems to have a closer relationship to Charles, according to both Reid and Alice. "What was his gift again?"

"Fear," Tinsley surprisingly answers, sounding haunted.

Right. The ability to read your fears and use them to fuck with your head.

The fact that he's the *psychiatric* medical director of the hospital makes me sick to my stomach.

Metal shifts and moves in Aiden's grip like it's something alive. It melds together effortlessly, smoothing itself into the shape he pictures as he outfits himself with metal gauntlets and a chest piece. "Kellan, Jackson, Reid, and I will be the only ones going in," he remarks while working on a whip sword next.

"Like hell you are!" I jump forward in my seat. "I'm going, too. I know I can't use the full strength of my gift, but that doesn't make me powerless."

"You think we can't handle him, beautiful?" Kellan challenges, throwing his arm over the back of his seat so he can see me.

"I can't handle you going into a fight without me, where I can't have your back! Aiden almost—" The words stick in my throat, emotions thrashing in my chest from the memory. I take a breath, slowing my words. "I don't care if you're about to fight the fucking Easter bunny. I'm going to be there."

Kellan chuckles. "I won't tell the Easter bunny you said that."

Dane slips his hand in mine, weaving our fingers. "I don't want to be separated, either," he tells me, his voice low. "But he's going to fuck with our heads. Our fears."

"Let him." My voice is hard, my stare pinning his with determination. "It's time I faced them anyway." Dane's brows lift in surprise, then sink as his gaze heats. "The more of us there are, the harder it'll be for him to use his gift. I don't think he'll be able to get inside all our heads at once."

"I'm sorry, but I think I need to stay here," Tinsley murmurs. "I thought I could, but I think I'd be too much of a liability with... my head." She smiles softly at Reid, whose lips turn down.

He squeezes her thigh. "Don't leave the car. Lay low."

Reid only shared a little bit of her past with GE and that they messed with her head. It makes sense for her to pass on this if she's only just gotten better.

Aiden's intense stare draws my eyes to his. I can almost see the argument forming to keep us here, but a small ding intervenes before he gets the chance.

Dane passes the phone to Reid. "Karl sent through a picture of where the doctor's holed up."

Pulling on the seat in front of me, I peer over Reid's shoulder. "Why is it so dark?"

Aiden extends his hand for the phone, and Reid gives it to him. He studies it for a few seconds.

"No windows," Kellan drawls after he takes a peek. He fists a hand and grins. "Looks like I *will* be able to test out my strength on him."

Aiden starts tapping the keys to send another message. "I want the full picture, first." A series of musical notes sounds only a minute later as messages flood in at once. He studies the screen, his expression darkening with every click to view the next image. He hands the phone to Reid. "He's not alone."

Fuck.

"How many others?" Jackson questions. His tone is the epitome of calm and unbothered. As if Aiden could throw out a crazy number and he'd still take it in stride.

"Too many to count. But they're all in cages or chained up," Aiden replies.

"Test subjects," Tinsley says, her voice low. She looks at Reid. "Be careful. If he's already messed with their heads..."

Reid doesn't flinch. "Don't ask me to save them, Tins."

She beats her hand against his chest. "Don't give me that crap, Reid! They're all worth saving. Like I was."

He holds her fist to his chest. She tries to yank it back, but he grips it tight. "No one is like you." He waits a breath, then continues, "I'll do whatever's necessary for us to survive, like I've always done. If they're a threat, I'll kill them."

She raises her fingertips to his face, tracing them over his hard expression. "I know. Just... try thinking of me."

"I always do."

Tinsley smiles, and they release each other.

Reid takes a final look at one of the pictures. "Let's go."

CHAPTER THIRTY-FOUR

RAEGAN

FOR A MOMENT, I have the disorienting feeling that we've jumped into one of the photos. Everything sways around me as my brain acclimates to our new location in limited lighting. Jackson steadies me while I help Dane on my other side. Kellan, Reid, and Aiden are in front of us, blocking our view of the board member where we'd seen him sitting at a table in the picture.

"Finally. I was beginning to think you'd never show up," the doctor's voice echoes in what sounds like a reprimand. "Charles requested that I join him and run away like a coward, but I told him I'd like to meet you myself."

We're standing among rows of tables with scientific equipment and computers on them. It looks like the lab of a mad scientist as liquid flows through tubes and drips into beakers. Another one is giving off an odd smell that makes me scrunch my nose when I first get a whiff of it.

A swift breeze brushes past my arm. Glass shatters, and one of the table's setups crashes to pieces, spilling its contents across the table and onto the floor. The awful smell dissipates.

The doctor sighs. "That was harmless."

Aiden flexes his wrist. The diamond blades of his sword separate to form the whip-like structure at his side. "What have you done to the people here?"

Beyond the tables on either side are rows and rows of cages stacked on each other until they disappear into darkness. It reminds me of the warehouse where we'd found Congressman Joe. The cages there had been empty, but these are full.

The prisoners on our right are hunched over or curled up. Silent.

On the left, they're banging the cages like wild animals.

I shift around the others to get a better look at Dr. James Richer. There's a single fluorescent light above him and his table, like a spotlight. He's wearing some sort of goggles on top of his thick white hair. If I didn't already know he's in his sixties, I would have guessed he was only in his early to mid-forties based on his appearance. The white lab coat is open to his buttoned and collared dress shirt and slacks.

"That would be a long list that neither of us has time for."

Kellan roars, lunging at him with his claws.

Something sharp rakes through my mind like talons. I scream and grab my head, dropping to my knees. Then it's gone, the feeling disappearing just as quickly as it came.

When I come back to my senses, I'm out of breath on the floor. The others are lying around me, and even Kellan is down on one knee.

The doctor is gone.

The light goes out, plunging us into darkness.

Fuck.

How much do I want to bet those goggles were for night vision?

Dane and I both activate our gifts, providing a small amount of light for our group. The combination of the deep red and soft white light casts an eerie glow on the immediate area. We may as well put a flashing arrow over our heads to tell him where we are, but I'd rather we have *some* light to see him if he sneaks up on us than be completely blind.

"Ah, pet. How I've missed you," Gordon infiltrates my thoughts, rising from memories I thought I'd locked away for good.

I try to ignore him, even though my body starts to remember anyway. The cool water tank that took away my troubles. His voice, the only thing keeping me company in the dark. My lungs constrict, forcing me to breathe faster.

James's and Gordon's voices start to blend into one, calling to me through the dark, and just like that I'm right back in the water tank where I can't move. I'm restrained so tightly that I can't do anything but listen. "I know how much you crave the dark, Raegan. You miss him. You miss the freedom he gave you. All you've had since they stole you away is trouble and worry. But Gordon gave you peace. Don't you miss that? Wouldn't you like to return to that peaceful state you'd been in where you don't have to feel so much?"

It feels like I'm spinning. I can't see or hear anything outside of his voice. I don't feel my body anymore. I'm floating. Trapped in the water tank as the words echo and repeat in my head. *"Did you have a nice dream?"* Gordon continues, and my stomach hollows.

A dream?

"You didn't actually think you'd escaped me, did you? You merely fell asleep in the tank again."

No. You're dead.

"Do I sound dead to you? Let me show you."

Something shakes me, and nausea burns up my throat.

Don't touch me!

My gift flares on reflex, and someone yelps.

I hear laughter. *"My pet is finally turning into the monster she was meant to be. Why don't you let it out? Prove to me you're not worthless."*

"—gan!" a faraway voice interrupts Gordon.

The restraints tighten like chains wrapping my entire body, suffocating me.

No! Let me go!

"I swore I'd never do that, beautiful," a rough, deep voice says above me. A whiff of musk and amber catches me off guard.

There's nothing to smell in the water tank.

Something strokes my palm in a soothing circle. "It's Dane. I'm right here, and I'm not going anywhere. You're safe. Gordon's dead. Come back to us," another voice pleads.

"Don't listen to him. Listen to *me*, Raegan," a third voice commands. "Look at me. Now."

I know these voices. They're... safe. I blink, struggling to focus in the dark, until I realize it's not pitch-black. The dark red and pale white light blinds me for a second.

"Useless," Gordon mocks, but it's not just his voice. It's someone else's, too.

"Good girl," the third voice croons. "Look at me."

A clash of metal in the distance startles me free of whatever trance I'd been in, and Aiden's face comes into view. Kellan's bear-hugging me from behind, and Dane's squeezing my hand at my side. He looks both relieved and... in pain?

"She's back," he breathes, exhaling sharply.

"What happened?" I ask, worry rising in my chest like acid.

Kellan releases me, and Aiden answers. "His gift, most likely. Jackson went after him, and Reid's trying to turn on the lights. Dane—"

"I'm fine. Let's go kill this fucker."

I squeeze his hand, and he flinches, pulling his hand away. "Dane?"

"It's nothing."

I'm still piecing myself back together, so I don't chase his hand. I hold mine out for it instead and wait for him to show me. He makes a face—like he'd really prefer not showing me—which only makes me want to see it more. Finally, he turns his hand over and reveals the bloody, tattered state of his hand.

I gasp, reaching for his wrist. "Dane!"

He pulls it out of reach and takes my hand with his other one. "You can look at it after this bastard's dead."

Aiden nods his agreement. "Kell—"

"I'll take point. You cover the back," Kellan growls, moving in front. Aiden shifts his whip sword into a shield as tall as him and three times as wide. It curves a bit overhead for added protection until I think he's out of metal.

We move down one aisle of cages. The people inside are crashing and slamming their bodies into the metal. Even through the noise, I can hear James's voice as clearly as if he's speaking directly in my head.

"You think you've fooled anyone, Dane? You should know better than anyone here. Grief is wearing a mask and telling the world you're fine when inside you're rotting. The more you tell yourself and those around you that everything is okay, the worse it gets. The more the rot festers."

Dane scowls.

"Don't let him get to you," Aiden orders. "He'll say anything to keep us distracted."

"We wouldn't want that, Aiden," James's voice echoes in our minds, giving us no clear direction for where he is. "You've already lost so many Guild members in this fight against GE. I'm not sure you could handle one more. It's a wonder anyone still follows you when you've failed at protecting your people over and over again."

A gunshot fires. Kellan widens his stance to block us. The bullet clinks to the ground.

"Good save, Kellan. You think you've become stronger now, but it's still not enough to defeat Charles. As long as he has your gift, strength will never be enough. You won't be able to protect them all. You're cursed to watch the others fall while only you survive."

"Oh yeah? Try saying that to my face, you coward," he snarls. "We'll see what words you have when I'm ripping your throat out."

There's another gunshot that strikes Aiden's shield with a hard *tink*.

Each fire of the gun catapults my heart into my throat as I wait to hear where the bullet lands. If I'll feel it or hear someone I love cry out in pain.

I won't let that happen.

Stopping, I send my gift through my feet to the floor, burying it beneath the surface to not give myself away. Dane and Aiden pause with me. It takes them only a second to realize what I'm doing as I seek out James. He can hide all he likes in the dark, but my gift will find and destroy him nonetheless.

James laughs. "You can try, Raegan, but you forget that I can hear your fears. What if you accidentally get Reid or Jack instead?" Metal rattles. "What if you kill all these innocent people?"

Fuck. He's hanging onto the cages.

"You really are becoming too dangerous to live… like Charles said. How long until you get so strong that you lose control? Until your gift becomes so hungry to devour everything in its path that you can't stop it? Until it kills the friends you've made. The men you love. You think you're a good person, but you're a villain in the making. All I have to do is kill one of the people in this room, and it'll be enough to set you off. You'll lose control of your gift, and all the people trapped in cages will die. All the innocent lives in the hospital above us will die. There will be no more redemption. Only feeding the world to your gift until it's satisfied."

My chest tightens as he gives voice to all my fears, making them feel more real. No, not just real.

Inevitable.

"Enough! Pick on me, asshole!" Dane shouts.

"They should kill you now to save the world while they still can. You're going to be the end of it."

"Raegan." Aiden draws my face to look at his. "What did I say?"

"Don't let him get to you," I repeat on a breathless whisper.

"Good. You let him get to you again, and I'll have Reid pull you out of here."

The threat is like a splash of cold water and a cattle prod to my pride. Gritting my teeth, I nod, and he releases me.

Another gunshot, but this time it's in a different direction. "You're right, Reid. She doesn't love you. You're both a classic case of Stockholm Syndrome. If you live long enough to try having a normal life, she'll realize you're nothing more than a cold-blooded murderer."

I hate that his voice is in all our heads at once, spilling our fears and secrets to the others. He's taking something personal and weaponizing it.

"And Jackson... I'm surprised you're not by her side when she means so much to you. Your arrogance will get her killed. She's going to die, and you won't be able to do anything to stop it."

The sound of a bunch of chains being drawn over a pulley and clanging metal suddenly fills the room with a deafening roar.

The cages.

We followed where we thought he went, and now we're surrounded.

A high-pitched sound rings in a single note, and if I thought the people in the cages were wild before, they completely lose it in response to that noise. They clamber and scream out of the cages, rushing toward us as if we're the threat.

"Fuck's sake," Dane mutters, grabbing my arm and pressing close. "They're just like the fucking zombies."

"But they're not," I remind him. I can't just kill them like I did the zombies. Not if they're only being controlled somehow by that sound. "We need to follow that noise and stop—"

The sound cuts off.

"...it," I finish.

The prisoners freeze.

"Found you," Jackson murmurs through the darkness. Something gurgles. "Your mistake was thinking I need my eyes to see. That sound led me straight to you."

Someone—James, I'm assuming—chokes.

The lights flicker—almost like they haven't been used in so long that it takes a minute for the electricity to power them on—before the room finally brightens. Reid appears beside us as we stare at Jackson doing something with James at the end of the aisle on the floor. The prisoners turn to see them as well.

They start running, a couple at first, and then the rest mob together toward James and Jackson.

"Jack!" I shout in warning.

He flies over them and drops at my side to one knee. Jack takes my hand and places something in it.

James's tongue.

For everything he'd said to me. I close my hand and send a burst of my gift through it. Then angle my hand and let the ashes fall to the floor. "Thank you."

He kisses the back of that same hand. "We should leave."

Aiden stares at the mob of prisoners surrounding James. "What did you do?"

"He's alive. And I left some knives for the prisoners to finish it," Jackson replies, his voice cool and dangerous.

"What about the others?" I look to the other side of the room where the more docile prisoners are still caged.

"We can't take all of them with us," Aiden says, then raises his phone to his ear. "I'm sending you coordinates. Have your FBI friend lock down the hospital and rescue the prisoners in the basement. They're likely gifted, so make sure only trustworthy agents are sent here. Oh, and there's a dead board member receiving justice by some of the prisoners, so I'd make sure they arrive quickly." Either I can't hear Elias's response, or he's so stunned by the information that he doesn't have time to say anything before Aiden hangs up.

"Karl!" I yell, cupping my hands around my mouth.

A man appears only a few feet from us, his mouth pressed into a tight line as he watches the brutality happening thirty feet away. He has the same blond hair as Harvey and crystal blue eyes. But his hair is cut short, unlike Sam's long and choppy length. His hands are casually tucked into his pockets. He looks displeased with what he sees, but not fearful or disgusted, either. I'm sure he's witnessed a lot of horrible things if James was the member he was tasked to watch.

"We're leaving. Reid can take you to your siblings," I explain.

"Where's Alice?" he inquires.

"With your other siblings getting them settled somewhere safe," Aiden answers.

Karl nods. "I'll keep an eye on them." He motions his chin toward the prisoners. "And on the people you've asked to come here."

Dane eyes the prisoners incredulously. "Is that safe?"

"I know how to keep them calm."

"Keep your phone on you. If something is wrong or you need something, let us know with that." Aiden fixes the shield to more manageable swords and armor on himself. I doubt it would have fit in the car if he hadn't.

"You'll tell me when he's dead?" Karl asks, his tone indifferent even though he's speaking about his father.

"Yes."

Chapter Thirty-Five

RAEGAN

Reid gets us back to Hype in the early morning before sunrise. We couldn't risk the long drive with the state of Dane's hand. There are muscles and nerves exposed from the breakdown of skin that puts him at risk of infection the longer it's untreated. We wrapped it with a sliced-up hoodie to help protect it until we got there.

While it takes Reid over an hour, it feels like seconds for us. I'm still reeling from the fight with James. From the fears that he'd revealed and now feel like an open wound for everyone to see as I silently bleed out.

Two hands cover each of mine.

Dane and Jackson.

"Come on, Rae. Let's go to the apartment for the rest of the night. We can put on a movie and cuddle under a blanket until you get hungry, and then I'll cook you whatever you want to eat."

"We're not doing anything until Cassandra heals your hand," I counter, my tone resolute. "That never should've—I thought I couldn't—Dane, I'm so sorry..." Each attempt is interrupted by emotion threatening to crack through. I'm not supposed to hurt the men I love. I'm supposed to protect them.

"You're a villain in the making."

"Stop." Dane tugs my hand, encouraging me out of the car.

Jackson twirls my hair together to the base of my neck, then pulls my hood up. He stays at my back when I move, like my personal shadow.

The others are already inside, so we exit quickly and go through the door with as little time outside as possible. Dane spins the second we're in and yanks me into his chest. For a few seconds, he just holds me.

"Just because he attacked us through you, doesn't mean it was you, Rae. You could never hurt me."

I draw a shuddering breath, clutching his back and burying my face into his hoodie. He's right. I've had nothing but control over my gift since training with Jackson and Kell. James picked at a sliver of worry in the back of my mind and made it feel like so much more in the moment. Even though it wasn't a fear I'd dwelled on for more than a few seconds. And I won't give it more than he already has.

"Thank you," I whisper. Slowly, I pull away.

Jackson smiles at me and tucks my hair behind my ear, following it to the ends and spiking my heart rate at the intensity of his stare. "Where you go, I go," he reminds me, but I know instantly what he's really saying. *Even if you became a villain, I'd be right by your side.*

The sharp click of shoes precedes Elias's appearance from the back hallway. One hand is seated in his pocket while the other flicks out to check his watch. "You're back earlier than I expected." He passes by Reid and Tinsley on their way to their apartment to rest as Aiden and Kellan join us.

"Reid teleported us back"—Elias's gaze flicks to the door, and

Aiden coolly adds, "With the car."

"I appreciate you not leaving it behind. My contact is enroute to the hospital as we speak. It's been put on lockdown until they can safely get the prisoners out. We already have a safe place where they can go."

Mm. Probably where they sent the trafficking victims to help them process everything. "One of my half-siblings is with them," I chime in. "I don't know what he plans to do, but he wanted to stay with the prisoners."

Elias nods, withdrawing his phone. "I'll let them know so there's no friendly fire."

"If you don't mind, Thorton, it's been a rough twenty-four hours. We can talk after we've gotten some rest," Aiden remarks.

"Of course."

Other voices draw our attention behind Elias. A group of Hype employees have stopped to stare at us and whisper. The bar must have closed recently if they're still up and cleaning.

"...her."

"Ruin..."

"...Raegan of Ruin..."

"...world breaker..."

"...of destruction better..."

A smack startles the group to look toward the bar. Ethan sets a box of liquor down. "The shift ended twenty minutes ago. Get a move on. Slowest one is on bathroom duty tonight."

The threat is like lighting a torch under their asses, and they scatter to whatever they are supposed to be doing.

"What the fuck was that about?" Dane demands of Elias, taking a step in front of me.

I touch his arm, and he immediately shifts back, but closer to my side as a show of support. "It's fine, Dane." I gave myself the Ruin moniker at the Pits fight, so I'm sure it's now making its rounds here. I can't say I'm thrilled about the other words I overheard, but it is what it is.

Elias gives me a look of sympathy. "If it bothers you, I'll request they stop. The toppling building has been a buzzing topic here when someone recognized it as your gift, and the word spread."

"No, it's okay. I went by Ruin at the Pits, so if any fighters from that night were here, they'd recognize it and use that name."

"It's what else your staff may plan to do with that information that concerns me. And how they react around Raegan moving forward," Aiden remarks.

Kellan crosses his arms and stares one of the staff down who'd been looking at me until they scurry out of sight. "Maybe we should host a Pits fight night here so they see Raegan's not the only one with a dangerous gift. We're all dangerous in our own way, and they should learn that if they haven't yet."

Elias appears unamused by that suggestion. Fighting for fun doesn't seem like his thing. "As you can see, there are quite a few things to catch up on when you're ready."

Aiden sighs, swiping a tired hand over his face. "We were only gone for a day."

"And your mission has resulted in a cascade of repercussions." He runs his hand down his suit jacket. "Get some rest. We'll talk tomorrow." Elias smiles and offers me a polite nod before he retreats to the back hallway.

"Fucking hell," Dane mutters.

"Come on." I loop my arm through his. "Let's find Cassandra."

"You're back!" Portia squeals and throws Cassandra's door open, leaping at me as a blur of color. Dane and Kellan are at my back while Jackson and Aiden returned to our apartment with our hoodies and incognito gear. After Dane's hand is healed, we'll be joining them.

"Portia? What are you doing here?"

"I filled everyone in on our day and played some games," she explains excitedly. "The others had a watch party for when the news would break on us taking down the GE building."

Kell barks out a laugh. "A watch party?"

"That's weird," Dane states flatly.

Portia shrugs and drags me further inside. "Since they couldn't be there with you, they wanted to at least cheer you on from here and make sure they didn't see anything *weird*"—she eyeballs Dane—"that you'd need to worry about."

"And?" Kellan prompts.

"Nothing to worry about!"

"I wouldn't say that," Fabian interjects from the living room.

"Ah! Reggie!" Gabe cheers on the couch with his hands up. "You're famous here now. They've come up with all sorts of nicknames for you downstairs. Raegan of ruin, ruin, world breaker, goddess"—he shakes his fists and opens them—"of destruction! Quite the list. I *may* have started the last one for the excuse to see you in a devastating dress and crown just to feed the fans."

I'm not sure how to react to any of that, so I focus on what he said last. "Fans?" Maybe he chose the wrong word. If anything, I expected fear now that they know what I can do.

"Oh, in the droves, my dear! Everyone was terrified of GE coming after us, but after what they've seen you can do, you're their shining beacon of hope! Of course, there are always haters, but Portia gave them each a good talking to with some wonderfully scary backup, and they've been quiet since."

"Oh... that's... okay," I manage, still processing.

"Good work, Rainbow." Kellan grins at Portia, who nods with faux seriousness.

Dane whispers in my ear from behind, "No going anywhere here alone." He lightly pinches my hip. I don't tell him that Jackson has been warning me of that since we started staying here.

Before, I argued it. Now, I might agree.

"Where's everyone else?" I ask the room.

Portia claps. "Oh! That's what I meant to tell you when I opened the door. Your friend just woke up! The others are in there."

"Evie?" She nods, and I hurry into the bedroom.

Cassandra helps Evie out of the private bathroom while Silas is seated on the bed.

"Welcome back," Cassandra greets us with a smile.

Silas jumps to Evie's other side to help support her weight.

"Evie! I'm so glad you're awake." I stay just inside the doorway to give them room to help her back in bed.

"Thanks. I'm glad to be up, too."

"How are you feeling?"

Silas piles the pillows at her back while Cassandra pulls the blankets up her lap. "I could eat," she admits.

"She's hungry," Portia reports from the doorway to the living room, as if answering someone's question. She turns back to the room. "Fabian says he's ordering. What are you in the mood for?"

"Anything. Whatever has the shortest delivery time," Evie replies, holding her stomach.

"Don't overeat or eat too fast," Cassandra warns her.

"Fabian's got it," Portia tells us, joining my side.

Silas looks past me, and I realize Kellan's now leaning in the doorway with his arms crossed. His gaze drops to mine. "Did you get them all?"

"Yeah. One didn't join the group, so we had to go after him. Otherwise, we would have been back a lot sooner."

He nods. "That's really good news."

"What did I miss?" Evie asks.

"Wait! Don't do a catch-up sesh without me!" Gabe cries from the living room. He's stopped by Kellan's large frame crowding the doorway. "Excuse me, large, tattooed man. News awaits!"

Kell raises an eyebrow at me. Smirking, I shrug. He turns, giving Gabe room to slip through.

"Before that, can you heal Dane's hand?" I direct to Cassandra.

"Of course." She looks around the room for him, and I realize he's still in the living area with Fabian and Zedd.

"Dane!"

"Yeah," he calls back, then appears in the doorway. "Fabian was telling me that some on the news are talking about the odd coincidence of two buildings collapsing the same way for the same company. Some are saying it's a coordinated attack."

"They can talk all they want," Kell drawls. "There's no culprit and no proof."

"The news is still fresh. Charles will probably have them backtracking before the sun is up," I reason.

Cassandra's already looking at Dane's hand, her brow pinched. She looks at me like she can tell it was my gift.

"Did they do that to his hand?" Portia asks, her eyes wide when she sees it.

I hesitate, tensing at the idea of admitting I'd hurt him.

Silas snorts. "I bet Dane touched Raegan without her permission and she clapped back." His words snap the tension.

"Fuck off, Silas," Dane retorts, although there's no bite.

"Both of you, be quiet so I can concentrate," Cassandra chides.

"Okay, *then* fill us in on what happened with the last guy," Portia whispers.

The shower screeches, making me cringe. It stops once the water shoots out. Jackson was already asleep when we returned from Cassandra's apartment after filling everyone in. Aiden texted he was meeting with Cibrina and would be back later. Dane was the first to pass out after turning on a movie, with Kellan not far behind.

I don't know if any of them got much sleep in the car since I'd slept the most between each stop. I won't be able to sleep until I've showered the last day off me, and then maybe I'll wake them up to join me in bed.

Once the water's to temperature, I slip inside and stand beneath the hot spray. The water pressure here is great—just like I remember it. I breathe a sigh of relief as it beats against my scalp and neck, then my back when I shift forward.

I stand there for a long time. Long enough that the heat soaks into my skin until I'm warm and languid. So long that the spray begins to itch, and I'm forced to turn.

Opening my eyes, I freeze when I see someone beyond the glass.

"It's only me," Aiden's smooth voice lilts.

I push the glass door open so I can see him better, and a flood of cooler air rushes into the shower, making me shiver. Aiden is leaning against the sink, one ankle crossed over the other, his hands in his pockets. He's wearing a soft, loose shirt that is starting to cling to his chest from the moisture it's absorbed. "How long have you been there?"

"Some time."

"Well, can I help you?"

"I was waiting for my turn, but I'm not sure if there's any hot water left."

Scoffing, I close the door to block him and the cold air. "Most people wait outside the bathroom."

"And miss the opportunity to see you?"

The shower door opens and reveals a now-naked Aiden. I don't move from my spot, blocking his entry. He steps inside anyway, letting his body press against mine to fit, and tugs the door shut.

My nipples are pebbled from the cooler air as they push into his chest, and a different kind of heat surges through my veins at the contact. "I didn't invite you in," I admonish, my voice breathy as I stare into his obsidian gaze.

He's looking at me like he wants to pick me apart. Learn me inside out and then put me back together again. "I've been thinking about what happened. What the doctor said."

My stomach drops. "Why? You said it yourself. He was only trying to distract us."

Aiden shifts closer, and I'm forced to step back. "Even if he twisted our fears, there was truth in it. I don't want to lose anyone else or put them in more danger. I've debated keeping Guild members here for the final fight. I wonder if it wouldn't have been better to keep refusing their help. Even if they hated my decision, they might be alive today. I argue constantly over the idea of locking you up until Charles is dead."

Once my back meets the tile, his thumb and forefinger pinch my chin, locking my eyes with his.

"If you break my trust like that again, I'd hate you."

"You'd be safe. Alive to hate me."

"You could never hold me. You know that."

"I still have the cuffs."

"That you need to defeat Charles."

"I'd take the risk for you. I don't think you fully grasp what lengths I would go to ensure you survive."

The memory of his unmoving body on mine hits me in the chest, squeezing until it's hard to breathe. "I do."

"No. I'd do more than die for you, Raegan. I'd gladly become your villain if it meant you were safe."

My breath hitches.

He leans close, his lips hovering over mine. "I love you more than anything. More than the Guild. More than my brothers. More than my own life. More than the world and the people living in it." His long fingers trail down my neck, down my chest to pause over my racing heart. Aiden pulls away so we can see each other. "Do you want to know a secret?"

Somehow, I manage a small nod.

"I never wanted to share you." I open my mouth to argue, but he presses a finger to my lips. "I was enamored with you the moment we met—before the others even came to the island. Maybe it was because I'd known you first, but when our group formed and I stepped up to lead it, I couldn't let you go. Even when I knew they had feelings for you, I couldn't step back. I'd rather none of us have you than the possibility that you'd choose someone else.

"And yet, at the first real challenge for your affection, I caved without hesitation. I kissed you first. I knew it was wrong. I'd failed as a leader in that moment, but I didn't care. Because when it comes to you, I can't think straight. I become so irrational, so crazed that even I don't know what I'm going to say or do next. That was warning enough for me to let you go. I tried, but I hurt you instead. I failed the *one person* I wanted to protect more than anyone."

He cradles my face. "There is no apology, no words that exist to express the regret, the guilt I have for what happened to you because I'd been so selfish. I'd refused to see what was right in front of me because I'd been so focused on denying everything I felt for you. If I could go back in time and fix things... kill Gordon before he ever laid eyes on you..."

I grasp his arm. "Don't. I don't want anything to change. We're all together now. Gordon is dead. You could lose the Guild. Promise me you won't try messing with the past, Aiden."

His eyes search mine as if looking for a hint of doubt. But he won't find any. Finally, he nods. "I can't promise that I won't get jealous. That I won't steal you away from time to time for myself. But I promise not to interfere with you and them. If you want all of us, then that's exactly who you'll have. I'll give you everything for as long as I live. So long as it doesn't put your safety at risk, it's yours. I'm yours."

"I want you alive," I tell him, my voice hardening with how much I need that. "If you throw yourself in front of a bullet for me again, I'm going to find the way to hell to drag your ass back here. And then I'll put *you* in those damned cuffs and a locked room to see how you like it."

My words draw a smirk to his lips. "Accurate for you to assume that's where I'd be."

I grab him by the neck and shoulder, yanking him down to kiss me. To fuck me against the tile until all our fears are too tired or weak to haunt us, and we can sleep.

CHAPTER THIRTY-SIX

RAEGAN

My BODY COMES ALIVE before my brain, pleasure unfurling through me with warmth. It buzzes under my skin, tingling my nipples and making my lower abdomen clench. I gasp for air, suddenly feeling deprived as my brain tries to kick online, but thoughts scatter when delicious pressure swirls my clit. An orgasm flickers in warning, and I push into the pressure for more. To send me over the edge where I'm teetering.

Cool air chills my nipples to frigid points. A warm mouth sucks on my neck. And fingers slide into my aching cunt, curling and pressing on the spot that has me seeing stars. One more flick of tongue and it's over.

I'm flying and falling at once, ecstasy hitting me in waves as I cry out and succumb to it.

A deep chuckle vibrates between my thighs, making my over-sensitized body shiver. "Morning, beautiful." I open my eyes to Kellan between my legs.

Aiden sucks on his thumb and forefinger on my right side before teasing my nipple as if he's determined to see them cut glass. Jack's on my left, kissing my neck and massaging my other breast.

I'm completely naked.

Dane bursts into the room, scrubbing a hand over his face. "Did you fuckers go without me?" His amber gaze settles on me, dragging down my naked body and feeling like embers. My chest rises and falls as I catch my breath, still waking up.

"Relax. I'm just getting started." Kellan chuckles and bows his head. A stroke of velvet coaxes a low moan from my chest.

"Goddammit." Dane grabs his dick through his pants. "I still need a fucking shower." He dashes to the bathroom, not bothering to shut the door before he wrangles his clothes off and hops into the shower that I doubt's even hot.

"See if you can get her to come before he's done," Jackson challenges Kell on a low chuckle.

That won't be hard, considering I'm already about to crest into a new one between his tongue and fingers.

Then Kell stops, raising his head like he's going to respond, and I grab his head and shove it back down. "Don't fucking stop," I order on a breathless command. "I'm so close. I'm so—" I inhale sharply as he adds a third finger and rubs my clit. "Fuck, fuck, fuck. Yes! Oh, please!"

Jackson sucks a nipple and at the same time Aiden captures my chin and kisses me. Pleasure zings through me like electricity, lighting me on fire and setting off another orgasm. It wrings my body tight, then leaves me limp.

Aiden rearranges me on his lap, holding my wrists over my head while Kellan frees his hard length at the foot of the bed.

My pussy throbs with the need for more. I stare at the cure, transfixed. "Yes. Fuck me, Kellan. I need it."

"Fuck, beautiful. You always know exactly what to say."

Dane runs out of the bathroom, everything but his hair dry as water drips to his chest and back. He's still hard as stone, the shower and time doing nothing to distract him from me.

I hold my hand out to him, urging him closer. "Dane—Ahh, oh fuck!" Kell lifts my leg and slowly pushes inside. He slides back to the tip, and my pussy nearly sucks him back in the second round.

Kellan growls. "You feel so fucking good. Like this should be illegal."

I rock my hips with his long thrusts, meeting him with every stroke that sparks a shot of ecstasy through my limbs. Dane stands at the edge of the bed, pumping his cock with a heated gaze. Licking my lips, I open my mouth to him. I remember how much he enjoyed eating me out with me on top, and I'm suddenly overwhelmed with the need to do the same to him. "Fuck my mouth, Dane."

He doesn't need to be told twice.

Dane crawls on the bed and straddles me as Aiden shifts to one side, still restraining my wrists. Jackson's forced to move from my breasts to avoid Dane's ass, but he easily shifts his attention to my clit instead, making my hips jolt from the contact and Kellan to groan when my cunt grips his shaft.

"Oh fuck, I thought you were going to squeeze my dick off. Do it again."

Jack chuckles, flicking my clit in a short burst that makes me gasp.

Dane holds his cock in my face, his face torn between the need to shove it down my throat and not wanting to hurt me.

I stick out my tongue in offering, and he balances the tip there while he grips the base.

"I'll go slow," he promises, sinking his dick down the length of my tongue and into my mouth. I close my lips around him, swirling my tongue and sucking him deeper. "Ohhh my fucking god, babe. Shit. Hold on." He draws back, panting. "Fuck, your mouth is amazing." Dane pushes himself back in, only stopping when he hits my throat and then cursing when I swallow around him. Thankfully, he doesn't stay too long and makes sure I have time to catch my breath between each slow thrust.

Kellan's groan joins his when my walls tighten on the verge of coming again. "So fucking tight." He drives into me again and again, his dick scouring that spot inside of me as Jackson rubs his fingers through my arousal over my clit. As Dane's cock plunges to the back of my throat at a slower pace.

Aiden breathes his own encouragement, his voice smooth as melted chocolate. "Look at you taking them both. But you want all your holes filled, don't you? You want our cum leaking out of each one, proving we all belong to you, isn't that right? Show me how much you love this, Raegan. Come for us."

I do. His command trips something inside of me like an invisible switch to my undoing. Dane shifts aside, giving me room to breathe as my body goes taut and pleasure erupts along every nerve ending. Kellan slams into me once more and stills, groaning long and deep while I collapse onto the bed.

Dane grips his cock, pumping it as he watches me come down from my high. It's hot when he gets himself ready, but something about him actively trying to get himself off when I'm right here bothers me.

"Lie down, Dane," I demand, turning on my side. Aiden disappears into the bathroom with Kellan while Jackson's shedding his clothes at the end of the bed. Dane lies back, his head on the pillows, and his hand still fisting his dick. I knock his hand away and grab the base, then swallow him whole.

"Ahh, fuck, babe!"

I fucking love making him talk during sex.

He slaps his hand over his eyes, his other hand gripping the bedding like a lifeline. He drags his hand up into his hair, grasping that next so he can look at me.

I'm looking right at him, smirking as I suck his dick down. He hisses through his teeth, struggling to maintain that eye contact and inevitably losing when his eyes roll back and he curses again.

A cool hand grazes my spine.

Jackson.

I pull my knees up, sticking my ass out to give him access while I continue drawing sounds from Dane that make my body tremble with excitement.

Jack grinds his dick across my core. It feels so fucking good that I moan around Dane, rocking my hips with Jack's movements to get the most out of it. Dane, in turn, releases a throaty groan.

"Ugh, yes! That felt so fucking good."

My shadow presses his tip to my entrance, then drives inside in a single thrust that hits so hard I think he might come out the other side. I nearly choke on Dane's dick.

Dane moans when my throat closes around him, and Jackson chuckles.

I withdraw to the tip, swirling my tongue around his head and teasing him when something touches my ass.

"Don't tense up," Aiden croons. He coats my entrance with lube, then pushes it inside with a finger. "Good girl," he praises when I force myself to relax. To breathe. Jackson and Dane pause, giving

Aiden time to prep my ass. There's no way he'd fit in this position to fuck my ass, too, so that helps me relax with the expectation it'll only be his fingers. Until something hard and smooth slides in and catches. "Very good." He steps back.

Jackson picks up where he left off, his thrusts directing my mouth over Dane's dick over and over again. I'm feeling so full, so good.

And then the butt plug starts to vibrate.

My entire body trembles and quakes from the vibrations. From the pleasure Jackson's been stoking to a steady flame.

"Oh fuck, babe. I'm gonna come." Dane grabs my hair and holds me down with his dick hitting the back of my throat. He comes down my throat, his body and dick twitching as he empties himself. Then he releases me, and I lick him clean. Dane has a full-body shiver. He sits upright and angles himself, grabbing my face and kissing me.

"You're fucking incredible," he breathes.

He leaves the bed, and I lean on my arms and face as Jackson fucks me with single-minded intensity and Aiden plays with the plug's vibration. I couldn't hold myself up if I tried. I'm lost in a sea of pleasure that's filling me to the brim. I'm not sure if I'm even breathing anymore, but none of it matters—nothing but the rising storm that's about to break does.

The butt plug twists and tugs, and pleasure bursts through me fast and hard. I scream, shattering to pieces.

When I come back to consciousness, Aiden's gently guiding a warm washcloth along my inner thighs.

He notices I'm awake and kisses me softly. "Shh, go back to sleep. I've postponed the meeting for another two hours. I'll wake you when it's time to get ready."

Jackson slides in next to me, while Dane's already on my other side. They both pull the blankets over us when Aiden's done, tucking me in between them.

My last thoughts are wondering where Kellan went before the warm press of bodies and my exhaustion pull me under.

Several sharp knocks on the door interrupt breakfast. Aiden sets his coffee mug on the low table and moves to answer it.

"Thorton." He checks his phone in his pocket, then returns it. "The meeting is in fifteen minutes. In your apartment."

"Something came up. May I come in?"

Elias strides into the apartment and stops between the kitchen and the living area, where the rest of us are finishing our food. There isn't much room in this tiny apartment, so Jackson and Kell are sitting on stools at the kitchen counter, and Dane and I are on the couch, eating at the coffee table.

Aiden returns to his chair in the living area. "Well? What couldn't wait fifteen minutes?"

"Good morning," Elias greets the room. "I apologize for interrupting your meal, but a business of mine has just been raided."

"I presume, if you've come to us, that means you suspect GE is involved?" Aiden surmises.

"I know they are. Which means everyone at Hype is in danger, as are the rest of the gifted under my protection."

"Wait. How would he know to go after you?" Dane chimes in.

"I imagine he's been desperate to find out where you've gone into hiding so he can have his revenge. Aside from my connection as the Tower landlord, it could be his contacts in the gifted trafficking network who gave him my name. If he's realized I'm also fighting his allies, and you and I have a larger relationship than landlord and tenant, he may suspect I'm the one hiding you."

Now that he says it, it's almost obvious that he would be our ally. We already have a connection to him from the Tower, but he's recently dismantled a trafficking empire—and customers of GE—and he owns plenty of real estate to hide us in. It was only a matter of time before Charles connected the dots.

"Did anyone get hurt?" I ask. "Or kidnapped?"

Elias shakes his head. "It was a by-the-book raid if you ignore the falsified claims granting them the warrant. The employees are being interrogated and then released. I have my lawyer already present to ensure their safety."

"If they already faked information to get a judge to grant the warrant, they could easily do the same to incriminate one or more of your employees," Aiden contests.

"I'm aware. I trust that the people I've sent to oversee the operations will be able to handle it. They're doing this in the public eye, so that does give us greater protection." He pauses as if gathering his thoughts in order before he continues, "Whatever move you're going to make against GE, do it. The longer you wait, the more at risk my people are now that my businesses have become a target."

Charles is trying to flush us out. Raid a business to see if we're there, and if not, go to the next one. How many businesses of Elias's can he go after before it pisses Elias off enough to give us up?

I glance at Aiden, who's already watching Elias. "Not yet."

Elias's expression darkens to one I've never seen before. He never gets upset. Not so visibly, at least. But I also know how important it is to him to keep the people he's taken in safe. And we're putting them all at risk by being here.

"Aiden, he's right—" I start, and he cuts me a look.

"Every time we've fought with Charles, he pushed us into it. Whether we were aware at the time or not, he crafted the event that forced us to react so we would do exactly what he wanted. We won't be reacting when we go after him. We'll actually be ready."

Elias's jaw tics. "My people are not collateral to your war, Adams."

"He didn't say that," Dane snaps. "Obviously, we'll do everything we can to help you protect them, too. Whatever we can do, just ask. But don't tell us to go in guns blazing without a real plan just to take the heat off your back."

Kellan laughs. "Relax, Rapunzel. Elias isn't used to the heat like we are."

"What can we do to help?" I ask Elias, my voice soft to counter the others.

He looks at me. "I'll handle it. But if he comes after Hype, there's nothing I can do to stop him from finding you and your Guild. What else do you need for your plan before this ends? How will you beat him?"

"The cuffs. He's too overpowered for us to face head-on. With the cuffs, he'll be an ordinary human who can be killed easily. It'll be a checkmate," Aiden explains. "And we have two sets. One from the late congressman and now a pair from Bea. That gives us two chances."

"Wonderful. What's stopping you from going after him, then?"

Dane scoffs. "The problem is how we get them on him."

"The guy loves to teleport," Kellan drawls.

"We've already solved that," Aiden remarks, his thumb tapping the rim of his mug.

"The Tower," Jackson inserts, and Aiden nods.

"You built something to block teleportation in the Tower with Cibrina and Reid," he says to Dane. "If we have that and can plant it in a room, then lure him to it, we'll only have to contend with his telekinesis."

And sleep and frequency gifts. The telekinesis gift on its own is difficult. But if he can't teleport, it just takes one of us getting close enough to put the cuff on.

"There's a problem with that plan," Elias remarks. "One of the developments that occurred before your return was that the Tower was seized. It happened several hours after you brought down the second headquarters, so it was most likely in response to that. As its landlord, I requested access, and I was denied with a court order spewing nonsense that I could have thrown out if I took it to court."

"How long would that take?" Dane asks.

"A few weeks to a couple months depending on how much influence he has to slow down the process. Seeing as he already has a judge and the police chief on board, I'd expect the longer timeframe."

I curse under my breath. "He'll find us here before then."

Elias dips his chin. "Precisely. The Tower is now locked up and guarded by police. You won't be able to get in without a fight with law enforcement. Even with your invisible team, there are likely alarms on the entry doors and guards posted within sight of them. I highly advise against conflict with them if you wish for the Guild to exist after GE is gone."

Damn.

Of course, he retaliated by taking our home.

"That's not a problem," Aiden replies smoothly. "We have alternative methods for entering and exiting the Tower than the front door. Do you know if anyone is inside the building?"

"I can't say I do. During the day, I would assume so. However, at night..."

Aiden nods. "We'll still assume there are or, at the very least, Charles has access to the cameras inside."

"Sounds like we'll still need some invisible friends, too," Jackson muses with a smile.

Elias fixes his cuffs and smooths his hand down the front of his jacket, his attention on Aiden. "I'll leave you to that planning, then, while I handle the rest. Once you have these teleportation-blocking devices, you'll be able to move on Charles?"

"Then we'll hunt him down."

CHAPTER THIRTY-SEVEN

RAEGAN

WE PULL INTO A bar parking lot in the middle of the night. I've been here before, but I'd been too distracted at the time to really take the place in. The bar takes up half of the building strip with its own parking lot and outdoor seating both in front and in back. String lights hang over the outdoor seating with warm lighting and an inviting atmosphere.

Television screens hang in the corners, protected by an attached gazebo, with different sports games that patrons cheer for. I can even hear them hollering for their teams inside.

"Must be a big game night," Kellan says, slamming the driver's door shut.

We pile out of the massive black car and stroll to the door. A bouncer shifts to block the entrance, then nods respectfully when Aiden's face is illuminated through the hood. The bouncers open the door for us and stare each of us down like they are memorizing our faces. They pause a bit longer on Alice—who is definitely too young to enter a bar—and Sam—who looks younger than he is—but he doesn't stop them. I guess Aiden bringing them is permission enough to let that slide.

"Welcome!" The bartender shouts over all the noise with a smile. "Take any seat you can find. Oh! Aiden!"

"Yahaira," he greets. I can only hear him because I'm so close. "Can we speak in private?"

"Of course! Jillian, cover for me, okay?" Yahaira flips the bar up and passes through, then waves our group after her. We walk through an employees-only door, then down a couple of hallways to an office door. She takes out a ring of keys and unlocks the door.

Jackson closes the door once everyone's inside.

"You're all going in?" she asks skeptically. "I think they have a patrol checking the floors at night. And I'd watch out for motion-sensor lights. Bobby said he saw lights popping on through the windows last night."

Pushing my hood back, I look at Alice.

"That shouldn't affect us," she answers, following my lead to reveal herself.

Yahaira nods and hands Aiden three keys. "We've had manual locks in place on each of the doors since the bunker was discovered. I know you can use your gift, but if you don't mind using these so we can put them back in place when you're done, I'd appreciate it."

"Thank Yaya," Aiden says, his hand closing over the keys. "Keep an eye out in case we were followed."

She laughs and puts her hands on her hips. "If anyone tries to interrupt the games tonight, all hell will break loose. Plus, there's a heavy mix of norms with us. You're safe from this side."

I give Dane a quizzical look at the term 'norms', and he whispers in my ear, "Non-gifted humans."

Ah.

Aiden unlocks the hidden door in the floor, swinging it open to reveal a pit of darkness. I swallow the lump in my throat. The mental wounds from James are still fresh, even though I've talked myself through it.

Dane finds my hand. "I'm right here, babe. I won't let go."

I nod, nerves twisting my gut the longer I stare at it.

"Jack. Scout ahead," Aiden orders. My shadow stalks to the opening and hops in, disregarding the ladder completely. Aiden passes Kell a flashlight. "Take point."

Alice extends her hand to Aiden and the last flashlight in his grip. "The least you could've done is pack enough for the rest of us. I'm not going down there without that."

"So much fear..." the bartender suddenly says, her voice sounding off. She reaches out to me, her gaze transfixed on me as she licks her lips. "Just a taste..."

Dane shoves me behind him, and Aiden snatches her wrist. "Snap out of it, Yaya."

She blinks, her eyes still focused on me. Then she looks at Aiden. "Sorry, Master. She smells so good."

"Fucking vamp," Dane mutters.

"Is that you, Dane? I hardly recognized you. I see you've come a long way from the last time I'd seen you."

"Fuck off, Yaya."

"Always so ornery." Yahaira shakes her head. Her dark eyes find mine. "I could help, if you'd like," she nearly sings, her voice a soothing lilt that tugs at my chest. "Take that fear away. Or just a nibble to take the edge off."

Dane's hand tightens on mine. "Don't accept it, Rae. She feeds on strong emotions, but if she takes too much, you'll be numb the rest of the day."

"That's enough, Yahaira," Aiden demands, his tone serious. "We'll take it from here."

She nods and smiles. "Of course. Good luck tonight." Yahaira waves, then leaves the three of us alone. The rest have already gone down the ladder into the tunnel.

Aiden closes the distance between us, and Dane moves to the side without letting go of my hand. "Most of this mission is going to be in the dark. Are you up to it, or would you like to stay in here?"

"You mean you're not just going to push me down there if I take too long?" I try to tease, but there's an unexpected edge to my voice at the recalled memory when he'd done exactly that.

Dane's head whips around to stare at Aiden in surprise.

Right. No one else knew what he'd done to try getting me to spill my secrets.

Aiden's eyes close, cutting me off from the spark of pain I catch there. "No." He opens them, his expression controlled once again.

I know it's unfair to jab him about it now. He's already apologized—already shared his regrets with me over what he'd done in the past. And now that he knows the effect the dark has on me, it's hitting him that much harder when he remembers what he'd done.

"I want to do this," I tell him honestly. Not that I'm fully prepared, or I won't have any problems. But I'll push myself to get through it because I won't let that fear hold me back. I won't give Gordon that control over me still.

He nods. "Dane and I will stay with you. If you need to leave, you and I will do that while the others finish the mission."

The out he's giving me releases the knot of tension in my chest.

Dane lifts his glowing hand between us. "I'll light our way."

Aiden takes the ladder first. He pauses a few rungs down and holds his hand out to me. I take it, turning and moving down until his body surrounds mine. "Tell me whatever you need, Raegan," he purrs in my ear. I nod, my body still stiff as we descend into the dark. "That's not enough. I need to hear your voice. Talk to me."

"I'm okay," I manage, focusing on my breathing and one step after another. There are a couple lights in the distance now that I can see the bottom, which I assume are Kell and Alice. The group is waiting for us; for me. I'm slowing everyone down. "I need to get off this ladder," I mumble to motivate myself to hurry the fuck up.

But Aiden hears it. He loops his arm around my front and scoops my legs out before we drop. Thankfully, it isn't more than four or five feet before we land, but it's still enough time for my stomach to leap into my throat as I choke on a gasp.

"What's wrong?" Dane whisper-shouts from above us. He rushes down the ladder and jumps to skip the last few steps.

Realizing Aiden's still holding me when Dane reaches us, I pat his chest. "Put me down. I'm fine. I was giving myself a pep talk, not asking for a trust fall exercise."

He sets me on my feet. "Let's catch up to the others, then."

The jump was a great distraction from the dark, but now that we're walking in it, my nerves are fried again. I keep waiting for his voice, waiting for the moment my mind taunts me.

Dane's hand and the flashlight on Aiden's phone light the way while they both stay on either side of me like guards.

There's a long stretch of quiet. Of shuffling feet and hushed whispers. Of breathing and scuffed shoes on stone. Enough quiet that I can feel the claws sinking into my mind, ready to bring me back to the water pod.

"You could have said something to me," Aiden begins, almost accusatory. I nearly trip with how quickly I halt. He takes my arm and keeps me moving. "Don't stop."

"Excuse me?"

"The dark. When I'd told you to take the ladder, you never said anything about it bringing up bad memories. Or you could have given me a half-truth that you were afraid of it."

"Do you think that gives you some sort of excuse for forcing me down there? For making me believe I was falling into a pit and might break something at the bottom?"

"All I'm saying is you could have given me something. That was all I asked for back then. Something real. That could have been it."

"And then what? You would have gotten off my back if I just told you I was scared of the dark? That would have been it?"

"Maybe. We'll never know."

Is he serious right now?!

I fist my hands, anger flooding through me at the *balls* of this man to put the blame on me for what he did. I'm preparing a slew of insults to slam him with when he tugs my arm to prevent me from knocking into someone.

"We're here."

Wait. Already? I look at him in surprise, and he smirks at me. Did he...? Was he just trying to rile me up to keep my mind off the dark?

"One tunnel down, one more to go," he says, leaving my side to unlock the next door.

That bastard. He did.

Dane laughs beside me. "Even I could tell he was just saying shit. You were so tense, though, and it seemed to be working, so I didn't say anything."

Damn.

Assholes.

I forgot how many damn stairs were in the tunnel between the bunker and the Tower. As much as I hate them and I'm gasping by the time we reach the wall leading to the final room, I'm grateful they were enough of a pain in the ass to keep my mind occupied. We've had to stay silent for the last twenty-minute stretch to make sure none of the wandering patrols could somehow hear us.

Kellan stops at the ladder, turning to wait for Aiden with the final key. Sam is fast asleep on his back, likely lulled to sleep by the constant steps up, up, up.

Dane tugs my hand, drawing my attention to Aiden gathering everyone around him.

"Partner up," he orders.

He'd already assigned who was with whom, so I move to Kellan's side and lightly shake Sam's arm. "Sam. Sam," I urge in a whisper. We have Alice and four of her siblings to help us sneak in and out unde-tected. Thankfully, Alice was the only one who hadn't known how to make other people invisible, so there was no training required.

I rub his back and then pat it a little harder. "Sam. Wake up." He drags his eyelids open, looking like I'd pulled him from a deep sleep. "Hey. Can you stand? It's time to move."

Sam starts to nod and gets caught in a yawn.

Kellan's already crouched because of the low ceiling, so it's easy for Sam to climb off when he's ready. I help make sure he's balanced before letting go. Aside from Kellan and his invisible partner, we're the only ones left. They vanish almost as soon as Sam is on his feet.

"Are you ready?" I hold my elbow out to Sam.

He takes it, his hold soft and light.

"You can hold on tighter," I tell him, worried his hand will slip if I move faster than him.

His grip tightens—barely—but I leave it alone. I shouldn't be racing around if we're invisible anyway. The rest of the group slowly comes into view, a thin, translucent veil shimmering over them, telling me they're invisible and I am too.

Aiden leads the way, climbing the ladder and unlocking the door. He pushes it aside, then climbs out with his invisible partner latched to his leg. The rest of us follow a pair at a time. Sam switches hands to my lower leg as we ascend the ladder, then back to my arm again when we're out.

We're in one of the kitchen storage rooms on the Guild Hall floor. The lights in the ceiling are dim like nightlights. It's enough for us to see each other since our eyes are already adjusted to the dark. I scrunch my nose at the foul smell. The food inside is spoiled.

We move in a line through the kitchen and bar to the open Guild Hall before the teams separate. There are five devices we need to acquire; one for each of us. Dane and Alice are picking up the controller device that he'll use to deactivate the rest before they can move them. They move in the direction of the infirmary while Kellan, Aiden, and Jack's team take the stairwell to the other floors.

Sam and I walk through the Guild Hall to the far end corner. There's enough moonlight pouring through the glass wall and half-dome ceiling that we can see fairly well. Tucked in the dirt of a potted plant is a black box the size of my hand with wires and things sticking out of it haphazardly like it was just thrown together. A green light blinks at us.

"Who's there?"

A light sweeps over us, and I freeze. Sam looks over his shoulder, then squeezes my arm. I turn, and the security guard is walking straight toward us.

Fuck.

Are we not invisible?

I look at my hands, but they still have that weird shine to them that says I am.

The guard gets closer, his flashlight moving back and forth over the area we're in as if he's searching for something here.

Did we mess up?

There's a low, flatline beep that makes all three of us pause to listen.

The green light is now a solid red light.

Dane's deactivated them.

A heads up that it would make noise would have been nice, Dane.

"What in the hell—" The guard pulls a radio from his hip.

Fuck a duck.

Sam lightly pulls my arm, dragging my attention from the other man to see where he's trying to get me to go. He brings us around the back of the potted plants while the guard starts talking on the radio.

"Hey, I might've got something here. Meet me on floor eleven. Yeah. The place with all the plants."

The guard strolls up to the potted tree just as Sam's hand covers the box. He doesn't grab it or move it, just holds his hand there as the guard leans forward to inspect the pot.

"I swear I saw something," he mutters, moving branches aside and looking at the other pots around it.

Sam carefully extracts the box—slower than a sloth, it feels like—until it's free from the dirt. He makes it just in time before the guard starts rooting around the dirt, mumbling to himself. The guard stares right through us to the wall and floor, looking around.

He brings his radio back to his face. "Never mind, I—"

Crashing echoes from the hallway. Where the offices are and...

...the infirmary.

Dane!

The security guard takes off running. I pull Sam up and grab his hand, taking him with me as I race after him. He taps my arm repeatedly. I ignore it at first, the worry for Dane taking over, before I finally realize he's trying to say something. Looking at him, he puts a finger to his lips, then points to my feet.

Right.

I slow enough that I can better control my steps. Heel to toe. Fast, but quiet.

We turn the corner down the hallway and nearly crash into a running Dane and Alice. I grab his shirt and push his chest at the same time as he grips my shoulder. Then he points behind us. Go back?

A text message alert rings between us.

"What was that?" a guard asks another, who grunts back.

Dane shoots a glare at Alice. She's trying to get her phone out of her pocket with the hand that's already holding the controller device while still holding Dane. It dings again. And again.

The sound of heavy footsteps picks up to a jog.

"Fuck's sake," Dane mutters under his breath. I can only hear him because we're nearly standing on top of one another. He pushes my shoulder to turn me around and get us moving. I do, holding Sam tight as we quietly run to the kitchen and storage room to wait for the others. Dane and Alice have their device, and we have ours, so we need to get the fuck away from the guards before something else tells them we're here.

I close the doors to the kitchen and the storage room, then turn on Alice. She's given the controller to Dane as she taps on her cell phone, her eyes scanning the message there.

"How could you have left the volume on?" Dane hisses.

She shoves the screen in his face for him to read. I shift against him to read it, too. The sender's name says Tobias. The first text is a date and time. The second, a string of numbers I'm guessing are coordinates. And the last text...

You forgot one.

"Dad," she whispers as the door to the storage room flies open.

Chapter Thirty-Eight

RAEGAN

I'm so distracted by the text and Alice's answer that the slight squeak of the door opening catapults my heart from my chest. I whirl around to see if we've been caught. It doesn't cross my mind in that second of surprise that we're still invisible as long as we're quiet. My thoughts are too stuck on *shit, shit, shit.*

Aiden frowns at me when he enters. The shadows caused by the dim lighting only make him look more intimidating, but I breathe a sigh of relief when I realize it's him. Dane tries to wave him over to talk, but Aiden shakes his head and points to the floor. He's saying to wait until we're in the tunnels.

Kellan and Jack arrive at the same time, anti-teleportation devices in hand.

Finally, we can go.

Aiden doesn't let anyone talk until we're on the other side of the bunker in the tunnel that takes us to the bar.

Kell leans his arm on my head, and I swat him away. "Were you the one causing all the ruckus, beautiful?"

"Nope. Not me," I reply, casting a side-eye to Dane, who, in turn, throws a glare at Alice.

"Don't look at me. Ask Harriet the Spy," he grumps.

Alice returns his glare. "Are you so old you forgot my name?"

Dane drags a hand down his face, then slides it through his hair. "Never mind. The professional teenage spy here touched something she shouldn't have."

"Hey, you said it was fine," Alice argues.

"I said that so you'd stop panicking and making things worse."

She gives him the middle finger.

Aiden sighs. "Let's hope it's not reported in, or Charles doesn't bother with it. Nothing says it was us."

"Was that why the guy on the radio called my patrol guy downstairs?" Kell asks, and I wince.

"Oh, yeah. That one was me," I admit. "But he didn't see us. He ran after the noise from Dane and Alice."

"Which was before Alice's phone blew up with text messages from Charles," Dane adds.

"What were they?" Aiden inquires.

"A threat." She looks over her shoulder at the rest of our siblings. "He has Tobias."

The others' expressions are divided between fear, resignation, and anger as three of them speak at once.

"—should've gone for him first—"

"—no way he can handle Dad—"

"—we're all screwed—"

Aiden's phone rings while they bicker. He holds his hand up, silencing the others.

"Who is it?" I ask, craning to read *Unknown Number* flash on the screen.

"Charles," Aiden answers, immediately switching the call to speakerphone.

"Guild Master," Charles greets, his pleasant tone icier than usual. "It's time we end this, don't you think?"

Aiden's smile is malicious. "I couldn't agree more. If you're calling with the terms for your surrender, however, it's too late. We're coming for you, Charles."

I wait for the GE president's laugh that usually follows whenever he or his company is threatened.

He doesn't.

"You've stolen assets, destroyed my properties, killed the board, and murdered Gifted Enterprise employees. I hope you're prepared for how I'll bleed out every member of your Guild before you. I'll break my mistake of a daughter as well as the other useless defects with you. But first, you're going to have to make a choice."

Dane's glaring at the phone, his hands clenched and jaw grinding while Kellan looks a breath away from exploding into his new draconic form. Jackson watches the phone with an intense stare, listening to every word like he's memorizing each threat he makes so he can mete out the punishment for it. Alice, Sam, and the others are clustered around us, fear sitting heavy in their postures and stares.

"A choice?" Aiden questions.

"I'm going to send you two coordinates. One will lead you directly to me. The other has some assets of mine being offloaded due to the shortage you've caused me. Alice has a third location, where you'll find the final spy child. Choose to save the others, or come for me. There won't be time to do all three. You have twelve hours before I go underground to rebuild Gifted Enterprise. I'd rather start this fresh with you lot gone, so I'm giving you this opportunity. I'm curious to see which you'll choose."

The call ends.

"Every time I think this guy can't get any worse, he proves me wrong," I mutter, glaring at Elias's TV in his living room.

"He's trying to split us up," Dane growls as we watch three real-time satellite views across the globe in three boxes.

That's right.

The locations are on separate continents, just to be sure we're as far away from each other as possible. And the satellites all conveniently allowed Dane to access these exact spots with crystal clear viewing.

The first one is an ocean port, where it's the middle of the night. On it, people in collars and chains are being loaded into a shipping container. His *offloaded assets*. Once they're in a shipping container and on a ship, it'll be impossible to find them. The ship coincidentally leaves the port in eleven hours.

The second is a building with a retracted roof on an island. Inside is Tobias, tied to a gurney and feeding blood into a large collection bag. The sun's only rising here, which means he's going to burn to a crisp by midday while his body is already drained. Charles is taking his gift for his use and killing him at the same time.

The last box shows a large house in a tiny island town. The location where Charles is supposedly waiting.

"That one's mine," Portia bites out, a sharpness to her tone that I've never heard before. I snap my gaze away from the screen for the first time since Dane pulled it up to look at her. She's leaning forward on the couch, her hands gripping her thighs as she focuses on the first one. She's dressed casually today in mini shorts and a halter top, her long brown hair falling in soft waves to her mid-back. As if sensing my stare, her vibrant green eyes meet mine with unrelenting will. "Let my group handle the one at the port."

I shouldn't be surprised she'd jump to help the ones about to be trafficked after what she went through. But hearing her story and seeing exactly how formidable Portia is when she sets her mind to something are two completely different things.

"Hold it there, Rainbow," Kellan drawls, his arm thrown over the back of the couch at the end while he fiddles with one of Jack's knives pointed into his thigh. Elias casts him a look of disapproval for the nickname, but Kell is already continuing. "Splitting up is exactly what he wants us to do. If we jump when he says, we're just walking into another one of his traps."

Portia pops up like she's ready to fight him. His grin sharpens. "I don't care if it is. We can't let them get away before they disappear to who-knows-where! This is their best shot to be saved."

"It's already too late. You'd never make it in time," Aiden counters.

She jabs a finger at Reid. He's standing behind the large couch, where Tinsley's sitting, his arms crossed with an expressionless mask in place as he regards the screen. "We would if he took us there. We could be there in minutes, right?"

Aiden frowns. "And take away our only teleporter until you're finished? I can guarantee it won't just be this one container. He'll throw everything he has at you to keep you occupied, if not to make you prisoners as well."

Portia's hands fist. "Then Reid can leave us there. We'll handle whatever he throws at us."

"I can arrange transportation home for us and the prisoners," Elias intervenes. "However, that would exclude us from your fight with the president, as I doubt we'd return in time."

Portia spins to me, her hair flying behind her as she bends and clasps her hands in front of her. "Rae, I know I promised to be there—"

"No, don't apologize," I say, stopping her. "I know you need to do this. And you *are* helping us. I don't think I could live with myself if we ignored them to go after Charles. I'll feel better knowing you're there to save them."

She pulls me into a hug. "Thank you! Thank you!" she breathes, her relief palpable. Portia stands and points at Elias. "Call the others and tell them it's time to kick some butt. Get ready and meet me at my apartment in ten." Kellan cackles at her ordering Elias around, and Dane coughs behind his hand. "Oh!" She spins to Reid. "I didn't even ask! Would you mind dropping us off there? Rae kind of already said yes, and I know you're her half-brother and would do anything to help her, and so this is kind of like helping her by helping me—"

Reid's eyes flick to mine while she rambles on. I give him a small nod—my way of agreeing that I'm asking for this, too. He puts his hand up. "Only if you stop talking."

"Yes! Thank you!" she gushes, already breaking that request as she runs around the couch to the door. Portia somehow stops on a dime in her heels at the door. "Oh, I didn't tell you where to meet us. My apartment is next to Rae's. The one on the right. 'Kay, bye!"

Elias sighs. "If you'll excuse me, I have some phone calls to make.

Good luck with your fight. If you determine the resources you need, feel free to send me a message. I can't guarantee when I'll see it, but I will as soon as I can." He smiles at me and bows his head. "Be safe, Raegan. For Portia's sake and mine."

I can't help but return his smile. "Thank you, Elias. For everything." The words don't seem like enough after all he's done to help us, to help the Guild, when he didn't have to.

"Thank you," Aiden offers him just before he leaves.

Elias pauses, glancing over his shoulder with a polite smile. "Of course. Don't die, Adams. Once this is all over, you owe me quite a few favors. We have a lot of work to do, you and I." He leaves without further explanation, the rest of us stunned into a moment of silence.

"What the hell does that mean?" Dane demands.

"We'll worry about it after this is done. There are two locations left," Aiden points out.

"We need to save Tobias," I point out what feels like the obvious answer.

"We'd lose Charles," Reid states flatly. "This is a taunt. Choose him to end this—and lose innocents—or try to save them, and he'll go underground and come back to kill us later, once he's rebuilt GE stronger than before. We need to kill him now."

Dane pulls a document up on the screen. "Remember how I said I'd uploaded a bunch of data from that island Charles had me and the others on? Well, it had the schematics and location of the machine my sister warned us about. That location matches where Tobias is." He faces Aiden. "Charles inadvertently led us there, and we could destroy that machine before more items are made. Even after he's dead, his scientists could keep making those things. We have to destroy it before they realize GE is done for and try to move and hide it."

I didn't need convincing to go to the island where Tobias is, but Dane brings up a good point. That machine should get destroyed while we're there so some scientist doesn't decide to use it against us after Charles is dead.

"Say we take Charles out now," I begin slowly. "What happens to the rest of GE? There are still agents and scientists out there, testing and brainwashing gifted. Those don't go away just by killing Charles."

Aiden answers without hesitation as if this has always been the plan. "Once the leadership has been removed, Dane can isolate each of the facilities from communicating with one another. They won't know anyone is gone and will continue to operate as usual. That will give us time to clear them out one after another. It may take some time, even with Guild teams assisting, but we will get it done. And with no Charles, the corrupt cops and politicians won't have guidance from him any longer. We'll keep eyes on them, but they should settle down."

Kellan snorts. "After Charles and the board are gone, the rest are probably just scientists and grunts. They'll be easy to finish off. So how do we save our girl's half-brother *and* kill Charles?"

"We split up," Aiden replies smoothly, saying the one plan I didn't want. He doesn't continue right away, before he shares the details with us. "Reid will take the Guild members prepared to fight with me, Raegan, and Dane to Charles's location. Then he'll bring Jackson, Kellan, and Tinsley to rescue Tobias and destroy that machine."

Jackson's head snaps to Aiden. He's been silent this whole time, letting everyone else talk and plan. Now, he's eyeing Aiden with cold, dark eyes. "No."

"There's no goddamn way I'm not going with you. We don't split up, Aiden," Kellan snarls. Small scales break out along the back of his clenched hand.

Aiden nods. "That's exactly what Charles believes. If he sees you or hears that you're there, he'll assume the rest of us are as well. He'll have his guard down. That will give us time to sneak in and plant the anti-teleportation devices somewhere in that building."

"I'll plant them," Jackson counters, refusing to back down.

"No. I'm sending you two because I need you to be in and out. Let him see you, kill anyone who's a threat, but then make a mess and get out without him realizing it. Then meet us before the fight. I don't plan on fighting Charles without you."

"You're making them a distraction," Reid muses aloud.

"It'll be more than that," Aiden continues, his expression firm. "Charles loves his traps. It's about time he falls into one of ours."

CHAPTER THIRTY-NINE

JACKSON

REID TELEPORTS US TO the center of the room with Tobias. Scientists look up, startled, before my knives find their throats and chests.

In and out. That's what Aiden said.

The longer we take here, the more time they're with Charles without us.

Kellan starts barking orders before the dead scientists even hit the floor. "Tinsley—check the island for any other prisoners."

He turns to the Guild members we brought and points at Tobias, "Get him loose and outside. Wait for Tinsley and Reid to get him off the island before anyone starts trouble."

The members with us will continue fighting and causing a distraction after we're gone. It's our job to weed out any strong players and eliminate them before we go.

"Jack and Reid. The machine."

Nodding, I find the nearest stairwell and hop down each flight to the bottom. Dane guessed they'd have it hidden underground with security. Reid follows, unable to teleport until he can see where he's going. There's a hallway with more doors, but the first one has the most noise coming from it.

Reid peeks through the square window. "Found it." He vanishes, reappearing through the window on the other side. A few button pushes later, and the door slides open for me.

We're standing on a balcony overlooking a massive metal beast at the center of the room. Workers are busy moving barrels and boxes filled with jewelry from the machine to another area. Another group checks and polishes the jewelry before placing it back on the conveyor belt. The machine pumps out curves of metal in different directions, each with their own shape and style. Monitors and tubes are a tangled mess around it.

It's an easy target.

Reid teleports to their level and starts killing everyone.

I push off the ground and aim for what looks like the power cord, slashing it with one of my larger blades.

It keeps running.

A battery backup?

A quick search reveals a wide panel in the back. I carve into the groove with my knife and force it open. Then slice through the wires with one hand and yank them out with the other. Electricity arcs through the panel, singeing my hand. A wire zaps, and I push it against another. The smell of burning precedes a loud *pop*, and then the panel catches fire. I stoke it with just enough air to feed it until I know the fire will keep burning without it.

I move to the rest of the machine, ripping it apart piece by piece. Destroying whatever I find. Carving out holes and weak points on every side. Then I grab the first gallon of gasoline I'd brought with me to chuck into those holes and around the outside. I empty it and do the same with the second gallon.

"You're going to blow the whole building with that," Reid remarks, suddenly at my side and covering his nose with his arm. He's covered in blood, but breathing easily. Killing the others hardly took any effort. They were worker bees, though, not agents.

Smiling, I reply, "That's the plan." I pull a matchbox from my pocket. Thumb the box and extract three matches.

Reid shakes his head and disappears. His task of getting me here is finished, so now he needs to meet up with Tinsley to get Tobias to safety. All that's left is the distraction and clearing the rest of the island. Kellan should already be on the latter part. I'll join him as soon as this is done. And then...

Rejoin Raegan.

I'll be there soon, little one.

No one will ever understand the way we feel about each other. It's more than love, lust, or obsession. It's a sort of bond that transcends all that. A soul connection. Where our lives are so intertwined that my heart beats in time with hers. Her happiness is mine. Her rage, mine. I'm her weapon, her beast, her monster.

I'll kill her enemies wherever they are and then return to her side.

I won't let her fight Charles without me. We'll keep this quick.

In and out.

Hopping to the nearest piece of furniture, I send a burst of air under me to keep propelling me higher. To the top of a shelving unit. To the edge of the balcony railing.

That should do it.

Flick the matches.

Deep breath.

Sulfur invades my lungs, and I get a burst of adrenaline. Of excitement. The flames flicker from the vents pushing air in here, so I create a bubble around them. A partial vacuum with enough air for it to stay alive until it reaches the machine without blowing out on the fall.

I toss them down.

They land with a soft tap on the gasoline, and the fire spreads in an instant.

Three.

Two.

One.

The machine explodes, metal and parts flying everywhere as a plume of smoke bursts free—destroying the floor above it. I shield myself with air to toss aside anything flying toward me. Whatever hasn't been caught in the blast catches sparks and ignites. The fire spreads, devouring the building. There will be nothing left when it's finished.

Now that my task's complete, I jump-fly up the stairs to the surface, then to the edge of the open roof to seek out Kellan. Guild members are fighting agents in one area. They don't appear to need my help, so I move on. A few more fights, but no Kellan. I take off to the nearest palm tree. If he's found a strong agent, then I'll help kill him so we can leave.

I start throwing knives as I soar from roofs and treetops, thinning the herd of agents.

The air shifts behind me.

Throwing my hand out, I counter whatever's flying toward me with a cushion of air. A large stone. It bounces back, then pushes against my barrier again.

Not thrown, then. Controlled.

Someone gifted.

A man in shorts and a floral vacation shirt and bare feet stomps on the ground below me. Rocks fly from the ground in various-sized chunks, then zip into the sky.

At me.

A swift flip and kick knocks the first stone back to the ground, and then I draw a massive gust of wind behind the flying stones to shoot them past me. I drop to the sand in a crouch. Straightening, I cock my head to regard the man who looks more like a tourist than a fighter.

We knew they would still have strong agents left. Royce and Thorne weren't the only ones. Was this one sent to guard the machine, or was he purposefully placed here by Charles to make sure our visit was an extended one?

A smirk creeps onto my lips. I can't help it. The idea of facing someone who might be a challenge is exciting. It gets my cold blood pumping and makes me itch to fight.

But this isn't a battle for who's the strongest.

Raegan's waiting.

I start plucking knives from my hoodie. They fall and then rise around me, hovering like obedient birds of death. "Let's make this quick," I casually remark.

The man swings his hand down. "I'm here to make sure you stay."

The air ripples behind me, warning me of the incoming pile of rocks.

And also... a new arrival.

Thrusting wind around him, I lift and throw him toward the water. As soon as he loses focus, the rocks behind me drop where they are. I send my knives at him where he's fallen. He touches the sand and walls of stone erect around him in a protective formation. My knives clink and clatter against the rock to the sand.

Kellan races to the walls with a roar, his fist raised and his body already covered in scales. The horns are a new addition, as are the size of his feet and hands. Raegan mentioned his updated transformation, but this is the first time I'm seeing it.

He punches the wall, and it shatters. Another wall is there to take its place. He swings another fist at it. Breaks it. Again and again, the agent nearly trips backward to keep putting walls between them until Kellan picks up speed and snatches him before he can get the next slab between them. Kell throws him further inland. Giant leathery wings and a thick tail spring from his back as he turns, then launches himself at the guy.

The agent grits his teeth with his arms crossed in front of his face, angled stone spiking from the ground to protect him. He's on the defensive from Kell. My wind and knives don't have much effect on his stone. But Kellan easily breaks through it as if it's made of glass.

While he's keeping the man occupied, I retrieve my knives and then follow after them at a leisurely pace. Kellan doesn't need my help, but I'll be here to slice the man's throat if there's an opening.

Kell smashes the rock and grips the guy by his hair, then jumps into the air. Once they're at least twenty feet up, he chucks the agent at the ground. The second he touches dirt, though, it caves to his will and curves to cushion the impact.

I send some knives at him just in case they can slip through, but he puts a dome of rock around himself.

Kellan flies at the dome, knocking a hole through it. Rocks fly out of it. He bats them aside, then shoves through the opening, and the rest of the dome collapses, revealing what he'd done in that instant.

It takes a lot to surprise me.

Kellan shredding the man with his elongated, sharp claws is not what I expected.

But I have no complaints.

In and out.

Chapter Forty

RAEGAN

Charles is on an island that's a ferry ride away from the coast. The entire island is a town. There are no cars, one main road, and a grid of houses. The town hall is at its center.

The town mayor is Charles Whitman.

One guess who that is.

Reid drops us off behind a building at the dock, where we'll draw the least amount of attention at midday. Part of me wonders if these coordinates were a way to wear Reid out, too. He's been hopping around the world to get everyone in position. Charles may not want him available as an escape route, and he used this to drain his strength before the fight.

Silas peers around the corner of the building. "There's no one here."

The main Guild fighters are with us to help with any obstacles sneaking into town hall. Or to draw Charles's attention away until we're ready.

Fabian pops a handful of peanuts in his mouth. "Maybe it's their lunch break."

Aiden strides to Silas's side to look for himself. "We knew he'd be expecting us. If he's cleared out the town in advance, that only makes things easier."

"Harder to hide, though," Dane adds.

Sam moves next to me, offering his hand. He and Alice wanted to join us on this final mission. Even though they're both terrified of their dad, they're putting their trust in us that we'll defeat him this time. Like Harvey had. I won't let Charles get to them like he did to Harvey.

I'll keep them safe, Harvey.

Reid, these two, and the others are the start of a family I never thought I'd have. I'll protect them just as much as the other family I've built with the Guild.

Smiling at Sam, I take his hand and hike the cloth bag over my other shoulder.

"We aren't hiding. Only you and Raegan are... at least until the anti-teleportation devices are in place," Aiden explains again. I've got three in my bag, and Dane has the controller and the last one.

Alice places a trembling hand on Dane's shoulder. He looks at her, and she glares daggers at him. "Yeah, I'm scared. What did you expect?" She forces herself to take a deep breath. "Let's get this over with. Either I'm dead tonight or maybe I'll sleep without nightmares."

They disappear for everyone else but me and Sam.

Aiden's gaze passes over the group. Silas, Evie, Fabian, Gabe, Zedd, and a handful of others. Cassandra and Cibrina are safe at Hype, ready for whoever returns first. "Let's go."

He leads the way, strolling across the boardwalk to the single main road and then following it. Past the little shops. Into the quaint neighborhood.

"Wait!" one of the Guild members shouts, running to grab Aiden and yank him back. The ground explodes where he'd been standing.

Bullets rain fire overhead. Aiden molds a shield to cover the front of the group. "Get behind me!"

Fabian takes the rear, his long tongue flicking out to catch the hot lead and swallowing it down. Silas covers above us with a shield of thick vines. Leaves and tattered greenery fall around us with every bullet. His jaw tightens as he struggles to consistently replenish the vines.

Evie brushes her hand along a length of vine, and it rapidly expands to cover more area. She follows that vine across the rest until we're fully covered.

The Guild member who alerted us to the buried explosive is squatting with his hand on the ground. "The road is littered with bombs. We can't go this way."

I kneel. "Yes, we can." My gift surges through my veins, eager to be used when I call on it. I send it into the ground and spread it under the road. The second it comes into contact with a bomb, it detonates. My gift branches out, setting them off in waves.

When my gift doesn't find anymore, I reel it back in. "It's clear," I report, standing.

"Ah!" Silas curses. "Fire."

The green barrier becomes an instant oven that fills with smoke. Flames eat away at the vines faster than he can replace them, and we find ourselves surrounded by agents.

"Ah, we found you!" Gabriel exclaims to the agents.

Zedd steps forward.

"Silas, Evie, Gabe, Fabian, stay with Zedd. The rest of you come with us to the town hall," Aiden directs.

"Block your ears," Zedd tells us. We stuff the plugs into our ears. I help Sam with his to make sure they're in all the way. He starts singing. His words are dulled by the plugs, but the melody is there. My eyes start to droop.

Dane shakes my shoulder. "Don't try to listen. Come on."

Fuck.

That was way too easy to fall for.

Aiden's already running toward the town hall with the others. Dane, Alice, Sam, and I follow, dodging the holes in the ground from the explosions. The double doors to the town hall burst open, and agents flood out.

"Fuck's sake," Dane mutters when we come to a halt.

Aiden withdraws his whip sword. "Sneak in while we keep them busy."

"Aiden—" I start to argue, but he cuts me off.

"I'll meet you inside. Get those devices planted. Then stay hidden until I get there."

"We're leaving now," I tell him, since Dane and I are still invisible.

He nods, preparing his weapon.

Dane and I skirt around the others, keeping a wide berth from the agents, then circle back around them to the open doors.

We creep inside, careful to keep our steps soft and deliberate on the smooth tile. The entryway is massive, like entering a mansion rather than a public government building. Everything is white except for the black tile floor. The walls. The ceiling. Most of the furniture. And then a gigantic chandelier hangs from the two-story ceiling.

Two opposing curved staircases greet us straight ahead. Black double doors are on our left, and another two sets are on our right behind a long desk. The receptionist is speaking into her desk phone. "Yes, sir. They've been split into two groups." A pause. "No. Not yet." Another. "Yes, of course. I'll be right there." She walks to the stairs, her heels clicking with every step. I watch her until she disappears down the hallway to the right.

If I assume she was talking to Charles, that means he's up there.

The sound of a doorknob jiggling snaps my attention to the door on the left. Dane's trying to open it, but it's locked. Sam and I walk over. Dane looks up when he sees us, then steps back and motions to the door.

I grab the knob and dip into my gift, shooting it through to the other side without touching the door. The knob disintegrates, leaving a hole in its place. The door falls open.

A room packed with people stare wide-eyed with fear at the creaking door and no one there. Some are clinging to each other, while others stand protectively at the front. They creep closer to peek through us.

"What was that?"

"What do we do?"

"Don't move. He said we'd be safe if we stayed in this room."

"But they could see us now!"

"Hurry! Help me block the door to keep it shut."

The ones in front grab the bookcases in the corner and start dragging them to the door.

We hurry out before they close it again and start barricading themselves inside.

"They're humans," Alice explains softly. "The ones who live here."

They're hiding.

From us.

We're the bad guys to them.

Dane squeezes my arm and shakes his head.

Right. We don't have time to worry about that. The point is that we can't use that room for our plan. We'll need to find another one.

After we've planted the devices, Dane texts the location to Aiden, and we meet in the foyer. Alice and Sam slip away for their next part, leaving the three of us in the open.

"This better work." Dane scrubs his hand through his hair, nerves making him agitated. "How much time do we have?"

"Not long, I'm afraid." Charles's voice echoes from the second floor. He's standing at the railing between the two staircases. "I wondered what was taking you so long to find me, but it appears you're waiting for something." He lifts his hand. "Let me ruin that plan."

Aiden swings his whip sword. It slashes through the railing where he stands, and Charles is forced to teleport. "Run!"

Dane and I dash down a hallway with Aiden covering us. Charles appears in our way with a laugh. I shove Dane to turn down the hallway to the left. This building is a maze with hallways and rooms galore. It's easy to get lost in it if we don't pay attention.

Something yanks us back off our feet. It's like a magnet drawing us in, and I remember how Charles had done that just before striking with a blast that hit every inch of our bodies at once. Reaching for my gift, I send an uncontrolled burst through the ceiling.

It's nothing but drywall and plumbing. There's nothing heavy as I'd hoped for to hit Charles with as it cracks and falls apart, but burst pipes flood the hallway. He drops us without the attack, and once again, we're rushing to our feet in the growing puddles.

"I can't help but notice you're more focused on running away than fighting. What are you waiting for?"

He shows up in front of us again. I drag Dane to a stop, switching directions as fast as possible on wet tile flooring without slipping. Dane does exactly that, his shoes squealing from the fast spin, but Aiden's right there to catch his other side and help me bring us back to the last hallway we'd passed.

Aiden doesn't know how to get to the right room, and I think Dane's already messed up the directions because he's missed opportunities where we could have turned.

We made sure to walk every hall before picking a room, so we knew how to get here. No matter which hallway we take, I can get us there.

The only question is, if we head there now, is it too soon? We only get one chance.

We're coming up to the room.

Do I take it, or keep running us in circles for more time?

I grasp the doorknob.

And I'm thrown backward, crashing into another door and room. Dane and Aiden run in after me. Charles blocks the door and only exit in the room.

"I think I understand now. You were trying to lead me to that room there, weren't you?" He uses his gift to block the doorway with all the furniture in the room. "You shouldn't have been so obvious by not fighting." He smiles, confidence dripping from him, while he looks down on us as if he's won.

"You okay?" Dane asks me, helping me to my feet.

"Yeah. Hurry," I urge, keeping my voice low for only him.

Aiden's dark stare is focused on Charles, who stands between me and him. I move up to his side, and he places his arm across me to keep me from getting any closer to Charles.

"You're still children playing checkers when I've been playing chess all along," Charles continues, enjoying his boasting. He's so self-assured that he's won.

It'll feel great to bring him down a peg or two.

"That's funny," I call back, and his attention zeroes on me. Good. Dane's already moved behind Aiden and toward the wall. "Aiden said something similar about you."

Charles's brows shoot to his forehead. "Oh?" His blue eyes slide to Aiden. "And how is tha—"

A sharp beep followed by four shorter beeps interrupts him.

Dane smirks from where he's crouched beside the device controller along the wall.

While Charles is busy looking at Dane, Kellan leaps out of thin air with a gift-blocking cuff. Charles sees him and knocks him back with his gift.

Click.

Jackson secures the second gift-blocking cuff around Charles's wrist and then stabs him in the neck. Blood sprays. Charles grabs at his neck, his eyes wide as he stumbles back. He chokes, blood dribbling from his mouth.

I'm barely breathing.

Somehow, it all worked.

It worked.

Relief floods through me in a wave, my body trembling from the adrenaline as I watch Charles bleed out.

We're free.

Harvey's siblings are safe.

The Guild is safe.

His chokes subtly shift to a chuckle. A low, terrifying laugh that gets louder with every breath.

He's breathing.

My heartbeat slows, cold fingers of dread dragging down my spine.

Charles lowers his hand, and I stare—stunned—as dark bronze scales spread from the side of his healed neck to the back of his hands, and his skin darkens with Kellan's gift. He clutches Jackson's knife in his other hand.

No...

Charles's laughter is unhinged as he takes in our shock. He digs his fingers behind the cuff and then snaps it free. "Did you think I spent years learning how to manufacture these cuffs with his gift without considering someone might try to use them against me?" He tosses the useless and broken cuff to the floor.

Kellan bares his teeth, his jaw feathering as he witnesses his own gift blocking us from winning. Jackson has moved to my side, his expression serious.

As long as he has Kell's gift, he's untouchable. We've blocked his ability to dodge, but what does that matter if we can never break that shell?

We need time.

It was a flaw of Kellan's for a long time. What are the chances it's still a flaw for him? If his clock runs out on his gift, it makes him vulnerable again.

Will we all survive however long that takes?

My stomach twists, not liking those odds. Kellan can outlast him, I'm sure. But the rest of us?

Charles keeps talking. "His gift may work on me directly, but every cuff, every collar, and piece of jewelry… they have a piece of me in there to protect myself. To counteract his gift if it comes into contact with my blood." He smiles at Dane.

Something Reid once said comes back to me, and my blood chills.

"If he feels cornered when it comes to Dane, he'd rather kill him for the emotional blow it will have on Raegan than allow someone to threaten him."

He would rather kill him.

Dane's gift is the only thing that can stop him now.

I run.

"Dane!" I shout as Charles raises his hand.

Dane's airborne.

I throw myself at him.

If I can knock him down…

If I can at least get between him and Charles…

Something slams into my gut, wrenching the air from my lungs.

DANE

WE HAD HIM. WE fucking. Had. Him!

The plan worked. We cuffed him. Jackson brutally stabbed him in the goddamn jugular with blood everywhere. He should have been dead in seconds. It should have been over.

Instead, he's laughing and boasting.

I clench my fists, shifting from my kneeling position to one foot on the ground in preparation to move.

My gift works.

It's the only way.

His teleportation is blocked, so he can't just run away like he always did. I can grab him. Block his gift to give the others time to kill him. I just have to hold on long enough... no matter what he tries to get me off him.

"Dane!"

Raegan's voice snaps my attention to her. She's in my sights for a second, running toward me, before the room moves.

No, not the room.

My body races to Charles midair. There's fuck all I can do about it, as much as I try to lean away. To move in any way that might change my direction.

Raegan is suddenly in front of me, and I drop.

She screams.

Time slows.

I force my head up, but it's like moving through molasses. My skin prickles as if her pain is electric, flowing through me and jolting my heart to beat double-time. And then the world becomes clearer. Sharper.

I'm on my feet, but I don't remember standing. Charles is holding Raegan off the ground by her throat. His other hand grips Jack's knife, where it's buried in her side.

Blood pounds in my ears at a dizzying pace.

"No. No!" I jump toward them. His hands are busy. I can grab him. I can save her.

The others are already shouting at Charles like me, racing toward them.

Something shoves me back so hard I fly off my feet and crash to the floor yards away. I blink away the disorientation. What did I hit? Kellan's lunging at them again, and I see him *bounce* off something a few feet from Charles.

But nothing's there.

Jackson's knives find the same invisible wall that throws them right back at us. He controls them before they do, but they're useless. He tries his wind. Aiden throws his shoulder into it and is thrown back.

"Thank you for volunteering, Raegan. You should have died a long time ago, so it's only fitting you die first." Charles twists the knife, smiling as Raegan's screams intensify. The sound shatters something in me.

"Stop. DON'T FUCKING HURT HER!" I run at them even though I know I can't get close. It doesn't matter. I won't stop trying. If there's even a second that one of us can get in, we have to find it. I'm repelled back. All the air knocks from my lungs at the impact. I wheeze and force myself to my side. To my feet.

I charge them again.

And again.

Tears flow freely down my face as I scream at him to stop. As I call her name. She doesn't respond. Not to me. Not to the others. Her eyes are closed, and blood leaks from her lips.

"Don't give up, Rae! Don't die. Please! Stay with us! Rae! *Rae!*"

Each time she doesn't answer, the broken pieces crack a little more like an icepick is hammering into my chest.

She can't die. She can't. I can't live without her. She's the only one who makes me feel whole. The only person I want to spend the rest of my life with. She deserves to live more than any of us. She deserves to live, dammit!

I slam my fist against the invisible barrier with my gift active, hoping it'll have some sort of effect. I'm thrown away again. I think I heard something snap with one of the falls, but I can't feel any pain. There is nothing but the sheer terror of watching Charles kill Raegan before our eyes.

"I'm going to squeeze the life out of you to make sure you're dead this time," Charles continues, his voice still businesslike as he strangles his daughter. "Do you hear them? I think your death will break them. Killing you will end this whole thing."

Raegan doesn't respond. She doesn't even look like she's breathing anymore. She's so very, very still.

Kellan dives at them from above, somehow sprouting wings and looking even more draconic than before. He's bellowing for Raegan to answer him. To fight.

Jackson's white as a ghost as he uses his gift to shove against the invisible barrier.

Aiden tries dropping the ceiling on him by slicing it up, but the fallen pieces are repelled from them just like us.

Alice and Sam are curled together in the corner, no longer invisible as they tremble and cling to one another and watch in terror.

Charles suddenly stiffens. He glances over his shoulder at Jack, then rips the blade out of Raegan. Blood steadily pours from her wound. He aims it like he's going to stab her other side, and then he relaxes. He takes a slow breath. "Take my oxygen again, and I'll fill her with holes before you can finish it."

Jackson's panting as if he's running out of air himself. Or maybe from the effort of holding himself against Charles's gift as he tries to push through.

"Rae! Rae, please! Open your eyes!" I activate my gift again, concentrating it on my hand as I approach the barrier. *Please, work. Cancel it.* I force my will over the single spot where my hand connects to his power.

This time, I'm not thrown backward.

I press harder, gritting my teeth as it pushes back at me.

Something cracks.

"Fight him!" Kellan snarls.

"Raegan!" Aiden and Jack's voices join in.

Chapter Forty-Two

RAEGAN

It's cold. And dark.

Am I still in the water tank? Was everything just a dream?

No. There's too much pain.

It's everywhere, seeping through my veins until I'm burning with it. I'm nothing more than a vessel for pain.

I'm saturated in it.

As if I'm floating in an ocean of pain and it's absorbing through my skin, infusing my lungs, my gut.

My stomach.

That's where I feel it the most.

So much pain.

Pain.

Pain.

"—gan!"

A fire burning the cold.

A livewire of heat threading through my limbs, pooling in my stomach.

Aching.

Begging.

To be used.

"Rae!"

"Fight him!"

"Raegan!"

"Raegan."

As my body warms, the distant voices become clearer. More familiar.

Dane. Kellan. Aiden. Jackson.

Consciousness comes rushing back like a speed train. Air, on the other hand, doesn't.

My hands wrap around whatever's cutting off my air on instinct, trying to pull them away as I drag my eyes open.

Charles.

We're still fighting him.

The men who mean everything to me are calling my name. Their voices are strained or rough with emotion.

But I'm also glad it's me and not one of them in my place.

I won't give up.

I promised I wouldn't die.

I won't lose.

I've barely used my gift in this fight. There's no way I'm out of it yet.

It hardly takes anything to draw it out; it's as if my gift's been simmering beneath the surface, ready and waiting to be let loose. Red lightning arcs and scatters over Charles's scales. It strikes him in the chest. The arm. The head. His side.

He doesn't budge from where he's standing.

But his grip loosens enough that I can breathe again.

I suck down air, focusing my gift on him to keep him distracted while I regain all the oxygen I lost. White-hot pain sears through my gut when I take too deep a breath, and I'm left panting and shaking.

"You can't hurt me," Charles reminds me, but I see otherwise.

My lightning doesn't penetrate his scales, but it still hurts. He's trying to hide it, but I can see the tiny flinches. The way he shifts himself with discomfort when it crosses his thickened skin.

It hurts him, but it's not enough to beat him.

Especially not in my current state. Not while I'm dizzy from blood loss. Or in so much pain I'm almost numb.

The others don't stop attacking the invisible barrier he has up between us and them. I see them repelled off their feet, then race back to try again. Their attacks are struck back just as much. All except Dane, who's holding his ground against the barrier somehow, his white light a single flame as it slowly forces a hand-shaped hole through.

Charles squeezes my throat again, and I gasp, digging my nails against his scales.

Fuck.

Think.

How can I beat him?

So much pain...

Darkness edges my vision. It's a sweet promise to return to nothingness. That numb, weightless feeling I'd once had in the water tank. There would be no pain if I give in to it.

No. I promised...

They need me.

And I need them.

I'm a world breaker.

Queen of destruction.

I'm Raegan of Ruin. And I won't go down without giving him my all.

I've fought through pain before. This is no different.

I draw out all of my gift. Everything I have, I release it.

My power erupts in a powerful blast. Everyone but Charles and I are slammed into the walls. Red lightning scores the room in jagged strikes that tear it apart. Chunks of ceiling falls. Whatever furniture was in the room disintegrates. The flooring cracks and turns to ash wherever lightning touches.

Charles chuckles. "You're going to kill yourself and all your friends in here before you can hurt me. And I'll walk out of here without a scratch."

More.

More wasn't the answer last time.

What else?

Black dots my vision.

Memories flash before my eyes, the past intermingling with the present.

Times on the island with the guys.

Seeing them again for the first time.

Thanking them for rescuing me from Gordon.

Them desperately trying to reach me while Charles has me in his grasp.

Love confessions.

Fun times with the Guild.

With Portia. Elias.

Hearing their voices as Charles steals the last bit of air.

Eating breakfast together with them at the dining table in the

Loft.

Training together.

Dane's gift making progress against his barrier like a beacon of light, penetrating Charles's gift. Kind of like...

Jackson telling me about his new move on the balcony.

Wait. Go back.

"I compress it..."

"It's the same amount of force contained in a more precise attack."

I don't have any time to think about it.

I let instinct take over to do it. Take all the power I have, everything I've released, and then squish it down. Compress that same power into something small. The lightning stops, and I can feel my gift disappearing from my extremities as I draw it tighter and tighter into a ball in my chest. I concentrate it down, down, down... until not a flicker of my gift is still visible.

But I can feel it.

All that power... all that force...

It's here in this tiny ball.

I send it to my hand.

My index finger.

And I point it at his chest.

I can't see anymore. I'm barely conscious, praying that I aim for his heart. As soon as my fingertip brushes against something, I let it go.

It's like pulling a trigger on a gun.

One second, the power is a massive energy at the tip of my finger, and the next, it fires and vanishes.

There's nothing left.

No gift.

And no air.

KELLAN

FOR ALL MY NEWFOUND strength, it does nothing against the force surrounding Charles and Raegan. Jackson struggles against that pressure as if he might somehow break through, and I do the same on the other side. No amount of slamming into it had any effect, so if we can find a way to meet its pressure with our own... maybe make it collapse...

Red lightning streaks across my vision, and I stop breathing.

"Raegan!" I roar, relief making me weightless when I see her eyes open. When I see her *fight*. It re-energizes my aching muscles from colliding with this barrier and the floor over and over again.

Her lightning strikes Charles in powerful, blinding blows. I can hardly see them through it.

I'm fucking coming, beautiful.

I ram into the barrier and get instantly repelled. It uses the same force we throw at it to send back at us. When I return, I lean into it, slashing my claws through it and meeting firm resistance.

Power explodes from Raegan and Charles without warning, slamming me into a wall. It crumbles beneath me, wood snapping and drywall collapsing like a wet paper towel.

My ears ring from the impact, and I shake my head to get it to knock off as I get my bearings. I'm in the next room.

Hope swells in my chest, almost making me giddy.

She's doing it. This was her gift. Her power.

I'd know it anywhere.

That blast was her attacking him with everything. Even if it doesn't breach his scales, it had to have broken that barrier between us and them.

I shove upright and race to the hole I made between the two rooms. My claws slash at the hanging drywall, clearing a larger space for me to fit through.

Cursing at the damn wiring in my way, I rip it all down and push through, then freeze.

No...

Where did it all go? Her gift... it's... gone.

Charles is still smiling. The muscles in his forearm are taut as he squeezes her throat.

And Raegan...

There's no sign of her gift.

No lightning.

Not even a reddish glow.

She reaches a hand toward his chest, but there's no strength to it, like a last-ditch effort to reach for something, before her hand drops.

"No!" I lunge forward. I'm only three steps in when a flash of crimson catches my attention, rooting me to my spot. Charles's eyes widen. Red cracks spread from his chest, breaking through his skin... his scales. It spreads up his neck, down his arms, and onto his torso. Blood tears streak down his face.

He drops her.

She lands on a cushion of air, then flies to Jackson.

I almost run to her. But I have to make sure this bastard is dead. I stalk to his body where he's collapsed on the ground. Raegan's gift is still making a mess of him, wreaking havoc inside too quickly for him to regenerate. But he still could.

Aiden appears beside me and thrusts his blade through one of the red cracks in his neck, pinning him to the floor. "Take his head," he demands.

I don't hesitate.

I use that crack in his armor to split his head from his body in a clean swipe. And I don't stop there. Every crack is a weak point I can rip through. Tear to pieces. Shred him until he's unrecognizable as once being human. At some point, the scales are completely gone, and he's nothing more than a pound of flesh and shredded organs.

I'm gasping for air when I'm finally done, my chest heaving as I stand there, covered in his blood and still not feeling satisfied.

"She's lost too much blood!" Dane cries out, and my heart tanks.

No.

We won.

"Keep feeding her air!" Aiden snaps at Jackson, his hands linked over top of one another as he does compressions.

Dane grabs her hand, holding it to his chest and rubbing his other hand up and down her arm. "Wake up. Please, Rae," he chokes out. "You won. You beat him. So *breathe*. Come back."

I fall to my knees next to him. She's lying on the floor, eyes closed, as Jackson guides air into her lungs and Aiden jerks with every thrust of his hands. The stomach wound is nasty, but it isn't leaking blood. Jack must be blocking it, but how much had she already lost? Her throat is mottled in nasty shades of black and purple that have me seeing red. But there's no one left to attack.

Gently gripping her leg, I bow my head over her. "Don't give up, beautiful. Fight. Don't let go. We're all here waiting for you. So please. Open your eyes."

"Come on, come on!" Dane pleads in a cracked voice.

Jackson's face is ashen as he presses his forehead to hers. He keeps his hand hovering over her mouth, pushing air into her lungs to make sure her body still has the oxygen it needs to survive.

"Go find Reid," Aiden commands. "Get Cassandra. Now!"

Yes.

Reid should be on this island somewhere still.

Dane and I storm the door. All the furniture is ash, while black soot streaks the door. I kick it down, and Dane runs through it to the hallway on the left.

Alice and Sam stand behind me. "We'll look for him too!" she declares. They go left as well, and I take the hallway straight ahead.

"Reid!" I bellow. "Reid!"

Goddamn it. He could be anywhere on this island.

Don't die. Whatever you do, don't. Die.

I clench my jaw to restrain the panic that has my heart thrashing in my chest. That makes it difficult to breathe. To think clearly.

Please don't die, beautiful. Hold on.

I keep running. I keep searching for Reid, shouting his name until my voice grows hoarse. Until every muscle in my body quivers from exhaustion.

But I don't stop.

I'll never stop.

I'll never let go.

CHAPTER FORTY-FOUR

RAEGAN

"—SAID NO, BUT YOUR men have recognized me as your best friend and number one person. If they didn't let me in to see you, there might've been some trouble with Elias and the others because I've been going stir crazy after Cassandra told me what she healed. If Kellan didn't swear to me that he ripped Charles's head off for stabbing you like that, I'd be giving your guys a piece of my mind."

Portia's voice reaches me in the darkness. A colorful light that beckons me to return to consciousness.

"Stop talking," Dane orders without any heat. Something gently strokes my cheek. "Rae? Can you hear me?"

Heat encompasses one side of my body, and the smell of citrus fills my nose when I breathe deeply. I peel my eyes open, sleep still weighing them down.

"Rae! She heard me!" Portia exclaims, bouncing forward, and entering my view.

Dane tucks hair behind my ear, his amber gaze warm. "How do you feel?"

I open my mouth, and it feels like sandpaper. "Thirsty," I gasp.

Something tugs on my arm when I try to move it, and I frown at the tubes attached to it. Dane is lying beside me in bed while Portia stands on the other side with a bright smile.

"You're all sorts of hooked up right now," she explains. "I'll call Elias to let him know you're awake so we can get you out of this stuff." She walks past Jackson to the bathroom.

He and Dane help me sit up before Jack brings a cup of water to my lips. I greedily gulp it down, gasping once it's empty.

The bedroom door—as I've now realized we're in my apartment at Hype—flies open with Aiden and then Kellan barreling through.

"Don't crowd her—" Aiden starts, but Kell doesn't hesitate to wrap me in his thick, muscular arms. He towers over Dane, engulfing my upper half while Dane cusses up a storm about how close his dick is to him.

Kell ignores him, crushing me to his chest. "You did it again. You scared the fuck outta me and I'm getting bitey as hell over it." He releases me, his mouth crashing into mine. His hands tangle into my hair, gripping me like he's afraid I'll disappear. I grab his arms—the only part I can reach with the tubes and wires linked to me—and kiss him back, my chest expanding as I'm filled with his love for me.

I'm breathless when he breaks away, his lips still hovering close to mine as he whispers, "Thank you for not letting go, beautiful. For staying with us."

He's close enough now that I run my fingers over his beard. "I have too much to live for to let go so easily."

Kellan grins and kisses me again before he's shoved away.

"At least let me get out of the way first," Dane snaps. He faces me again and kisses my temple. "Are you hungry? I'll make you whatever you want to eat."

My stomach growls at the promise of food. "I'm starving," I admit. "Whatever's quickest to make would be great."

He nods. "A smorgasbord of breakfast, coming right up." Dane squeezes my hand and slides from the bed.

"Our doctor and Cassandra are on their way up with Elias," Portia announces from the bathroom doorway. "I'll let them in."

Jackson sits at the edge of the bed, taking my hand and holding the back of it to his lips. He closes his eyes and inhales deeply. When his eyes open, they're bleeding with dark obsession and violence. I scared him again, too, and he's fighting the need to let it out through bloodshed. There will be plenty of time for that soon.

"He's dead?"

"He's dead," Aiden confirms first, standing at my other side. "Kellan tore him to pieces, and we burned them to the bone."

Thank fuck.

I close my eyes, breathing through my nose.

He's dead.

The leader of Gifted Enterprise, who has haunted us for most of our lives, is dead.

Their business front is destroyed.

Their board is dead.

We did it. And we survived.

I'm grateful I'm still in bed as my body shakes with relief. I cover my face as emotion builds behind my eyes, and I draw a shuddering breath.

The bed dips on Aiden's side, and I'm carefully pulled against him. "You did it," he murmurs in his smooth, cognac voice. "It's over."

I grip his soft shirt with my free hand and let a single tear fall.

Jackson crowds my other side until I'm trapped between them, hidden from the world as I let it all go.

It takes a week of recovery before Elias arrives unannounced with a demand. "Without Charles around to back the corrupted officials, my legal team had the court order seizing the Tower thrown out. Law enforcement has been forced to leave the premises effective immediately, and we retain full control over the building moving forward." He fixes his tie and clears his throat. "With that now settled, please go home."

He leaves without another word, and Kellan roars with laughter. "Did he just tell us to get the fuck out?"

"Sure sounds like it," Dane mutters.

Jackson hums into my hair. His arm is slung over my shoulders as I lean into him on the couch.

Aiden stands from his chair. "He's right. We've overstayed our welcome and I, for one, am looking forward to going home." He holds his phone to his ear, most likely calling Cibrina. "Tell everyone to pack their things. We're returning to the Tower in two hours."

"What about Alice and the others?" I ask, worrying where they'll go now that Charles is dead. I've been visiting them since my energy returned two days ago, but we'd always avoided the topic of what was next for them after a small Guild team rescued their mother and unborn sibling and brought them back here. We've been content in this bubble of our win while living at Hype to talk about plans for the future.

"There are apartments available in the Tower if they'd like to come with us," Aiden replies easily.

I nod, pushing to my feet. "I should go talk to them. And Portia, to let her know we're leaving."

Dane stands. "I'll come with you to make sure Alice doesn't start shit."

I don't bother telling him that he's the only one she usually gets an attitude with now. They're already like bickering siblings, and something about that makes me happy.

We walk to the apartment they all share. Elias offered the last two units for them to split, but they're all so used to sleeping on floors that they felt more comfortable sticking together.

One of my half-siblings—Wendy—answers the door after I knock. "Hey," she greets with a smile, stepping aside so we can enter.

"I have some news," I share with her and the room. Alice is preoccupied staring at whatever show is on with Michael and Ben. Sam is tucked away on a chair in the corner with his noise-canceling headphones while reading a book. Karl, Tobias, and Sophie are sitting together on the kitchen stools, and Lance and Brinley are seated on the floor playing a card game.

The room is filled with white-blonde heads and blue eyes, apart from Alice, Ben, and Brinley, who share Charles's black hair like Reid.

When Sam is still preoccupied, I stride over and lightly tap his book. He looks up and catches the rest of the room watching us. His face flames as he drags the headphones down around his neck.

"It's okay, I just wanted you to hear this, too," I murmur softly, just for him. Then, in a louder voice, I address my family. "The Guild is going home to the Tower. It's a big skyscraper with plenty of room for all you, if you'd like to come with us."

"What are we supposed to do?" Wendy asks from the door, crossing her arms. She's the same age as me, part of the older half of brothers and sisters.

"That's up to you." The room fills with chatter, the consensus a growing concern with what's expected of them next. "If you want to use the Tower to take more time and figure out what you want to do now, then you can. If you want to join the Guild with us and use your gifts as a job, to contribute to society in a good way, then you can do that, too. Or if you want to leave and explore the world, then no one will stop you. I'll see if we can put some money together to help you get started, at least."

Dane gives me a look. I don't know what the Guild's financial status is now that Charles is gone, but I'll work as many jobs as I can to make enough so they can afford to live for a little while at least. They deserve to see more of the world now that they have the freedom to do and go where they want.

"What about GE?" Karl, the oldest, inquires. "They're still out there."

"We're going to hunt them down until there's nothing left," I reply. "You don't have to worry about them."

"I'm not. I want to help," he states coolly. "If that's part of what your Guild is doing, then I'll join it."

I try to keep my happiness contained that he might want to stay. "You don't have to join the Guild to help us get rid of GE. You could stay at the Tower with us to help, and then do what you want after."

Sam grasps my wrist. He shows me a message he typed on his phone screen.

I want to join.

I dip my chin, unable to stop the smile that takes over. "Of course. You're already part of the team."

"That better include me, too," Alice chimes in, jutting her chin out and crossing her arms. "I saved your asses more than he did."

"That's funny," Dane slides in with a taunting smirk. "Because I remember you blowing things up that were only supposed to be on fire and then giving away our position on those missions."

Alice jumps from the couch. "None of those were my fault, and you know it! Tell them how I'm the real MVP. You wouldn't have won without me."

Dane scoffs. "We all know that title belongs to Rae."

"Guys. There are no titles," I reason, then add under my breath, "But if there was, it goes to Cassandra."

They both whip their heads to look at me incredulously. Apparently, I didn't say it quiet enough.

I shrug. "It's the truth. *Anyway*," I emphasize, getting us back on track. "If you are coming with us to the Guild, even if it's just to stay until you figure things out, meet us downstairs in an hour and a half with whatever you have."

Less than a week later, a Guild strike team is gathered in the gym. We're decked out in protective gear and armed with weapons, although most of us don't need them. They're merely there for back-up.

The hunt for every last vestige of Gifted Enterprise starts today.

Our team has nearly tripled in size since the days of our island raids. Aside from the usual Guild crew, half of my siblings and another dozen Pits fighters have joined us.

Only the older siblings are joining these missions: Karl, Sam, Wendy, Michael, and Alice. Tobias is staying at the Tower with the younger four.

Aiden steps forward, drawing everyone's attention. "After we killed Charles, Dane gained access to more of the GE locations still operating around the world. He's been covering operational messages to those sites to keep them unaware of their president's death. While they should be unprepared for our arrival, that does not mean they are unequipped to fight. Be on your guard and don't go anywhere alone. Team up. And don't damage the computers. Dane will be pulling data off their servers to search for other locations, and then he'll wipe them.

"We'll be taking down a site a day. This strike team will split into three groups: rescue, data extraction, and offense. It is the rescue team's job to get any prisoners to safety, the data extraction team to pull the information Dane needs, and offense will eliminate GE employees and destroy the facility once the first two teams are clear."

Aiden continues with the explanation of how we'll travel there for the newbies who didn't island hop with us before. Evie waves when he explains her gift and the tub that we'll all get in, and then he nods at Reid as he covers the potential side effects of the teleport.

Once he's finished, he surveys the room. "Any questions?"

No one speaks up.

"Let's go hunt."

EPILOGUE

AIDEN

NINE MONTHS LATER

The Guild Hall is alive with merriment for the holiday season. Garlands and wreaths dress the large beams overhead and spiral the thick columns with twinkling lights. The hidden stage is open and equally decorated while members fill the tables closest to it. If they aren't singing along or shouting words of encouragement to whoever's performing, they're talking and laughing with one another.

Aside from the holiday, there's a bigger moment we're all celebrating today.

Yesterday, we took down the last Gifted Enterprise facility.

After Dane compiled locations from Charles's computer, we've been taking them down one by one. Our Guild has now doubled in its membership from rescued gifted who didn't want to go home or wanted to help us save others.

Now we can finally celebrate the complete annihilation of GE.

And remember those who we lost in the fight.

We've put up a memorial wall in the Hall with pictures of everyone who gave their lives for this. Who sacrificed everything to free gifted from GE and the fear of being hunted.

The ache in my chest when I think of them hasn't faded—even nine months later.

"Don't you look morose on this happy occasion," Cibrina teases lightly as she strolls to my side with a celebratory glass of champagne. She hardly consumes alcohol, so seeing her with the flute is a surprise.

I drink my bourbon. "My thoughts wandered away on me."

Cibrina smiles at the tables singing along with Kellan, who's on the stage belting out "Blue Christmas" in his deep voice. "Maybe you should join them. Sing along and forget any lingering troubles for a while. You deserve the break."

"We all do," I counter.

She nods. "Of course. But you and I both know that our break won't be for very long. You should enjoy it while it lasts."

I take another drink, then tap my finger on the glass. It's a conversation we've had before that we've pushed to the side in favor of focusing on GE. But now that they're gone, there's nothing stopping us from turning our attention to it.

Avoiding it would be foolish.

It's only a matter of time before people learn of our existence.

The ratio of gifted to norms is increasing exponentially with every generation. It makes me wonder if one day everyone will be born with some sort of gift. And with how powerful some of them already are today, what kind of future will they have if that kind of power goes to someone who isn't good?

And with Charles dead, that protection across media and governments to keep our secret is gone with him. Elias has been helping in our efforts to remove news stories and videos posted online that expose gifted individuals who weren't careful enough. It's become a whole department and floor in the Tower.

As much as I hope the reveal doesn't happen in our lifetime, we need to prepare for it.

My gaze falls on Raegan in the front row, cheering on Kellan with Dane on one side and Portia and her guys on the other. Reid, Tinsley, Alice, and Sam are seated at the same table while the rest of Raegan's siblings are at the next table over. Evie and the other lead members are at the table to her left. Mallory sits with them, and her four-month-old puppy—that Raegan suckered me into—is curled on her lap.

Raegan's buffered by family—chosen and related by blood. This was what I wanted for her.

My biggest worry now is how the public would perceive her gift if it ever came out. And others like us whose powers might be considered too dangerous.

Even if the gifted community is outed, I have to keep her safe.

We will keep her safe.

"You're right. Let's enjoy tonight. We can talk about the future tomorrow," I reply.

Elias has already scheduled a meeting with me after the holidays to discuss how I'm supposedly repaying all his favors.

"Any word on Detective Unger?" I inquire.

"Still missing." Cibrina offers me a consoling smile.

The murder investigation has essentially dropped since Detective Unger disappeared not long after I'd been rumored to have died. Jackson was prepared to wear Thorne's face and be seen by the cameras to get me out of it, but thankfully, it didn't need to go that far. I told him I'd rather Dane fake some evidence than try that plan, but he shrugged and said he'd keep it on ice just in case.

So long as it's not in one of our freezers, I don't care.

The tax audit came back clean with a nominal amount that had to be paid. Dane removed all the damaging articles and posts about the Guild, and we've been busier than ever. The frozen offshore account was confiscated, unfortunately, but we'll be making that money back over the next year or so. Now that income is flowing in, it's less of a concern. That had always been backup money anyway.

"I know that's not the way you wanted the issue resolved, but him missing is better than having to prove Thorne's alive," Cibrina continues.

"I'd rather be done with it so it doesn't loom over us like a dark cloud."

She smiles. "I understand. Now go to Raegan and enjoy yourself tonight. I'll keep an eye on any over-exuberant shenanigans with Penn and Quinn. Take the night off. Sing something for us," she adds, laughter sparkling in her eyes.

I'd rather make Raegan sing for me in other ways, but I keep that thought to myself.

I raise my glass to her. "Thank you. Make sure you enjoy the party, too."

Her glass clinks with mine. "I always do."

EXTENDED EPILOGUE

Raegan

"It's bubbling. Is it supposed to be bubbling?" I ask Dane, concerned I'm already screwing up my assigned task.

Kellan dips a finger into the sticky substance and licks it clean. "Tastes good to me."

Dane smacks him over the head with a spatula. "Don't stick your finger in the food we're all going to be eating. Did you even wash your hands? Get out of the kitchen!"

Smiling at the two bickering behind me, I stir the liquid as I'd been directed to. Watch it. Stir it. Don't let it burn.

Kell bumps into me, knocking me forward.

A swift breeze pushes me back before I fall onto the hot metal pot.

"Rae! What the fuck, Kell? This is why you're banned from the kitchen!" Dane pulls me away from the stove to look me over.

Kellan steps protectively between me and the stove as if it's the one at fault. "Shit, beautiful. I forgot how small Old Red's kitchen was. Are you hurt?"

I swat him away. "I'm fine. Now watch out so I can get back to stirring before I ruin it."

Kell tries to stay by my side, but Aiden pins him with a dark stare. "Out."

He shrugs, turning to the cabinet and pulling out some liquor. "I'll make us some drinks. What do you want with our festive meal, beautiful?" He gathers them between his fingers in his two large hands, strolling around the island to the open side before setting them down.

Aiden's sitting at the other end of the island peeling and slicing apples into a bowl while Jackson's perched in the middle of the island with one foot up and the other dangling. Whenever Aiden gets distracted by us, he uses his gift to float an apple slice to himself. I'm still waiting for Aiden to realize half of his work has been eaten. He would have been done already if not for Jackson's snacking.

"I'll have whatever you're making," I answer Kellan.

Dane turns the fire down on my burner. "Let it simmer for another couple of minutes and then take it off the heat."

I nod, making note of the time so I don't mess it up. When he said he was making a big dinner for tonight, I asked if I could help. It's the perfect night at Old Red with holiday music playing in the background, white string lights hanging along the brick walls, and a tree in the corner with small presents underneath. A fire plays on repeat on the television to add the crackle and ambiance without the heat. After dinner, we'll open the presents and relax for the night.

It's our first night back at Old Red since Dane and a few Guild members helped renovate it. The dorm-style rooms are gone, replaced with larger rooms for each of us with attached bathrooms. My bedroom is the largest with a bed big enough for the five of us. The truck bays have all of Kellan's project cars and Dane's bike. Aiden's still shopping for a new car since he sold his Aston Martin. I'm also in the market for a car since Kell's been giving me more driving lessons. We're going to find one that I can use for getting around and in street races.

I turn off the burner and shift the pot back.

"You finished?" Kellan hands me a drink. It tastes like peppermint and cream.

"Mm, this is delicious," I moan.

He grins. "Good. Get your sexy ass into the living room then, and we can sing and dance to some music before food's ready."

I turn to Dane, but he answers without me having to say the words. "I've got the rest. Go dance." He starts to wave me off, then pauses. "Wait. Come here." Dane hooks his fingers into the tie at the back of the apron, tugging me back. He pulls me into a kiss, his hand cupping my face as he presses his warm mouth against mine.

I sink into him, gripping his shirt as my heart flip-flops in my chest.

He releases me with a smirk, and I realize he'd untied and removed my apron. He points to the words on the front: Kiss the Cook. He licks his lips, tasting me. "Go before I decide I'd rather eat you."

Kellan laughs and smacks me playfully on the ass to get me moving to the living room.

I push him back, laughing and dancing as I move backward to the center of the living area. He pushes the low table out of my way, giving me more floor to work with as I start to move with the music. I'm wearing a sexy red velvet dress that flares into a short skirt rimmed with white fluff. It moves when I sway my hips. Shimmies with me.

Kellan cheers me on from the side while the other three's eyes are locked on me. Their attention feels like heat from the sun. Warm and burning at the same time. Like my heart catches fire and makes my chest ache with how much I love them. And how much I feel loved by them.

This is everything I've ever wanted and more.

I finish my drink before long, then call out a bathroom break. My body's buzzing between the alcohol and music that Kellan turned up so loud, I could feel it vibrating through me like at the clubs.

The bathroom door bursts open as I'm washing my hands, and Dane stands there, his amber eyes molten as they stick to me like honey. He's on me in seconds. Kissing me. Holding me in his arms.

I melt into him, grasping at his shirt and pressing my body to his. When I find the stiff outline of his dick in his jeans, I rub against it. Warmth pulses in my chest, slithering to my core.

His hands run down the back of my dress to my bare thighs, lifting me in one smooth motion to straddle him. He turns us, gently setting me on the bathroom counter and pushing my back to the mirror. I recently got my phoenix tattoo redone over my scars, so he's careful with the bandages as he moves me around.

I moan into his lips, using my heels to lock him in place as I grind against him.

"Fuck. I need you, babe." Dane kisses down my neck, his hot tongue swiping my collarbone. He pushes my underwear aside, sinking a finger—and then two—inside when he feels how wet I am.

My head drops back and smacks the mirror, but I'm too busy rocking over his fingers to give a shit. "Yes!"

Dane removes his belt in a frenzy, whipping it out and then yanking his pants undone with one hand. All while he continues to kiss and lick my skin. Tasting me. Savoring me. He scoops my breasts free of the dress, piling them on top so they're lifted and exposed. He sucks a nipple into his mouth while shoving his pants and briefs down, kicking them out of his way.

I bury my hands in his hair, holding him to my chest as I roll my hips and gasp at the building pleasure. Pleasure coils in my lower abdomen, tugging and urgent with every swipe of his tongue and slow thrust of his fingers.

Then they disappear, but I'm empty for only a second before he slides his dick into my pussy with a loud groan. "Fuuuuckk. Goddammit, Rae. You feel. So. Fucking. Good," he grunts between thrusts, his hands gripping my thighs and golden-brown eyes drinking me in.

My mouth parts, helping me to breathe through every strike of his dick. My face is flushed from the alcohol and pleasure combined as I watch him watching me. As desire collides with a base need to feel him inside of me.

Before long, I'm calling his name through a climax, white-knuckling the counter as ecstasy pulses through me. My orgasm triggers his, and he holds me tight. Even when his muscles grow slack, he doesn't let me go. He presses his lips to mine. Again. And again. "I love you, Rae. I love you so fucking much."

"I love you too," I murmur softly, stroking the side of his face.

A voice clears.

We both look at the open door.

The other three are standing in my bedroom, watching.

"Where was our invite?" Kellan drawls, his grin feral as he takes in my disheveled appearance.

"I took your food out of the oven when the timer went off," Aiden states, pulling his tie loose. "The apple pie is in the oven. Make sure you take it out when it's done."

Dane untangles himself from me, then helps me to my feet. He plants another soft kiss to my lips. "I'll go finish dinner."

Jackson cocks his head, a feral smile curving his lips.

My heart pounds with excitement as the three of them watch me hungrily, waiting for me to make the first move.

Slowly, I slide the dress from my shoulders. Down my hips until it falls to the floor. My underwear is next, leaving me naked except for my heels. I remember how much Kellan liked me in those.

"Come and get me."

ACKNOWLEDGEMENTS

Thank you first and foremost to my readers.

To the ones who have been with me since Ravage first released, or even its ARC, thank you from the bottom of my heart. Your support since day one means the world to me.

To members in the Rookery who have shared reactions, support, and encouragement, thank you!

I'd like to give another shoutout to my editors, Steph and Zee, who are both amazing people and help elevate these stories and make them stronger.

Thank you Clair for your alpha and beta feedback. Reading your reactions always makes my day.

Thank you to all the amazing artists who have fed my character art addiction. I'm in love with every piece and still gush about them to others.

To my husband, I love you so much. I'm too awkward and shy and embarrassed to talk about what I do with others, but you're my biggest cheerleader and make me feel like I can do anything. <3

To my family who buys my books even though I warned against reading them, thank you for your support. A special shoutout to my parents who raised me to love reading and getting lost in other worlds. And for listening to all the details involved in being an indie author every step of the way (because it's a lot!).

Writing about Raegan and her men has been a wild ride of emotions. I'm sad to say goodbye to characters who've lived in my head for so long, but I'm also looking forward sharing new characters and stories.

Thank you for reading Raegan of Ruin.

<3 Rook

Want to receive a bonus scene?

Or maybe stay up to date on the newest releases?

How about early access to ARC or giveaway opportunities?

Sign up for A. L. Rook's newsletter to stay in the know of all things

Rook's books.

Scan or click the QR code below, or go to the website to sign up

@

www.alrookauthor.com

Join the A. L. Rook Reader Group on Facebook

The Rookery

@

www.facebook.com/groups/rookery

Or scan the QR code below

STALKING LINKS

amazon.com/stores/author/B0CYQJ2GWL

facebook.com/groups/rookery

instagram.com/alrookauthor

tiktok.com/@alrookauthor

WEBSITE: https://www.alrookauthor.com

NEWSLETTER: https://subscribepage.io/rooknewsletter

SPOTIFY: https://open.spotify.com/user/31g47djeh3oqclz7y
yaag2hwvtom?si=ca7e308dc7ec4b2c

FB PAGE: https://www.facebook.com/61557109453545/

ABOUT THE AUTHOR

A.L. Rook is an avid reader and has been dreaming of becoming an author since the first grade. She's been thinking up and writing stories ever since. Her favorite stories are dark contemporary or fantasy romance with strong characters that leave a lasting impression. When not drinking exorbitant amounts of coffee while writing, she can be found reading, binge-watching various shows, or traveling.

If you want to stay up to date on release dates, news, or for a chance at extra teasers and giveaways, follow Rook on her socials and join her newsletter.

9 781964 190082